**The time had come, Will decided, to reveal
certain truths to Quirk.**

"Mattrax," he said, "the dragon who governs this northern tip
of the Kondorra valley, which we are oh so lucky to be in right
now, is fifty yards from snout to tail and considered runty for
his kind. It gives him a shitty attitude, but it's hard to pick out
because all the dragons in the Consortium have shitty attitudes.
They live in vast fortresses, surrounded by guards picked from
the arse-end of humanity, who love nothing more than to go
around beating their arbitrary rules into the people who live
near them. And then every year they send out tax collectors
to steal as much of your coin as they can simply so they can
sit on it and feel fucking pretty. The only time they drag their
sagging guts out of their caves is so they can steal a few cattle for a midafternoon snack, and literally shit on the people
whom they govern. That is, in fact, a little game for Mattrax. To
see how many people he can hit with a single bowel movement.
As a species they are so comfortable with the idea of being evil
overlords that they actually hold gatherings from time to time
in the core of an active volcano. That is who you study. Tyrants.
Arseholes with wings."

# THE
# DRAGON LORDS
## FOOL'S GOLD

## JON HOLLINS

www.orbitbooks.net

Copyright © 2016 by Jonathan Wood
Excerpt from *Dragon Lords: False Idols* copyright © 2016 by Jonathan Wood
Excerpt from *The City Stained Red* copyright © 2014 by Sam Sykes

Cover design by Kirk Benshoff
Cover illustration by Karl Simon
Cover copyright © 2016 by Hachette Book Group, Inc.

Orbit
Hachette Book Group
1290 Avenue of the Americas
New York, NY 10104
orbitbooks.net

First Edition: July 2016

Orbit is an imprint of Hachette Book Group.
The Orbit name and logo are trademarks of Little, Brown Book Group Limited.

The publisher is not responsible for websites (or their content) that are not owned by the publisher.

The Hachette Speakers Bureau provides a wide range of authors for speaking events. To find out more, go to www.hachettespeakersbureau.com or call (866) 376-6591.

Map copyright © Tim Paul

ISBNs: 978-0-316-30823-6 (trade paperback), 978-0-316-30825-0 (ebook)

Printed in the United States of America

RRD-C

10 9 8 7 6 5 4 3 2 1

For Tami, Charlie, and Emma

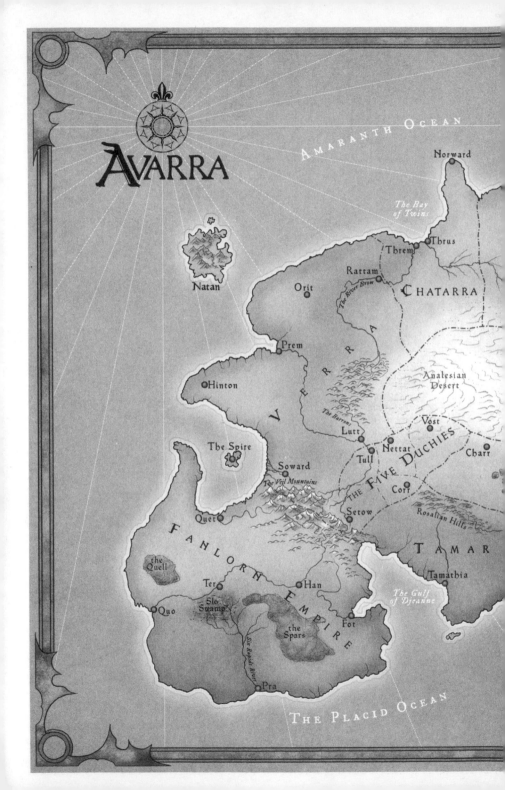

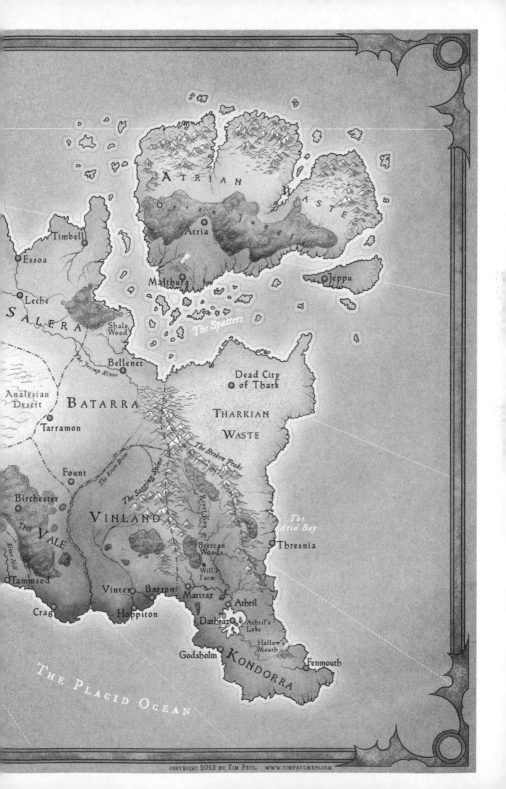

ATRIAN WASTE

Osten Jung

Atria

Malthura

Jeppu

Timbell

Essoa

Leche

SALERA

Shale Wood

Bellenet

The Yessup River

The Spatters

Dead City of Thark

Analesian Desert

BATARRA

THARKIAN WASTE

Tarramon

Fount

The River Brim

The Broken Peaks

Birchester

The Sagging Spine

River Kon

VINLAND

THE VALE

River Nill

Tammsod

Vinter

Barton

Breccan Woods

Will's Farm

The Arid Bay

Thresnia

Crag

Hoppiton

Mattrax

Athril

Dathrar

Athril's Lake

Godsholm

Hallow's Mouth

KONDORRA

Fenmouth

THE PLACID OCEAN

"Oh, for a muse of fire."

*—Henry V*
William Shakespeare

# PART 1:
# A JOB DONE RIGHT

# 1

## Will

It was a confrontation as old as time. A tale begun back when the Pantheon of old first breathed life into the clay mold of man and set him down upon the earth. It was the tale of the untamable pitted against the master. Of the wild tearing at the walls of the civilized. It was man versus the beast.

Will placed each foot carefully, held his balance low. He circled slowly. Cold mud pulled at his feet. Sweat trickled down the crease between his eyebrows. Inch by inch he closed the distance.

The pig Bessie grunted at him.

"Five shek says she tips him on his arse," said Albor, one of Will's two farmhands. A strip of hairy gut was visible where he rested it upon the sty's rickety old fence. It was, Will had noted, significantly hairier in fact than his chin, which he scratched at constantly. Albor's wife had just departed the nearby village for a monthlong trip to help look after her sister's new baby, and Albor was three days into growing the beard she hated.

"I say it's face first, he lands," said Dunstan, Will's other farmhand. The two men were a study in contrasts. Where Albor's stomach swayed heavily over his gut, Dunstan's broad leather belt was wrapped twice around his waist and still flapped loose beyond the buckle. His narrow face was barely visible behind a thick cloud of facial hair, which his wife loved to excess. She had a tendency to braid sections of it and line it with bows.

"You're on," said Albor, spitting in his muddy palm and holding it out to Dunstan.

Will gave a damn about neither beards nor wives. All he cared about was his father's thrice-cursed prize sow, Bessie. She had been his dancing partner in this sty for almost half an hour now. He was so coated in mud that if he lay upon the sty's floor, he would have been virtually invisible. He briefly considered this as a possible angle of attack, but the pig was as likely to shit on him and call it a good day's work as anything else. There was an uncanny intelligence in her eyes. Still, she was old and he was young. Brute force would win the day.

He closed the distance down by another inch.

Bessie narrowed her eyes.

Another inch.

Bessie squealed and charged. Will lunged, met the charge head-on. His hands slammed down hard against her sides.

Bessie flew through his mud-slick palms and crashed all of her considerable weight into his legs. The world performed a sprawling flip around Will's head, then hit him in the face.

He came up spluttering mud, and was just in time to hear Dunstan say, "That's five shek you owe me then."

Bessie was standing nonchalantly behind him, with an air of almost studied calm.

Will found his resolve hardening. Bessie had to die. With a roar, he launched himself at the pig. She bucked wildly. And yet still one of his hands snagged a bony trotter. He heaved upon it with all his might.

Bessie, however, had lived upon the farm longer than Will. She had survived lean winters, breeched piglets, and several virulent diseases, and was determined to survive him. She did not allow her limb to collapse under Will's weight, advanced years or no. Instead she simply pulled him skidding through the mud. After several laps, he appeared to be done. With her free hoof, she kicked him in the forehead to emphasize the lesson, then walked away.

"I think you almost got her that time," Albor called in what might be generously described as an encouraging tone.

Will did not respond. Personal honor was at stake at this point in the proceedings. Still, there was only so much mud a man could swallow. He clambered to his feet and retreated to consider his options.

Dunstan patted him on the shoulder as he collapsed against the fence. Bessie regarded him balefully.

"She's too strong for me," Will said when he'd gotten his breath back.

"To be fair, you say that about most girls," Albor told him.

"I have to outsmart her."

"That too," Dunstan chipped in.

"Don't usually work, though." Albor chewed a strand of straw sagely.

"This," said Will, his temper fraying, "is not so much helpful advice as much as it is shit swilling in a blocked ditch. That pig has to become crispy rashers and if you have nothing helpful to add you can go back to picking apples in the orchard."

For a short while the only sound was Bessie farting noisily in her corner of the sty.

Above the men, thin clouds swept across a pale blue sky. The distant mountains were a misty purple, almost translucent.

Will softened. None of this was Albor's or Dunstan's fault, even if they did not want to see old Bessie taken to the butcher's block. Deep down—deeper perhaps now than at the start of his ordeal—neither did he. Bessie had been part of this farm as long as he could remember. His father had sat him upon her back and had him ride around the sty, whooping and hollering, while his mother stood clucking her tongue. Dunstan and Albor had been there, cheering him on. Even old Firkin had been there.

But now Will's parents were gone to an early grave, and Firkin had lost his mind. Bessie was old and would not sow anymore. And Will was the unwilling owner of a farm on the brink of ruin.

"Look," he said, voice calmer, "I want Bessie dead no more than you do, but I am out of options. The Consortium increased taxes again, and paying them has left my coffers bare. If I am to have a hope of surviving another year, I need to put her to the knife and sell her pieces for as much as I can get. Next winter she'll be blind and hobbled and it will be a kindness."

Another silence.

"You can't wait a little, Will?" said Albor, straw drooping in the corner of his mouth. "Give her one last good year?"

Will sighed. "If I do, then there won't be anyone to slaughter her. This whole place will be gone to the Consortium and I'll be in a debtors' jail, and you two will be in old Cornwall's tavern without any sheks to pay for his ale."

At that threat, the two farmhands looked at each other. Finally Dunstan shrugged. "I never liked that fucking pig anyway."

Albor echoed his sad smile.

"That's more like it," said Will. "Now let's see if together three grown men can't outwit one decrepit pig."

Slowly, painfully, Will, Albor, and Dunstan hobbled back toward the farmhouse. Albor rubbed at a badly bruised hip. Dunstan was wringing muddy water out of his sodden, matted beard.

"It's all right," said Will, "we'll get her tomorrow."

Later, the farm's other animals locked away for the night, straw fresh on the barn's floor, Will stood in the farmhouse, heating a heavy iron pot full of stew over the hearth. A few strips of chicken roiled fretfully among vegetable chunks.

He never bothered naming the chickens. It was easier that way.

He sighed as he watched the stew slowly simmer. He should be checking the cheese presses, or scooping butter out of the churn and into pots before it spoiled, or possibly even attempting to tally his books so he could work out exactly how much money he owed folk. Instead he stood and stared.

The nights were long out on the farm. It was five miles through the fields and woods down to The Village. The distance had never seemed far when he was a child. But that was when his parents were alive, and when Dunstan and Albor, and even Firkin, would all have stayed to share the supper, with laughter, and jokes, and fiddle music lilting late into the night. That was when performing the chores around the house had never seemed exactly like work, and when stoking the fire so it warmed the whole room had never felt like an extravagance.

The firelight cast the heavy wooden cabinets and thick oak table and chairs in guttering light. Will tried to focus on that, not the shadows of the day. Maybe Bessie did have one more litter in her. Maybe he could give her one more year. A good litter would bring in enough coin. Or near enough, if the taxes didn't go up again. And he could scrimp and save in a few places. Maybe sell a few of the chairs. It wasn't like he needed more than one.

Yes. Yes, of course that would work. And Lawl or some other member of the Pantheon would manifest in the run-down old temple in the village below and shower them all with gold. *That* was what would happen…

His slow-bubbling thoughts were interrupted abruptly by a sharp rap at his door. He snapped his head to look at the thick oak slats. Outside, rain had begun to fall, tapping a complex undulating rhythm against the thatch roof above his head. It was over an hour's walk from The Village. Who would bother dragging themselves out here at this hour?

He had half-dismissed the sound as a loose branch blowing across the yard when it came again. A hard, precise rap that rattled the door latch. If it was a branch, it was a persistent one.

Removing the stew pot from the fire, he crossed the room quickly, unlatched the door, and opened it onto a cold and blustery night.

Four soldiers stood upon his doorstep. Their narrowed eyes stared out from beneath the shadows of their helms, which dripped rainwater down onto their long noses. Swords hung heavily on their large belts, each pommel embossed with an image of two batlike wings—the mark of the Dragon Consortium. Sodden leather jerkins with the same insignia were pulled over their heavy chain-mail shirts.

They were not small men. Their expressions were not kind. Will could not tell for sure, but they bore a striking resemblance to the four soldiers who had carried off most of the coin he'd been relying on to get through the winter.

"Can I help you?" asked Will, as politely as he was able. If there was anything at which he could fail to help them, he wanted to know about it.

"You can get the piss out of my way so me and my men can come out of this Hallows-cursed rain," said the lead soldier. He was taller than the others, with a large blunt nose that appeared to have been used to stop a frying pan, repeatedly, for most of his childhood. Air whistled in and out of it as he spoke.

"Of course." Will stepped aside. While he bore the guards of the Dragon Consortium no love, he bore even less for the idea of receiving a sound thrashing at their hands.

The four soldiers tramped laboriously in, sagging under the weight of their wet armor. "Obliged," said the last of the men, nodding. He had a kinder face than the others. Will saw the lead soldier roll his eyes.

They stood around Will's small fire and surveyed his house with expressions that looked a lot like disdain. Large brown footprints tracked their path from the door. The fourth guard looked at them, then shrugged at Will apologetically.

For a moment they all stood still. Will refused to leave the door, clinging to the solidity of it. Grounding himself in the wood his father had cut and hewn before he was born. As he watched the soldiers by the fire, his stomach tied more knots than an obsessive-compulsive fisherman.

Finally he crossed to them, the table, and his stew. He began to ladle it into a large if poorly made bowl. He wasn't hungry anymore, but it gave him something to do. These soldiers would get to their business with or without his help.

As he ladled, the lead soldier fiddled with a leather pouch at his waist.

"Nice place this," said the fourth, seeming to feel more awkward in the silence than the others.

"Thank you," Will said, as evenly as he was able. "My parents built it."

"Keep saying to the missus we should get a place like this," the guard continued, "but she doesn't like the idea of farm living. Likes to be close to the center of things. By which she really means the alchemist. Gets a lot of things from the alchemist, she does. Very healthy woman. Always adding supplements to my diet." He patted his stomach, metal gauntleted hand clanking against the chain mail. "Doesn't ever seem to do any good." He looked off into the middle distance. "Of course my brother says I'm cuckolded by a drug-addled harpy, but he's always been a bit negative."

The guard seemed to notice that everyone was staring at him.

"Oh," he said. "Sorry. Obviously none of that is related to why we're officially here. Just wanted to, well, you know..." He withered under his commanding officer's stare.

The lead soldier looked away from him, down to a piece of browning parchment paper that he had retrieved from his pouch. Then he turned the gaze he had used to dominate his subordinate upon Will.

"You are Willett Altior Fallows, son of Mickel Betterra Fallows, son of Theorn Pentauk Fallows, owner and title holder of this farmstead?" he asked. He was not a natural public speaker, stumbling over most of the words. But he kept his sneer firmly in place as he read.

Will nodded. "That's what my mother always told me," he said. The fourth soldier let out a snort of laughter, then at the looks from the others, murdered his mirth like a child tossed down a well.

The lead soldier's expression, by contrast, did not flicker for an instant. Will thought he might even have seen a small flame as the joke died against his stony wall of indifference. The soldier had the air of a man who had risen through the ranks on the strength of having no imagination whatsoever. The sort of man who followed orders, blindly and doggedly, and without remorse.

"The dragon Mattrax and by extension the Dragon Consortium as a whole," the officer continued in his same stilted way, reading from the parchment, "find your lack of compliance with this year's taxes a great affront to their nobility, their honor, and their deified status. You are therefore—"

"Wait a minute." Will stood, ladle in his hand, knuckles white about its handle, staring at the man. "My lack of *what*?"

For a moment, as the soldier had begun to speak, Will had felt his stomach plunge in some suicidal swan dive, abandoning ship entirely. And then, as the next words came, there had been a sort of pure calm. An empty space in his emotions, as if they had all been swept away by some great and terrible wind that had scoured the landscape clean and sent cows flying like siege weaponry.

But by the time the soldier finished, there was a fury in him he could barely fathom. He had always thought of himself as a peaceable man. In twenty-eight years he had been in exactly three fights, had started only one of them, and had thrown no more than one punch in each. But, as if summoned by some great yet abdominally restrained wizard, an inferno of rage had appeared out of nowhere in his gut.

"My *taxes*?" he managed to splutter. He was fighting against an increasing urge to take his soup ladle and ram it so far down the soldier's throat he could scoop out his balls. "Your great and grand fucking dragon Mattrax took me for almost every penny I had. He has laid waste to the potential for this farm with his greed. And there was not a single complaint from me. Not as I gave you every inherited copper shek, silver drach, and golden bull I had."

He stood, almost frothing with rage, staring down the lean, unimpressed commander.

"Actually," said the fourth soldier, almost forgotten at the periphery of events, "it was probably a clerical error. There's an absolutely vast number of people who fall under Mattrax's purview, and every year there's just a few people whose names don't get ticked. It's an inevitability of bureaucracy, I suppose."

Both Will and the commanding officer turned hate-filled eyes on the soldier.

"So," said Will, voice crackling with fire, "tick my fucking name then."

"Oh." The soldier looked profoundly uncomfortable. "Actually that's not something we can do. Not our department at all. I mean you can appeal, but first you have to pay the tax a second time, and then appeal."

"Pay the tax?" Will said, the room losing focus for him, a strange sense of unreality descending. "I can't pay the fucking tax a second time. Nobody here could afford that. That's insane."

"Yes," said the guard sadly. "It's not a very fair system."

Will felt as if the edges of the room had become untethered from reality, as if the whole scene might fold up around him, wither away to nothingness, leaving him alone in a black void of insanity.

"Willett Altior Fallows," intoned the lead soldier, with a degree of blandness only achievable through years of honing his callousness to the bluntest of edges, "I hereby strip you of your title to this land in recompense for taxes not paid. You shall be taken from here directly to debtors' jail."

"Oh debtors' jail," said the fourth guard, slapping a palm to his forehead. "I totally forgot about debtors' jail. Because," he added, nodding to himself, "it's not as if you can appeal the ruling while you're in the jail. Nobody's going to come down and listen to you down there. But when you get out, you can totally appeal. I think the queue is only four or five years long at that point. Though, honestly, I would have expected it to be shorter given the fairly high mortality rate among inmates in debtors' jail..." he trailed off. "Don't suppose that's very helpful, is it?" he said to the room at large.

Will could barely hear him. This could not be happening. Every careful financial plan he had put together. Every future course he had plotted. Each one of them ruined, ground beneath the twin heels of incompetence and greed, became nothing more than kindling for his fury. Rage roared around him, filled his ears with noise, his vision with red.

He tried to say something, opened his mouth. Only an inarticulate gurgle of rage emerged.

"Chain his hands," said the lead soldier.

Something snapped in Will. Suddenly the bowl of stew was in his hand. He flung it hard and fast at the lead soldier's face. It crashed into his nose with a satisfying crunch, shattered. Pottery shards scored lines across the man's face. He'd made that bowl as a boy, he remembered now. A simple pinch pot; a gift for his mother. He'd meant it as a vase but hadn't been old enough to know what a vase had actually looked like. He'd flown into a temper tantrum when he first saw her eating from it. And now it was gone. Along with everything else.

The soldier reeled back, bellowed. Will was barely paying attention. He was already lunging for the larger pot, iron sides still scalding from the heat of the fire.

A guard beat him, steel-encased fist slamming into the pot, sending the contents flying.

Will could hear steel scraping against leather. Swords leaving their hilts.

He brought the ladle round in a tight arc, smashed it into the lunging guard's cheek. The man staggered sideways. Will came up, was face-to-face with the fourth soldier. The soldier's eyes were wide, panicked. Will stabbed straight forward, the spoon of the ladle crashing into the guard's throat. The guard dropped to the floor choking, a look of surprise and hurt on his face.

And then the last guard's sword smashed the ladle from Will's hands and sent it skittering across the floor.

Out of daily kitchenware, Will reconsidered his options. The lead guard was recovering, snarling, red blistering skin bleeding openly. The fourth guard was still gasping, but the other two both had their swords up. They advanced.

As most other options seem to lead to rapid and fatal perforation, Will backed up fast.

"Not sure you're going to make it to jail," said one guard. He was smiling.

The other just stalked forward, weight held low, eyes narrowed beneath dark brows.

Will glanced about. But his mother had always been strict about leaving the farm outside of the house and that habit had died hard. There was no handy scythe, no gutting knife, not even a shovel. His foot slipped in one of the muddy footprints the guards had left on the tile floor. The grinning guard closed the gap another yard.

"Stop fucking about and kill the little shit stain already," snarled the soldier with the blistered face.

The words were the catalyst. Will unfroze as the guards leapt forward. He tore out of the kitchen door, heard the swish of steel through the air, waited for pain, and found it hadn't come by the time his feet carried him through the threshold and into the darkness.

He abandoned the spill of yellow light and tore toward the barn as fast as his feet would carry him. There was a way to fight back there. A way to stop this. There had to be.

"After the little fucker!" The rasping rage of the burned guard chased after him.

"He hit me." The bewildered burble of the fourth guard.

"I'll fucking hit you if you don't bring me his spleen."

The other guards were hard on his heels. Rain slashed at him. Will hit the door of the barn, bounced off, felt the sting of it in his shoulder, his palms. He scrabbled at the door, flung it open. A sword blade embedded itself in the frame as he darted through. A guard grunted in frustration.

Everything was shadows and the smell of damp straw. He could hear the cows, Ethel and Beatrinne, stamping and huffing. The soft lumbering snores of the two sheep, Atta and Petra. It felt like home. Except the guards behind him were some awful violation. Some tearing wound in everything he held dear.

He looked around, desperate, panic making the place unfamiliar. A blade. He needed a blade. The scythe—

"Torch it." The words barely penetrated his consciousness. But then he heard the strike of a flint, the whispered roar of flame igniting. Yellow light blazed in the doorway. He watched the torch as it flipped end over end to land in the straw.

He rushed toward it. Flames raced toward him. He stamped desperately at them.

The second torch hit him heavily in the chest. He staggered backward, slapped desperately at the flame that started to lick at the front of his jacket. In the handful of seconds it took to extinguish, two more torches had arced into the barn. One landed in the hay pile. It flared like kindling. By the time Will was halfway to the pile, the smoke already had him hacking and coughing.

The cows were awake now, starting to realize they should panic. The guards shouted to each other outside the door.

This was his *home*. This couldn't be.

But it clearly was.

He stopped, stood still, fire and smoke swirling about him, the cries of panicking animals filling the air. He was frozen between the future that he had held and the shattered pieces of the present at his feet.

Something splintered. He looked up, fearful of a falling beam. Then the sound of skittering hooves made him realize it was the gate of the pen that he'd been meaning to fix for more than a month now. And then Ethel's shoulder checked him as she scrambled out of the door.

*Cursed cow,* said some part of his mind. *When she comes back tomorrow she'll be full of rage that she hasn't been milked and her udders are heavy.*

But there wouldn't be a tomorrow. Not if he didn't get out.

He started to move again, to look for a way out that was not blocked by soldiers and swords.

For the first time ever, he was glad that the farm overwhelmed him. That there were rotten boards up in the hayloft that he hadn't got round to fixing.

He dashed to the ladder, threw open the door to the sheep pen as he went past it. The rungs were rough, slightly spongy with rot. He climbed upward into clouds of smoke that drove him to his knees, hacking, coughing.

He scrambled forward, elbows and knees supporting his weight. He thumped his head against the barn roof, felt his way along the wall, until the wood bowed beneath the pressure. His lungs burned. Bracing himself, he kicked once, twice. The boards gave way on the third heavy kick. He cleared a wider space with the fourth and fifth, shoved through the gap, grabbed the edge with his fingertips.

He hung in the darkness for a moment, smoke pouring out around him, obscuring his vision. How close had he put the vegetable cart to the back wall? The last thing he needed now was to break his neck on its edge. But there was no time to dredge for the memory.

He kicked off blindly, flailed through space.

He landed on the cart's wooden boards with a crash that jarred him from head to heels. His teeth clacked shut so hard he thought he heard his gums groaning. Spots of light danced in the night sky.

A shout crashed into his swampy thoughts. A guard had circled around the barn, seen him jump. He didn't have time to get his bearings, only to run. So he put his head down and did just that.

A fence lurched at him out of nowhere. The rain was coming down hard now, and the wood was slick as he tumbled over into a field. Wheat slapped at him, tall enough to get lost in.

He tumbled forward, barely thinking, just putting one foot in front of the other, simply getting away, and leaving all his hope behind.

In the end, a tree put paid to his flight. Not one to suffer fools or hysterical men lightly, it hit him forcefully with its trunk. Will took the opportunity to sit down heavily and not think about much at all for a while.

Eventually he came back to himself. Not fully. Not enough to totally take in the events of the evening. But enough to know that he was lost, that it was raining, and that home was not an option.

A moment of confused and painful thinking followed. His home was gone. Irretrievably, irreconcilably. The culmination of the bad luck that had begun with Firkin losing his mind, and moved on with the death of his parents. His future was gone. His dreams too. He would not find a way to make the farm profitable. He would not find a good Village girl to bring back. There would be no one to fill the old farmhouse with light, and love, and song. He had failed his father and his mother both in a single night. The chance to achieve their dreams for him had been stolen from him.

As for the future... That was beyond him. Instead he aimed for something less ambitious. Like where in the Hallows he had ended up. When he solved the problem, he did not arrive at a particularly reassuring answer.

He'd headed into the Breccan Woods—the vast tangle of untamed forest that lay to the north of his farm. It was a hard enough place to navigate in the bright of day, with a known trail beneath his feet. It was a downright foolish place to be at night. The shadows were not safe—every mother told her child so. Goblins, ogres, and worse called this place home. And yet, he had apparently decided that a headlong dash for the hills super-seded anything resembling common sense.

He shivered. He needed shelter. He needed rest. He needed time to come to terms with a torched home and a warrant for his death. Because that was what it would be. *Gentle* and *under-standing* were not the words one usually used when describing the soldiers employed by the dragon Mattrax. If you resisted their edicts, they would not simply sit you down with a warm cup of mead to gently explain the misunderstanding. They were generally recruited more from the stick-a-sword-in-your-guts-and-kick-you-into-a-ditch mold. On a good day, at least, your friends would find you before the rats did.

This did not feel like a good day.

His body ached, but—given the trouble he'd been through to keep it in one piece that evening—Will decided to stumble forward, and look for a place where he could avoid freezing to death.

The going was slow. Trees hid most of the moonlight, and what came through seemed reluctant to show him where any obstacles might lie. Stones stubbed his toes, tangles of roots and vines tripped his heels. Rain dripped onto him, seeking out the gap between his collar and his neck with unerring accuracy.

He was shivering hard when he came upon the rock face. A ragged wall of granite twenty yards in height, where the land stepped up toward the mountains at the valley's edge. Such diminutive cliffs were a common enough feature of the landscape, often forming natural boundaries between farmsteads. More to Will's purpose, they tended to contain caves.

All he had to do was find one that didn't contain a bear.

*Lawl—father of the Pantheon Above, lord of law and life*, he prayed silently as he felt his way along the rock, *I don't know what I did to make you piss in my stew tonight, but I hope you can find it in your heart to forgive me.*

No sooner was the prayer uttered than the rock gave way beneath his hand. He stumbled forward, almost cursing, before he realized that the opening was in fact a cave entrance. *Well, that's service for you*, he thought. *Thank you, kindly.*

He stepped under the lip of the cave's entrance, the relief from the rain instant. He sighed, heavily, inhaled—

—and then rather wished he hadn't.

He'd never smelled anything quite like it. If a bear lived in this cave then it had died here. After a rather violent bout of diarrhea. Possibly brought on by the excess consumption of skunks. Who had also died of excess diarrhea. Several weeks prior.

He gagged slightly, and hesitated. But then, who was he to question divine providence? And while the smell of rot might normally attract predators, this was rancid enough that even a crow might decide it had too much self-esteem to stoop to the cave's contents. And it wasn't as if the world was overabundant with options for him at this moment.

Pulling a mostly dry rag from his pocket, he covered his nose and pushed deeper. Despite the rag, the stench grew with each step. When he could take it no longer—his revulsion a physical wall he could not push past—he backed up a step toward the cave entrance and simply lay down. The rock beneath him was cold and hard, but thankfully lacking in murderous intent. He looked back toward the cave entrance, the world outside. He could just make out the forest, a dark blue smudge in a field of black. He looked away, and rolled over, searching for a more comfortable way to lie—

—and collided with something small, furry, and warm.

Will shrieked.

He had always hoped that in a situation like this he would be able to describe the sound as a bellow, but it was definitely a shriek.

Fortunately, from his ego's point of view, whatever he had collided with let out an equally shrill noise. Less fortunately, something else echoed the sound. And then something else. And then ten more voices took up the cry. And ten more. A rippling wave of tremulous, unmanly sound, rushing back through the cavern.

And then, in response, a wave of light came flooding back. Torches flaring brightly in the dark. The light reached Will just as he made it to his feet.

He looked out onto a cavern packed from wall to wall with small, green figures. Feral faces with pointed snouts and pointier ears. Little black eyes screwed tight in anger. Teeth bared.

The shadows of Breccan Woods were not safe, he reminded himself. This one particularly so it seemed, housing as it did an entire fucking horde of goblins.

*Lawl above,* Will thought, *you're an absolute bastard.*

# 2

# Lette and Balur

The problem with adventuring, Lette reflected, was that it was a crap way to make money.

She wiped sweat from her brow. Gods-hexed mountain pass. Weren't mountains supposed to be cold and snowy? What was she doing sweating her ass off this high up?

But she knew the answer to that question, and she didn't like it. Instead she turned again to the more nebulous arena of finance. Specifically, how it intersected with her chosen career path.

Adventuring had seemed such a good idea when she'd started out. Punching monsters for a living. Receiving riches and glory in return. And there really was glory. She knew at least three people who had had songs composed about their endeavors. Four if you counted "The Ballad of Fairthroat the Man-Whore" but that one didn't end with Fairthroat in possession of all of his anatomy, so the glory thing was questionable there.

And yet, even assuming you got a song, and that then someone managed to reconcile the sweaty, bloodstained social deviant in front of them with the shining idealized figure they'd heard songs about, you were still left with the fact that any riches coming your way would be the result of a significant amount of violence and personal harm. And violence and personal harm had a way of spiraling out of control. Very far out of control. Lette refused to look back over her shoulder. Instead she concentrated on the fact that she was ready for a steadier lifestyle.

"What about a bakery?" she said out loud.

Her traveling companion looked at her for a very long time.

Balur was approximately eight feet tall, lacked any body fat whatsoever, and owned a tail. He was an Analesian, one of the lizard men from the Western deserts. His yellow eyes regarded her narrowly from a broad, elongated face. They peered out from between large brown scales, thick and knobbly like fist-size stones.

"No," he said after a pause. His voice sounded like rocks grinding. He shook his head slowly. "No," he said again.

The Analesians were a hard people. Lette had heard a rumor that their language had forty onomatopoeias for the noise a man's head made when it was crushed beneath your war hammer. She had never quite managed to find the right time to ask Balur if this was true.

"You just say 'No' automatically now," Lette objected. "You didn't even think about it." So far Balur had rejected swordsmithing, blacksmithing, farming, horsebreaking, and exotic dancing as potential career changes. To be fair, Balur's skill set was largely limited to hitting things very hard with a hammer, but that's why the smithing ideas had been so promising. To Lette's mind he was simply being obstinate.

"Look," she said, pointing ahead, "see that?" The crest of the mountain pass was finally approaching. Beyond it lay the Kondorra valley, vibrant and fertile. "That's a fresh start. That's a new page in the story of our lives. We can be anything we want to be once we cross that line. *Anything*."

Balur nodded. "Yes," he said.

Lette's face lit up. Finally progress. Finally the thick-skulled oaf—

"I am wanting to be a mercenary," Balur finished.

Lette groaned. "Oh yes," she said. "Because that's working out *so* well."

The wind shifted briefly, blowing up the mountain rather

than down. For a moment, the smell of smoke and carrion filled her nostrils. She groaned again.

*Eyes forward. A fresh start. A new beginning.*

Balur strode on. Then on the crest, the liminal point, the start of something new, he paused. He held out a thick, four-fingered hand toward Lette. "I am not having the hands for baking," he said. "I am having no nimble fingers."

"You could just knead the dough," Lette suggested. Balur required a more solution-oriented outlook in her view.

Then she was on the crest of the past beside him, and the whole of her future was spread out before and below her. The Kondorra valley.

The sun was low, on this early edge of autumn. Its glare was still partly occluded by the mountain peaks around her. It sent flat shafts of light streaking across the trees that flowed down the mountainside below them. Distant, at the valley's floor, the forest broke open into fields, a patchwork of farmland that stitched its way up the valley's far slope, until rock and scree took over at the hill's summit. In this light, the slow, sluggish river Kon marking the valley's base was transformed into a line of white fire.

It was a world to itself, the valley. A microcosm. She could see castles, like children's toys, lakes, a swamp, and even something that could conceivably be a volcano. It was all small and perfect from this distance, like a picture painted into a book. Nothing spoiled by the proximity of reality.

"Look at that," Lette said again. She pointed. "We can be anything we like down there."

Balur shrugged. "I am liking being a mercenary."

"What about a butcher?" Lette suggested, a momentary flash of inspiration striking her. "You could still kill things if you were a butcher. Cattle. You'd be perfect for it. A swift blow to the skull, each one."

Balur cocked his head to one side. "Butchery is being mostly knife work," he said.

"I do knife work," Lette said. Her fingers flickered, and a knife appeared there, skittered away, appeared in her other hand. "You just slaughter cattle."

Balur thought about it more. The slow gearwork of inhuman thinking. "Would the cattle be fighting back?" he asked eventually.

Lette had to take a moment for that one. "Cattle?" she asked, double checking.

Balur nodded. "Would they be being much of a challenge?" he said. "I am not wanting to go soft, being a butcher."

Lette blinked, once, twice. The question did not go away. "Cattle is fucking cows, Balur." Lette clarified for him. "They do not fight back. They eat grass, get their heads caved in, and then become delicious meaty snacks."

Balur weighed this. "I am thinking I still prefer being a mercenary," he said after a while.

Lette resisted the urge to grab Balur and shake him. Though in fairness that was mostly because she couldn't really reach his shoulders. Or shake him even if she could reach them. Instead she pulled the heavy bag of gold coins off her waist and thrust it at him. It was the only half-decent thing to come out of the disaster that lay behind them.

"Look at this, Balur," she said. "This is anything we want it to be. New lives. Better lives."

Balur's eyes narrowed. "Is it also being wine and whores?" he asked.

Lette shook her head. "You are a foreigner from a far-flung land. You are meant to be exotic and interesting."

Balur shrugged. "I am being eight foot tall and am possessing odd syntax. That is being interesting."

Lette considered whether to stab him in the crotch or the eye.

She was saved from the agony of indecision by a small, screaming figure abruptly launching itself from a hiding place behind a rock and flinging itself at her. A goblin, she realized. It flew through the air and seized the purse from her hand.

"Mine! Mine! Mine!" it screamed as it landed and tore off down the path away from them, short legs pumping furiously. "I gots it! I gots it! It's mine!"

The goblin got exactly one additional step farther before Lette's dagger caught it in the back of its neck, neatly slipping between two vertebrae and making a mess of its cerebellum. The goblin was dead before it hit the ground.

"See," said Balur. "You are being good mercenary. You should be playing to your talents."

"My talents have caused a lot of human misery," Lette said, walking over to the goblin and plucking the knife from its back. The body resisted giving it up. She disliked killing goblins. They were weirdly sticky creatures. She always had to spend forever afterward cleaning bits of them off her blades.

She bent to pick up the purse—

—only to have it snatched from before her, as another goblin hurtled out of its hiding place and took off across the path.

"Barph's hairy ball sack," she cursed. "How many of these bastards are there?"

Perhaps learning from his slowly cooling companion, this goblin did not scream. He just legged it. Unfortunately, any attempt to leg it when you are only four foot tall is significantly limited by stride length. Balur was not similarly restricted.

His war hammer descended. The goblin stopped being a small, ugly humanoid and instead became a small, ugly bloodstain.

"Gods' spit, Balur, careful of the damned purse!"

"It is being fine." The lizard man rolled yellow eyes behind nictitating membranes.

Lette sighed heavily. She might as well berate a rock. Instead she turned her attention to their surroundings. Woods had arisen almost as soon as the pass started to descend. A thick tangle of trunks and underscrub. It smelled damp and loamy. Too many hiding places.

"I hope you spot a pattern developing!" she yelled to however many other goblins were left lurking around them. "You take the purse, you die messily." Even goblins should be able to understand that sort of equation.

Apparently not.

A bush rustled. Then the goblin appeared, shrieking like a kettle on the boil. It grabbed the purse and hurtled off, still screaming, all flailing, gangly limbs.

Lette sighed. This one was faster than the others. Its torso was a tiny round ball suspended between long knobbly legs and arms. Still, it was not faster than her dagger. The blade appeared again in her palm. She took aim.

And then goblins fell like rain.

They were in the trees. Ten, twenty, maybe more of them. All screaming. All leaping. All armed with jagged rusting knives.

Lette loosed her dagger. It never made it to the one with her purse. Instead it caught a goblin in the neck as it leapt into the blade's path. The screaming creature was pinned to a tree, went still.

"Gods' spit on all of them."

Then her sword was out. She cut the legs out from beneath another goblin even as it tried to land on hers.

Balur's war hammer whirled. Bodies impacted against its broad head fast enough that the sounds blurred together. Lette leapt into the space he'd opened.

A goblin lunged at her. She turned the blade, slit its throat, but another had circled behind her, lunged for her hamstrings. Balur brought down his war hammer in a hard vertical arc. A goblin disappeared beneath its head. Lette wondered if the Analesians would describe the sound as more of a squish or a splat.

She caught sight of the goblin running off with her purse. It was twenty yards away now, the distance increasing rapidly. An ugly little head bobbed about on its undersize body. Not a large target. Another dagger appeared in her hand. She breathed slow. Cocked her arm.

Something hard and sharp impacted against the spiked pauldron protecting her right shoulder. Her arm jerked sideways. The knife flew wide. Cursing, she whipped round. Her sword blade buried itself in a goblin's neck. Blood sprayed, it kicked, died.

Lette tried to yank the sword free. It did not come. She shook the blade. The goblin flopped and spasmed but refused to come loose. He was a corpse puppet on the end of a single, very sharp string. She cursed again. Why in all of the Hallows were goblins always so damn sticky?

Two goblins, sensing her slowness with the overburdened blade, circled to either side of her, closed in.

Her sword shook. The corpse flopped. She cursed.

Then at the same moment, the goblins leapt. They struck identical poses: great bounding arcs, knives clutched in both hands behind their heads.

Lette wondered where they learned the move. It had to have been learned. The symmetry was too perfect. Did goblins run combat drills? If so, they shouldn't. The move told her everything that was about to happen. It took half the fun out of combat.

She pivoted on one heel, brought the other up and round in a short sharp circle. She caught one of the goblins in its midriff as it flew through the air. Its ribs cracked, the angle of its flight changing, becoming shorter and more terminal. It slammed into a nearby tree. The contents of its skull became a red smear.

Lette had already moved on, using the momentum of her kick to whip her goblin-encased sword around. The second goblin slammed into its dead compatriot, sheathed the protruding sword tip in its gut. It screamed, jerked, and remained firmly lodged on the blade.

"Oh gods' piss on it!" The sword, now effectively a club made of small dying creatures, was too heavy to be practical. Four more goblins were closing fast.

Balur's hammer descended, one, two, three times. This time it was definitely more of a "squelch" sound, Lette thought. Balur caught the fourth goblin around the neck with his free hand. He held it aloft. It kicked futilely at the air.

Lette looked around. The goblin with the purse was gone. She was surrounded by dead and dying bodies. She looked up, to the Pantheon Above. What had she done to piss them off? She said her prayers, paid her dues at temples. What sort of divine comedy had they devised for her? *Assholes, all of them.*

She turned on the dangling goblin, another of her daggers in her hand. The blade was short and bright, catching the sun as she advanced. The goblin was momentarily distracted from Balur's fist on its neck.

"You," she said, pointing at the spasming creature. "You are going to literally spill your guts. And as you do, you are going to tell me everything. Where in the Hallows is my purse?"

"Thrasher," the goblin gasped. "Thrasher took it. Ran with it." The goblin was a potbellied thing. Its skin the same dirty greenish brown she associated with the gastrointestinal aftermath of one of Balur's Analesian curries. Its eyes were large, round, and dark. Although there was the chance that Balur's squeezing was altering their natural shape.

"I don't need his god's-hexed name." Lette advanced with the dagger. "I need his location."

"Needed the money," the goblin continued gabbling. "For the down payment. Had to have it."

Lette closed her eyes. She didn't want to know. She just wanted to know where the cursed creature with her purse had gone to. But...

"Down payment?" Balur rumbled.

The goblin twisted to look up at his captor. "For bakery," he squeaked.

*A divine pissing comedy.*

"Bakery?" Balur repeated. He look at Lette. She refused to meet his eye.

"Oh yes." The goblin nodded, trying to smile through his evident pain. "We think there is a big market for goblin pastries. Very delicate. Melt in your mouth. We have very nimble fingers." The goblin took a break from vainly trying to peel Balur's fist open to wiggle a hand at him. The fingers were indeed long and slender.

Balur nodded sagely. "That is being a good point, that," he said. "Nimble fingers are being important for baking." He looked at Lette significantly.

"Oh give it a fucking rest."

"Yes," the goblin jabbered, too preoccupied with its own survival to pick up on basic social cues. "You see. You see. But money, you see? Money is the problem. Need to have money to buy a bakery. For the down payment. High start-up costs for bakeries. Very high. And the Merchants Guild. They won't lend us the money. Goblins have shitty credit record, they say. Cultural and historical activities not conducive to large-scale financial loans, they say. But we need money to make money. Financial trap, we say. Plutocratic bullshit, we say. Racist fucks, we call the Merchants Guild. And so they kick us out. And now we are here. Engaging in cultural and historical activities not conducive to large-scale financial loans. For your purse. For our bakery."

He stared at them wildly. Trying to stretch his squished face into a toothy, pitiful smile.

Lette closed her eyes. "Why the hell do I still not know where this whoreson Thrasher is? Why do I not know where my fucking purse is?"

She was shouting. This was her new start, gods piss on it. Her new beginning.

The goblin swallowed. "He is," he stuttered. "He is..." He started again.

"Oh just get rid of it," Lette snapped, her patience finally reaching its breaking point. "I'll track the other one down and find our purse myself." She could see the trail of broken branches and matted-down grass leading away from the skirmish. It would be an easy enough trail to follow.

Balur gave a satisfied nod, and the muscles in its arm bunched. The goblin screamed.

"Gods, Balur! Not like that!" He'd been about to crush the goblin's skull. Lette pulled at her hair. "We are trying to be better people, remember?"

"You are trying." Balur was belligerent.

"Just throw it away, and I will track this arsehole, Thrasher. You can kill him instead, all right?"

Balur sighed heavily. "Fine." With a casual sweep of his arm he flung the goblin away.

Unfortunately, the parabolic flight of the goblin intersected directly with a tree trunk five yards away. There was an ugly cracking sound. What was left of the goblin slumped to the ground.

Lette just looked at Balur.

He opted for indignance. "What? What?" He rolled his eyes. "That was being a genuine mistake."

Lette sighed as she looked around her. Dead bodies. Blood and carrion. Crows already circling in the air above, their calls long and mocking.

*Her new start.*

As she stalked deeper into the woods, one word seemed to sum it all up.

"Shit."

# 3

# Ill-Met by Moonlight

Will stood, momentarily paralyzed by the vision of a cave full of goblins.

*Run!* screamed a small and eminently sensible part of his mind, but for some reason his legs weren't paying attention. They, it seemed, were more fatalistic. They would only carry him from so many attempts on his life in one day before simply giving up and accepting the fate as inevitable.

"Sorry," he heard himself. "Wrong cave. My one's a few entrances down."

He went to take a step away from the goblins but his cowardly legs were still not on the same page as the rest of him.

A low growl seemed to rise from every small mouth in the room, a whisper brought to the volume of a roar by the sheer density of the bodies packed into the space before him.

"I'll be off then," he said, more to his own anatomy than to the crowd. His knees shivered in response, but he thought the movement boded collapse more than any sort of horizontal traction.

Suddenly a bloodcurdling howl rose through the night. It hollowed out all of Will's resolve, left him a quivering shell.

He found himself thinking of the Pantheon. Of Lawl, father of the gods. Of Lawl's wife, Betra, mother to all. Of their children, Klink, Toil, and Knole—gods and goddesses of money, labor, and wisdom. Of Lawl's daughter-wife Cois, goddess of lust and desire. Of Betra's husband-son Barph, god of revelry. Who could he pray to? Who might, against all the odds, send him aid?

*Fuck it,* he thought. *I'll slaughter a whole damn army of pigs to the first one of you lot who helps me out here.*

Apparently the Pantheon had about as much faith in him as he had in them.

His arms, more cooperative than his legs, rose up over his head. His spirits almost rallied as he felt movement in his petrified legs, but it was only him sinking to his knees.

*Wait,* said the small voice inside him, the one that had advised retreat, *that howl came from behind you...*

*Shut up!* yelled the panicking component of his mind. *I don't have time for your shit. I'm busy dying, gods curse it.*

Something massive bowled past Will. He felt the wind of it as it passed him, the bass growl of its roar in his chest, the pounding of its feet through the rock beneath him.

Then silence. A moment of absolute silence.

Then wind. A violent swishing noise.

And then the sound of death.

Will had grown up on a farm. He had raised enough livestock to know that sound. The sound of flesh tearing, bones breaking.

But it wasn't coming from him.

He dared to open one eye.

Divine intervention. At first, that was the only explanation that came to his mind. That somehow his prayers had worked. That Lawl had really stepped down from the heavens and come to intercede on his part. That a divinity had finally come back to Kondorra. Just for him.

And then, he got a look at the creature, and while there were stories of Lawl, and Betra, and Barph, and the rest of the Pantheon taking on some odd forms over the years, nothing he'd ever read was quite like this.

It was a creature perhaps eight feet tall, made entirely out of vast slabs of muscle, and spackled with cobblestone-size scales that glistened bronze in the firelight. It wielded a massive war hammer, the head of which scythed through the pressed ranks like a blade through wheat. Small bodies flew, anatomy distorted, fluids flying in great spraying arcs. The scent of blood and shit filled the air.

The goblins screamed, panicked, tried to flee back into the dull dead end of the cavern. A few brave souls leaked around the edge of the creature's arc of death, fled toward the entrance. They raced past Will, and he tracked them as they hurtled toward the night.

And that was when he saw her. The angel to pair with the demon deeper in the cave. She was etched in moonlight, sweat-slick hair pulled back into a haphazard ponytail, mouth set in a grimace of rage. She held a sword in one hand, a dagger in the other. She slit the throat of the first goblin that tried to get past her, cut the legs out from beneath the next. It collapsed on severed knees, screamed so hard it retched.

The vast lizard demon waded into the cave, splashing death upon the walls and floor, and the woman followed, ending the lives of those initial survivors one by one with sharp, careful precision. Like a surgeon following in a butcher's wake.

Could they be demigods? When the gods manifested, they usually had just one thing on their mind. Anyone unfortunate enough to fall under their glamour and be impregnated was rarely allowed to go full term, though. The Pantheon's offspring—demigods—simply sowed too much chaos in the world. They were too powerful, too unpredictable. The balance of nations could be knocked askew.

This butchery, though. Its scale. Its efficiency. It still felt almost divine to Will. The pair were quiet in their work. After the initial howl of the charge, there were no more battle cries, no more declarations of righteousness. All around them the goblins screamed, but the pair worked with a grim set to their jaws.

But as he watched, Will decided, no. Not divine. While the

scale and the proficiency of this slaughter was a new vista for him, this was still quotidian butchery. There were no lightning bolts, no quakes of telekinetic power. Just blade, and blood, and bone.

So who in the Hallows were they?

Eventually the slaughter was done. All about them were the dead and dying. The pair stood, panting, looked at each other, sighed, and shrugged.

"See," said the lizard monster in a voice that sounded like rocks grinding together, "that is being more fun than baking."

"Shut up and start looking for the purse," said the woman. She wheeled round suddenly, stabbed a finger out at Will. "You," she said. "Have you seen a purse?"

Will stared at her. His life did not make sense to him anymore. He remembered a metaphor his father's old lost farmhand Firkin had said to him, in one of his increasingly rare sober moments. He said it was as if the narrator of his fate had needed to step away for a moment and handed the reins to an angry toddler—a god's hand sweeping through the bricks of his life and knocking everything to the floor.

"Me?" Will said, to the woman pointing to his chest.

"No," said the woman, shaking her head, "the other helpful bystander standing just behind you."

Caught off guard, Will looked over his shoulder. There was no one there. Then his mind processed. He looked back to the woman embarrassed.

He could see her better now. The goblins' torches littered the floor. Her face was angular, hard, flat planes coming to abrupt angles at her cheekbones and jaw. She was dressed in boiled leathers studded with steel. A hodgepodge of plate mail was strapped to her shoulders, arms, and shins. The sharpness of her features carried through to her eyes, bright and alive in this field of death.

Behind her, the massive lizard man was holding two dead

goblins aloft by their ankles and shaking them. A few scraps of leather and dirt fell from them, along with a fairly large quantity of blood. There was no purse, though. The lizard man grunted and slung both bodies toward one corner of the cave. They landed with a crack of breaking bone that made Will wince.

A hint of sympathy entered the woman's face. "Not how you spend your typical evening?" she asked.

Will shrugged helplessly. "Not even a typical day."

The woman cracked a smile at that. The hard planes of her face transformed, curves appearing out of nowhere at her cheeks, and even a small dimple revealing its presence.

"I'm Lette," she said. "That's Balur."

Will stared at the lizard man. Balur. The word sounded foreign. He had the feeling that this was a moment when curiosity might equate to a feline fatality, but he couldn't quite help himself. "What is he?" he asked.

"An obstinate idiot," Lette said without a pause.

Balur shook out two more goblins and flung them at the corner. "You being flirting is not helping us find our purse any faster," he said without looking up.

"At least," she spat back, "my version of flirting is a little more sophisticated than whipping my britches off and proffering some coin." Without pausing for breath she turned to Will and said, "Get any ideas and I shall feed you your own testicles."

Will was still watching events through a thin haze of confusion. His head still hurt from running into the tree. He wanted to sit down and ignore everything in the hopes that it would go away. Except Lette. He thought Lette could stay.

He realized he had not introduced himself. "I'm Will," he said. "I'm a farmer."

Lette nodded. She looked back at Balur. "How about farming?" she asked the lizard man, apropos—as far as Will could tell—of nothing. "Working with your hands. Very physically demanding, farmwork can be."

Balur grunted. "Bad for reflexes. Ruin muscle memory," he said, leaving Will none the wiser.

Lette sighed, sank to her knees, and started rummaging through the possessions of the nearest corpse. Behind her, Balur had moved on to a different part of the cave. He shook out two more goblins, then, disappointed, flung them away to start a new pile.

As they landed there was a muffled yell.

Balur hesitated, arm still outstretched from his throw. "Got a live one," he said.

Will's stomach tightened, a sharp knot lodging near his kidneys. He looked back at the entrance to the cave. He could slip away. They wouldn't notice. He could...

He could what? Run into more trouble? It was unlikely he would come across any other well-armed strangers to brutally slaughter all of his problems. Given the many and various ways the world had tried to screw him over this night, staying with Lette and Balur actually seemed the safer option.

Lette had her short sword out once more and was advancing on the source of the sound, Balur by her side. They slowed as they came close. Then with a speed that surprised Will, Balur darted forward and grabbed something. It wriggled and writhed in the lizard man's massive hand as he held it aloft.

It was bigger than the goblin corpses littering the ground. And it was wrapped in ropes. Balur had it by its ankles, but it still took Will a moment to realize the massive scruff of hair at the bottom was a man's hair and beard.

"That's not a goblin," Will said, just in case stating the obvious would help.

"Might be in league with them," Balur said, eyes narrowed at the struggling form. Grunts and squeaks emerged, and Will realized that one of the ropes had firmly gagged the man. "Maybe be killing it just in case."

"In league?" Will said incredulously. "He's tied hand and foot."

Lette nodded. "Farm boy makes a compelling case."

"I am still thinking I should perhaps be squishing it. Just in—"

"I'm still thinking about spaying you," Lette cut in. "Put the poor bugger down."

Grudgingly, Balur lowered the man to the ground. Lette's knife appeared in her hand, apparently without having traveled through the intervening space between it and the sheath at her waist. The knife flashed in a single stroke, and the bonds fell away.

A dirty, disheveled man emerged from the looping mass of rope, shouting as he came. He was naked except for a pair of discolored undershorts, and a fairly thick coating of mud. He was rail thin, but with a small potbelly sticking out, as if he had at some point in the past swallowed a child's ball and it had obstinately stuck in his system. His arms too were more muscular than his frame might suggest, and his hands were disproportionately large. His face was almost entirely lost in a shock of hair and beard, long, tightly curled bristles standing out in wild clumps.

"Varmagants!" he was screaming. "Barph-cursed wotsits! Menagerie! Cursed and hexed vermin! Thy cannot prevent me. I am the inevitable! I am the word of the future that shall come! I am the inescapable odor!"

Both Lette and Balur took a step away from the man. Lette's sword was up once more.

It was rather a shock to Will that he recognized the man.

"Firkin?" he said.

Lette glanced at Will, quick and darting. "You know him?" she said fixing her attention back on the raving, half-naked man.

Will took a step toward him. And, yes. Yes he did. It was indeed his father's old farmhand, Firkin.

Memories flooded Will. Sitting with his father and the farmhands on a summer's day, all of them laughing at Firkin's tall tale. Up on Firkin's shoulders, his mouth full of stolen apple flesh, racing across a field, his father chasing and cursing. Watching Firkin tell jokes as his father branded the pigs. Passing bread out of a kitchen window while his mother's back was turned, Firkin gathering the rolls up in a fold of his shirt. Sitting and talking about dragons and dreaming of revolution. Watching Firkin tickle the cow's backside with a porcupine quill and then watching as the cow's kick sent him halfway across the yard. Laughing so hard he thought some part of him might rupture. Firkin and his father standing in the yard, yelling at each other, red-faced. Will and Firkin sitting slouched beneath a tree, daydreaming about stealing a dragon's gold from beneath his nose. Firkin drinking so much he fell off the table, and his father, not far behind him, laughing so hard he joined him on the floor. His mother slapping Firkin full across the face, the red handprint standing out stark on his pale skin. Firkin telling him that he didn't want company right now, and the first feeling of utter rejection in his life. Then riding a cow, madcap down a hill, Firkin running behind full tilt, switching its behind. His mother holding him, sobbing and shouting at the same time. Asking his father where Firkin was. Days spent listless and wandering. Then a meal interrupted by a knock at the door, his father rising, words exchanged with an unseen man, voices rising, the scuffle of violence, and then Firkin framed in the doorway, his father on the floor, lip bloody, horror in Firkin's eyes. Then Firkin from a distance, a shadow shape that haunted distant fences. Riding with his father into town and seeing a man shouting at people who weren't there—he only recognized him as Firkin as they passed him on the way home. The moment when he realized he was used to that sight, not bothered by it anymore. His father's funeral—seeing that familiar shadow that used to haunt the fences. Watching Firkin being thrown out of the tavern again. Again. Again.

And now here. Firkin. The village drunk. The village crazy. A man who seemed to be waiting for everyone to forget why they gave him the dregs from their plates, the spare copper sheks they couldn't spare.

Firkin chose that moment to vomit noisily and messily over the floor. It was a practiced movement—tip and pour. He straightened, wiping his mouth. "Darn varmints," he said. "Gone went fed me some of the pootin'."

Nobody seemed up to the task of asking him what "pootin' " was.

Balur regarded the filthy, scrawny man and then shrugged. "Is looking goblin-y to me." He hefted his hammer.

"No!" Will yelled, darting toward the old farmhand. "No, he's not. He's a friend."

Firkin narrowed his eyes at Will. "I don't like you and your bunk," he said with surprising clarity.

"I am saving you from poor taste in friends," Balur said, not relaxing his grip on the hammer.

Firkin assessed the massive lizard man, stuck out his lower lip, and squinted with one eye. "You's a biggun," he said. "I like the bigguns. Carry more of the ale for me. Down to the merry lands, and we all drown happy like." He smacked his lips twice.

"We can't kill him, Balur," said Lette from behind Will and Firkin, sounding slightly exasperated. Will felt a wave of gratitude flood through him.

"We can be," said Balur matter-of-factly, causing the wave to break. "Be being simple. I be bringing down this hammer with speed of a certain amount. His head is going crump, and we are having a dead man there."

"Well, I know literally you can kill him…"

"Thank you," said Balur, readying himself once more.

"No!" Will shouted again. "He's my friend. He helped raise me."

Balur gave Will a skeptical look. "Maybe I should be killing him to be saving you from your poor taste in friends, then I should be killing you to be saving Lette from her poor taste in men. Everybody be being happier then."

"No!" Will said, starting to feel repetitive, but not sure what other words might save him from a homicidal lizard man at this point in the proceedings.

"If we're saving me from my taste in friends," said Lette to Balur, "maybe I should be killing you then."

The hammer blow continued to fail to fall.

"Look," said Will, reaching out to Balur, imploring, "he's just an old drunk, who the goblins found and tied up. Who knows how long he's been captive? He needs some kindness, not death threats." That, at least, seemed obvious to him. A little piece of the world he could have make sense.

"Was all part of my plan," said Firkin, tapping the side of his nose. "Right where I wanted them."

"You're not being where I want you," Balur groused, but he finally put down the hammer. The head rung as it struck the stone ground, a sonorous bass note. Will had no idea how he'd been able to hold the weight of it for so long.

"Let Firkin just stay for the night," Will said, turning to Lette, now that yet another threat had been averted. "He'll catch his death out in the rain, and you only just saved his life from the goblins."

Lette nodded. "Be a shame to put good work to waste. He sleeps downwind of me and there'll be no complaints."

Balur grunted. Possibly in agreement.

"Hey," Lette said as if struck by a sudden thought, putting a hand on Firkin's shoulder. "Don't happen to have seen a purse, have you?"

"I seen the world," said Firkin, eyes fixing on some far-off point. "I seen the plans. I seen the writing on a turtle's back. I seen the insides of a cow." He nodded, self-satisfied. "It was warm in there," he added.

"Right," said Lette. "I'll just look over here then."

As the search continued, Firkin drifted away toward the cave entrance. Will was worried he might wander into the rain, but he stayed standing there, half-sketched in moonlight, staring out into the night, muttering obscenities to himself.

Behind him, Lette and Balur seemed to be losing what little good temper they'd had.

"Where in the name of Cois's cursed cock is it?" Lette spat. "Where did that little fucker put it?"

"Maybe you were tracking him wrong. Maybe this is being the wrong cave."

"Oh, it's insulting my professional skill set is it now? That's how you're going to fix this situation? By pissing me off so much that I gut and skin you and sell your hide. Except, oh wait." She struck the side of her head with the heel of her palm. "It's fucking worthless. If I just hung a ball sack from a stick and carried it about with me it would be very little different from having you around."

Balur shrugged. "Be being a better conversation starter too."

Joining the conversation, Will realized, would be a little bit like holding his hand in a flame to see how it felt. Lette captivated him, but the piles of corpses around the room were a useful reminder that she could back up her threats if she wanted to. And then, despite all this sensible thinking, he found his jaw starting to move

"Could he be right?" he said, pointing to Balur. "Could there be another cave?"

Lette rolled her eyes and set her jaw. "Look around you," she said. "There are sixty-four corpses here. We left eighteen others back up at the mountain pass. That means they need to scavenge enough wildlife to support eighty-two souls. That means a range of twenty or more miles in any direction from here. That means that if any other tribe came within that distance they'd fight until the others were dead and their eyes boiled down to surprisingly tasty after-dinner snacks. Which means that unless I'm a complete fucking idiot who couldn't track her own grandmother from the bedroom to the privy, then this is the only fucking place the goblin that stole my purse could have gone. And yet that fucking purse is not fucking here."

Another dagger appeared as if by magic in her hand, and she flung it at one of the piles of corpses. It buried itself up to the hilt in a dead goblin's back. She spat after it.

There was, Will thought, something very sexy about Lette's competence. The area of expertise was utterly terrifying, but, on the other hand, it was significantly more exciting than butter churning, or animal husbandry, or any of the other interests the Village girls usually pursued.

"Could the thief have dropped it?" he said somewhat against his better judgment. He was trying to keep in mind that the moth tended to come out of confrontations with the flame rather the worse for wear, but it wasn't helping much.

Lette closed her eyes.

Balur grunted again. "Running pretty hard, it was," he said. "And it was being focused on not dying more than it was on being rich."

Lette groaned.

"It was being easy enough for us to miss," Balur continued. "We were being focused on the beast instead."

Lette clawed her hands down her face.

"Might be a drop even," Balur went on. "Someplace special hidden like. Be dumping the stuff there and be returning for it later when the coast has been cleared. Be throwing it up in a tree even. Makeshift drop."

"Shut up," said Lette. "Just shut up." She sank to her knees. "Gods' hex on it all."

Will almost reached out to her, to put a hand on her shoulder, but he saw Balur shaking his head.

"I had a coin once," Firkin commented from the front of the room. "But she left me. Cantankerous bitch."

It happened so fast, Will almost missed it. A roar of rage from Lette. The blur of her limbs. And then she was across the room, knife in hand, holding Firkin's collar by the other, pressing him up against the wall.

"You fucking—" she started to snarl.

"Excuse me?"

A new voice—the tone deep but feminine—brought Lette to an abrupt halt.

They all stared at the newcomer standing in the entrance of the cave. She wore a gray traveling robe, hood pulled up to obscure her features. Dark-skinned, long-fingered hands were clasped in front of her. Looking at them, Will found himself thinking of small blackbirds.

For a moment everything was very still.

"By Barph's ball sack," Lette said, not letting go of the squirming Firkin. "How many people are going to wander into this cursed cave tonight? Is there some gods-hexed sign I missed?"

"Like you were missing a goblin tossing all our gold," Balur murmured.

Lette whirled, pointed the dagger. "Don't you even fucking start."

"You know," said the figure, "I think this is the wrong cave after all." There was a tone of refinement to her voice that made Will straighten up a little, and run his hands down his shirt to smooth it. The action mostly served to spread the blood-stains out.

"I'll j-just be going," said the robed woman, and stepped away, back toward the sheets of rain that blanketed the night.

The tremor in her voice caught Will's attention, though. He saw water dripping from the front of her hood in an almost steady stream. Her robe swung heavily. She was soaked to the bone.

"Wait," he said. "You can't go out."

The others looked at him. Even Firkin, still pressed up against the wall.

"She's soaked to the bone." He pointed out to the room at large. "She'll catch her death."

"You be saying that a lot, I think," Balur said. "Unhealthy obsession."

Will stared around at the sixty-four goblin corpses. But, yes, of course, he was the one with an unhealthy obsession. Though, given the size difference between him and Balur, he decided to keep that opinion quiet.

Instead he just said, "It's been that sort of night."

Lette let out a small huff of laughter. She let Firkin go. The disheveled man collapsed away from her. "Come in then," she said to the woman in the cave's entrance. "Let's get a fire going and try to salvage what's left of this shit show of a day."

# 4

# Quirk

Lette studied the woman in the cave's entrance. The way she held her weight on her feet. The position of her hands as they hung at her sides. The way her eyes moved.

Lette relaxed. Whoever this woman was, she was not someone who carved her way through life with steel. She had taken Lette's words of invitation at face value, rather than as an invitation to remain somewhere Lette could keep an eye on her. She was another one like the farm boy, Will.

Well...not exactly like him.

There was something to the farm boy. She could not put her finger on it exactly. Though she thought perhaps she would like to. He was not thick in the chest and arms the way she had liked in some of the mercenaries she had known. But there was none of their preening pride in him either. And he was lean, and had the hard, flat muscles of a man who worked with his hands for long days and nights. She had known a boy like that once, a long time ago. He had been sweet. And when she had left him he had borne the same utterly idiotic expression as well. As if her kicking him in the balls was the first time he'd realized he had them.

And still, despite her assessment, when the woman in the cave entrance finally started to move, Lette instinctively dropped a blade into her palm. Then, grimacing, she slipped it back into its sheath.

Maybe Balur was right. Maybe the only thing she was suited

to was death and mayhem. It would be hard to explain away the maim-first-and-use-torture-to-ask-questions-later instinct if she was trying to live the life of a seamstress.

She was not the only one watching the newcomer. Balur had narrowed his eyes. "Why were you hesitating before you were coming in?" he growled.

The woman froze once more. Lette could just make out her eyes beneath her hood, large and brown. There was a fright in them, yes, but it was not alone. Curiosity lingered there as well. Not exactly what Lette expected.

She could feel the weight of the blade in her sleeve.

"Had it crossed your mind," Will said stepping forward, utterly oblivious to danger, "that she might be intimidated by the large lizard man covered with other people's blood?"

Balur shrugged. "Goblin blood. Goblins are not being people."

"Well actually—" the woman in the cloak said, then hesitated. Her gaze flicked out from beneath her hood, nervous and quick.

Could it be a ruse? It was difficult to mask the signs of readiness, but it was possible. Lette was doing it herself now. Long days of practice and punishment let her hold her shoulders loose, keep her fingers curled slightly.

Yet with one flick of her wrist...

She found herself thinking of Will. The look of horror that would be on his witless face if a blade buried itself in the woman's throat. That shouldn't bother her, but it did. A bit. Well, a very little bit. But even that infinitesimal hesitation was new.

Maybe it was change. Maybe she was changing.

She risked giving the farm boy an appraising look.

Balur's attention hadn't wavered. "Actually what?" he growled at the woman.

"Well," she said again. Lette saw her lick her lips. "All I really meant was that there was an interesting treatise written in the previous century by Friar-Abbot Matteson about whether goblins were intelligent enough to be qualified as people, or whether they were a lower life-form more akin to animals. He, you'll probably be glad to know, agreed with you. That their personhood was negligible. But on the other hand, he was also a big proponent of using broccoli as a siege engine. That's pushed a lot of the current academics in the other direction. The current wave of thinking is that if goblins were treated civilly they would behave in a more civilized way. The trouble is, of course"—she laughed slightly, a nervous chuckle—"finding a town that wants to make that gamble should we prove to be wrong."

Considerable silence met this statement. Firkin seemed to have no patience for it.

"Knew a goblin once," he said. "Called himself Marvin." He nodded a few times. "Lots of bones in him," he added after a moment's thought.

The silence decided to hang around a little longer.

"You are talking a lot," Balur said eventually. His eyes were still suspicious slits.

"Yes," the woman agreed. "As the young man pointed out, I'm rather nervous. And I do tend to ramble when I feel that way." And then with absolutely no segue whatsoever, "You're an Analesian, aren't you?"

Lette noticed that Balur's hammer's head had left the ground. Not by more than half an inch, barely enough to be noticeable, but enough to make the mask of nonchalance that much harder to maintain.

"How are you knowing that?" Balur sounded belligerent. Lette knew he could get terribly precious about his exotic mystique.

"Well," the woman coughed twice, "the Analesians are pretty much the only race of eight-foot-tall sentient lizards, which does narrow it down a bit."

"She's got them smarts," said Firkin, still lingering by the wall where Lette had pinned him. "All in her head and coming out her mouth." He nodded. "Like when you squish them ants' heads."

"Look." Will tried to step between Balur and the woman. Lette couldn't decide if he was brave or stupid. Or possibly a dangerous mix of both. "I don't think we need to threaten violence to anyone just because they read a book once in their life. Can't we just make a fire, and all dry out so we make it to the morning?"

For a moment, Lette allowed herself to step away from herself. Step away from her frustration, the tired ache in her bones, the girlish intrigue in Will and what he could do with those heavy callused hands. For a moment she was nothing but steel. A blade.

*Firkin was at the cave entrance. He was slow, but unpredictable. He should be the first to go. The knife in her hand loosed at his neck. Will was the next threat, young and strong as he was. But Balur would move before Will did. The farmer would be stuck staring at the blood fountaining from Firkin's neck, aghast. Balur would turn him into a stain on the ground before he figured out what he wanted to do. That left the woman. Also unpredictable, but off-balance now. Lette could close the distance, sweep a knife blade across her eyes, slow her down, then she and Balur could deal with whatever she threw at them. It would all be over in seconds. And then...*

No.

Lette stepped back into herself. Away from the cold analysis of murder. That was not who she was going to be here. There was, she was beginning to realize, a point when paranoia stopped being a helpful survival tool, and became more of a social impediment.

"Yes," she said to Will, forcibly ungritting her teeth. "A fire. That sounds lovely."

Balur looked at her perplexed. She tried to look at him with the daggers she was restraining herself from throwing.

Several of the goblins' torches were still burning. She started to pick them up, pile them together in the center of the room. Will, though, stepped toward the woman.

"I'm Will," he said. "Pleased to meet you."

Lette hesitated, watched the woman's hand snake out to meet Will's. She could throw the torch, strike the woman in the face...

The woman's grip looked frail in Will's big hand. "My name is Quirkelle Bal Tehrin," she said. She had a slight accent. Southern, and unless Lette missed her mark, Western as well. "People in this part of the world tend to call me Quirk. Very nice to meet you."

They shook hands. Lette watched their palms. But Will didn't convulse. Didn't pull his hand away with a cry. Didn't start to choke on his tongue or grab his arm in sudden agony.

Lette gently set down the torch she was gripping.

"I'm a farmer," Will continued. "That's Lette"—he pointed toward her—"and that's Balur. They're..." He hesitated. "Very nice but violent strangers." He shrugged nervously. Lette found she could live with the description. "And that's Firkin," he said, and hesitated, "he's...erm..."

"I am the moonlight's breath," said Firkin. "The shadow and the blade. The voice of the one to come charging out of the night cloaked in red, and fire, and death! I am the sound that cannot be unheard! I am—"

He interrupted his own diatribe with a resounding belch, then stared off into space.

"Yes," said Will, "he's that."

The woman, Quirk, nodded, taking it all in. She was still wearing her soaking-wet cloak. Still shivering.

"So who are you?" Lette asked, gathering up another pair of torches. She was aware of Balur standing between them and the cave exit, appearing to be at rest, and actually being very far from it.

"She just said," said Will. Lette briefly wondered how he'd managed to make it this far through life without dying. Perhaps she wasn't the first kindly stranger to stumble into his life and save him from impaling himself on his own guilelessness?

"I'm a thaumatobiologist," said Quirk, who was apparently quicker off the mark, "if that's what you mean. I'm based out of the Tamathian University."

Tamathia. South and West. Lette kept her smile from her lips, but it was there all the same.

"You gonna talk," Firkin spat from where he sat at the cave's mouth, "use them real words."

Balur grunted. "May all the Pantheon be helping me, I am agreeing with the crazy man."

Firkin stopped staring at the night, turned back to them. "Get out of my brains, monster man," he growled. "Leave them be."

Balur cocked his head. He was not, Lette knew, used to people taking that tone with him. Still, she was less interested in Firkin's ability to shorten his life expectancy than she was in Quirk's brief autobiography.

"Tamathia?" she said. "That's a few hundred leagues from here." She was reassessing the woman yet again. No one came a few hundred leagues without a few tricks to keep them safe.

"Three hundred and sixty-nine as near as I can estimate," Quirk said in agreement. "But the Kondorra valley is the only place with dragons on the continent, so it was the place I had to come."

Will actually stepped away from her. There was a look on his face...Lette tried to evaluate. Was it disgust? It seemed out of place on his simple face.

"The dragons?" he said. And there was definitely an edge to his voice now. "You wanted...You came from far away to see... The gods-hexed *dragons*?"

No, Lette thought, it wasn't disgust. It was hatred—a sword hidden in this haystack of a man. And maybe Quirk wasn't the one she should be reassessing.

What did she know about Kondorra? That a loose association

of merchant dragons ruled over it. That they ran some of the most successful trade routes on the continent. That you only attacked their caravans when you were desperate or very sure they couldn't track you down and use your intestines to string you up from the nearest hanging tree.

Quirk, it seemed, was also having trouble reevaluating Will after this abrupt emotional turn. "Yes," she said, a touch of defensiveness in her cultured voice. "Well, I think I said I was a thaumatobiologist."

Will stared at her blankly.

"I think," Lette said, voice held steady as a dueling blade, "that perhaps that word needs a little more explanation."

Quirk looked at them, for all the world like a kicked puppy. "Thaumatobiology?" she said. Then with a note of pleading. "You don't...? Not one of you has ever heard of the field?"

"I know what a field is," said Firkin, a touch indignantly. "Took a shit in one just the other day, so I did."

"You work for the dragons?" Lette saw her own slow-growing suspicion writ large on Will's features.

Quirk shook her head violently. "For...?" she managed. She still seemed bewildered by this line of questioning. "I *study* dragons."

Again the room seemed to stop, everyone trying to process. The fire crackled in the middle of the room now, heat starting to rise.

"*Study?*" Will still seemed uncertain as to whether he should exchange his hatred for incredulity.

"Yes." Quirk was earnest. "Thaumatobiology. The study of magical flora and fauna." She looked around at them, seemed to resign herself. "Plants and animals," she said, a little sadly.

"You have been studying plants?" Balur seemed outraged by the idea.

"Well, yes." Quirk nodded. "Very useful area, actually. I mean, if you just talked to Will here, I'm sure he would be full of all sorts of valuable information about crop rotation, and what fields are best for which sort of planting. That sort of information is invaluable. Not to mention the healers who use plants in their poultices. And the dye makers who need to collect the right types of berry. All of them are expert biologists in their own fields. My field just happens to be magical plants. Though really my main interest is thamatofauna . . . well megathaumatofauna."

It was very quiet, but Lette could just make out Balur's growling. He did not do well with polysyllables. It made him feel like people were trying to get one past him on the grounds that he was foreign.

"So . . . really big magical creatures," Lette hazarded.

"Yes," Quirk said. Lette couldn't help but feel the woman's smile was a little patronizing.

*Magical.* Lette thought of those 369 leagues the woman had crossed.

"So," said Lette, allowing the dagger to once more slip from its sheath into her palm. "You're a magician."

It made sense now. Quirk wasn't balanced because she didn't need to be balanced. She wasn't quick because she didn't need to be quick. Her weapon moved as quick as thought, as swift as a whispered word. She could flay them all with her mind.

Lette's only hope was a dagger thrown fast enough, unexpected enough.

"Oh." Quirk almost seemed to stumble without actually going anywhere. "No. No not at all. Not in any way, shape, or form. Well, I mean . . . not anymore anyway. Not now. No."

Lette did not allow her arm to slacken for an instant. "Being a magician," she said, "is not exactly something one can give up." It would be like giving up being someone who breathed air, or who ate food with their mouth. Magicians just were. Sometimes some member of the Pantheon, be it Lawl, or Cois, or Klink, or Toil, or any other of the fickle bunch would reach down their divine finger and plant it in a mother's swollen belly. And the child was touched, and would be forever. That was not a palm print that simply washed away.

"I am," Quirk spoke awkwardly, "reformed. I have stepped away from practicing the magical arts, and now simply study the phenomena in other creatures."

Balur hefted his hammer up onto his shoulder. "You are saying that you can be doing magic, but that you are choosing to not be doing it?" To describe his tone as dubious would be like describing the Cois—hermaphroditic god(dess) of love, fertility, and loose morality in general—as being a little bit forward with the ladies.

Quirk straightened, pushed her shoulders back, held her chin high. Lette thought she was probably trying to appear defiant. Unfortunately all she was really achieving was to remind people of how haughty magicians were said to be.

"That," said Quirk in an austere tone, "is exactly what I chose. I chose to be in control of who I am and what I do."

Three hundred and sixty-nine leagues. On her own. Without a single spell? Lette wasn't sure she quite believed that. But she did believe that Quirk wanted it to be true. The question was how in control the woman was. And how much warning would there be before she slipped?

Balur was shaking his head. "That is like owning a hammer and trying to put in nails with your hand."

Quirk didn't let go of her rigid pose for a second. "The problem arises," she said, "if every time you use the hammer you accidentally bludgeon three or four people along with the nail."

And suddenly, without warning, she won Lette over. A chord ringing out that was too much in tune with the one thrumming in her own breast. That desire to be better. That struggle.

"Come on," Lette said, stepping toward Quirk, the weight of the blade strapped to her wrist suddenly forgotten. "I thought the whole point of this fire was to make sure you didn't freeze. Get that cloak off and come closer."

# 5

# The Problem with
# Dissecting Dragons

Will watched Lette approach Quirk, watched her shoulders finally relax. A letting go of some inner tension. For some reason she had switched from treating Quirk as if she was some barely contained bag of knives and ferrets, to more like she was the poor, cold woman she appeared to be.

He was making the opposite journey.

*Study dragons?* The only reason Will could think of for that was if you were looking for weak points. And this woman seemed to be missing both the army and the suicidal tendencies that usually accompanied that exercise.

Quirk shrugged off her cloak, then searched for a patch of floor relatively clear of intestines and bodily fluids where she could lay it out to dry. Beneath the cloak she wore a simple pale green dress bound with a blue cord. It was not much drier than the cloak.

Without her hood to hide her face, Quirk looked to be in her early forties, curly black hair cropped close to her skull. She was broad-featured—wide nose and lips. A line of gold studs stitched its way up her right ear. There was a direct, no-nonsense quality to her gaze, though the lines around her eyes seemed to suggest a smile was not hidden too deeply.

She settled herself down by the fire, Lette beside her. Firkin ambled over from the cave entrance, all joints and gangling limbs. Then came Balur. The lizard man at least still seemed to be nursing the suspicions Lette had released.

*Study dragons.* Will felt his knuckles clench, unclench. Clench again. *Study the fuckers that took my farm from me.*

He breathed steadily, waited for his vision to broaden back from the pinpoint it wanted to become. He opened his hands, joined the others at the fire. Staring at this woman suspiciously wouldn't help much. It was like his father used to say: A breeched calf didn't turn itself around just because you gave it the stink-eye. You wanted to sort out a problem, you better just get elbow deep in cow vagina.

His father, Will reflected, had not had much poetry in his heart.

Still, the advice was sound enough. "I'm sorry," he said, to Quirk, doing his best to keep his voice calm. "I'm still having some trouble with the bit where you actually study dragons."

"Really?" Quirk's eyebrows lifted in what appeared to be genuine surprise. "Well, they're fascinating creatures. And we still know barely anything about them. We haven't a clue how they generate the fire they breathe. Some sort of flammable fluid secreted from a sac inside the cheeks or throat is the most likely explanation, but then how do they light it? And how do they even get off the ground? The sheer mass of them speaks against it. The ideal of course would be to get to dissect one—"

"Dissect one?" Will wasn't sure if he should laugh or shout in anger. "Of course. Just walk right up to a member of the Consortium and ask if you can slit them up the belly." He put a hand to his head. "Gods. Study them? Have you ever even seen one? You don't..."

He trailed off as Quirk avoided his eye. *It couldn't be...* But the facts were there in front of him, writ large in her body language.

"Wait," he said. "You study dragons and you've never even seen one?"

"Well, I've seen...drawings," said Quirk defensively. "And I have read some very detailed, albeit partial, descriptions of them. Though some did seem like they exaggerated a little." She chuckled slightly to herself. "One of them described a creature over twenty feet long. Can you imagine? I mean, the flight mechanics are improbable enough for a creature half that size—"

"Twenty feet?" Will cut her off again. "You think twenty feet is improbably long for a dragon?" His laughter felt almost hysterical. This was deranged.

"Well, obviously," said Quirk, shuffling back from the fire a little. "I mean just think of the thrust needed to get something..." And then she finally caught on. "You've seen a dragon? Actually *seen* one? Living?"

"Seen one?" Will spat. "I've had my whole fucking life ruined by one."

"And it was over twenty feet long?" Quirk asked with, Will thought, a certain amount of callousness.

"Great big varmints." Firkin decided to chime in. "Rats of the sky, I say. If rats breathed fire and ate cattle, like." A dreamy look entered his eyes. "Oh that'd be a rat, that would. I'd like one of those rats. Keep him as a pet and call him Lawrence."

The time had come, Will decided, to reveal certain truths to Quirk. "Mattrax," he said, "the dragon who governs this northern tip of the Kondorra valley, which we are oh so lucky to be in right now, is fifty yards from snout to tail and considered runty for his kind. It gives him a shitty attitude, but it's hard to pick out because all the dragons in the Consortium have shitty attitudes. They live in vast fortresses, surrounded by guards picked from the arse-end of humanity, who love nothing more than to go around beating their arbitrary rules into the people who live near them. And then every year they send out tax collectors to steal as much of your coin as they can simply so they can sit on it and feel fucking pretty. The only time they drag their sagging guts out of their caves is so they can steal a few cattle for a midafternoon snack, and literally shit on the people whom they govern. That is, in fact, a little game for Mattrax. To see how many people he can hit with a single bowel movement. As a species they are so comfortable with the idea of being evil overlords that they actually hold gatherings from time to time in the core of an active volcano. That is who you study. Tyrants. Arseholes with wings."

He was he realized, leaning forward into the fire. Spittle sprayed with his words, the rage in his gut boiling hotter than the flames.

"They took my farm," he said, and he felt his eyes sting. "They took everything from me. Everything. The farm my mother and father had built with their own hands." The thought was almost too raw for him to utter. "And now I'm sitting in a cave that smells of dead bodies and shit."

Balur shifted uncomfortably. "Being sorry for that," he said, tapping his stomach. "Raw goblin...Never be sitting well."

There was nothing but silence for a long time.

"Well, the problem is," Quirk said, sounding apologetic, "thaumatobiologists stopped going out in the field a hundred years ago or so. Self-preservation, really. There was a high propensity for them to be consumed by the subjects they were studying. In fact, if my research is correct, I'm the first thaumatobiologist to attempt the field study of dragons in approximately two hundred years."

There was, Will thought, an unwelcome note of pride slipping into her voice at the end.

"No," he said. "The problem is that you're studying them, when really what we should be doing is killing them and selling them for parts." The laugh that came up from him was an ugly, unfamiliar thing. That was something else Mattrax had given him. Bitterness. "At least," he said, "that way I'd have enough money to pay off my taxes and get my farm back."

"In my experience," Balur said, pulling a small steel flask from his belt, "if you are needing coin, it is best to be just taking it."

Will heard his bitter laugh again. It sounded no better this time around. "The only one with any coin around here is Mattrax."

Balur unstoppered his flask, swigged, and smiled, showing every one of his stained yellow teeth. "So be stealing from Mattrax."

*Steal from Mattrax.*

Memory rushed over Will like a wave, carried him to another time, another place.

It was a sunny afternoon. His back was pressed against a tree. There was a blue sky above his head. Birdsong and laughter. The memory was a collage of details scattered over a sketched in world. He was young. What...? Six? Perhaps seven? His father had sent him to pick up apples in the orchard before they rotted but he was shirking his duties. So was Firkin.

The man was... Was he so different back then from the man Will had met in the cave? His beard was cropped more closely, perhaps. But his hair was still wild, though perhaps more in the way a hare is wild than a wolf. And the potbelly was yet to fully manifest. There was less gray and more brown about his temples. And the eyes... They stood out clear in the memory. There was a calmness there that no longer existed.

Eighteen years ago. Barely any time at all, and somehow a lifetime as well.

"It's good here, Firkin," Will had said, his voice reedy with youth, the words spat around a mouthful of apple.

Firkin had nodded, taken the time to swallow his own mouthful before replying. "You da runs a good place."

"No." That wasn't what Will had meant. "This place." He swept his arm expansively. "Kondorra. The valley."

He expected Firkin's smile. Firkin had a smile that shone in rooms like the sun shone through the window. He had a smile that got in your belly and lifted it up like it could carry you away over the hills.

But Firkin didn't smile. Firkin grimaced instead. "She's seen better days, Will. This valley has."

Will didn't understand. But he didn't want Firkin to know he didn't understand. Firkin didn't treat him like he was little. Firkin treated him like he was big. And Firkin was funny too. He told jokes that made Ma cluck her tongue. Will didn't want Firkin to start thinking he was little and stop telling jokes.

"Yeah," he said instead. "But the dragons keep it nice."

He'd seen Mattrax once. And if he was honest it had been terrifying. The crashing of his wings. The roar of his voice. The panic of the animals. His mother's sharp shriek. The tightness in his father's eyes. But afterward...Afterward there had been something magnificent about the vastness of the dragon, of knowing that he was *theirs*. Of knowing that he had chosen to take Kondorra and make it his special place.

He knew about the gods, of course. His ma and pa had taken special care to make sure he knew Lawl, and his wife Betra, and their children, Toil, Klink, and Knole. But the gods got confusing with Cois who was Lawl's daughter and Toil's sister-daughter. And then there was Barph, the absent god, who was Cois's son, but also her lover, and who was Betra's daughter too.

Will really didn't understand Cois at all.

But in the end it all came to the same thing: No god had manifested in Kondorra in years. That was what everybody had said. In contrast, Mattrax was *real*.

Which all added up to considerable confusion on his part when Firkin cuffed him on the back of the head. "Don't you ever be saying that. You hear me, boy?"

Firkin's eyes were glittering hard, and there were no smiles in him as he glared at Will.

Will felt his lip start to tremble, felt tears pushing up behind his eyes.

"Oh Cois's cock," Firkin said, rolling his eyes. "I didn't mean..." He pulled Will to him in a rough hug. "And pretend I didn't say that about Cois and her...his...pissing god. Oh and pretend I didn't...You know what?" He held Will by the arms, and held him so he could look him in the eye. "The gods have abandoned this valley, so as long as you don't tell your mother I said so, piss on the gods. Even though Cois would probably enjoy it."

Will didn't know exactly what Firkin was talking about, but he knew his ma would do more than cluck her tongue at that. He giggled through his tears.

"I'm sorry I had rough words for you," said Firkin. "But you've got some things backwards there, and they rubbed me backwards, and some beasts don't like that, if you follow me."

Will sniffed, and nodded. "I follow." And that was mostly true.

"You weren't here before the dragons," Firkin said. "And sometimes I forget that." He let Will go, and grabbed another apple off the ground. He took a bite. "Not that it were all that," he said, still chewing and spraying chunks of white apple flesh across the orchard in a way that kept Will smiling. "Lords will always be lords, and taxes will always be taxes, and nobles will always be colossal bastards all the world over." He leaned in and nodded sagely. "They say you're a bastard if you don't know who your pa was, but if a man can tell you who his pa was eight generations back...that's when you know you've got a real bastard."

Will's tears were long forgotten by now.

"No," said Firkin. "It weren't perfect, but it worked. People bitched and moaned. I bitched and moaned, for that matter. But we got by. Wasn't no golden-age bullshit, like some will tell you—"

Will giggled again.

"—but it were all right."

Another grimace. "Then Mattrax and the rest of those..." He hesitated. "Well," he said with another knowing nod, "maybe you're not quite old enough for me to use the word that really describes those dragons. But they came along. And there was a fight."

Will was old enough to know that there had been a war. He'd seen the grave markers around the temple in the village. He'd heard the scraps of stories his ma exchanged with those who came to buy eggs and milk each morning.

"Why'd folk fight, Firkin?" asked. He'd never quite understood that bit.

"Well." Firkin shrugged. "The nobles may be bastards, but they also know that if some great fire-breathing beast out of legend lands himself in the middle of a field that you should probably go stab him before he eats up too many of the farmers. That's the idea about taxes, you see? The farmer pays them, and the noble uses them to pay the soldiers to stab stuff before it eats the farmer. We've lost that idea since Mattrax and his lot came along. Now the soldiers are more likely to stab the farmers. But that was the original idea."

"The dragons ate farmers?" Will had definitely never heard that before.

"Mostly they ate the soldiers actually." Firkin shrugged. "Touch of irony there."

"So what if they hadn't attacked?" It seemed to Will that if this whole attacking thing happened then everyone would be happier, along with Firkin.

"Well," said Firkin, ruffling Will's hair, "in that case the dragons would have gone and eaten all the nobles, and if there's one thing the nobles like even less than dragons eating all the farmers, it's dragons eating all of *them*."

Will had never truly considered what Mattrax ate before. Thinking about it now, he felt again some of the fear that he'd felt when he'd seen the dragon fly over him. And while he was mostly convinced Firkin was telling him a tall tale, given Mattrax's size, the dragon *could* eat a person. Will shuddered slightly.

"So pretty much the dragons ate the soldiers, and then they ate the nobles," Firkin went on. "And somewhere along the way, the farmers started fighting too."

"Why?" So far it seemed to Will that nobody had actually been threatening to eat the farmers and the whole thing still felt a lot like a giant misunderstanding.

"Because they were fucking idiots," Firkin said, with a certain amount of feeling.

Something about the way he said it felt odd to Will, even at six years old. "Did you fight?" he asked.

Firkin shrugged. "Let me just figure out how to tell this, would you?"

Will mimed buttoning his lips. Firkin laughed. Buttoning his lips always made Firkin laugh. And that made Will laugh, though he did his best to keep his lips shut.

"So the farmers fought. And they did it because...Well, men and women get used to a certain way of living. And even if it's not a great way to live, they'll oftentimes fight to protect it. They get scared of a future they don't know. Like a room you've never been in before and there aren't any lights. So you stay in the room you know, where the lights are. You understand?"

Will nodded. He understood enough.

"And to be fair, when you know the next room has a dragon in it, then you're probably smart to stay where you are," Firkin said with a strange, sad smile. "And I think that back when they started out, the farmers really thought they had a chance. Gods still manifested in Kondorra from time to time back in those days. And they seemed to think that the great father Lawl, or the protective mother Betra, or hardworking Toil, or someone would come and deliver them from their woes. Even if all a god normally did when it was manifested was whore around and break bits of the world." He shook his head.

Will risked a question. "What's whoring around?"

Firkin looked at him and grimaced. "It's...it's a bit like

running round all the farmhouses and sticking your finger in all the pies, and licking the finger in between without washing it. Except worse."

Will imagined every mistress of every household in a rage at him, and wasn't entirely sure what could be worse than that. Still, he let the issue lie for now. Firkin's story was a good one.

"Did a god come?" he asked.

"The gods did jack and shit, Will," Firkin said and threw away his apple core so hard it broke in two when it hit another tree. "Not a sight nor a sound of them. Not even hardworking Toil, who some said was patron of this place. Not protective mother Betra. Not law-obsessed Lawl. None of them. The farmers got eaten up along with everyone else."

"All of the farmers," Will asked incredulous.

"Not all of them, you dolt," said Firkin with a roll of his eyes. "I'm still here, aren't I? Your ma and pa are still here. But enough." His voice grew somber. "Enough got eaten up. Until we gave up, said enough, said we'd do whatever the dragons asked of us."

"What do they ask of us?" Will was trying to imagine Mattrax swooping down off a mountain and landing in front of his mother's kitchen door, and demanding a pie from her.

Firkin smiled, big and broad, and absent of all mirth. "Little things, Will. Little things. They asked us to live in fear. They asked us to give up anything we held dear whenever they wanted it. They asked us to live in poverty. They asked us to scrape by in the dirt when once we used to walk...maybe not tall, but not stooped either."

And Will thought again of the shadow in the sky, of the panic in the fields, and of his mother's scream. And he thought of other things too. He thought of the times he had gone to bed hungry. He thought of the hours his father spent repairing rusting farm tools. He thought of the uniformed men and women who came each year and took away the small coffer of coins his father kept in the corner of the kitchen.

And in his mind that shadow in the sky grew, and the sun didn't shine so bright above his head.

But above all, one thing troubled him. "Firkin," he said, "why didn't you fight?"

Firkin gave another small sad smile. "Nobles aren't the only one who don't want to die," he said.

And that did seem reasonable to Will. So he switched to a new line of thought. "We should kill Mattrax now," he said. The job had clearly not been done right when the dragons first came; he supposed it was up to him now.

Firkin laughed out loud at that. Normally Will liked it when Firkin laughed. It meant something funny had just happened. But now he had an unpleasant feeling that the funny thing was him.

"What?" he said. "He's a bad guy. You said."

"Aye." Firkin nodded. "And I'm glad you listened and you figured that out. But a lot better than us have tried to kill the dragons and they haven't had much luck so far. And while I'm not so keen on being eaten up by a dragon, I'm even less keen on being flayed alive by your ma when I tell her how you've been eaten up."

And that did seem like reasonable logic to Will. But it also led to an impasse. There was a bad guy, someone to be defeated. In all the stories his ma and pa had told him, all the fairy tales and religious fables, the bad guy was faced down and eventually slain.

"So what do we do?"

And then, all of a sudden, there truly was joy in Firkin's smile. Will felt his stomach swelling and getting light, and he felt the sun once more, as he leaned back against the apple tree.

"That's why I like you, Willett Fallows," said Firkin. He pulled out the flask he always carried with him and took a quick tug from it. "Always thinking right. And, no, I don't think we can kill old Mattrax up in his fortress, but I know what I'd like to do."

"What?" Will was all ears.

Firkin grinned as broad as the horizon. "Why, young Will, I'd like to steal from him." He leaned in close. "And I know exactly how to do it."

# 6

# Worst-Laid Plans

The whole memory flashed through Will in an instant. Balur spoke and a moment later he had the taste of fresh apple in his mouth. And then, a moment after that, he tasted all the ashes of the broken promises that had come on that moment's heels.

He looked over at Firkin, hunched over, staring at the fire, eyes and mind lost. And he felt anger, a clenched fist in his gut. It was another new experience, this rage that lurked inside him.

"Oh," he said, turning to Balur, with a degree of aggression that the lizard man's size should have dissuaded. "It's that simple is it? Just take the gold from Mattrax. From a dragon in, wait...what did I say again? Oh yes, an entire fortress full of guards! Because that's the first time anyone in Kondorra has looked at their shitty life and said, 'Wouldn't life be better if we just took all the gold from the dragons?' Because not one evening has been spent in a tavern fantasizing about just that thing. Because we've all had better things to do...Actually I take that back. We *have* had better things to do. We call them 'not being killed by a dragon.' It's a fun way we like to spend our lives round here."

Balur curled back his lips and revealed his teeth for a moment. Will felt his stomach try to bore into the ground beneath him. "Be being a touchy little fucker, aren't we?" the lizard man said.

Will swallowed, breathed, and looked at Lette in the faint hope of support. "It's been a rough day," he managed to get out.

"Well," said Lette, looking at Balur, "if we've lost the fucking purse, and no one here has the coin to hire us, then we'll have to find a mark or move on."

Balur arched...Will wasn't quite sure what it was. The bony ridge that stood in for his eyebrow, he supposed. "There is being no more baking for you, then?" he said, equal parts arch and nonsensical as far as Will could tell.

"Oh shut up and give me the flask." Lette reached out and Balur tossed the thing over to her. She took a swig, and smacked her lips. She was graceful, in a way, Will thought. Not the way that courtesan's were in the stories the tinkerman told down at old Cornwall's tavern. The grace in stories had less...brutality to it. Still, Lette's was a grace of sorts.

"You'd not be denying a man a wee sip of the nectar now, would you?" said Firkin, a wheedling edge sneaking into his voice, eyes large, round, and fixed on the flask. "Not just because he called all your mothers whores?" He smiled and showed the scattered remnants of his teeth.

"When did you...?" Will started.

"A man can mutter, can't he?" yelled Firkin. Then he turned to Lette, stretched out his hands. "Please," he implored. "I need it to live."

Lette seemed unconvinced and glanced at Will. "Noisy drunk or quiet drunk?"

Will grimaced. He would like to give her good news at some point. "Pretty much just this all the time."

Lette rolled her eyes and passed the flask.

"Hey," Balur objected.

Lette waved him away. "There's plenty for everyone."

A faint glugging sound came from Firkin as he upended the flask. They watched him pour. When the growl from Balur began to make the cave's rock floor vibrate, Will laid a hand on Firkin's arm.

"Maybe—"

"No!" Firkin screamed. Alcohol sprayed across Will's face, into the flames, where it hissed and spat. "The fire!" he went on screaming. "In my belly. My balls, man. I need it in my balls! I need the fire. I am the flame! I burn! In my balls!"

He hiccupped loudly, blinked twice at Will, went to take another swig, and collapsed backward. The only part of the performance that shocked Will was that he managed to keep the flask upright the whole way down.

Will plucked the drink out of the old farmhand's fingers. Firkin started to snore. Tentatively Will held it out to Balur, who snatched it back with a sour expression. Then he looked at Firkin. "Least he is being quiet. Probably is being worth the trade-off."

Quirk was watching all of this with a look of slight confusion. This was, Will gathered, not exactly how things went in the halls of academia. She shifted her weight and he half-expected her to get up and leave, but she simply leaned forward, looking back and forth between Lette and Balur.

"You wouldn't seriously propose," she said, "to steal from a dragon's lair?" She paused, seemed to consider the corpses spread around them. "Would you?"

Lette and Balur exchanged a glance.

"I am not knowing," Balur said finally, voice grating out. "I have been doing stupider things."

Lette snorted. "Speak for yourself."

Will's brow furrowed. "Trust me, there's nothing you could have done that is stupider than trying to rob a dragon."

Balur's mouth opened.

"Don't you fucking dare." Lette's tongue lashed out as quick as one of her knives.

Balur rolled his shoulder in a tectonic shrug.

"It would be amazing to see a dragon actually guarding his hoard," said Quirk with what Will could only call an inappropriately dreamy tone. "It's very rarely been seen." She smiled ruefully. "I suppose it's because you're eaten almost immediately after you see it." She nodded to herself. "That does seem far more likely now that I know how big they are. Even if flight doesn't." She looked up at Will. "You're absolutely sure they fly?"

Will looked to the others for support. "You study dragons for a living and you're not entirely sure if they fly?" he asked.

"Dragons don't live in Tamathia any more." Quirk sounded distinctly huffy at this point. "The last one was killed before the Thirsk uprising ten generations back."

"Killed?" At first Will thought he must have misheard her. But then she nodded.

Will reeled. That simple up-down movement of Quirk's head was like a slap in the face. For all his life the impossibility of killing a dragon had been a given. Dragons were as much a part of the landscape as the mountains, as the earth beneath his feet. They were everlasting, immovable. The idea of one dying from old age was almost beyond his comprehension. But killed? That was even more insane than the idea of robbing one.

"How?" he asked. "Where?" Even the idea of dragons beyond Kondorra's borders was lunatic.

"Oh," said Quirk, without any acknowledgment of the violence she was doing to his worldview. "This was back in Tamathia around two hundred fifty years ago. You see, according to the records I've found, dragons used to be far more common in Avarra. Clashes between human settlements and dragons were quite common. But with our advancing technology we apparently got quite good at killing them. The assumption was we'd killed them off, up until the Kondorran incursion thirty years ago."

Will was reduced to blinking. *Killed them off?* How come no one had ever mentioned this to him growing up?

"We still have accounts of the battles," she went on. "They would go out with..." She trailed off, stared into space. "Gods,

I always thought they had the numbers wrong. But groups of about fifteen hundred or so. A small army, I suppose. A thousand archers—five hundred for each wing. Arrows couldn't penetrate the scales on the body, but the leather of the wings was vulnerable to them. Then there would be two hundred pikemen positioned to swipe at its guts when it came in to attack. They would just have to stand in front of the fire and hope they weren't too savagely burned when it was their turn to finally poke at the dragon's guts. Horrific losses, of course. But they went mad for that sort of thing back then. Anyway, once they finally got the dragon on the ground, there were three hundred axe men to finish the job." She shook her head. "They called it sport. A massacre isn't a sport in my opinion." She hung her head sadly.

"I think," Will said, "that I would like to live in Tamathia." He spoke with the same half-dreaming tone as Quirk had when she talked about live dragons.

Lette grunted. "You've got dragons. They've got gods manifesting. That's why uprisings are so common. Knole and Cois showed up a decade or so ago, and there was a civil war. Took them years to build back up. Made them very insular." She rubbed the back of her neck. "You have to buy your way in."

"Another reason to rob that dragon," Balur rumbled.

Having one more dream kicked out from under him was not what Will needed right at that moment. He landed back in reality, hard. "It's impossible to steal from a dragon," he snapped. Then he rounded on Quirk. "Or kill one. They're like shit. No one wants it but everyone's stuck with it."

Balur regarded him coldly. "Can steal from anyone."

Will's bitter laugh was back. "Really?" he said. "Really?" He suddenly wanted to strip Balur of his arrogant ignorance. "All right then. Mattrax lives in a cave up in the mountains. And around the whole cave...I mentioned the fortress full of guards didn't I? So the gold is in the cave. And so is Mattrax. All day.

All night. Guarding it. Along with the guards. He leaves only once each day, to go and stretch for an hour and perform his ablutions on some poor unsuspecting bastard like me."

Balur looked amused. "So—" he started.

"No." Will cut him off. "You don't. Because the cave's entrance has a massive portcullis over it. An ironmonger's wet dream. The whole thing operates on a pressure plate. And about the only thing big enough to trip the mechanism is the gods-hexed dragon you're trying to steal from."

Lette's eyes were narrowed. Will could see the gears working behind them. Some sort of professional pride was at stake. "Wait," she said, "it's built on a castle. The guards must..." She trailed off looking at Will expectantly.

"Sure." Will nodded, the bitter bite of his words still souring his mouth. "The guards have an entrance to the cave beyond just the portcullis. They use it to go into the cave once a day with a great big juicy oxen for Mattrax to snack on. But where is that entrance? Or do you people honestly keep forgetting about this giant, guard-filled fortress I keep mentioning? Because I keep on mentioning it."

Balur was looking at him, a considering expression on his face. "How are you knowing so much about this cave and this fortress? Have you been casing it?"

Will's eyes slipped to Firkin again. He tasted a mouthful of apples and ash...Suddenly he just wanted the conversation to be over.

"Casing it?" Will laughed awkwardly. "I'm a farmer. I told you, everybody around here wants to steal from Mattrax. Everybody talks about it. Everybody knows. Mattrax doesn't care who knows these sorts of things. Because it doesn't matter. He's impregnable." He spat at the fire. The phlegm—suffering the same fate as any hopes of robbing Mattrax—evaporated on impact.

Balur was still considering him. "You are telling me," he said, "that everybody in this part of the land could be telling me that Mattrax is having a pressure plate to be operating his portcullis that is being keyed specifically to his weight? Every last one?"

He'd done it now. He'd let his anger—and, just maybe, his desire to impress Lette with his knowledge—get the better of him.

"Well," he hedged. "Maybe not *everyone.*"

"Anyone?" Lette pressed.

"Well," said Will again, trying to find a way to sidle out of the specifics. "I was told," he managed. "So, yes, someone else knew."

"Who?"

*This,* Will thought, *is why I can't outsmart a pig. I never consider the next step in the chain of events.*

Will chewed his bottom lip, then looked at the hairy, stinking man sleeping next to him. "Firkin," he said finally.

Universally around the cave, eyes were narrowed.

"Him?" asked Lette and Quirk in harmony.

"Barph's syphilitic ball sack," said Balur.

"Yes, him," said Will, defensive despite himself. "It was when I was a child. Before he"—he gestured vaguely with his hand—"took to drinking, I suppose."

They all just stared at him. He sighed. He was going to have to go through it with them. Or at least some version of it. "This was back when I was a kid. We used to talk about it. Just a game or..." He shrugged, trying to shed the bitterness and the disappointment. "I don't know what he thought it was. But it was all shit." He looked down at Firkin. And still couldn't quite manage with hate. Not quite with sorrow either. There was still too much nostalgia mixed in there with it all.

Another memory. This one with sharper edges than before. Sitting on his mattress, the curtain that gave him privacy from his parents pulled tightly closed. The paraphernalia of rebellion was laid out on the cot before him, scavenged from the farm and his mother's kitchen. He examined his treasures with intensity: a rusty old butter knife, the stub of a charcoal pencil, a scrap of wax paper, a fistful of sticks sharpened to points, a trowel—

Rustling behind him made him sweep up his sheets to hide everything, but when he turned around and saw his father peeking around the edge of the curtain he knew it was already too late. He'd been caught.

"Hey there, young'un," said his father. "What have you got there?"

His father had a round, open face, sun-bleached hair, and hard, tan skin. To Will he seemed more enduring than the rocks in the hills, more powerful than any of the gods. Only his mother seemed to know more about the world.

Resistance was futile.

He explained slowly, in stops and starts. What it was. What it was for. "Firkin has a plan, Da," he said finally. "A way to fight back. 'Cept not fighting like with fists. Like you told me not to. But like a way that'll hurt the dragons without us getting hurt. He's figured it all out. He has." He tried to get his da to understand with the intensity of his emotion.

But his da smiled, that indulgent smile of a parent amused at his son's foolishness. And Will seized up his trowel and wielded it defiantly, uncertain of what he could actually do with it, but desperate for a totem of his certainty, his defiance.

"He does, Da. *He does.*"

His father's smile faltered, and he nodded his head, and sat down on the edge of Will's bed. "How about you put that down and we talk about this?"

"He does, Da." But Will put the trowel down. More than a little of him was glad he had not gotten into trouble for that.

"Firkin told you about the fighting when the dragons first came, did he?"

Will nodded fiercely.

"That was a scary time. A whole way of life changing. A whole way of life being ripped away from us. And we were all scared, and we all fought—"

Will might be six, but he could see where this was going. "I know he didn't fight, Da. He told me." His da was about to tell him about how Firkin was a coward, he knew. He was about to say Will shouldn't put his trust in the man, but Will had listened to Firkin. They had talked about this as men. His da had no words to dissuade Will of what he knew of Firkin.

Will's da nodded, slow and steady as the season's ticking over. "Aye, lad. Do you know what he did do?"

Hesitantly, Will shook his head. Firkin had remained tight-lipped on this subject.

"Firkin didn't go to the fields or the forests to fight, Will, that's true enough. But he didn't stand by. He didn't run or hide. He wasn't a coward. He was... The word people use is, *strategist*. He told us *how* to fight, if you understand me. He was the one who knew where we should be. How we should get there. What we should do when we got the there. How best to achieve our goals. He knew things that no one else knew. And I still don't know how. If he had other men and women who told him things. Sometimes he would go off and wander, and maybe then he found things out. I don't know. But round in this part of the valley, he was the most important man in the fight."

Will's da put his arm around Will, pulled him close.

"We lost, Will," he said, and there was a world of heartbreak in his voice, a sadness that at six years old Will could only just begin to understand. "That's what all Firkin's plans came to. Mattrax sitting up in his fortress sending his guards to take our money. And it's not that they weren't good plans, Will. They just weren't good enough."

And with those words, Will understood a little more about heartbreak. His da looked down, and understood, and he held Will a little tighter.

"I love Firkin like a brother, Will. I fought for him too back in the day. But the dragon war, our loss…that broke him a little Will. Like a plow that won't give you a straight line."

He looked down at Will, and his words died out. There were none left that could help.

Will looked around the cave, focused on Lette's expectant face. And he wanted to please her, to tell her what she wanted to hear.

*That's probably what Firkin felt,* he thought. But Firkin was passed out drunk on the floor. Firkin was a weak man. Will wouldn't be like him.

"So," he said, "because of everything I know, you're probably thinking I know how it can be done, and you can use me to plan something." He grinned at them without an ounce of mirth in his body. "Except, all my knowledge does is tell me that it can't be done."

There was a long pause after that. Will finally began to relax. Maybe he could salvage a decent night's sleep, and plan out the rest of his life in the morning.

Then Balur looked over to Lette, and said, "What are you reckoning?"

Lette rolled her shoulders in what might have been a shrug. "Always a way," she said.

Will felt his jaw tighten. He was terrified that they'd actually try it. That they would think that their competence with goblins was somehow enough to let them pull it off. Then not only would he be running for his life from the Consortium, but he'd be doing it with all this guilt on his hands.

He tried to lay out the impracticalities for them. "The only way to get that portcullis open would be to get everyone from the village to go up into the mountains and stand on it."

Lette nodded. "Yes," she said. "That would work." There was a matter-of-factness to her tone that worried Will.

"No," he said, "it wouldn't." But he could almost see the set of scales behind Lette's eyes, weighing the opportunity. "The villagers would never go. They have this silly little thing called a desire to live through to tomorrow."

"We could be inciting them." Balur nodded to himself.

Will laughed. "With what? There's no money to tempt them. That's why we're talking about robbing a dragon in the first place." He shook his head. "Unless you know someone who can cook up enough Fire Root potion to drive an entire village into a homicidal rage." He snorted.

Quirk straightened suddenly. "I could do that," she said. She sounded surprised. Then she caught Balur's expression. "Alchemy," she said quickly. "It's sort of a hobby for me. I find it...relaxing." She checked Balur's expression again. "It's not magic!" she said defensively. "I told you. I swore that off."

"No!" Will managed. What had he done? Somehow everything had gotten worse.

"Oh," Quirk said quickly, "I'm not advocating for any of this, of course. All just a thought experiment, of course. Except it really would be fascinating to see what sort of lair a dragon has. What it collects. That really would be a coup."

"A coup?" Will clutched at his head. He'd had Quirk marked as the sane one, despite her odd notions about the local overlords. She had exuded an aura of intelligence. But it turned out that what she really was, was a carefully created human mask over a sack full of crazy.

"You're all mad." Will pawed at his forehead. "You think you can feed an entire village fermented Fire Root? I mean what in all the Hallows is your plan for that? Are you going to mix it with the bread?"

Lette and Balur exchanged a glance. "That," said Lette, a note of admiration in her voice, "is a really good idea."

"No!" Will screeched again. He looked around for a safe

harbor in the shit storm of madness. Firkin was still snoring on the floor. And Will knew that when he was looking to Firkin for sanity then things had really gone awry.

"Say..." He could barely get the words out, but he forced them. "Say that all works. What do you then do about the giant fucking dragon that would notice his front door being forced open?" He pointed at Quirk. "What do you do about all the people you just sent to their deaths? Do you have a potion to fix that too?"

Quirk shrugged. "Well, it depends how much Snag Weed grows in these woods, I suppose."

Will reeled. Sitting down as he was, he reeled. "Oh." He threw up his hands. "We're poisoning Mattrax now, are we?" He shook his head. "Of course we are. And how are we doing it? I suppose we're drugging some oxen he's been given to eat, and having him chow down on that. Just smuggling it into the castle disguised as guards or something?"

Silence followed this. Will took a breath, let it out as a sigh. Finally.

"Gods," Lette breathed. "You really have thought this all out, haven't you?" she said.

Balur was nodding. "You are being really very good at this," he said.

No. No. No. No. No. Will clutched his temples.

"Why?" he asked them. He was begging them, really. He grasped around for something they couldn't twist. "You're talking about poisoning the villagers' morning bread. Mattrax doesn't eat until the evening. So your plan requires him to hold off on killing the villagers stomping around on his pressure plate all day?"

Balur looked to Quirk. She shook her head. "On a creature that big, Snag Weed would give you a few hours at the most." She caught herself. "I mean, academically speaking. Obviously a few hours to study an unconscious dragon would be amazing, but I'm not condoning any of this." She sounded neither convincing nor convinced.

Balur's shoulders slumped. "Goddess Betra's saggy tits," he said finally.

Will knuckled his forehead, trying to push the tension out of it. He was done. He should let it go.

When he opened his eyes, Lette was looking at him intently. "How would you deal with that, Will?"

There was an edge to her look, almost a hunger. It gave him pause.

"How would I...?" he started. "By not trying to rob a dragon in the first place." How had she not picked up on that?

But Lette wouldn't stop looking at him, wouldn't stop smiling. "You already know the answer," she said. "I know you do. You've already figured it out."

Will clamped his lips shut very tight indeed.

Irritation flicked across Lette's face. Her eyes narrowed. "Okay," she said. "We bring the villagers up to the portcullis, open the door. The dragon comes, and scatters the villagers. So"—she turned and smiled at Quirk—"no one is killed."

"No one?" Balur cut in. "What is being the point of this plan?"

Lette closed her eyes, took a deep breath.

"Okay," she said, "probably some guards," she said.

"Guards?" said Quirk.

Lette's breath was considerably deeper this time around. "They're arsehole guards," she said. "They took Will's farm from him. Now can I get back to figuring this out?"

Will felt like saying, "No," but he wasn't sure about the wisdom of that.

"Okay," Lette said. "We've opened the door. The villagers have fled. And..." She thought. "Okay, we've got to poison the dragon later. So..." She pointed at Will. "Someone hides inside the cave. So they can wait for the dragon to be poisoned, for it to fall asleep."

Balur nodded. "I am liking this." Then his almost-eyebrows furrowed. "Where are you hiding?"

Lette looked at Will expectantly. "I don't know," she said. "I should be able to find some shadow in a cave to hide in..."

Will tried to keep his lips shut. He really did. But he honestly wasn't sure if she was bluffing. And he knew, knew for a fact, that there were no safe shadows in Mattrax's cave. Mattrax wasn't stupid enough to leave any, gods' hex upon him. If she went in, she would die.

He looked at her.

She would die.

*Bugger it.*

"The locking mechanism," he finally blurted.

Lette cocked her head. "The locking mechanism?" she said. "How would I get in there?"

"Well..." Will sighed. But he couldn't have her life on his hands. "To operate a portcullis that size you need a very large chain, so there's a very large hole cut into the rock for it. It leads down to the locking mechanism that's buried beneath the plate. That's the weak point in the whole setup." He looked at her, grimaced. "You can slip through that hole and hide down there."

Balur clapped his hands. Slowly a broad, beatific grin spread across Lette's face. "Of course," she said, still grinning. "Of course." Her grin was still getting broader. "The coup de grâce."

# 7

# The Coup de Grâce

Will was grimacing again.

"That's it," Lette said. "That's the whole plan, isn't it? The one you and Firkin came up with." She didn't wait for any acknowledgment from him. "We drug the villagers. We take them up the mountain. They open the portcullis. Mattrax comes bellowing. They scatter. But before they do, I sneak in, hide in the locking mechanism. And I can pick it. I know how to do that. So I sit there. Everything settles down. And then I set to work on the mechanism. Rig the counterweights so all it needs is a small weight, not a big one. In the meantime, someone sneaks a drugged cow to the dragon. Night falls. Mattrax falls over unconscious. You guys sneak up the mountain, step on the sabotaged pressure plate, waltz in, and clean out the dragon. Done."

Will hung his head. But there was no getting away from it now. "It's Firkin's plan," he said. He pointed at the messy sprawl of a human being. "You've seen him. You know what he's like. It won't work."

But Lette shook her head. "It *wouldn't* work. Because you didn't know how to drug the dragon. Because you didn't know how to pick the lock. Because you had to worry about the guards. Because you're a farmer. But," she said grinning, "we aren't."

And for a moment, just a brief instant, something like hope flickered in Will's chest. A momentary glimpse of the future that might be. As quickly as he could, he blew that flame out.

"I am seeing a three-person plan," Balur was saying. He pointed to Lette. "We are needing you to be up there and be hiding in the mechanism. We are needing someone to herd up the villagers. And we are needing someone to be taking the drugged cow into the fortress and to be feeding the dragon."

"And someone to drug the cow," said Lette, looking at Quirk.

Quirk looked like a deer caught in the glare of a midnight torch.

"Who is saying the alchemist cannot be pulling double duty?" asked Balur. "It would be good to be having her in the fortress so she can be making sure that the drugging is going as planned."

"Wait," Quirk managed. "This was all just an academic exercise."

Lette arched an eyebrow at her. "This works," she said, "and you get undisturbed access to that dragon for as long as he's unconscious."

Will had to say it would have been more reassuring if Quirk had not licked her lips at that point.

"I don't—" Quirk started.

"Yes, you do." There was no give in Lette's voice.

Balur smiled. There were far too many teeth involved. "So that is being it," he said. "Three people for a three-person plan."

"I want Will," Lette said.

Will felt his heart stop in his chest for one beat, two. He tried to speak. To tell them this was all madness.

But the vision of that beautiful future he and Firkin had imagined was flickering in the back of his skull again, like a candle fighting a hurricane of common sense.

"Why are you wanting the farmer?" Balur asked. "He is being just a farmer."

"It's his plan," Lette pointed out.

"What?" scoffed Balur. "It is not seeming fair to you to take his plan from him?"

They were, Will thought, discussing him as if he were a chicken sitting on a table, neck snapped, and feathers plucked.

"I don't—" he started, but they ignored him.

"It's not fairness," Lette said. "It's practicality. Plans change. They adapt on the fly. He knows the most about the dragon. He's a virtual dragon-thieving savant. I want that in our back pocket."

Balur still looked as skeptical as it is possible for an eight-foot-tall lizard to look. "It is not even being his plan. He is saying it's the drunk's plan."

"Fine." Lette was unperturbed. "We bring the drunk too. We have to split up anyway. Best we both have access to this information."

Balur arched an eyebrow. "Access to diseases and halitosis?"

"Don't I get a say in this?" Will finally said.

Lette looked at him. He felt she would look at him the same way if he challenged her to see who could kill the most goblins in a minute.

"Really?" she said. "You really don't want this? You don't want everything you ever dreamed of as a child to come true? You don't want Firkin to finally have his day in the sun? You don't want Mattrax to look around his bare cave and see all his wealth, his power stolen from him? Stolen by you?"

Lette's voice was low, seductive. Will was slightly aware of Balur, behind Lette, rolling his yellow eyes. But he didn't care.

"And," Lette went on, "when you've taken everything from him—just the way he took everything from you—you'll have enough money to buy ten farms. You'll be absolutely, absurdly rich. You can leave this whole valley. You can walk away from the shadow of every dragon if that's what you want. Be your own man, free from debt, from worry. A young man with the means to cut his own path in the world."

How did she know him so well? How could she land words with the same accuracy as she flung her blades? But he knew resisting this now would be like resisting the ground when you fell from a tree. She had done it. She had delivered the coup de grâce.

He looked down at Firkin. At his old friend. Maybe not his friend for a long time now. But if he could recapture the magic of those summer afternoons, planning and laughing...Could Firkin recapture something of the man he had once been?

Finally he nodded. Lette smiled.

"Well," said Quirk, "I suppose if everyone is getting involved..." No one was paying her any attention, though.

Abruptly, Firkin sat up, stared about wildly. He pointed at Balur. "Dibs on inciting them there villagers," he said blearily. "All about the inciting, I am, so I am." And with that he collapsed back to the ground and began to snore.

# 8

## Morning Breaks

Quirk was dreaming. Something to do with a cat, and research papers, and a dragon telling her that the average feline academic record was pitiable. And Quirk kept trying to tell both of them that the room was on fire, and they had to get out. But the dragon told her he was an expert on combustibles and she was talking nonsense. And the cat just kept on trying to tell her about how conflicting models of the universe could be unified by its yarn theory. And all the while heat and light was growing.

She came awake sweating. The sun was in her eyes, lancing between treetops, thrusting into the cave entrance, and landing with a crash at the back of her eyes. She rolled away, blinking and groaning. Her head felt foggy. She had vague memories of Balur's flask, which, in the startling light of morning, she was convinced had contained some form of liquid fire.

From behind the shelter of her eyelids she cursed herself. She shouldn't have drunk anything. That was a mistake. Drink made your control slip. And she could not afford to let that happen. Not again.

But she had been excited. She remembered that. Almost celebrating.

What had she been excited about again?

She experimented with opening her eyes again. Her hypothesis that now she was facing away from the entrance of the cave would lead to a more muted, digestible visual palette bore fruit.

Unfortunately it was Firkin's fruit. He squatted, stark naked three yards from her, scrubbing himself vigorously with a pinecone.

"Taking care of them varmints," he said with a cheerful smile. It revealed fewer teeth than it should.

Quirk closed her eyes again. Fast.

"It's easier to let him just get it over with." Will's voice was apologetic. "Otherwise he'll just do it later somewhere far more public."

Quirk didn't really care if it would have been more public. It wouldn't have been so close to her face.

She pushed the thought down, inhaled calming breaths, ran the mantra through her mind. *Be the surface of the lake,* she told herself. *Be the absence of the wind.*

Slowly she went through the exercises she had been taught by a priestess of Knole, goddess of wisdom. She found the inner font of quiet. And encased in the silence of her mental oasis, she put the pieces of the previous evening back together. Will. Lette. Firkin. Balur, the Analesian. It came back to her. The whole night. The whole plan. The dragon.

The surface of the lake tremored, then boiled, exploded.

She sat up hard and fast.

*The dragon.*

She could see one. Touch one. She could poke it, and prod it, and measure it. She could assess the texture of each scale, could see how each limb articulated. Each aspect of it could be a paper she would publish. The sharpness and position of it claws. The contents of its spoor. The girth of its loins.

Her breath was coming fast, her heart thumping a syncopated beat against the battering-ram rhythm of her hangover. A dragon. She would see a dragon.

*Be the surface of the lake. Be the absence of wind. The absence of sound. Be the lacuna in the world.*

*No. Fuck the lacuna in the world.* She was going to see a dragon. *A fucking dragon.*

She fought for control. She had known this was coming. This was why she had come to Kondorra in the first place. This was the valley's promise. Cut off from the rest of Avarra except for a few profitable trade routes. And full of dragons. Dragons risen out of history that was almost legend. Only here in all the world, in a southeastern spit of land shielded off by low mountains. Keeping themselves to themselves. Waiting. Waiting for her to come and reveal all their secrets.

*Be calm,* she demanded of herself. *Be detached. Be the academic. And if you can't be detached, then you must abort. Walk away from this.*

She tried not to laugh at that. Walk away. As if she could.

*You have to,* insisted the quiet voice of reason. *You have fought too long and too hard for this to throw it away now.*

She stood slowly, calmly, moving her limbs with a dancer's precision. She could feel the Analesian watching her. Another reason to go outside, to refresh herself away from stale air and the corpses of goblins. She could already hear flies buzzing.

She walked toward the light of day, feeling the kinks of a night on a stone floor slowly starting to come out of her limbs. *Think this through. Be rational.*

First there was the fact that this was a criminal undertaking. She had not expected that. She'd known the dragons played some sort of social role in Kondorra, but sovereign lords? She supposed she must have heard that somewhere between Tamathia and Kondorra, but she had heard so many things. Gods. Overlords. Predators. Myths. Livestock. War beasts. And one woman who insisted at great volume that they were all her lovers and had curious peccadillos concerning goats' milk. Picking the truth out of guesses would be like reaching into the Tamathian library and at random trying to pick out the exact book you wanted. The only people who could have told her the situation for what it was were the merchant guilds that regularly interacted with Kondorra. But they and their numerous guards had made it abundantly clear that they had had no time for an itinerant scholar.

So here she was, helping thieves and rogues plan to rob a dragon. Here she was fully intending to participate in a crime. She had devoted herself to a life of learning and quiet worship of Knole.

*Oh to the Hallows with it! She would be getting to poke a dragon in its gods-hexed belly and seeing if it giggled in its sleep! Knole—goddess of wisdom, knowledge, insight, and academia that she was—would give her right tit for an opportunity like that.*

The surface of the lake, when she summoned it, was rippling with motion. She breathed slowly, walked out of the cave, let the heat of the sun sink into her aching body.

Next was the fact that people's lives would be put in danger by this undertaking. Not just hers but the lives of everyone she had said she would give Fire Root potion.

*Gods, she had said that. How much had she had to drink?*

*But she could give it to them. She really could . . .*

Lette had promised to save the villagers' lives. Well . . . sort of. But even that thin promise still left her conscience with the guards who served Mattrax. All of them. Balur had said he wanted to kill them. Of course he had. That was his people's way. She had read about Analesians. A hard people growing up in an even harder land. Scrabbling for survival among the cliffs and sands of the Analesian desert. Creatures that fought for every moment that they drew breath, killing their food, killing each other, right up until the moment they were killed themselves.

She could not be party to that sort of violence.

Could she?

The dragons' soldiers were villains. The dragons were villains too. She could excuse the reptiles though. They were not human. You couldn't apply human rules to them. They had their own rituals and needs that were not necessarily compatible with those of human life. That was simply how thaumatobiology worked. But the guards...The guards chose to steal and to kill. So didn't they deserve...?

Not by her hand. That she had sworn. That was inviolable.

But by her will...?

No. She couldn't be responsible for that either.

*Poke! Poke! Poke!*

She clenched and unclenched her hands. Started to go through the ritual stretches, each one designed to bring body and mind into closer alignment. Each one stilling the surface of the lake inside. Each one canceling out a breath of wind that disturbed its silence. Each one making the calm more perfect.

"What in the name of Lawl's black eye is this thing?"

Quirk was yanked from spiritual and physical alignment back to earth. Her psyche landed with a bump. Lette was standing a few yards away. She was pointing at Quirk's cart.

"That's my cart," Quirk said. Because it was.

Lette appeared unsatisfied by this answer. "And how in the name of all the gods did it get here?"

The surface of the lake was not smooth. Not at all.

"I had it with me last night," Quirk said. She could feel heat of the sun on the side of her face.

"So where in the Hallows is your horse?" Lette asked. "Where's the gods-hexed yoke for a horse? Where's the bridle and tack? Where are the fucking reins?"

The heat of the sun, and the heat of her dream. The heat of fire, balling, collecting in her palms, her fingertips.

Quirk breathed slowly, clenched her fists. She hoped the mercenary didn't notice the wisps of smoke escaping between her fingers.

"It's a thaumatic wagon," she said, speaking slowly and carefully. "It runs on a thaumaturgic engine."

"That being," Lette said, "the thing in the middle that looks like the offspring of an oven that got drunk and opened its doors to an alchemist's toolkit?"

"Yes." Quirk kept her answers simple, her exterior calm. *Imitate what you shall become.*

She could hear feet behind her, Lette's...exuberance... attracting attention. From the slight wince she saw cross the mercenary's face she assumed Firkin had refrained from adding clothes to his morning ensemble.

Still Lette was not distracted. "What happened," she hissed, "to the bit where you said you don't practice magic anymore?"

Another calming breath. It was easier to achieve this time. Quirk understood people's distrust of magic. She distrusted magic and she was a practitioner of the art. Nobody liked being proven wrong, and that was doubly the case when you were dealing with the fundamental laws of the universe.

"I don't practice magic," she said. "The person who created the engine does. I simply bought the engine from him, and now employ it."

"You employ magic?" Lette said. She did not sound impressed.

"Like a small business owner," Balur said from over Quirk's shoulder, in a poor imitation of helpfulness.

Quirk took the moment of Lette's distraction to further cement her serenity. "I'm not entirely certain," she said, "that I understand your concern."

That brought Lette's attention back to her. "My concern?"

Quirk was fairly sure that Lette's laugh was not genuine.

"My concern," Lette said, "is that I spent the night sleeping a few handful of yards from a magical bomb you did nothing to warn us about."

"It's not a bomb," Quirk said as reasonably as she could manage. "It's an engine."

"An engine is just a bomb that hasn't happened yet."

Quirk opened and closed her mouth. She wasn't quite sure

what to make of that. And yet that phrase "a bomb that hasn't happened yet" struck a little close to home.

"Life experience is coloring the world a shade not everyone is seeing for Lette," Balur supplied.

"Shut up, Balur." Lette's anger was not ebbing away.

Quirk thought she should tell Lette about the mantra, and inner calm, about the surface of the lake, and the absence of the wind. But she thought she should do it at a more opportune moment when she was less likely to be gutted for it.

There again, this seemed like the approximate point in proceedings when Will—

"Maybe we should all just take a moment," Will said.

Quirk smiled. He was a good man. Naïve, and likely to die soon, but good. And that counted for something.

"It is quite safe," Quirk said. "I assure you. And it has made transporting all of my equipment much easier. But it has traveled three hundred and fifty leagues without the slightest glitch. I am sure it will be fine now."

Lette curled her lip. "I do not like magic." She said it quietly. Because it was close to what Quirk knew she really meant. She was scared of magic.

"Me too," Quirk replied.

Balur laid a hand on Lette's shoulder, rubbed it almost affectionately. "There is being no magic in Kondorra. The gods have all been buggering off and leaving it to the dragons."

Quirk cocked her head to one side. "Is that true?" she said to Will, unable to restrain her curiosity. "I hadn't thought of that. Is there magic here?"

Will's look of conciliatory patience slipped several notches closer to frustration. "We haven't been abandoned by the gods. Is that what people outside of Kondorra think? No, they didn't come to our aid in the dragon wars, and no, admittedly none have manifested here in a long time, but the seasons still come as Lawl dictates them, the crops still come just as Cois and Toil command them, babies are still born healthy and whole just as Betra would have them, coin still flows as Klink desires, the skies don't fall. Knole does whatever she does. All the god stuff takes care of itself. And we don't get them coming down making demigods, and causing chaos and wars."

"But," Quirk pressed, still not quite able to stop, "what about mages?"

Will threw up his hands. "Fine. I don't know about bloody mages."

Balur shrugged. "I was hearing that you were all worshipping the dragons instead of the gods, and that you were all having orgies with virgins, and that then you were sacrificing them."

Lette looked at Balur like he was something diseased. "Where in the Hallows did you hear that?"

Balur shrugged uncomfortably. "Was being some guy in some bar." He rubbed the scales on the back of his head. "Was being half the reason I was suggesting we were coming."

Lette shook her head. "I should have fucking known."

Will was looking at them all, slightly aghast. "Don't you know anything about Kondorra?"

Lette gave him a mildly pitying look. "This is the arse-end of Avarra. Who do you think is out there talking about it?"

Will shook his head. Quirk doubted he had ever seen much outside of this tail end of the valley.

Lette affected a sympathetic look. "Don't feel bad about it. At least it means that there's no one out there talking about what an oppressive shithole this place really is."

Will sighed heavily. "You know what?" he said. "It's too early for this. Let's just go eat, and try to work out if we really meant what we said last night."

They had really meant it. Quirk was surprised by how rapidly that became apparent over their makeshift breakfast. Even Will, though he put up some token resistance, quickly conceded to the gravity of events. A good man, a naïve man, but a man with a stomach full of rage too, no matter how well he hid it. He wanted to hurt the dragon.

And then, with the plan settled, it was time to put it into action. And so she was sent out into the woods to look for herbs.

"This is being a thing that is taking a long time," Balur said from where he leaned against a nearby tree, quietly wringing the neck of grammar.

Lette had assigned the lizard man to protect her as she looked for ingredients. The woods, Will had said—repeatedly in fact— were not safe. But Quirk had traveled more than three hundred leagues. She had crossed the wooded valleys of the Vale. She had kowtowed to war chiefs, hidden from spiders, drugged tribes of orcs, given gifts to elven kings, and...

*No, she was not thinking about that.*

—and had survived to tell the tale. Lette knew that about her. Or suspected enough of it to know it wasn't likely that Quirk needed protection. No, Balur was not there to protect her. He was there to keep her there.

Quirk bent, picked up the lower branches of a hawthorn bush, checked the scrub below, and tried to figure out how she felt about that. Was she thinking of running? Was she going to go through with all this?

"Snag Weed is picky about where it chooses to grow," she said. "It likes shade, but not too much, the damp, but not too much, clay soil, but not too much." There was peace in the litany of facts, something to calm the questions quivering in her gut.

She found what she was looking for, and threw the handful of Snag Weed into her thaumatic wagon, which trundled through the woods after her. They had a fair amount now, but not enough, she suspected, to knock out a dragon of the proportions described to her.

"I am not knowing why we are needing this Snag Weed anyway," Balur groused.

"I think," Quirk said, as carefully as possible, "that the group seems to think that not having to fend off an enraged dragon would be the safest way to address the proposed plan."

Balur snorted. "Red of tooth and claw. That is how adventures should be. The testing of oneself against the fury and the rage. The animal inside being let loose. To be living at the edge of oneself and one's civilization. To be being honest with oneself about what one is being."

Quirk didn't answer that. That was a dangerous conversational path for her to be wandering down. Instead she moved to the next hawthorn bush, lifted it up.

"The plan is sounding good," Balur said. "But plans are always being that way. They are always sounding like you will be waltzing into somewhere and will then be two-stepping out while one's shit is smelling of roses. But what is actually happening is you are waltzing in and you are having your skull smacked, and then you are eviscerating your foes with your jaws, and you are staggering out with your shit smelling of your internal bleeding." He hesitated. "To be using one specific example."

Still Quirk held her tongue. She tried to concentrate on the large Snag Weed plant before her. All she had to do was take it and leave.

But there were ripples on the surface of the lake. Worries skittering through its waters like panicked fish.

*No killing.* Lette had said that. Except for the guards. But she had been appeasing Balur. She hadn't meant it. Had she?

Something calm and simple. That was what she needed. That was what the plan promised. Right? No bodies. No worries. Everything simple. Everything calm. She gripped the Snag Weed at its base, close to the root.

"You be trusting me," Balur said. "We will be seeing that dragon, and soon the mountains will be running red. Weed or no weed."

Flame blazed in Quirk's hand. Bright and sharp. The Snag Weed's small purple flowers blackened and curled. In an instant all she was holding was a fistful of ash.

She straightened, glanced at Balur. He hadn't noticed. She fixed on a smile like a rictus. "Nothing here," she said. "Let's try looking somewhere else."

# 9

## Strange Brews

The morning staggered into afternoon. The afternoon stumbled on and eventually evening fell. Balur's narrow tongue licked the air. The smell of Quirk's brewing painted the sky around the cave mouth, thick and heavy, coating the back of his throat like blood. He moved away, deeper into the woods. Lette would be being upset at him if he was ripping the drunkard's head off.

He found Lette alone, beyond a stand of trees that masked her from the cave. She didn't turn to face him, but he could read the subtle tides of her body language as she relaxed minutely in his presence. They were tribe. Stronger together.

It was ten years now. Ten years that they had been fighting, killing, and fucking side by side. Ten years cutting a bloody swath out of the Analesian desert, through Salera, Batarra, and Vinland before finally crossing the Kondorran peaks and descending into...

What was this being?

Opportunity? Futility? Complete and utter shit show?

He was knowing half the answer. He was knowing what this was to him. Kondorra was having dragons. He had not been knowing much else about Kondorra, but he had been knowing that. So this was being his chance to bloody his hammer's head on the skull of a dragon. This was being his chance to feel the breath of a beast roasting his skin. This was being his chance to show a dragon's tooth to one of the skinny little human girls he liked so much, and to be seeing her eyes go wide. This was telling tales while ale was making his blood grow hot in his veins.

But that was not what this was being to Lette. This was being something else to her. But he was not knowing what. And that was worrying him. Tribe was knowing tribe. That was how it was supposed to be being. That was how it had been being for ten years.

She had found him in the desert. Ten years ago. She had come into the sands leading a pack of scholars. Tribe to each other but not to her. They had paid her coin, and pointed at the desert, and told her they wished to plunder its depths.

They had thought of the desert like a virgin child, standing for her first night on the brothel balcony. Balur had grown up in the desert. He knew it for what it was. The cruelest of killers. She had many the faces, the desert, and, yes, many treasures, but she gave none of them up. She stole life, either quick and savage, or slow and with a smile.

Lette's employers—no matter that they called themselves scholars—were being a bunch of idiots.

Not that any of that had been concerning Balur at the time. He had been too busy dealing with the fact that the desert was busy killing him.

He had gone three days without water then. Fifteen without meat. The scales had hung loose on him. His tongue had been a stick of wood in his mouth. His eyes had burned. The skin between his scales cracked and ran with blood so thick it could scarcely flow. Thought was almost gone from him.

He had taken shelter in the ruins, was hunkered between half a sandstone column and a broken-down stump of a wall. Some temple perhaps. Half lost in the dunes. Like him really. And he had given up. Even the need to survive not enough to drive him on anymore. He had curled up upon himself and waited for the end.

And then he had heard them. Heard her. She was telling them

to set up camp because a storm was blowing, she had told him later. And she was stifling laughter at their inability to do so.

"Literally had to tell one of them to try not to club himself in the head so often while driving in a tent peg," she had said. "Good thing I was too parched to piss myself."

While he had heard the words, none of the sense of them had made it into his skull. Scholars. Idiots. Whatever they were, Balur had seen them as one thing.

Food.

He had sunk into the sand—so only his spine, nostrils, and eyes showed—and slithered forward. Slow. So slow. It was easy to be slow when he was more than half-dead already.

He had taken one scholar before they knew he was there. Hands reaching up and unseaming the man's belly before they understood what was going on. Burying his face in the man's guts and feasting on blood. Feeling slick viscera slide down his dry throat. His empty stomach clenching in response.

The scholars had stepped back, shocked, aghast. And he had smiled. There was no time to be shocked in the desert.

And then, just before his claws had closed around the second one's throat, Lette had been there.

She was small. That had been his only thought. And then, as he went to crush her, *small and sharp*. Her blades sliced at his scales, at his weak, cracking skin. He tried to swat her. She had darted away. *Small, sharp, and fast*. And then a thought to sum all those up. *Annoying*.

He had gone at her then. With all that was left of his fury and strength. Great swipes of his claws that sent her leaping back, crashing off ancient architecture. She scrabbled up a wall, a column. He beat it down. She rolled free, and he stomped with a foot. She leapt out of the roll. He grabbed a scholar, bit deep, trying to recover his strength. She flung a knife at his eyes. He used the scholar as a shield. She had closed the distance, struck at his hamstrings. He kicked her away. She flew, but rolled as she landed.

So it had gone. On and on. Trading nicks and cuts but never landing a killing blow. And then the scholars were forgotten. Even the dead ones leaking out precious fluid into the sands. It was just the dance of combat. Just the testing of skills. Just the two of them, feint and counterfeint. Seeing who could deliver the mortal blow. Seeing whose strength would falter first.

And then finally his strength would carry him no further. He fell. Waited for her blade to follow suit.

When he had the strength to see why it hadn't, he saw her on her knees, panting, unable to get up.

They had lain there, side by side, while around them the sand began to howl.

A week later they had crawled out of the desert together. And they had been together ever since.

Tribe.

And now...

"What are you thinking?" he rumbled. Subtlety had never worked for him. He treated conversations like he treated fights. Hit hard and directly until something cracked and leaked.

"It's a good plan," she said quietly, still not looking at him.

Balur considered. "You are sneaking out here to be staring morosely into the middle distance so that you can be thinking about what a good plan it is?" He nodded. "I am believing that I am smelling the odor of bull's dung."

"What if I told you I didn't want to talk about it?" She sounded petulant. Probably because she knew she would not win this fight.

"Tribe shares with tribe."

"Your tribe is dead." She knew pretending to misunderstand this point annoyed him.

"My old tribe was exiling me. That is making me anxious to not be repeating the experience with my new tribe."

She turned finally. There was a tightness about her eyes. "That gold we had was a new start, Balur. It was a way to get started in Kondorra, away from gods, and kings, and wars, and backstabbing, and bullshit. It was a different kind of life. And now it's gone. And we're back to doing the same thing."

Balur nodded. "So we will be making more gold. We will be finding that new life in a short while. Maybe somewhere that is having slightly fewer dragons after all."

Lette shook her head. "I know that. That's not what worries me."

"What is it that is worrying you?" Balur had enough respect for human syntax that he worked hard to avoid sounding like a pirate.

"That now that we have a plan—a good plan—I'm glad we lost the gold."

Balur was not subtle, but he knew how to kill silently, how to slip into an enemy's camp without being detected. And that was how he kept the smile in his heart hidden.

"I am thinking," he said, "that this is being less to do with the plan, and being more to do with the planner. I am thinking that you are out here to be trying to put out the flame in your britches."

Lette hesitated a moment, then grinned. "The only one with flaming britches is you after that whore in Vinland."

That killed Balur's smile a little. He nodded in acquiescence. "That was being a miscalculation," he conceded.

Lette grinned, teeth pale in the waning light. Balur grinned back. Behind them, Quirk's voice rang out. "Potion's done."

"Come," said Balur. "Night is falling. Potion is being brewed. And you are having a whole village to fuck up."

# 10

## Mugging Ethel

The problem with high-risk adventuring, and other acts of derring-do, Lette thought, was that they mostly involved just sitting around on your arse. No ancient and mysterious cult had ever bothered to build its temple within an easy morning's ride of a city. No long-dead king ever bothered to be buried anywhere near where he had actually ruled. And considering the frequency with which terrible beasts terrorized villages, they tended to live remarkably far from them.

Even the more lowly adventurous acts—mugging two soldiers and a cow, for example—seemed to involve lurking in a yew bush for such an inordinate amount of time that several bards would start composing ballads about the pair of you.

The soldiers in question, and their truculent bovine captive, were half a mile away. The road—little more than a loose mixture of gravel and mud—wove drunkenly down a hillside and up another before disappearing out of sight toward the local village. On either side, barren pasture spread out, pockmarked by a few sagging trees. A few sheep observed the scene, as morose as the day's weather. Rain seemed on the cusp of falling, but had yet to gather its nerve to properly pour down.

Like the pregnant clouds above, Lette's impatience was growing.

"I was telling you to be taking a nap this morning," said Balur, who it seemed had decided to do an impression of her mother. "You are always being cranky after early morning crimes."

She looked over at Balur, squatting beside her in the bush. Well, mostly on top of the bush. The bush was not really up to concealing the lizard man. But when he was sitting still enough, and curled up on himself, Balur could look remarkably like a piece of the landscape. A particularly stupid piece of the landscape.

"Did I say anything?" she snapped. "Any complaint?"

"You were breathing angrily," Balur deadpanned.

"Is this more tribe bullshit?"

"You are breathing very shrilly when you are being angry," Balur told her, still without inflection. "I am thinking you have a tendency to narrow your nostrils. It is likely being related to why you so often lose at cards. Too many tells."

"I'll tell you where to shove that tail in a moment."

It would be easier, Lette reflected, if Balur was wrong. But she had been up early. And she was cranky.

With Quirk's potion brewed, the next step had been to introduce it to the villagers' morning bread. And if there was one career worse than mercenary and itinerant adventurer, it was, in Lette's most sincere opinion, being a gods-hexed baker. Up at the arse crack of dawn. Before it even. Not even the arse crack, but instead that strange mutant tuft of back hair that announced the arse crack. That moment when the rooster rolled over and thought, *Fuck it, everyone can hang on another fifteen minutes or so.*

She was sincerely glad that Balur had not taken her up on that particular career path.

What was worse, she had needed to wake up not only in time to be at the baker's at the same time as the baker, but in time to travel the two leagues from the cave in the Breccan woods so she could be at the baker's at the same time as the baker. The whole thing had almost gone to the Hallows when she'd nearly alerted the baker to her presence by yawning at considerable volume. Still, when the baker had stumbled blearily into his storage closet to investigate the noise, she was up braced against the roofbeams, and the fool had never even looked up.

She had dropped down behind him, slugged the base of his skull with a weighted cosh, spilled some milk on the ground to make it look like he'd slipped, dosed the dough, and bugged out.

And then she had not napped. And now here she was waiting to steal a cow, and regretting it, and unable to complain about it because for some gods-hexed reason she had decided to make her closest friend in the world a smug, sarcastic arsehole.

There again, thinking about it, that was probably why he was her closest friend in the world.

She sighed. She wanted a better life, but she was having a very hard time being the better person that required.

She watched the soldiers, watched the cow, watched the sun rise in the sky. She cursed each one in turn.

There was rustling from behind her. She grimaced. She would have preferred to leave Will, Quirk, and Firkin far away from this part of the heist, but Will and Quirk needed to be here so they could change into the soldiers' outfits after the mugging, and no one was willing to leave Firkin alone to his own devices for even a second.

She turned around to see which one of them was trying to ruin everything. It was Will. Despite herself she felt the harshness of her expression soften.

And then he went and ruined it by opening his mouth.

"Ethel?" he said.

She narrowed her eyes. "No. Lette. We've been hanging around each other for the past two days."

"No." Will shook his witless head. "I know that cow. That's Ethel."

Lette closed her eyes. *I know that cow.* She'd suspected that Kondorra would be rural, but this...? This is why she liked working in cities. The fetishes were a little more predictable there.

"I am not supposing that means you can be talking it into being our accomplice?" Balur asked.

"Do either of you remember," Lette hissed, "the part where we're supposed to be ambushing people?"

"That's *my* cow," Will said obstinately.

"Technically it is not being your cow." Balur insisted on dragging this out.

"I raised her from a calf," Will objected.

"The reason we are being here in the first place," Balur pointed out, "is that the dragon Mattrax was confiscating your farm, including"—he paused for just a fraction of a moment—"Ethel."

For a blessed moment, Will held his tongue. Then he appeared to reconsider the whole being-sensible thing. "But they're taking her to be eaten," he said. "For Mattrax to have as some sort of pre-dinner snack."

"Yes," Lette hissed. "That's precisely why we're taking her, filling her full of drugs, and feeding her to him. It's your cursed plan."

"But," Will said yet again, "she's *my* cow. I raised her."

Lette clawed at her face, and checked the road. The soldiers were very close now.

"Get back in your hexed bush," she hissed at Will.

But instead of doing that, Will seemed to take it into his head to step into the road.

"Hey," she heard him call out. "That's my cow."

She exchanged a glance with Balur. "Maybe," he rumbled, "this is being a very cunning distraction."

Lette considered. "Him being gutted by two soldiers is a cunning distraction?"

Balur paused. Then, "It would mean that we are only splitting the haul among four instead of five."

Out on the road, things were not going so well. A prime example of that being that both soldiers had drawn their swords. They regarded Will with a mixture of suspicion and disbelief.

As if watching a mouse saunter out of its hole, climb up onto their dinner plate, and politely demand the cheese.

"You fucking what?" said one.

"He said it was his cow," said the other.

"That's funny," said the first.

"Not that funny," said the second.

"He don't look like Mattrax," said the first.

"He didn't even have a punch line," continued the second.

"And this is Mattrax's cow."

"Now your mother's face, that's funny."

"And unless you is, Mattrax—" the first went on, addressing Will now.

"And that," said the second, "was a punch line."

"—then you better get the fuck out of my way."

They were dissimilar men. One short, one tall. One fat, one lean. One with lank, greasy blond hair, one with tight brown curls. One pale-skinned, one dark. In fact, the only thing uniting them was the same look of growing contempt on their faces.

"That," said Will, enunciating clearly, "is *my* cow."

The first soldier looked at the second, then back at Will. "You," he said, "is one stupid fucker."

Lette couldn't say she disagreed at that moment.

"We could," Balur whispered contemplatively beside her, "always use him being gutted as a cunning distraction, whether he intended it or not."

Lette sighed. Part of her was tempted by Balur's suggestion. Yes, Will was a good-looking young man, but there were plenty of good-looking men in the world, and many of them could be bought with coin. Except this was Will's plan. And while his knowledge might not extend to the simple mugging of two idiotic soldiers, it almost certainly extended to the layout of Mattrax's castle and how best to get a drugged cow from the entrance gates to Mattrax's cave.

Also, allowing her newfound companions to be killed as a

distraction was probably not completely in line with her desire to be a better person.

She stood up, pushed out of the yew bush, and made for Will. The guards started back. Which, she noted with a tinge of professional pride, meant that they had had no idea she was there.

Then Balur rumbled to life. "Fine then," he grumbled, as he unfolded to his full height. At this the soldiers started considerably more. Lette's mood stopped brightening.

"What the fuck is this?" said the first soldier.

"This," said Lette, looking up and down the empty road, "is bloody amateur hour apparently." She pointed at Will. "Get back in your bush."

"But we can't..." he started. "She's *my* cow."

Lette shook her head. "Yes," she said. "I know. You have made that point repeatedly. But we need a cow, and"—she pointed to the empty fields all around them—"we are a little light on them at the moment. So we need that one. So please get back in your bush and let the grown-ups take care of this."

"You clear this bloody road now," said the second soldier, waving his sword vaguely at them. "This is Mattrax's business. And it don't need to be interrupted by...by..." He considered Balur. "Things like you."

Lette turned to him. "Can you just be quiet, while I talk some sense into my colleague here for a moment?"

The soldier opened his mouth.

"It is being best to just go along with her," Balur said. "There is being no reasoning with her when she is being like this."

The soldier shut his mouth again.

"I would like," Lette said to Will, "to say that I am very sorry that this cow once belonged to you. But I'm not. I legitimately don't give a shit. I just need a cow. Because doing so will allow me to get my hands on so much fucking gold, I can actually smelt it down and make myself an entire herd of golden fucking cows, should I so wish. So you are going to get out of my way, stop interfering with my cow thievery, and get back in the gods-hexed bush. Do you understand?"

Something in her tone must finally have broken through. Will looked away from his cow, and back to his bush.

"Thievery?" said the first soldier. "You think you is—"

Without looking, Lette flicked out her arm. A dagger appeared in the guard's throat, buried to the hilt. He dropped to the ground gurgling.

Balur shook his head. "I was warning you. I was being very clear."

The second soldier's mouth was open. For a moment only air hissed out. Then with a howl he flung himself at Lette.

Or, to be more accurate, he flung himself into the head of Balur's war hammer, which was traveling toward him at considerable velocity.

He also dropped to the ground. There was no gurgling this time.

Lette looked at Will still frozen on the path. "Well?" she said.

He looked from the bush to the dead and dying soldiers. He shrugged. "Doesn't seem to be much point going back in there now."

Balur pulled Lette aside as Quirk and Will started to put on their purloined outfits.

"What?" she snapped.

"Are you being all right?"

It took Lette a moment to realize that Balur was genuinely concerned. "Yes," she said, almost bemused enough to stop being irate. "Of course. Why?"

Balur's narrow tongue tasted the air. He glanced at Will. "You were saving him," he said. "You were not waiting for them to attack him, for them to be being distracted. You were standing up and putting yourself in danger."

Lette looked at the two guards, now both dead and naked. "Danger?" she scoffed.

"It was not being much," Balur said with a shrug. "But it was being a little. An unnecessary amount."

Lette shifted uncomfortably under his gaze. He was getting at something, and she wasn't sure she liked it. "So what?" she said.

Balur shrugged again. "Maybe it is being nothing," he said. "I am only thinking that the Lette from outside the Kondorra valley would not be doing what you were doing." He stared up at the sky, gray with clouds. "It is just being that things like that, they make me worry that you are becoming a better person."

He left her with that. And she took it with her, as she left the others and climbed up into the hills that would lead her to the mouth of Mattrax's cave.

# 11

# Nom Nom Prophecy Nom

When Balur was finally of the opinion that Will was suitably cowed, would stop bellyaching about Ethel, and would just go about feeding her drugged arse to Mattrax, and when he was equally convinced that Quirk's ardor to get up close and personal with a dragon would cause her to keep the farm boy in line, he grabbed Firkin by the scruff of the neck and steered the tottering drunkard toward civilization. Or what was trying to pass itself off as civilization in this arse-end of Kondorra.

Balur had not seen the village himself, but after visiting the baker's this morning, Lette had described it as "a blackhead of humanity, waiting for the fingers of oppression to burst it."

Firkin, for his part, seemed happy to be pushed and prodded along. He muttered to himself. Balur braced his mind for the open sluice gate of cloacal verbiage, and attempted listening for a moment.

"—concerned with money. That's their problem. Shiny stuff. That's what they think about. I can make stuff shiny. Shine it up real good. Bit of fish oil. Shine myself up. Glistening in the sun I'll be. They'll all be wanting me then. Mattrax will take me home and call me his dandy. And he'll feed me all the livery bits of all the cows. Shiny as a button. And they'll fight for me. And then I shall say to dance. Dance for my favor. And round they'll all go. And then they'll try to put their hands on me, but they won't be able to. Slippery, fish oil is. Slippery *and* shiny. Twice as good as gold, fish oil is."

Balur slammed the sluice gate shut so hard it echoed inside the confines of his skull.

Incite villagers to riot. With Firkin.

It was like being given a wet noodle and being told to flog a man to death. Like most things, it would be easier if he just did it with his fists.

The village, when he finally saw it, was larger than he had expected. Forty houses perhaps, clustered about the main road. A tavern, with a battered sign that read simply, "The Stuck Pig." Several stores. There was even an undertaker's with coffins stacked up outside, though Balur was not entirely certain how reassuring that was. There was a temple too, which was well maintained despite the likelihood of a god manifesting there being approximately equal to Balur's chances of finding a virgin in a whorehouse.

Everything was built sturdily from timber, with a mixture of thatch and slate crowning the walls. Several buildings were whitewashed, and the tavern even looked as if it had received a coat of real paint at one point in its life.

Yet despite all its solid bones, there was something despondent about the village. Nothing exactly sagged, and yet the buildings all looked as if they were getting ready to settle into a solid slouch. The road was not well tended, and neither were the houses. The ivy that grew looked less picturesque and more like some rash that had gone too long untended.

Balur looked over to Firkin, who was still muttering to himself. "So," he said, "what is it that this place is calling itself?"

Firkin looked up at him, the coals of some unknown fire dim in his eyes. Whether it was madness dwindling or just beginning to burn, Balur couldn't tell.

"The village," he said nodding.

"Yes?" Balur asked. Though that had surely been completely obvious. It was unlikely he was asking the name of the copse of trees just off to the left.

"The village," Firkin repeated.

"What's it called?" Balur repeated the question.

"The village," Firkin said for a third time.

Balur tugged his war hammer free from its restraints on his back. He could be explaining this to Lette. She would not be minding so much.

Then, from out of nowhere, the thought struck him that the old man might not be gibbering complete and utter nonsense.

"Wait," he said. "The name of the village is being The Village?"

"The village," Firkin said again, then, recognizing his signature on the death warrant in Balur's eyes, turned in a complete circle and shrieked, "Yes! I went to say yes. Betrayed by my own tongue. My lips are sleeping with the enemy. Fraternizers the pair of them. I don't trust them!"

The trick to this, Balur thought, was going to be making sure that Firkin didn't say a single gods-hexed word.

The streets of The Village, Balur noticed as the road brought them closer, seemed uncommonly busy. And as he took a mental head count—and plotted out the best path to batter through the crowd, should the unlikely but possibly pleasant scenario of that becoming necessary arise—he realized that almost everyone from the village must be on the streets. They milled about aimlessly, bumping off walls and each other.

"What is being the matter with them?" Balur pulled his hammer loose again. The crowd-battering scenario was seeming more likely all of a sudden.

"Juiced them, she did," said Firkin, teeth clattering around the words. Yellow, they might be, but Firkin had a surprisingly large number of teeth given his lifestyle. "Put the juju in their minds and their guts. Full of piss and fire. And fiery piss.

Though there's an ointment for that." He nodded to himself, mop of hair flopping back and forth with the motion. "Good 'un that is."

Balur licked the air. It tasted unpleasantly of Firkin. But beyond that the slight waft of humanity was on the air too now. And yes, the flavor of it was skewed a little out of true. Something of Quirk's potion. That heady, bloody scent that clung to the back of his throat.

They were past the second house of the village before people noticed them. Even then, as heads began to track them, the gazes seemed half turned inward. Balur looked at one woman, middle-aged, wiry arms and paunchy belly, her graying hair scraped back beneath a bonnet that might just once have been white. Her pupils were too large in her gaunt face, not quite focused on him. Her head was cast back slightly, nostrils flared, mouth just open enough for him to make out her tongue flicking back and forth, licking the back of her teeth. A noise somewhere between a growl and a moan drifted up quietly from the back of her throat.

They were all like that. Not quite present. The same slightly defeated, underfed look. Beneath the rising flavor of Quirk's potion, despondency laced the air of the village. These were people who had given up. Quirk's potion was working in them, brewing and churning in their heads and hearts, but whatever primal rage it was trying to kindle was buried so deep, the fires would not catch.

Slowly, as they walked deeper into the village, the crowd was pulled to them. Men, women, children. All of them stumbling after Balur and Firkin. By the time they reached the heart of the village they were completely surrounded.

Balur turned in a complete circle. How did one incite a riot? Balur's normal technique was to kill a few important-looking people. But no one looked important here. And besides, he wasn't sure how many villagers he could honestly afford to reduce to meat mush. Who knew how many he would need to tip the scales that opened Mattrax's portcullis?

Which left him with words.

*Cois's curse on all their cocks.*

"Citizens," Balur started, because that seemed to be the way most speeches started. "Wait...Villagers," he amended. "You are being oppressed by the dragon Mattrax." He upped his volume. "You are being robbed of your gods-given right to be tearing flesh from bones with your teeth!"

*Wait...*He hesitated. *Was it that humans were liking to rip flesh from bones with their teeth? He should be paying more attention to them in general.* He pictured Lette with a turkey leg. *She was seeming to like that. Yes, he was being on the right path.*

"You are being penned like your animals. You are being robbed of your pride. You are being robbed of tribe. Of the path to war. You are being—"

He cut off as he felt a slight impact against his belly. He looked down. A man in his forties, a farmer perhaps, with a thick beard covered with bows and braids, stood looking at the large branch he had just used to strike Balur's stomach. He stared at it in his hands, hit Balur experimentally again. The stick bounced off Balur's scales. If he hadn't been looking down, Balur might have missed it.

The farmer looked up at Balur and dropped his stick.

*Fine then,* thought Balur, *killing a couple of them it was, then.*

"Balls!" The shrill cry came from beside him. He looked down. Shit. He'd forgotten about Firkin. The deranged little man was stepping in front of him, yelling at the top of his lungs.

"You have balls!" Firkin yelled. "Right there, in the front of your britches. I know they're there. I'm having a pair right there in front of me. Can't get away from the damn things. Follow me like a shadow. A shadow that ignores the sun. Like demon's work."

"All right," Balur rumbled, "it is being time for you to be shutting up."

Firkin ignored him. "You remember your balls, you bunch of weasel fucks?" Firkin screamed. "You!" His finger lanced out, bounced off a woman's skull. "You remember your balls?"

She stared at his finger confusedly, jaw opening and shutting with a slight clacking sound.

"You remember when Mattrax told you not to use them?" Firkin shrieked.

*Fine then.* Balur cracked his knuckles. *Firkin's blood would be the first libation to bless the earth.*

"Why the piss-balls are you listening to a great big flying lizard?" Firkin asked the crowd.

Balur cocked his fist.

And then suddenly the crowd came to life. A sound rising out of them. Something like a groan, and something actually like a word. A great "boo" echoing out of every mouth.

Balur hesitated. Was this... working? Surely...

"Flying lizards?" Firkin was an animated bundle of stick limbs thrashing around Balur. "That's fucking mad that is. Mental buggery. Great big lizard. Got wings. Flies around? Fuck that." He pointed at them. "Fuck it! That's an atrocity that is. That's pissing in the eye of the natural order of things. Bigger something is, more on the ground it should be. Stands to reason. They should burrow. I could respect a burrowing dragon. Maybe. But a great big flying one? Balls to him. Your balls. Your ones."

Whether he was pointing or flailing, Balur couldn't tell.

"But he said you couldn't use your balls, right? Right?" Firkin screamed. "And you listened because he said it with his big old teeth. Oooooooh." Firkin pantomimed fear. "His big old noshers and nashers."

"Oooooooh," the crowed echoed, and looks of genuine fear seemed to push up out of the stupor that had claimed them.

Balur shifted. Firkin had them, there was no doubt about that, but with Firkin at the tiller the direction was never entirely certain. And to Balur the world suddenly seemed full of rocks to crash upon.

"Fear the noshers!" Firkin yelled. "Fear the nashers! Stands to reason. Not mad are we? Not great big flying dragons? No! Good people is what you are. Stand-on-the-ground people. Where-we-belong people. Except we belong above dragons. Smaller than them. Up nearer the top. But he's on top. Because of his nashers.

"Well fuck his noshers, I say." Firkin grabbed at his shirt and ripped it off over his head. He struck at his pigeon chest. "But who listens to me? I'm just poor old glug-glug Firkin, I am. All booze and madness, you say. You say it because you live with a dragon on top, when he should be below. You live in a world all topsy and turvy. Standing on the birds next, you will be. And why? Because of noshers."

Firkin stared around, balefully. A rumble rose in the crowd. A belligerent grumble.

"Noshers," Firkin repeated. "Noshers. Noshers. Nashers! And noshers! And nashers! And nosh! And nash! Nosh! Nosh! Nosh!" He slammed the word into them over and over, arms pistoning wide then crashing together, the clap a counterpoint to his words. The word took hold, spread like a rash through the crowd, came back at him.

"Nosh! Nosh! Nosh!" The crowd chanted.

Balur gave up. He had no idea what was going on anymore.

Firkin was a dervish around him, whirling and pirouetting, beard flopping back and forth. Just as the crowd seemed ready to burst with sound, he brought his arms crashing down—a conductor silencing his orchestra. The crowd fell still.

"We don't have noshers," Firkin said. He sounded sad. "Not like that big old lizard. We've got little wee ones. Ones that could fly with the birdies. Float away maybe. Can't bite a dragon with noshers that fly away. Be all gummy, that would."

The crowd rumbled assent. Balur wondered if they'd noticed if he walked off and sat down for a bit.

"But"—Firkin's voice dropped down to a stage whisper—"what if we had a nosher of our own? What if we had the biggest and sharpest nosher of all? A nosher to nosh on dragons. To bite and dig deep. A nosher to make that big flying lizard up and soil its britches. Enough to make it hand back those balls of yours. What would that be?"

The crowd, it seemed, was as clueless as Balur.

"What if it were foretold that the nosher would arrive today? Here and now. Among us. What if there was a great and terrible prophecy that the nosher would nosh among us? That he demanded us? Demanded our balls! That our balls should be there to nosh with him. To nosh back upon the noshers. What if prophecy lived and breathed among us?"

Balur's brows knit. A champion. Firkin was promising them a champion.

Where the hell were they to be getting a champion from?

Balur had let this go on too long. He had given Firkin too much rope. Not just enough to hang himself, but to hang them all.

The little man had moved some distance away from Balur. The lizard man started wading through the crowd of humanity. Firkin saw him coming, and danced away farther. "Today is the day our balls say no more! Today is the day our champion liberates them. Today is the day we stand by his side, our britches bulging with life and potency, and we put the dragon Mattrax where he belongs! In the ground!"

Balur was almost in range. "Now wait—" he started, but then even he could not hear his voice above the cheer that erupted in the heart of the village square. A baying, howling cry of bloodlust finally let free of the leash. Men and women and children threw back their heads and bellowed out Fire Root–induced rage.

"Mattrax's cave!" Firkin howled, his nasal shrill somehow

cutting through the sound of the crowd. "He waits for us at the entrance to Mattrax's cave! Waits with our balls!"

For a moment the crowd stood there, silent, eyes wide, mouths hungry. Then the words sank home, hit deep in their drug-addled minds.

As one they surged forward, a barking, roaring mass of unhinged humanity. Heading for the hill, for the cave, for Mattrax. And this, Balur realized, was it. The tipping point had been reached and passed. Though what it was they had tipped into, he was not sure.

Beside him, Firkin reached down and picked up a beetle that had just dragged itself out of a puddle. He dropped it into his mouth, crunched it, and smacked his lips as he watched the retreating crowd.

"Inciting violence," he said, "always gives me a powerful hunger." He grinned at Balur, eyes glittering with the flames of an internal fire. "Let's go do it some more."

# 12

## The Great Big Flying Lizard

Perched high above the floor of the Kondorra valley, encased by the protective walls of his mountain, atop a pile of gold so vast that a thief had actually drowned in it once, the dragon Mattrax was possessed of a powerful urge to shit on all he surveyed.

The arse-end of the Kondorra valley. The field-strewn, forest-clogged, scraggly arse-end of it. That was what they had seen fit to give him. Him. Mattrax. He who had melted the faces of a thousand foes. Who had carved the guts from ten thousand more with his gilded claws. He who sat upon the wealth of ten kings. That was what the Dragon Consortium had given him. The northern tip of the valley. A region so remote, so sparely populated, that the single most important human settlement was known as... The Village.

It wasn't even "The Town." You couldn't even pretend that it might get round to calling itself The Town sometime soon. To be honest "The Hamlet that Had Rather an Inflated Opinion of Itself" might be a more accurate name. And then there were the farmsteads, scattered like warts on a whore's arse. And populated with human pus. And what was worse, far, far worse... *poor* human pus.

That was what was so galling about it all. If the hills here had been shot through with valuable ore. If gold or diamonds had glittered in deep mines. If perhaps instead of farmsteads there were the mansions of a wealthy elite scattered among the hills, then perhaps that would relieve some of his frustration. But, no. It was peasants, illiterates, and the mentally disturbed. That was who he oversaw. Them and not another soul.

Mattrax shifted on his pile of gold. A crown and several ruby-studded necklaces tumbled down, clattering against silver platters, tiaras, and loose gemstones. The massive coils of his body twisted, leathery wings stretching slightly as he settled into a new position.

His thoughts turned with his body, headed toward darker territory.

Dathrax. The bloated, fat, lazy, son-of-an-iguana Dathrax. Sitting fat and happy one province to the south, lauding his dominion of Athril's Lake. Fishing towns. Not just one town. But towns. A plurality of towns. All the citizens with pockets stuffed fat from the profit of their stinking hauls.

The taxes. Mattrax almost groaned at the thought of them. He stroked his own belly with a single gilded claw, imagining the carts coming in, axles creaking under their loads. Great sagging chests, overstuffed, coins positively bursting out of them, begging to be raked by his talons.

And none of it his. All Dathrax's.

He could take Dathrax, of course. *Would* take Athril's Lake from him in time. But that required an army. And an army required coin. And coin required something fucking more than an arse-load of squelching, stinking peasants to tax.

But that was all he had.

And so all that he could truly do was stretch his wings, take to the air, and shit on it all.

# 13

## Ethel's Party Invitation

Will clutched the leash that was tied to Ethel's neck in a grip so tight his nails threatened to break the skin of his palm. It was old rope, fraying and rough. He imagined how it felt around her neck. The slow friction of it, working back and forth, the mounting irritation. He thought of the rough pebbles of the road beneath her hooves, so different from the grass meadows she had ambled through all her life.

He thought of the dragon Mattrax's jaws settling about her neck.

"Are you crying?" Quirk, walking beside him, looked as if she was assessing him for some hidden injury.

Will turned away, allowed his purloined helmet to hide his face. It wasn't difficult. The guard whose clothes he had taken had been a fat-headed man and the thing hung loose on him. Everything hung loose. Chain mail clanked around his thighs. The sword belt kept slipping. His britches pooled in his oversize boots. It would have been uncomfortable enough even if it were not soaked through with blood from where Balur had slammed a war hammer into the former owner's chest and punched a large portion of his lungs out between what was left of his ribs.

The same way Mattrax's jaws would crush the life out of Ethel.

"I knew her since she was a calf, is all," Will said, trying to keep his voice steady. "My pa birthed her, but I raised her for the first years. He used to give me the younger animals to look after. The ones headed for pasture anyway. I mucked her out. Kept her hay clean. Cleaned the burrs off her coat."

Quirk nodded sympathetically. "That's a hard thing," she said. "To be there for both the start and the end of a life. I cannot imagine wanting to be there for the whole of that journey."

Will nodded, permitted himself a sniff.

Quirk rested a hand on his shoulder. "Honestly, it's impressive," she said. "Your drive to see this through. Passion for revenge conceived in the heat of the moment can be hard to sustain, especially when you are faced with the need to sacrifice things you have loved." She smiled at him, full of understanding. "Regret is not weakness, Will. It is a demonstration of humanity, of compassion."

Will nodded again, grateful. He was glad Quirk was with him in this. It would be harder with Balur or Firkin. People who could not understand.

"Now," Quirk said, "please hold Ethel still. I have at least a gallon of this potion to force into her."

They spent the rest of the morning and most of the early afternoon climbing the great zigzagging road that led up from the valley floor. It slowly switched back and forth as the landscape transformed from fields, to forest, to rock and scree.

Finally, the gate to Mattrax's castle loomed before them—a great monstrosity of oak that couldn't have made Will feel more unwelcome had the iron studs that punctuated its surface been arranged to read "Piss off." Around it, rock had been piled into a gatehouse built along a similar theme. Beyond it, a jagged crack in the rocky ground pitched down into a dry moat. And beyond that, Mattrax's fortress rose.

If the gatehouse was unwelcoming, the fortress was positively rude about the whole notion of visiting. It was an ugly towering slab of unfriendly rock, spilling shadow and hate onto the valley below. Carved directly into the surface of the mountain, its walls were polished smooth to give attackers no place to gain a foothold. The crenellations jutted forward at a sloping angle to make the use of ladders more difficult and to provide routes for boiling oil to be poured down upon anyone clustered in the moat below. Arrow slits peered down upon the whole affair, and a pair of eyes could be seen behind each one.

Who exactly it was that Mattrax imagined would be attacking the castle was beyond Will. Did he picture some mass suicidal urge gripping the valley below? Everyone marching here en masse to batter their brains out against his castle walls? The only threat Will could possibly imagine was another dragon, and one of those would just fly over any fortifications while arrows bounced off its skin, slowly charbroiling all the archers until Mattrax bothered to come out and have a proper fight. Assuming Mattrax would bother. It would be like the fat, lazy bastard to just sit there and wait until the other dragon got bored and flew off.

Much like the guard sitting atop the gatehouse wall gazing down at Will, Quirk, and Ethel right now.

The guard scratched one of several chins that filled the space between his chain mail and his helmet. "What," he said, "in the name of Betra's sagging tits is wrong with that cow?"

Ethel, it had to be admitted was acting... strangely.

In order that the Snag Weed not render Ethel immediately unconscious, and so that she could get to Mattrax's fortress under her own steam, Quirk had put the potion in a series of pigskin bladders that she had forced down Ethel's gullet. The idea was that the bladders would dissolve slowly in Ethel's stomach acid, releasing the potion and permeating the meat only after the moment of death. Ethel's stomach however, was a little ahead of schedule, and she was not reacting terribly well.

Her head lolled first to one side then the other and her tongue flopped back and forth from her slack mouth as she did so. Her laconic nature faded as one's eye traveled from head toward rump. Her front feet shifted unsteadily, but her back legs were stamping like those of an enraged bull. She held her tail aloft and was whirling it in circles so rapidly it was practically a blur. Will almost expected her hindquarters to take off the ground.

Will glanced at Ethel and then up at the guard. In his experience, Mattrax's soldiers didn't know much about cattle.

"She's, erm…" He shuffled options in his head. "In heat."

"She's what?" The guard kept scratching at his chin.

"In heat," Will repeated. "Like…mating season."

The guard squinted. Will risked a look at Quirk. She was squinting at him too. Which didn't really feel like the right attitude to Will.

"It's a horny cow?" said the guard eventually.

"Yeah." Will shrugged again. Then risked an, "Obviously."

Quirk emitted a sound that distinctly resembled choking.

The gate guard hadn't left himself much leeway for additional squinting, but he gave it a noble effort. His eyes were barely open as he examined Ethel.

"Something funny about that cow," he said. "I don't trust it."

"Please," said Quirk, "it's just a cow. It's for Mattrax. It's his dinner. How much damage could it cause?"

Unfortunately, Will thought, being polite was as likely to mark them as suspicious as being in possession of a cow that was evidently tripping balls.

Having no room to squint further, the gate guard chewed his lip instead.

"Could be a ruse," he said. "That cow could be full of enemy combatants."

Both Will and Quirk regarded Ethel.

"Full?" Quirk hazarded. "Of…how many?"

Will supposed that that was as valid a question to pull from the ether as any other.

"Could be dwarves," said the gate guard, doing an impressive job of seeming to be guileless.

Quirk held her arms out measuring the cow. Which, Will thought, was perhaps humoring the madness a step too far.

"You're worried that this fully alive and healthy cow also contains...perhaps two dwarfs?"

"Could be pixies," said the guard quickly. "They're bloody small, they are. Could have a hundred pixies in there. That could be a whole fake cow full of pixies."

Quirk shook her head sadly. "Actually," she said, "pixies are a highly individualistic society. Gatherings of any more than three or four rapidly devolve into violent confrontation. They tend to use flower blooms as weapons, though, which means their territorial displays are often mistaken for adorable demonstrations of cuteness, but actually they're quite feral in their..."

She finally seemed to notice Will's horrified stare. "Ix-nay on the knowing it-shay," he whispered. Entry into Mattrax's guard did not require a significant level of education. In fact, the mindless following of orders was far more cherished than independent thought.

The guard spat—a brown gobbet that arced down and splattered next to Will's boot. "Might be some sort of bomb," he said. "Someone made her eat it and now it's making her funny. Someone bites into her and she goes boom. That's more than my job's worth. I don't want to let in no exploding cow."

Quirk, Will noticed, seemed to be finally running out of patience. She was repeatedly opening and clenching her fists. Her knuckles were white, but her palms were bright red.

Violence, pain, death, and the impressive meltdown of the plan in its infant stages seemed inevitable, and just as Will was working out if there was time to flee for his life there was a great rumble from the mountainside. His eyes left the guard and flicked left to where, fifty yards or so below them, soldiers were milling about on a broad shelf of rock. Something in the rock itself was moving. Something grating against stone.

*The portcullis,* he realized, the entrance to the cave, to the gold, to revenge. It was so tantalizingly close.

And then Mattrax appeared. A vast uncoiling mass of scale and muscle. His head was titanic. As big as an oxcart, small fiery yellow eyes dwarfed by the huge underslung jaw. Teeth jutted up like broken yellow branches from his mouth. A crest of spines crowned it. His scales were a dull red, the color of raw meat left out for a day. His wings were held half-spread, almost impossibly large. The flesh stretched between each elongated, thorny joint was almost translucent, thick with veins.

The dragon yawned lazily, snapped halfheartedly at some guards, and then launched himself into the air, rising rapidly on quick, powerful strokes.

A low moan drew Will's attention to Quirk. She was no longer a quivering arrow of rage. Her hands were not clenched. They were wide open, held almost in supplication. She was staring at the dragon in awe. As the beast disappeared into the low clouds, she flicked her gaze to Will.

"We *have* to get in there," she breathed.

Will, for his part, was having his own trouble controlling his emotions. But it was rage instead of awe that bubbled inside him.

"Then convince Captain Arsehole to let us in," he hissed back.

"Look," said Quirk loudly, turning to the guard above. She had her teeth bared in a rictus smile. "What if we just killed the cow here and now? Then you can see if it explodes or not, or if a hundred imps leap out, or anything. Would that make it easier?"

For a moment, Will's world seemed to stop. A single heartbeat thundered through his chest. He turned to Quirk. She turned back to him. A big soft smile on her face. She turned it back toward the guard but kept her eyes on him.

"You'll have to do it, I'm afraid," she whispered from the corner of her mouth. "I'm a pacifist."

"What?" The word squeaked out of him. "I'll have to what?"

He could, he supposed, deal with the death of Ethel in the abstract. Eventually, given time, he could, perhaps in the peace and quiet of his home, imagine handing her over to soldiers who, far out of his sight, would hand her over to a dragon. He might even—with several weeks to think it over, and a number of strong drinks inside him—be able to take her to the cave entrance himself. As long as he were able to shut the door tight before the inevitable slaughter began.

But here? Now?

He stared into Ethel's eyes.

Each one rolled independently in its socket.

"Go on then!" yelled down the guard. "Do it then!"

"To be honest," Quirk whispered, "I'm surprised she's survived this long given the quantity of Snag Weed we put in her, so if you could kill her first that would be a huge weight off my conscience."

Will felt his jaw clenching. The red rage brimming up in him. But he took a breath, turned back to Ethel. He put a hand on the side of her head. It lolled away from him and a slurred moo dribbled out from between her lips.

"Look," said the guard, "I'll help you out. I'll go and get my crossbow, and if it's not dead by the time I get back then I'll kill you and the cow. Sound fair?"

Quirk spread her arms, exasperated. "We're guards the same as you. Look at our uniforms." She sounded slightly injured that the disguise wasn't proving to be more effective.

"You might just be wearing them," said the guard, and Will's heart skipped a beat. "Or you could be pixie-stuffed puppets for all I know."

"I already explained the unfeasibility of—"

But the guard was already gone. Quirk whirled on Will.

"Go on then," she said. "Do it already."

Will felt the weight of the purloined sword on his belt. He felt the warmth of Ethel's fur against his palm.

"I can't." He felt helpless.

"Look." Quirk leaned in close. "There is no version of this plan—of *your* plan—where Ethel survives. There is only a version where we survive. And I am not dying outside this castle, pincushioned by some mouth-breathing imbecile because you can't bring yourself to kill a dying cow. If I die here, it is going to be at the hands of a brutal monstrosity like a respectable thaumatobiologist. Now pull yourself together and stab that cow."

Ethel's rolling head slapped into his stomach, her nose smearing snot over the loose-fitting breastplate.

How many days had he drunk Ethel's milk? How many years had her cheese been a constant of his life? Her butter? She was his sustenance.

He held on to her head, cradled it gently in his arms. Her tongue probed sloppily at his elbow.

"Weren't you a farmer?" Quirk said. Much of the sympathy seemed to have boiled off from her voice. "Didn't you slaughter animals all the time?"

"Not the ones I named," Will said. "Not the ones that were part of my family."

"Look," said Quirk, leaning in close. "Who would you rather see killed here? Me or the cow?"

"I know the cow better." It was out of his mouth before he'd really thought about it.

Quirk struggled to respond to that for long enough to allow the guard to return above. "Oh good," he said. "I was hoping you would have waited. Now let me see how I aim this thing again."

"Will!" Quirk wasn't whispering anymore.

Will held Ethel's head. He thought about how she had supported his life for so many years. How she had helped bear the farm on her back.

But the farm was gone. And now there was only one way left she could serve him.

He pulled the sword free from its scabbard in a single fluid movement, and slashed at Ethel's throat.

The blade wedged into the flesh after about half an inch. He heaved. It jerked another quarter inch.

Ethel brayed, kicked.

Will jerked on the sword, horror mounting behind his eyes. If its previous owner had not been lying dead on a road, Will would have hunted him down and beaten the basics of blade maintenance into him. He'd owned sharper butter knives.

Ethel's wavering legs went out from under and she crashed to the ground. The weight of her slammed into Quirk, slapped the woman to the ground.

"Oh gods." Will tugged the blade free. More blood sprayed up, coating his face. Ethel screamed, kicked. Quirk screamed along with her.

"Oh Lawl's black eye on all this shit." Will brought the blade down with a dull thwack.

It took another minute of hacking and sawing before Ethel finally lay still, in a spreading pool of her own blood. Quirk had managed to extract herself from beneath the dying cow and was trying to wipe the worst of the gore off herself. Will just stood there dripping, trying to keep his gorge from rising. He failed.

Above them, the gate guard looked vaguely disappointed. "Fine then," he said. "Come on in then. Welcome back to Castle Mattrax."

# 14

## Gaffes and Gatekeepers

Lette had lain hidden among the trees as Mattrax emerged from the mountainside. She was around two hundred yards shy of the portcullis, where the tree line ended and loose rock and shale began.

She had a rough idea of what to expect from a dragon, of course. Her childhood had allowed for some schooling. She had read some histories. She knew it would be large and powerful. And she had killed some large, powerful creatures herself. A wendigo in the mountains east of Saleria, tall enough that it made Balur look like a toddler. A wyvern in northern Vinter, although that was so drunk from eating fermented grapes that it was literally pissing itself in the battle. And there had even been the demigod in Batarra—some spawn of Toil's that had somehow made it to its early twenties, and blessed with the gift of compelling people to work themselves to death on a regular basis. Fortunately, when it turned its glowing eyes on Lette, her work had been to kill demigod arseholes.

Still, even when compared to the semidivine walking upon the earth, this was different.

Mattrax was not just large. A horse could be large. A tree. A house perhaps. These were simple things of a size the mind could grasp in a single glance. Mattrax was large in a far more complex and profound way. He was large in the abstract way that major pieces of a landscape were large. In the way countries were large, or rivers that took months to travel from their source to the ocean. He was so large that it was difficult for Lette to think of him as something truly alive. He had seemed more like some part of the mountain that happened to be able to leave and fly around for a bit.

And she was going to steal from him.

He would be right there next to her, and she would steal from him.

He would be drugged, of course. But could you really drug something that large? Could they really have assembled that much Snag Weed?

And more to the point, how in the name of each and every god of the Pantheon was she going to stop Balur from trying to kill it? The bigger the beast the more he seemed to want to test himself against it. He suffered from an almost suicidal form of machismo.

This, she thought, was going to be a very long and harrowing day.

But first Balur had to get up there, the villagers in tow. First they had to herd the drugged idiots onto the platform, to the pressure plate hidden there. First they had to open the way.

She heard them before she saw them. Her first impression of them was one of baying, braying, belligerent sound. It crashed and careened up through the forest toward her hiding spot, whooping and hollering as it came. She clambered a few branches higher into the pine tree she was using as a lookout, just in case.

Despite their vocal enthusiasm, though, when the Kondorran villagers came into sight, yelling and gnashing their teeth, they were also panting a bit. It was a good six or seven miles from the village on the valley floor to here, and the last two miles were nothing if not steep. It was difficult, Lette supposed, to keep up your deranged enthusiasm for murder when you had a forty-five-degree angle to conquer. When you stabbed a mountainside it would always resolutely refuse to bleed.

As the villagers hit the end of the forest, she could see they were definitely running out of steam. They stumbled out into daylight, started grinding to a halt.

Where the hell were Balur and Firkin? They should be here, driving this rabble on. She scanned the trees below. If Balur was late because he was busy digging a shallow grave for Will's drunkard friend, he was going to have to dig a second one for himself…

Then she spotted them, picking their way up the mountainside. For some reason, Firkin was perched between Balur's shoulder blades, slapping the top of his head and shrieking, "Gyah! Giddy up, you fine steed! Onward and upward, you magnificent beast of burden!"

Even as she clambered down the tree to meet them, she found she was actually impressed at Balur's restraint.

"Come on," she called as she reached the pine-needle-littered floor, "they're flagging."

"*They* are bloody flagging?" Balur groused as he reached her. "Have they been needing to carry a squirming gods-hexed fool up the mountain? Because I have not been seeing that."

"You're eight feet of muscle and rage," she said, reaching up to pat his arm. "Stop being such a complete pussy. It's unbecoming."

Balur grunted.

Firkin for his part whipped repeatedly at Balur's head and neck. "What is this?" he shrieked. "Tally ho and sally forth! Tally forth to Sally the ho! Lovely girl. Very welcoming. Onward!"

"What exactly is his role being in this whole plan?" Balur asked. "Because I would be liking to change it to being a sack of bloody meat."

"He's important to Will, and Will is important to the plan because he came up with it," Lette said.

"But he was coming up with it already. What are we still needing him for?"

"For when you inevitably fuck it up." Lette felt that this state-ment was not entirely without precedent.

Balur considered this for a moment and then nodded. "That is being fair enough."

Lette grinned and turned back to pursue the swarming vil-lagers. "Oh Betra's tits," she swore.

The villagers had come to a halt just shy of the rocky lip that served as the entrance to Mattrax's cave. The fifteen or so guards who stood watch over the portcullis were eyeing them suspiciously, shifting spears and swords from hand to hand.

Overly aware of the guard's scrutiny, Lette scuttled out of the trees and toward the crowd. As she approached she was aware of a susurrating grumble rising up from it. She pushed into the edge of the mass.

"—no bloody prophet," she heard someone grumbling.

"Not got any noshers now, have we?" said another.

"Not going up bloody there all by myself," came another voice.

"Said we was going to get a bloody prophet."

"I figured he'd be leading the bloody charge. Get himself in all the danger."

A number of belligerent ayes came in response to this. Lette turned to Balur—bulldozing a path into the crowd behind her—and arched an eyebrow.

"Prophet?" she said as acidly as possible.

Balur shifted on his massive feet. "Ah," he said. "Well." And then, "You are seeing..."

"No, Balur," she told him. "I am not seeing."

"Firkin was using a little bit of artistic license when he be motivating the crowd..."

"Inciting!" Firkin screamed from his perch. "I do not moti-vate. I incite. I excite! I titillate! I ferment!"

"He is being difficult to keep on a strict party message," Balur said with a shrug.

For her part, Lette did her best to maintain her frosty demeanor while again being impressed that Balur had not reduced Firkin to a messy stain on the Kondorra landscape.

"You could be being a prophet," Balur suggested.

"I could not be being that, numbskull," Lette snapped back, suddenly finding it easy to be frosty once more. "I am meant to be sneaking unnoticed into the gearworks of the door that your crowd is meant to have opened already. I can hardly be leading the charge and then hoping no one notices me."

"Oi!" shouted one of the guards from the safety of the lip. "Fuck off!"

The time had come, Lette decided, for executive action. "You," she snapped at Firkin, "you got us into this mess, get us out of it."

Firkin stared at her wide-eyed for a moment, made a number of rude hand gestures, and then shrieked. "Crowd! Villagers! Mindless minions of the mighty word of the prophet! Mud pies and squat froglike fat faces! Inbred swine! Melting pot that was melted maybe just a little bit too much! I bring the word of the prophet unto you and thou shalt hear his command and say, why yes of course, that sounds like a reasonable course of action, I think I will do that right away pronto, thank you very much for providing my previously worthless existence with such out-standing advice, it is the lightness in my eyes and the breath in my heart. And thus shall I say to you as he said unto me—"

Here Firkin paused, and Lette was amazed to see that a hush had fallen over the crowd, as they all stared up at Firkin.

Firkin grinned savagely and thrust a gnarly finger at the guards. "Get those fuckers!" he yelled.

As one the crowd turned to face the guards—

—and hesitated.

"Erm," said one loud voice.

"Yeah," said another.

"About that..." supplied a third.

"Again," added a fourth, "I don't mean to harp on this, but didn't it seem like the prophet was actually going to be here. I thought there would be more actual leadership."

"He's the voice of the prophet," said another, and the attention of the crowd shifted back to Firkin.

Lette hung her head.

"Why are we listening to Firkin anyway?" someone else chimed in.

*A fine question,* Lette thought.

"You go ahead and attack if you're so bloody keen," said someone else, clearly getting sick of this whole business.

"You know," Balur said, "I am not hating that idea."

Lette groaned. All they needed to do was get a bunch of villagers onto a pressure plate. That was it. Why was that so hard? Why did people have to die for that? Why couldn't anything just be clean?

But Balur was already off and running, leaving all her doubts in his dusty wake. Firkin yelled and screamed, flapping about on Balur's shoulders, clinging desperately as Balur shifted his war hammer from his back to his fists.

The crowd and the guards stared, stunned, as this lone, towering figure charged toward fifteen blades.

A guard captain was the first to recover. He started yelling. Soldiers stumbled into formation, tried to get their spears up.

*Poor bastards,* Lette thought.

Balur hit the wall of guards like a battering ram. Spears snapped as points struck his armor, his thick hide. His hammer swung. A guard's chest shifted from concave to convex. The man brayed blood in a short coughing bark that signaled the end of his life.

This was it, Lette knew. This was the moment when the crowd would either move with them, or abandon them and flee. The tipping point.

"Gyah!" she yelled, as if driving a herd of horses into a gallop.

"Get on with you! Get up there! Do your Lawl-hexed prophet some pissing good, you worthless sacks of shit!"

The crowd hesitated a moment longer, watched as Balur caught a sword in his fist, yanked the soldier on the other end of it toward him, and head-butted the poor bastard into oblivion.

"Do it!" Lette screamed. "Fucking move!"

And much to her shock they did.

*A motivational speaker,* she thought. *Perhaps that's the path ahead.* Then she was running after the crowd, harrying and shouting as she did so.

The guard captain, it turned out, was not as stupid as Lette had hoped. Balur was, he recognized, not someone his troops were going to beat. He also recognized the weight of Balur's war hammer. Inhumanly strong, Balur might be, but he was not indefatigable. He would tire eventually. Until then containment was key. The crowd, on the other hand, was more easily handled. Rapidly he shouted orders, only two of his quickest soldiers dancing around Balur, poking and prodding at him and desperately flinging themselves out of his way. The rest of the guard simply swarmed round him.

The crowd clashed against the guards. They outnumbered them to be sure, but solid steel would take care of that quickly enough. Lette tried to get a good line of sight as she worked her way through the crowd. A dagger found its home in a soldier's throat. Another was backed into by a villager staggering away from a spear-wielding guard. He flung his arms up in shock and pain. The soldier took advantage of the villager's kind offer and gutted him.

Lette cursed. This was supposed to be clean. Hell, it still could be. All she needed was one big push, one surge up onto the lip. The pressure plate would be there. And then the villagers could scatter.

"Push!" she screamed. "Push!" She was at the far edge of the crowd now, up on the lip itself, where Balur had made a mess of one guard but was still being tormented by the other. "Push!" she yelled again.

A guard yelled. She flung a knife. It speared his eye socket and he dropped. She needed to be able to disappear, to drop from notice and be poised for the moment when the gate rose. But it was not coming. The moment was hung stubbornly in stasis.

The crowd quivered under the guard's onslaught. But then the guards were dropping back, regrouping. The villagers hesitantly, but undeniably, advanced. Lette realized this was going to work.

And then, all of a sudden it was not.

All of a sudden, everyone was standing still.

All of a sudden, there was the sound of wings beating in the sky.

Whoomph.

Whoomph.

Whoomph.

Mattrax landed with a crash of air and dust, wings spread, mouth wide, his snarl shaking the air. His massive head swung back and forth, looming over everyone. His tail lashed out, sent villagers flying.

The whole cliff side shook with the power and the weight of him. The world shrank down to the single point that was him, his eyes, his jaws, his teeth. All sound was the sound of his roar. All the wind was the beating of his wings. All the ground was the tremor of his footsteps. He defined the world.

In the face of this onslaught, in defiance of this oblivion of the senses, Lette saw Balur roar. It was a lost sound, hurled into the fury of Mattrax's roar and flung away. But it was his roar. His will. His refusal to bow. And Balur charged Mattrax.

Lette watched Mattrax, as the dragon watched Balur's approach. Together they both watched the lizard man as he raised his war hammer, watched him roar, veins standing out on his neck, as he gave the blow his all.

It never landed.

Mattrax flicked a forepaw at Balur, a small casual movement. Balur flew. He traced an arc through the sky, made contact with the trees, and crashed down through branches, a beaten, broken toy.

The crowd watched him, turned back to Mattrax, took stock of exactly how fucked they were, and ran like Lawl had set all the demons of the Hallows upon them. Lette could see Firkin bobbing and flailing in their midst, howling along with all the rest of them.

But she did not run. She did not even back carefully away from the stone ledge.

Because the cave was open. Mattrax stood directly atop his pressure plate, screaming and roaring at the retreating villagers. Behind him the cave entrance was wide open. The portcullis that guarded it stood wide open, a beckoning black maw.

She could see the black iron chain that held the gate to its counterweights, each link thicker than her waist, disappearing down through a hole carved into the rocky floor. She could fit in there. She could do exactly what she had come here to do.

She just had to get past the notice of Mattrax and the guards first. And there was no time to sneak, no time for subtlety, no time for anything but putting her head down and running hard.

The only real drawback of the plan that she could see was that it was complete and utter suicide.

She pressed into the cliff face. In a moment it wouldn't matter anyway. The guards were going to spot her, point her out to Mattrax, and she would be looking at the inside of his gullet within moments.

*All because I trusted a plan a farmer came up with.* She shook her head. *I should have told him to shove his plan, and whisk me off to some new farm so we could roll in the hay and raise pigs.*

The thought came unbidden, but before she had a chance to beat it back into whatever dark corner of her subconscious it had crawled from, a noise came from above like a pair of massive bellows filling. She glanced up. Mattrax was breathing in, the air seeming to catch in his gullet.

Oh, all the gods' hex upon it, she knew what happened next.

Mattrax exhaled.

A roaring sheet of flame filled the world, whistling past her, scorching her skin. It raced after the fleeing villagers. It smashed through Mattrax's own guards. She heard screams, saw someone staggering out of the blast, skin sloughing away from bone.

For a moment she was paralyzed, held in place by the horror of it, the magnificence. So much power. Such raw rage excising life from the land. And then she realized: This was it. This was the moment she was waiting for.

She put her head down. She ran. She shot past Mattrax, past the cave entrance, and straight to that dark, dank hole into which the portcullis chain disappeared. No guard cried out. No guard pointed and screamed. They were all too busy being roasted alive by their infuriated master.

She slammed into the chain, grabbed a handhold. And then, lithe as an eel, slipped down into darkness and safety.

# 15

# The Belly of the Beast

Like all castles, Mattrax's mountain fort had been constructed with one goal in mind: to repel attackers. A series of walls surrounded the keep, each protected by a gate offset from the one before, the layout of which would force assailants to zigzag back and forth, taking the longest path possible, all the time suffering the withering blows of the castle's defenders.

An additional consequence of this strategy, Will discovered, was that it made it painfully difficult to drag a dead cow through the place. The experience, he was finding, was making him significantly less fond of Ethel.

"Thrice-cursed daughter of a cow whore," he muttered as he tried to get a better grip on her hoof. "Why did I ever feed you any single extra grain of corn? You fat fucking..." He descended into muttered curses.

"I don't know what you're complaining about," Quirk grumbled, shoving her shoulder into Ethel's dragging arse once more. "You're a farmer. Physical labor is what you do all day. I'm built for academia."

"Aren't you a wizard or something?" Will was increasingly skeptical of this. He'd seen her brew her potions, to be sure, but alchemy and a working knowledge of herbalism was not summoning mystical forces and spitting in the eye of the gods' immutable laws. Still, it seemed like the sort of thing that could really help them out now. "Can't you cast a spell and make the cow float or something?"

"I am trying," Quirk said, face buried in Ethel's backside as her feet dug at the ground, "to give that up."

"What the hell does that even mean?" Will asked. "What sort of wizard doesn't want to cast spells? Isn't that the whole point? Power and riches summoned by eldritch forces?"

"The sort," Quirk snapped, "that has a functioning moral compass."

"You're here to rob a dragon!"

Quirk popped her head up over Ethel's rump and eyeballed him very hard indeed.

Will became abruptly aware that he was wearing a dead man's armor, standing beside a dead, drugged cow in the center of the enemy's castle, surrounded by guards armed with a large assortment of pointy metal. Quirk's eyebrow slowly inched its way up her forehead.

Will ducked his head and started heaving on Ethel's forehoof.

They had navigated the second of the three gates that led to the keep when it became abruptly apparent that something was very much awry. Will's first clue was a roar so loud that the ground shook. Ethel's dead flesh quivered with the force of it.

Will and Quirk locked eyes immediately. Barely controlled panic reflected barely controlled panic. Will took a breath, did a quick mental inventory of the steps in his plan. And yes, he was sure. There was no point that called for the bellowing of an enraged dragon. In fact almost every step of the plan was aimed at completely avoiding that outcome. Something was very, very wrong.

"Do we bail?" Quirk whispered, once whispers were audible once more.

Before he could answer, there came a rushing, whispering, roar. The sound of fire. The sound of Mattrax incinerating someone.

*Lette!*

No. He shook his head. *No, she couldn't be dead. She was too smart, too tough for this.*

*It's your fault,* said a small voice in the back of his head. *This is your plan.*

No. He shook his head. *I was trying to talk them out of it.*

*Yeah, great job you did there. The way you told them the exact plan that you and Firkin used to discuss. That was a great way to tell them not to do it. And now Lette's dead. You should have told her to shove the plan, and then whisked her off to some new farm so you could roll in the hay and raise pigs.*

She's not *dead.*

"Will!" Quirk's whisper forced its way into his consciousness. "Do we bail?" She looked down at the cow, back at the gate.

Will hesitated.

"Gods' hex on it," said Quirk, "this isn't worth it. I'm—"

"No," Will snapped. Quirk froze.

"We have to leave," she implored him. "Something has gone very wrong."

Will nodded slightly. That did seem like the most likely turn of events. "But," he said, "I'm not sure how us dropping everything and running screaming for the hills makes us seem less suspicious."

Quirk chewed on her lip.

"We stick to the plan," he said. "We feed Mattrax Ethel. We hide in the vault while he passes out, and we see if we can still meet up with Lette."

"And if we can't?" Quirk's wide eyes and skittering fingers made it clear she didn't really think that this was a question.

"Then," Will hissed, "we're still in a vault full of gold with an unconscious dragon." He tried to keep his temper under control. He wanted to be the one panicking. It wasn't fair that Quirk was taking up all the panicking time that they had. "We shove our pockets full of coin, you take your measurements, or whatever it is you want, and we sneak back out through the castle under cover of darkness."

Quirk hesitated. Will wanted to go over and shake her. "It's the only way," he told her. Because it was.

Still Quirk vacillated. Will decided actions spoke louder than words. He grabbed the hoof once more. "Come on," he said, starting to heave. A moment later he felt Quirk throw her weight into the cow's back end. They recommenced their crawling pace forward.

Will breathed a sigh of relief. While disaster seemed to have fallen, they had at least avoided compounding the issue.

"You," barked a voice from behind them. "Stop what you're doing right fucking now."

*Of course,* thought Will. *I forgot. The gods hate me. Lawl, Betra, Klink, Toil, Cois, Knole, even absent Barph—the whole bloody lot of them. Sitting up in the heavens, they have hexed me and each and every element of my life. They have marched through kicking and shrieking, trying to make sure they've covered every conceivable way to screw me.* Will found that he almost admired their thoroughness. It truly was divine.

He turned slowly. Quirk still had her shoulder to Ethel's rump, her feet still pushing at the ground. Still desperately fighting against reality.

She went nowhere.

The soldier bore down on them. He was a large man, the noseguard of his helmet bent askew, and a large livid red weal where Will had flung soup into his face several nights before.

Will froze, tried to swallow against the sudden dryness of his throat, failed. A tiny overture of discomfort heralding the pain to come.

The soldier cuffed Quirk over the back of the head. "Did I or did I not tell you to get your face out of the arse-end of that cow?"

Quirk turned abruptly, and Will was surprised to see her fists were balled. Where was the pacifist now when he needed her?

This was not the moment to start a fistfight. This was, in fact, pretty much the opposite of that moment. This was the moment when they desperately, desperately needed to go unnoticed.

Then the soldier's eyebrows arched. Quirk stumbled, managed to turn the raising of fists into a pathetic salute. The soldier sneered. Will tried his best to turn away.

"Mattrax has had another of his hissy fits," the soldier said finally. "Going to need more guards down on his portcullis." He pointed to Quirk. "Move your arse."

Quirk remained frozen in her salute, a look of mounting horror on her face. "But..." she said, "the cow. For Mattrax. It is. I mean it is for him. It's his supper."

*No!* Will wanted to shout at her. *Shut up! Agree! Nod. Smile. Do anything you have to do to get him to leave and to take all his attention with you.*

*Brilliant idea,* said the smaller, more hateful voice that resided behind the panicky one. *Leave yourself alone in the castle. Try and haul Ethel by yourself. Gods, you are absolutely chock full of terrible ideas, aren't you?*

Quirk was still frozen, as if some part of her anatomy had glitched, a piece of the clockwork of life come undone, and the artifice of the whole charade suddenly revealed.

"This cow is Mattrax's dinner?" said the soldier without any apparent concern. "Well, let me take a moment to see if I give the slightest of fucks." He placed a finger on his chin. "Nope. Appear to be all out of fucks." He leaned in, his undamaged cheek turning as red as the burned one. "I told you to get your maggoty little arse down to the gate before I deliver you there in a bloody gods-hexed pile! Am I bloody clear?"

Quirk took an involuntary step away from both the soldier's flying spittle and Ethel. She looked at Will imploringly.

He was going to have to do it. He was going to have to open his mouth.

"I really need—" he started, dropping his voice an octave.

The soldier backhanded him without looking, the metal of his gauntlet splitting Will's lip. "You need to learn to shut up when you're not being spoken to. And—" He paused, considered, then finally turned to Will. Will's heart stopped for a moment, then appeared to decide to try to bore a way out of his rib cage.

"—as funny as it would be," the soldier went on, "to watch your stupid arse try and do this on your own, you probably try to remember the invention of the fucking handcart." He shook his head sadly. "You country recruits. I swear you get stupider every batch we pull in." And he turned away without giving Will a second glance, saw Quirk still staring at him.

"Well?" He veritably exploded. "What gave you the impression you should still be bloody standing there? Move!" And finally Quirk did, going back the way they had come, almost at a run, casting distressed looks back at Will.

Will sagged against Ethel, then realized that moment hadn't arrived yet. The soldier still stood a few paces from him, staring at Quirk's strange retreat. He shook his head again.

"Barph's hex on their brains," he said quietly. And then strode away.

The soldiers of Mattrax's castle were, Will discovered, no more full of the milk of human kindness when they were at home and helping out their fellows. In fact, whatever milk they were filled with, Will suspected it was spiked with bile and tasted much like fermented piss. Requests for directions to the much-rumored handcarts were met with blank stares at best, and long tirades about his dubious parentage at worst. It was late afternoon by the time he finally found them. There was no way to get Ethel on without hacking her to pieces, and while Will had some experience at butchery, a blunt soldier's sword was not the ideal tool for the job. On the plus side, by the time he was done there was no way to notice the bloodstain that marked the fate of his armor's previous owner in among all the others.

The sun was low in the sky as he squelched toward the keep, leaving dark red footprints in his wake. His passage drew enough attention to make his hands shake, but all the soldiers gave him a wide berth.

*What was I thinking?* he asked himself as he trundled the remains of Ethel and her wake of attendant flies through the keep's main gates. *I'm a farmer. Not a thief. This is absolute madness.*

He looked around the main entrance hall of the keep. Half-remembered conversations with Firkin flickered through his memory. Down. He remembered that Firkin had known that there was a path down here.

Not just a path. A ramp.

He saw it, off to his left, a torchlit archway, a spiraling floor that led down and away.

Would this make Firkin happy? Should he have brought the old man in here, somehow? It was an impossible dream. No subterfuge would have been possible with Firkin in tow. But... could seeing this plan finally put into practice heal whatever wound it was that kept driving the old man back to the bottle?

There was no way to know, and no time to ponder. So Will just went through the archway and into a spiraling descent. The path led down. And down. And down. Torches set into rough iron brackets in the wall seemed spaced farther and farther apart. Their flames spat and flickered. Soot stained the walls around them.

What was left of Ethel was beginning to smell. Not the natural, bloody smell of fresh meat either. There was a slightly-too-sweet tang to the odor rising from her. Unconscious flies littered the handcart. The Snag Weed was working.

Glancing behind him, Will hesitated. Down in the valley, Quirk had given him a final vial of the potion to rub into the meat before it was delivered to Mattrax. A just-in-case backup to ensure full perfusion.

*What if it's not enough?* nagged the voice in the back of Will's head. *Quirk had no sense for how big Mattrax is. She doesn't know anything about dragons. What if he digests food differently?* Will didn't know much anatomy, but he knew enough about animal husbandry to know that most creatures were unwieldy bastards who delighted in fouling human plans.

Again, none of those thoughts helped. He was committed now. He upended the vial of potion, let the contents glug out over the meat. Quickly he rubbed it into the meat, fresh blood squeezing between his fingers. When he regripped the cart's handle, it felt slippery beneath his slick fingers.

Trying to keep his breathing steady, he made two more circuits of the descending ramp before it opened out onto a small, dark room, containing one guard, one stool, and one very solid-looking iron door covered with so many spikes that Will wondered if its creator was trying to compensate for something.

The guard beside the door did not so much sit upon his stool as sag around it. It appeared like some curious outgrowth of his posterior—like some foreign object left in a tree and slowly absorbed by the growing wood. His chain mail stretched over his gut, then finally gave up, leaving an exposed stretch of skin, which he scratched at idly. He was covered with a sheen of sweat. The few torches that guttered against the walls cast off more heat than the stone walls and low ceiling could shed.

"You're late," he said in a voice that seemed to bubble up from the spreading swamp of his chest. "Hours fucking late."

"I, erm, had, err, trouble with the cart," Will said.

The guard belched. "Good thing for you Mattrax took it all out on those poor bastards guarding his front gate. Otherwise…" He shook his head, setting off a series of small tremors that caused landslides of wobbling flesh to run down his sides.

Will worried that if he sweat any more he would simply melt and run between the flagstones below.

"Well," he managed to get out, though his voice shook, "I'm

here now." The artificial cheer in his voice sounded like hysteria even to him. "Just let me on through and he'll get his supper."

The guard's eyes, perched precariously above the sloping hills of his cheeks, retreated deeper into valleys of creased skin.

Will nodded at the door in what he hoped was an encouraging fashion. Sweat dripped off his nose with the motion. "You know," he said, "I'll just pop in and get everything laid out for him." He was increasingly aware that he had absolutely no idea what he was talking about.

The guard's eyebrows were struggling to clamber out of the creases around his eyes and up his forehead. "Go in?" he burbled. "What is it? Your missus left you? Gambling debts?"

Will saw he had no option but to resort to monosyllables. "Huh?"

"Normally they're more weepy," the guard went on. "The suicidal ones."

"Erm..." was as far as Will was willing to extend his vocabulary.

The guard broke into brief, gasping laughter. His gut shook and Will had the distinct impression that if the chain-mail shirt could have given him a reproving look it would have.

"Go in?" gasped the guard, panting from the apparent exertion. His cheeks had turned a dangerous shade of purple. "Go in?" He gasped again, pounded at his chest with a hammy fist. "Nobody goes in, you fucking numbskull. That's his lord high Mattrax's personal abode that is. That's no place for mere mortals. And it certainly ain't the place for fuckwitted young fools like you. Now—"

He reached over, grabbed a short lever previously hidden among the spikes on the door, and yanked on it. The bottom third of the door lifted up, making a flap.

"—shovel all that meat through there and get out before the Hallows take you."

It was short and bloody work. The guard made faces as Will did it. "Fuck. Can tell you was late. Smells something awful that does."

Will's own stomach roiled, but it had little to do with the meat. He was meant to be in that cave. He was meant to be spooning this shit into Mattrax's mouth. Except now he wasn't in there and the meat stank so highly of poison that even this bubbling cesspit of a guard could smell it over his own overpowering body odor. And so Mattrax would smell it. And he would see Lette as she emerged from her hiding place—assuming she was even still alive—and he would devour her instead of poor Ethel, who had now died for naught. And then, when Balur and Firkin showed up he would eat them as well. Quirk too, like as not.

As for himself, he would be lucky if he was eaten. The soldiers would take turns seeing how deeply they could stab him without killing him, until he was more wound than man. And then they would leave him by the gate to bleed out as a warning to others who thought that anger counted for more than good sense.

The last portion of Ethel landed with a slick slop on the far side of the flap. There was a wet sound as it slipped down a ramp into the darkness beyond. The guard cranked on his lever, and the flap shut.

Will stood staring at the closed exit.

"Go on," belched the guard. "Get out."

Will turned away, walked on heavy feet. But even as he passed under the arch and back onto the spiraling path that led upward he knew there was no way out.

# 16

# Strong Drinks and Weak Minds

Far below Mattrax's castle, down at the floor of the Kondorra valley, Balur watched as the sun, tired of the drudgery of the day, slowly collapsed behind the peaks of the valley wall. Shadows stretched. Darkness descended.

It was possible, he thought, that when even Firkin questioned your actions, you had made a miscalculation. However, Balur found it was also likely that he didn't give a shit.

If he was being honest, it all came down to one thing: He was embarrassed. He had talked the big talk. He had told Lette to expect a certain amount of violence. He had told himself that he would not be forgotten. This was to be his moment of glory. Something wondrous and wonderful.

But what had Mattrax done? Had he suffered? Had he bellowed in fear and pain?

No. Mattrax had barely even noticed him. Mattrax had dismissed him. With a flick of his claw. Not even a full swipe. And Balur had not even landed a blow. Hadn't even left a dent to be remembered by. It was pathetic. It was beyond pathetic. Mattrax wouldn't even remember him for being pathetic. It was…forgettable.

That was the truth, if Balur was being honest. But Balur was well on the way to ensuring that he wouldn't have to be honest with himself for much longer. He was drinking, and he was drinking heavily.

This was the source of Firkin's objection. Not that Firkin seemed the type to usually oppose the heavy consumption of beverages. In fact, if anyone seemed likely to be a proponent of consuming Barph's nectar—as the bards were wont to call a mug of ale—then usually it was Firkin.

The problem was, Balur supposed—with what little senses were left to him—that they had spiked the ale with all that was left of the Fire Root potion.

It had seemed like a good idea at the time.

He had come to in the woods below Mattrax's cave, stitched with splinters, muscles aching. The crowd had gone, fled back down to The Village. Mattrax had swaggered back into his cave. The gate had shut behind him. Of Lette, there had been no sign. Of Firkin, unfortunately, there had been ample sign. He had been in front of Balur, attempting to shake him into consciousness. And Balur had sat up, and taken stock. He had grown embarrassed. And he had decided then and there, that this would not abide. A growl had risen out of him. No...if he thought back, that was not how it was being. The growl had not been coming out of him. It had been being him. He had been becoming the growl. His muscles were a growl. His thoughts. His footsteps as he strode down to the village.

This.

Would.

Not.

Abide.

He had been embarrassed. The village had embarrassed him. Firkin had skittered and scampered after him, barking words. Questions, he supposed, but knowing Firkin it had as likely been a dissertation on the advantages of fornication with squirrels. He had not really cared. Growls did not listen. They rumbled with hatred. They grew. They exploded.

The villagers would be easy to track, he had told himself. They would be easy prey. He could slip into their homes silently. He could be the monster beneath their beds. He could rend them, drink them, bury his face in their bowels.

But he would not. They were not worthy to be part of him. No. Instead they would submit and be the gods-hexed extensions of his will that he needed them to be.

And if they refused...Well, burying his face in a few bowels always seemed to turn him into the persuasive type. It was one of those funny human peculiarities he had trouble wrapping his head around.

When he had arrived in The Village he had found them all huddled in the tavern. His head had cracked the lintel above the door as he strode through it. That had failed to improve either his mood or his audience's disposition. They cowered.

"Useless." His growl had become a word. He had grabbed a villager by the neck, hoisted him aloft. His growl had grown, became a command. "Fight," he had barked into the man's face.

Not only had the man failed to fight, but he had also lost his own battle with continence. Balur had dropped him in disgust.

"Fight!" he had roared at the tavern's occupants. "Find your balls and fight!" The balls part had seemed a popular part of Firkin's speech as he recalled. He had not been above pandering to the idiots if it was truly necessary.

From the reaction he had received, he had wondered if it was a translation problem. Perhaps "fight" meant something different here. Something along the lines of "grab the nearest piece of furniture and cower behind it while all the time making a telltale whimpering sound."

Firkin had stepped forward at that point, had puffed out his chest. Balur could sense the air entering the scrawny man, could almost feel it becoming gibberish inside that pigeon chest. He grabbed Firkin by the neck, squeezed off that air. Firkin did actually fight. It was that act alone that had convinced him to not squeeze any harder. He dropped Firkin and let him gasp a bit.

What was wrong with these people? Could they truly be so cowed? This morning...

And then he had remembered. Somewhere in his rage and his embarrassment he had forgotten. Drugs. Quirk's potion had been in them. He had scrabbled at the pouch at his belt. Lette had not used all of it. Something about not wanting to poison everyone. Some weak-willed swill like that. Lette really needed to remove her head from her posterior and get back to kicking arse and taking gold.

He had stared around looking for some bread to mix the potion with. For some reason, none had been readily apparent. He had grabbed the villager who had refused to fight him, shook him a couple of times to make sure he was focusing, and demanded, "Where is the bread being?"

"The bread?" the man had replied. Well, he had whimpered a lot, had his head banged against a beam, and then said, "The bread?"

"Where is it being?"

The man had just cried. Balur had not understood it at all.

He had then become vaguely aware of something tapping at his waist. He looked down. Standing there had been a man in his fifties. He wore an apron, a mustache, and a prominent bald spot. In his nontapping hand he had held a mug of ale.

"Perhaps," he had said, voice shaking, "you just fancy a brew? I think it's been a long day for everyone."

Balur had considered this suggestion. Finally he nodded. The man had wilted visibly, a sigh exhaling.

"This is being a good idea," Balur had told him. He had been pleased that someone here beside himself had finally shown some initiative. "You will be fetching me five barrels."

"Five?" The man had sounded horrified, though for the life of him Balur had not understood why. He had looked around the room, reevaluated.

"Four will probably be covering it. You are largely being gutless, I suppose."

The man had whimpered and retreated. Balur had waited with

poorly concealed impatience. Beside him, Firkin had seemed to have recovered enough to be considering opening his mouth. Balur had given him a long look that he believed suitably conveyed how sick he was of Firkin's bullshit and false promises of prophets, and that if he opened his idiotic mouth to give voice to more idiotic suggestions, he would soon find his idiotic tongue wrapped around his idiotic neck. Firkin had seemed to possess enough sense to understand that at least.

Finally the man had appeared along with several others and the requisite barrels. They had fetched five after all. Using his claws Balur had yanked off the barrel lids, and upended the vial of Fire Root potion over them all, ensuring a liberal amount went into each barrel. He had dunked his arm in each one and swirled it around to ensure a good mixture. He licked a single talon clean. The Fire Root tang had been a powerful kick at the back of his throat. The growl in him had grown.

"Drink!" he had barked at the crowd.

Maybe it was him. Maybe it was his accent or his syntax. Sometimes humans did have trouble with that, though he was trying to make this fairly pissing simple for them all. Maybe they were all just horribly inbred and stupid. That would help explain Firkin, for one thing.

Actions, he had decided, would speak louder than words.

He had picked up the hapless, soiled villager who knew nothing about bread, and had dunked him headfirst in the ale. He held him there until he felt the man's chest buck, and he started to kick. That should be a good long swallow.

The man had come up barking, braying, and finally, it seemed, with a bit of fight in him. Balur was satisfied.

"Drink!" he had barked at the room once more, and this time a very pleasing crowd had formed around the barrels as the villagers had scrambled forward to comply.

Lette could say what she liked about his leadership skills. This was proof he could command the masses.

After that, there had not been much left to do until the villagers had drunk their fill, and replaced all their cowardice with a bellyful of alchemically induced murder-lust. And that had led to contemplation, which had led to morose pondering upon Mattrax's dismissal, which had led to embarrassment, which had led, inevitably, to a need for drink.

By that point most mugs had been smashed over someone else's head as the villagers raged and smashed at the confines of the tavern. So Balur had just grabbed a barrel, raised it to his lips, tipped, and poured.

He had lowered it with a satisfied smack of his lips, and seen Firkin's slightly horrified expression. There was a moment of suspicion that perhaps that had not been the smartest thing to do, and then the Fire Root had taken that idea out the back and kicked its head in.

And Balur had drunk.

Everyone had drunk.

He drank again now. Feeling the fire expand out from his belly, into his arms, his fingers, his legs. He was a growl no longer. He had transcended the growl. He was an openmouthed howl of rage into the night. He was the imminence of violence. He was the potential for devastation. And he was tired of waiting.

Above him, hunkered down in his pathetic cave, Mattrax was sleeping. Sleeping and not even thinking about him. Well, that would change. Mattrax would think of him long and hard. Or at least for as long as it took Balur to cave in his skull. Balur was rather beyond the specifics of timing by then.

Finding the door proved difficult. Simply tearing a hole through the cowshit and straw of the tavern's outer wall less so. He sprang, howling into the night. Baying and screaming, the villagers followed hot on his heels.

# 17

# The Smartest Man in the Room

*Bugger,* thought Firkin as he started off after the crowd. *This is about to go as well as that time I put a ferret in my britches.*

# 18

# Nom Nom Ethel Nom

Mattrax chewed upon his dinner disconsolately. The meat they had brought him tasted funny. Maybe it was time to bring back the position of official taster once more. They never seemed to work out, though. He always got peckish while waiting for his cow, and ended up eating them.

He shifted irritably on his pile of gold, sending coins skittering in rolling cascades. He picked up a crown with a single claw. The gold was pure, thick, worked into a design so fine that in places the metal had the texture of paper. It was a technique from a lost age. He thought he had pried it from some scholars who themselves had scavenged the thing from the tomb of a Vinland king. Some lunatic who had dedicated himself and his kingdom to Barph. Some fool willing to dedicate himself to a life of indulgence and pleasure.

Mattrax breathed out and the crown melted in the corona of his fire. He smeared the dripping slag on the wall of his cave. He was thinking of coating the whole thing in gold. The stone was ominous, yes, but dreary too. It would be glorious to have a golden cave. He bet stupid Dathrax didn't have a golden cave. Dathrax—living in the middle of a lake. He would have gold and Dathrax would have mold. He snorted at the thought.

Still, melting his own gold was a lot of work. Maybe he'd reintroduce slavery. The Consortium had ruled against it. One of their annual meetings at the Hallows' Mouth volcano.

Something to do with riling up the masses. But there were no masses up here. Just idiots, like those ones swilling around his cave earlier. Gods, they had been annoying. And his ridiculous, pointless guards. Just standing there, dying. Did he have to do everything himself?

He stifled a yawn. He was feeling unexpectedly sleepy. Probably all the murder earlier. Idiot guards exhausting him like that.

He took another bite of his meal. What was wrong with this meat? He took a few more experimental mouthfuls, trying to identify the flavor. Were they trying to spice his meat now? Gods.

He contemplated leaving it where it was. But he'd eaten three of the guards earlier and plate mail always upset his digestion. Some simple cow meat would be good for him.

He gave into another yawn, and then settled in to chow down.

# 19

# A Familiar Face

While he had never given it too much thought, Will had always had the impression that he could describe himself as a strong-willed man. Stubborn, his mother had called it. And his father. And both Albor and Dunstan, at least every other day working on the farm. But Will just understood he was a man who knew his own mind, and who had the strength of resolve to see his plans through.

That said, there was only so long one could hide out in a latrine at Castle Mattrax. Willpower could last only so long against that stench.

He slipped out into the keep grounds. The sun had descended behind the peaks of the mountains, and night had mercifully fallen. In the safety of shadows and starlight, he should be able to slip out of the castle and...

And...?

He honestly wasn't sure. The plan was clearly in violent disarray. Maybe he could reconnect with Quirk. Maybe he could find Balur or Firkin. Or at least their grave markers.

Gods...

He shook his head. He had enough concerns to deal with in the present moment, without trying to work out the ones he'd have to confront in the future. Those would simply have to form an orderly queue and wait their turn.

He slunk slowly along the wall leading to the first of the inner gates, trying to plot out a route using half-remembered maps outlined in half-remembered conversations with Firkin half a life ago.

The problem, he concluded, was that the castle was pressed up against a mountain on three sides. It was distinctly lacking in side doors. And, as his entry to the castle had shown, the one door that did exist was guarded by arseholes.

He needed a good cover story. Some sort of urgent task that he had been sent upon. Something that even one of the spite-filled, gutter-minded guards could believe in.

He sighed. This castle was supposed to be difficult to break *into*, not *out of.*

"Hey! Hey, you! I said hey!"

Will froze, and instantly regretted it. If panic hadn't seized him for just that fraction of a second perhaps he could have pretended that he hadn't heard, that he hadn't understood. Perhaps when he broke into a run he could have made a half-believable excuse. But now all he could do was stumble five miserable yards before he was intercepted.

The guard was running as he approached. He arrived panting, then doubled over, armor clanking as he sucked air in and out.

"Hey," he said, still panting. "I mean, hi. That is hello." He doubled over again, sucked air. "Sorry, running in this stuff..." He gestured at the armor with his hand. "Does me in every time."

"Erm..." Will said, feeling that he had some requisite part to play in the conversation, but not really knowing what it was, now that it apparently wasn't screaming and running for his life.

"Sorry," said the soldier. "Always horrible at introductions. General shortcoming in life. I think I do all right once I get past them, but they're always sort of the inciting moment that I need to get past. So then I don't get to the bit that's past them, because

I'm stuck on them. And it's horribly awkward." He looked up, looked around. "Sort of like this actually."

"I'm...sorry?" Will tried. He wished he knew magic like Quirk. Something that could open up a hole in the ground and swallow him.

"Oh don't be. Not your problem at all. Totally mine," said the guard. And then, "Oh bugger, I forgot the bit where I tell you my name. I told you I'm horrible at these things."

It was slowly dawning on Will that there was something horribly familiar about this man.

"I'm Bevvan," said the guard. "You're Will, right?"

Will's stomach lurched. Then it lurched again. Then it did a rather complicated gymnastic routine for good measure. Will tasted his own bile, which apparently preferred to take more of a bystander role in the back of his throat during such performances.

Will opened his mouth to fill in his part of the conversation again. He was pretty sure that some stringent denials went here. Instead all that came out was a wheezing, croaking sound, like the death wail of a particularly flatulent frog.

"Probably don't remember me." Bevvan the guard shook his head sadly. "I don't have one of those memorable faces. At least that's what my wife's always telling me. She says it's sort of plain and doughy and she wants to forget it." He laughed. "She's a funny woman. But yes, I was one of the guards that came to your farm the other day. Had to take your farm away. That whole clerical misunderstanding."

Oh gods. Oh gods why was he hated by the heavens so much? Had he forgotten to pour a libation one day? Had he blasphemed one time too many?

"No." His tongue felt like a stick of wood in his mouth. He forced the word out around it.

"Yes!" said Bevvan, all smiles and joviality. "And now you're here! I'm so glad you landed on your feet. I mean, that was horrible luck about the farm. It looked like debtors' jail for you for sure, I thought. But here you are all safe and sound."

Muscles in Will's face were starting to twitch. Some expression had to be formed, but each part of his anatomy seemed to have its own idea about which one. His eyebrows were jerked back and forth, his mouth curled and sneered.

Bevvan grinned in much the same way as a man would, should his brains be replaced by a jug of milk.

Then abruptly, he looked over Will's shoulder and shouted, "Hey, Joeth! Joeth! Come and look who it is! It's Will!"

The time for filling in gaps in the conversation had clearly come and gone at this point, and Will had failed spectacularly at that. Now his options became, in some respects, even simpler. He had to flee. To simply put one leg in front of the other and push.

He placed his right leg in front of his left. He bent his knee—

Bevvan landed a meaty arm upon his shoulder, preparing to spin him around to meet Joeth as he strode toward them. On the point of rapid departure, Will was decidedly off-balance. Instead of either running or turning, he instead collapsed sideways, smacked his head against the wall, and got to think about how terrible a blacksmith Mattrax employed if these were the best helmets he could produce.

"Will?" said Joeth, reaching the staggering pair. "Who the piss is Will?"

Finally Will found his tongue. "Me?" he said. "I'm nobody." The other soldiers had clearly all hated Bevvan. Joeth's reluctance to be there interacting with them was writ large on his pinched, weaselly face. If he could, he would make this another pitiable nonevent.

"Fucking right." Joeth spat a stream of brown phlegm onto the ground at his feet and turned to walk away.

"No," Bevvan persisted, because apparently he was some Hallow-spawned demon dressed up in the skin of a bumbling imbecile, "Will. You remember. From the other night. We took his farm and were going to put him in debtors' jail. And then he ran into the barn and we set it on fire. And Kurr kept telling us how he was going to kill him. He'd burned his face and was terribly upset. But look! We didn't kill him! And he's enlisted! I mean, isn't that a funny coincidence?"

Joeth, it turned out, was not as stupid as Bevvan. It wasn't that surprising. Will used to own stools that weren't as stupid as Bevvan.

He got almost an entire stride before Joeth caught him by the shoulder and threw him to the ground. Will kicked out hard, felt a satisfying crunch as his heel connected with something hard, and then a less satisfying thump, as a wailing Bevvan collapsed on top of him.

"Joeth!" he howled. "What are you—?"

"He's not a fucking soldier, you dim-witted son of Cois. He was condemned to debtors' prison and burned off half of Kurr's face. We tend not to enlist fugitives. If we tended not to enlist idiots then arseholes like him might not sneak in here to get up to whatever the fuck he's been up to."

Joeth, it turned out, was not a mumbler. Indeed he shouted this into Bevvan's tear-streaked face with almost perfect diction, and at considerable volume. He attracted considerable attention. By the time Will had fought free of Bevvan's weight, several pairs of hands were ready to help him to his feet. And then to help him slam face-first into the wall. And then to hold his hands at an excruciating angle behind his back while they were bound together.

Conversation had failed. Fleeing had failed. Will could only hope that when it came to dying painfully he would prove himself equally inept.

# 20

## Ignorance Is Bliss

Always a light sleeper, Lette—who was at that moment sandwiched between a gear the size of a wagon wheel and a chain thicker than her own waist—had rarely been pleased to hear the sound of snoring. Balur was a snorer. His mouth would flop open as he slept, and from the back of his throat would emerge a sound that she could only liken to two mountains making love. A guttural gasping rasp that sawed through her mind and erased sleep from the list of options that the night held for her. She had once trekked an additional mile through a kobold-infested forest just to escape the sound.

This snore was different, though. This was a deeper, rumbling sound, like fresh earth settling itself. It made the rock reverberate around her, deep and sonorous. It was the sound of a dragon snoring.

Mattrax was drugged up to his eyeballs.

Slowly, with exaggerated care, Lette began to move. She had spent the first hour of her seclusion learning how to navigate the portcullis lock in the dark, charting out crawl spaces, gaps in the pressure plate's mechanics. The next hour she had spent firming up her understanding of the mechanism, its operation, its critical junctures, its weak points. Then she had waited. She had expected to have heard Quirk's and Will's voices. But there had been simply the sound of Mattrax moving around, huffing and grunting to himself in injured tones. What in Toil's name a dragon rolling in gold and food had to complain about escaped her, but at least the fat sack of fire had shown no sign of suspicion. All the job had really required so far was flexibility and patience.

Neither was she worried about the blow Balur had taken in the earlier confrontation. She had seen him shake off worse. The Batarran giant they once fought had literally picked him up and used him as a club to try to smash her. Right up until Balur had gotten an arm free, torn off the giant's thumbnail, and used it to slit the giant's wrist. Sailing a hundred yards or so into some trees was eminently survivable.

No, what worried her was that Balur's part of the plan had already gone awry and he was the one other member of their current team who had professional experience. Now she was relying on a university professor and an angry farmer to keep her safe from being roasted alive.

What if Mattrax was *not* drugged? What if he was simply asleep? Rumor had it that dragons could detect the removal of even a single coin from their stockpile. Lette had her doubts about that, but removing several sacks full of gold and jewels could definitely tip the balance against them.

So she moved slowly, soundlessly, letting one movement flow into another—a slow, sinuous unfurling of her body as she emerged into the cave and the night.

She stood stock still—a shadow among shadows—and took stock of the cave. She had only glimpsed its contours in the mad dash to hide. It was larger than she had expected, the floor smooth and sandy. The bulk of the cavern was curled away from the portcullis, so she could see neither Mattrax nor his pile of gold, only a faint red-yellow glow smudging through the deepening shadows.

She herself stood near the cave entrance, within arm's reach of the portcullis. Moonlight spilled between the iron beams, painting a chessboard on the floor before her. There were only two guards. That was a stroke of luck, at least. There had been far more earlier. Two guards simplified things considerably.

Moving at an almost imperceptible pace, she crossed the mouth of the cave. Her feet were silent on the sandy floor. Her shadow fell away from the guards. The rumble of Mattrax's snores stayed constant. Neither guard turned around.

She let a knife drop into each hand. She cocked one arm. She threw.

The blade whistled between the grille of the portcullis and landed with a solid thwack in the back of the first guard's neck. He dropped with a slight gurgle, and the heavy thump of lifeless limbs.

The second knife was already in her hand. She cocked her arm once more.

"Cois's cock!" The second guard shrieked, jumped almost half a yard. Lette tracked her with ease.

*Her?*

She hadn't had much time to observe Mattrax's forces, but he seemed as blinkeredly misogynistic as the armies belonging to most rulers she'd met.

And didn't she recognize that voice?

"Quirk?" she whispered.

"Lette?"

It *was* Quirk. Lette could even make out the bloodstains she had made when stealing the woman's armor. But...

"What in the name of the Hallows are you doing *outside* the cave?" she said. "Wasn't the whole plan that you'd be hidden in here helping me move the gold until Firkin and Balur arrived with the wagon?"

Quirk hesitated. Lette gathered breath for a whispered harangue. Then she noticed the other woman's shaking hands, her ragged breathing. Quirk kept looking over at the dead guard, kept opening and closing her fists.

"It's okay," Lette said. She needed Quirk calm and functional.

This wasn't the end of the world. She could get Quirk inside easily enough. Then another thought struck her. She looked over at the body.

"Wait..." she managed. "Will?"

Quirk shook her head vehemently. "No. No," she said. "He's trapped inside."

"Trapped?" That was not the sort of word Lette liked to hear when in the middle of a job.

"That's not what I meant." Quirk shook her head with the sort of violence Lette usually reserved for jobs that required particular prejudice.

"Maybe," she said, "you should start at the beginning."

So Quirk did. Then she jumped to the end. Then to some point in the story halfway through, and from there leapt about like some deranged jackrabbit until finally Lette could piece the whole mosaic of disaster together.

"But is Mattrax actually drugged?" she asked finally. Quirk had proven elusive on this one point.

Quirk worried her hands several times. Lette cranked up the intensity of her glare several notches. If Quirk couldn't manage calm, then cowed would be a close enough approximation.

"I don't know," Quirk said miserably.

"And is Will inside this cave?"

"I don't know," Quirk said again, equally miserably.

Lette clenched her jaw tight and did not say a number of things that she would have liked to.

"Right," she said eventually. "Well, in that case, the first thing to do is to get this portcullis up. You're sure there are no other soldiers about?"

Quirk shook her head. "They seemed stretched a bit thin after Mattrax killed off the previous guards. They just put the two of us down here."

"Okay. Let me get back down in the mechanism so I can open up this portcullis. That way if everything goes to shit, at least

I have a way out of here." And without waiting for a response, she slipped down the hole back into the portcullis's inner workings. She wriggled forward until she found the fist-size gear she had identified earlier. Five swift blows with the hilt of her dagger and it fell out of alignment.

She threw herself backward as, around her, the mechanism blazed to life. Cogs whirled, chains shrieked, and counterweights fell with a resounding crash. A moment after it was all over, Lette heard Quirk's shriek as a brief punctuation to the whole event. Alone in the darkness, she permitted herself a roll of her eyes.

Then she waited. Waited for the roar. For the crash of Mattrax's feet as he descended upon the gate. For the heat of his flames roasting the rock around her.

But all she heard was the slow, steady rumble of his snores.

She smiled. Despite it all, something had actually gone right.

# 21

# Something Going Right

High above Lette, in the belly of Mattrax's castle, an alarm bell rang loudly.

"What's that?" said a guard, looking up.

Much to Will's chagrin, however, he did not remove his knees from Will's kidneys.

"What's his bloody nibs doing opening up the gate?"

Will thought this was an excellent question and one that the guards should probably go and investigate posthaste, and he would have happily offered up that opinion had not his mouth been, at that precise moment, pressed directly into the mud by several meaty hands.

"Who gives a fuck?" said the guard Will had come to identify as Kurr. He, Will had also discovered, was the guard whose face he had burned with soup. There were, he thought, extenuating circumstances surrounding that situation, which, again, he would have been willing to discuss at considerable length. The dialogue Kurr was more interested in, though, was the one going on between his steel toe caps and Will's ribs. He kicked Will again. Hard.

Will brayed pain into the mud.

"If Mattrax wants to go flying, let him go. Give us another hour before he comes back and eats someone," said one of the guards holding down Will's legs.

Another kick. Tears ran down Will's cheeks.

"He don't go bloody flying about at night," said the first guard. "Sleeps for bloody hours that bastard does."

"That is true," said another voice.

Another kick.

"I said, who gives a fuck?" Kurr was a man of narrow focus, Will was learning.

"Well," said the first guard, "all I'm thinking is that here we are with this intruder—"

"This whoreson," said Kurr, giving Will another kick. Will bucked ineffectually.

"Yeah," said the first guard. "This whoreson. But he's an intruding whoreson."

"You got a point?" said the guard up by Will's head.

"Well, it just seems," said the first guard, "that here we are with this intruder—"

"Whoreson."

"Intruding whoreson—"

"Seriously, just get to your fucking point already."

Will couldn't agree more.

"So here we are with this intruding son—"

"Yeah you said that already."

At this point the first guard seem to lose his patience a bit. "I bloody know I've said it three times, but every time I say it you go and bloody interrupt about how you want to know more. If you shut your fucking trap you might actually learn something. Like how to wipe your arse probably, you smelly arsehole."

There was silence for a moment.

"Uncalled for," muttered the guard near Will's head.

"So an intruding whoreson. And we know Mattrax sleeps through for a solid night's sleep every night." A pause, which allowed Kurr to get in another kick. "Except now the alarm is going off to say his portcullis is opening."

Another longer pause. Will braced for the next kick.

"Oh," said Kurr at last. "Balls."

"Shit," said the guard at his head. He let up with his hands. Will pulled his mouth out of the mud, gasping and gagging.

Kurr filled his vision. "Who did you come with, arse-wipe?" he spat. "Who's down there?"

"There's no bloody time for that!" yelled the first guard, grabbing at Kurr's shoulder. "He's tied up. Let's just get down there, kill whoever is crapping on our evening's entertainment, and then come back here and finish him off. He's not going nowhere."

Kurr's face twisted in irritation. Then finally he spat in Will's face and stood up. "Go anywhere," he growled at Will, "and I'll kill you."

That, thought Will, was not much of an incentive considering his other option was to stay exactly where he was so Kurr could kill him.

He watched his trio of torturers run from him, heard other boots pounding past. Everyone heading to the portcullis.

Lette must have opened it, he realized. Because she hadn't known about the alarm bell. Because he had never told her about the alarm bell. Though, to be fair, he'd never known about an alarm bell. Firkin had never mentioned it.

In the end, though, he was forced to conclude that trying to figure out his own level of culpability was probably less productive than actually sitting up, escaping, and attempting to rescue Lette from the castle's-worth of guards that were about to descend on her.

On the other hand, his ribs were making a pretty convincing counterpoint about the merits of curling up into a fetal ball and sobbing.

The process of sitting up was long, laborious, and punctuated with curse words that he thought even Firkin might shrink from.

Getting from his arse to his feet was even worse. He tottered across the keep grounds, gasping, head spinning.

Lette. He needed to get to Lette. He wasn't sure why, or what help he could offer, but surely...surely that was what he had to do. He couldn't just leave her to die. Will didn't know much about what was going on anymore, and perhaps the middle of a robbery was an odd time to find his moral compass, but still, he knew that you did not run from a fight and let your friend take all the blows.

*More blows.* He cringed inside. He wouldn't be surprised if he pissed blood tomorrow. But he kept moving.

He staggered toward the keep, a plan forming in his mind. Inside the torchlit entrance hall, he searched desperately for a sharp surface. He found it in the form of an axe lying abandoned in a weapon rack against one wall. Carefully he backed up to it, then pushed his bound wrists against the blade.

A minute later, taking a break from massaging life back into his numb hands, he tried the pad of his thumb against the blade of the axe. It was far sharper than the sword his captors had confiscated from him. He hefted it, tested its weight. He nodded to himself. Perhaps not as good as his father's old wood-cutting axe back on the farm, but he suspected it was good enough to do some damage, and it was light enough to be wielded single-handed.

So armed, he turned to the dark spiraling corridor and began to descend.

# 22

## The Beast Wakes

Quirk stood in the depths of Mattrax's cave and gaped. She had never seen anything like it before in her life.

"Betra's sagging tits," Lette breathed. "I've seen gold in my time, but this..." She trailed off with a small sigh of contentment.

Quirk took note of the gold for the first time. *Yes,* she supposed, *there was a lot of it.* Coins, crowns, medallions, necklaces, brooches, bracelets, scepters, gilt frames, earrings, emeralds, rubies, topaz, diamonds, pearls...

She looked away, disinterested. She looked back to *him.*

Mattrax slumbered atop his treasure trove. A vast coiling column of muscle and scale. His wings drooped down forming leathery blankets over the slopes of his hoard. His head was a vast angular wedge. Each nostril was wide enough that she could thrust a clenched fist into it and barely tickle the fine hairs that lined it. Each claw upon his foot was longer than her forearm.

She could hardly breathe. Her chest felt full of air, the confines of her ribs too tight for her lungs. The room was bright despite the cloying night. The edges of the world were fading to mist.

She walked toward the dragon as if in a dream. Coins and jewels gave way beneath her feet as she mounted the hills of his fortune. She stretched out her hand. She had to touch him.

Would he feel rough? Smooth? Warm? Hard or soft? Would the skin give beneath her hand?

She remembered the first time she had touched magic. A

child in the dark of her parents' hut. Hiding from her brother, Andatte. Curled up in a nest of dirty laundry while he tried to seek her out. Half-asleep. The heat of summer mounting where she lay. Becoming almost unbearable, almost beautiful. And then the sense of something pushing through that heat. Some vast, unknowable intellect manifesting in it. And it was reaching out to her. Pressing through layers of reality. And she had reached out, pushed back. And then...they had touched. Been briefly connected. She had touched something that had redefined her utterly. Left her branded. Left her different.

This felt like that moment.

She was vaguely aware of Lette scooping vast armfuls of wealth into her pockets, letting out small giddy noises.

Quirk was almost annoyed. Such petty concerns in the face of such...such...magnificence. Was the woman blind to the beauty of the world? Did she spit in its eye on purpose?

*No.* Quirk stilled herself. Nothing was going to spoil this for her. This moment would be pure, unsullied by the world, by her past, by her need for constant control. This was what she had worked so hard for, for all these years. She wouldn't let anything ruin it now. She could feel the heat of Mattrax's breath gusting over her hand, playing between her fingers—

A noise from the mouth of the cave. A shout. And another.

Quirk froze.

"Shit," Lette cursed.

And no. No. This couldn't be happening. This was her moment.

Another shout.

"Balur," Quirk breathed. "It's Balur. And Firkin. With the wagon and the sacks. That's all."

She reached once more for the beatific peace of biological rapture. Toward epiphany. Toward Mattrax.

From the cave entrance came the sound of steel clashing against steel.

"Lawl's balls!" Lette cursed again. Then the mercenary was moving. She dashed along the contours of the golden hoard, heading back toward the cave entrance. Rivers of coins tumbled and tinkled in her wake.

As she dashed past Quirk, the ground gave way.

*No. No!*

Quirk lunged, desperate, grasping. Her fingers were almost there, almost touching Mattrax's skin. But there was nothing to gain purchase on. She felt herself falling. She screamed. Everything was slipping away from her. Epiphany fluttered away.

Then she was tumbling, arse over heel, landing unceremoniously, feet in the air, hands splayed and empty.

For a moment, Quirk lay and seethed. She recognized the signs, felt the mask of control slipping away. *No!* screamed some last rational part of her. *No! That's not what this is. Not what this was meant to be! This was my moment.*

She picked herself up. Her teeth gritted. Her palms hot. Steam rising from between her fingertips.

Someone was running around the corner of the cave. A guard, chain mail glinting in reflected moonlight, mouth open in a yell, sword raised. He saw her, let loose a fresh howl, and charged.

Quirk did not see the man. Not as he was here and now. She did not see the cave around her. She did not feel the hot breath of Mattrax gusting over her.

Instead, she felt the hot breath of the Tamathian scrublands blowing at her back. She saw the shallow sloping hills of her childhood, dotted with scrubby bushes that held more thorns than leaves. She saw a bandit dressed in tatters charging, scimitar raised above his head, the desperation of a starving man glinting in his eyes.

*No!* screamed the voice. *This is over. This is past. This is not who you are.*

But the mask of control was slipping, almost gone. And in her rage, her frustration, her fear, Quirk reached up and tore it away.

She reached out her hand. Heat rose in her palm. She felt divine power within her. She felt words she had never learned forming on her tongue, words that pushed back at the skin of reality stretched over the world. Felt them punch through.

The guard was almost on her. His sword hung above her head.

The heat in her palm became a physical pain. A scalding, searing expression of hate and rage. She howled, loud enough to match the guard's battle cry.

And then, there, in the darkness, she gave birth to fire.

# 23

# Hammer Time

*Fire Root,* Balur thought in one of his increasingly rare lucid moments, *is being the absolute shit.* He had heard certain whores discussing the improvements certain herbs and powders could bring to their area of expertise. But, honestly, they were going to have to try mass murder while high on this stuff. This was being absolutely fucking great.

"Whee!" he cried, spinning in a circle, war hammer held out at full stretch, feeling his shoulders take the weight, his heels spinning on the sandy floor, watching the bodies flying through the air. Their blood painted the air in spiraling arcs, glistening like streams of rubies. He could smell it, like a shooting star exploding in the back of his throat.

He hadn't expected to find guards here. He was unsure what he had expected now. But it hadn't been them. Not that he was sad about it. Rather, when he had come running out of the woods below the cave and seen them streaming out of the castle gates, he had let out a howl of joy. At his back, the villagers had echoed the sound.

The guards had turned, seen them, charged. The two forces had crashed into each other like newlyweds.

Balur reached out, grabbed someone nearby, bit their face off, and laughed giddily as blood ran down his chin.

This was what he lived for. This moment. This surrender. To say farewell to thought, to morals, to civility. To live beyond the boundaries of culture, and societal norms. This was life at its most pure, its most bestial. This was life without pretenses. All masks removed. Life reduced to meat, and bone, and fury.

He pirouetted, brought his hammer up, clean through the body of...someone. Factions were meaningless at this point in the fight. The head of the hammer glistened above the fray, dripped blood. He brought it down and listened to the meaty crack of impact.

Someone stabbed him. He felt the blade find a spot where his scales met, its tip slide inside him, puncturing muscle. He felt the pain, bright and hot. He laughed again, grabbed the sword blade, and then its owner. The sword wielder's neck snapped in Balur's fist.

He descended into a bloody haze. The world was red and wet for a while. When he emerged he was, for a moment, disoriented. He pummeled a man in the face, trying to get his bearings.

People were screaming, running, pushing to get past him. Villagers and guards alike. "Dragon!" they screamed. "Dragon! Mattrax wakes!"

And then Balur saw it, bright and beautiful, blossoming in the back of the cave. Great gouts of fire that sparkled yellow and red in his dilated pupils.

*The dragon.* That was why he had come here. To show the world that he could defeat a dragon. To make the dragon know his name even as he took its life.

Some small, sobering part of Balur saw that fire and questioned if, just this once, wisdom shouldn't be prevailing over bravado. A larger, drunker part of his mind shouted at that part to be fucking off. He was totally knowing what he was doing. Why was the other voice always nagging at him with its rational good sense? He was being a *warrior,* gods' hex upon it. He was having to do certain things because they were being there. His actions were not having to make sense.

He set his shoulder and charged into the depths of the cave, toward heat, fire, rage, and glory. Bodies bounced off him, scrambling to get away. All around him screams rose.

"The dragon!"

"The dragon!"

"It's going to kill us all!"

*No,* thought Balur with a drunken grin. *I am.*

He rounded the bend in the cave, skidded to a halt.

Quirk stood there.

No, floated there.

The thaumatobiologist's feet were a clear foot off the floor. Her robes billowed around her, rippling through the heat haze. She held her arms out, palms raised.

And she was beautiful.

Ribbons of fire danced from her hands. They wove together in complex patterns of slaughter. A hapless guard was caught in a stream of liquid flame. He didn't even have a chance to scream. His blackened body skittered and danced. The dead lay all around her.

She didn't say anything, didn't fix her gaze on anyone. She just wove her ribbons of fire back and forth in front of her. Where they struck the floor, explosions bloomed, spattering the bodies with glowing shrapnel.

*I,* thought Balur, taking the scene in at a glance, *would be totally hitting that.* Then his eye fell on the dragon beyond her.

Mattrax lay slumped over a vast hoard of gold and jewels, wings splayed in a sloppy half-collapsed pile. Drool was spilling from one corner of his mouth in a thick, ropy stream.

Momentarily, Balur lost the power of speech. All he could utter was a single, guttural roar of hate. Rage. Bloodlust. Desire. He *wanted* that dragon. He wanted its blood on his skin. Its bone shards stuck into his cheeks.

Waves of rage carried him forward, a misty cloud of hallucinogenic fury. He ducked and darted through Quirk's tapestry of fiery destruction. Mattrax loomed in his vision, the vast face eclipsing everything else. The dragon was his world. Its death at his hands was as inevitable as the turning of the sun in the heavens. His hammer was above his head. His muscles burned with power, with the churning potential of death.

He brought the hammer down, felt the impact run up his arm, felt the hammer head glance off the scales. He stepped back, slipping in the piles of coin that mired his feet.

For a moment he thought he had achieved nothing. That this was all just a paltry lie, some drug-addled fantasy he had concocted to make himself feel better about the ignominy of his earlier defeat.

But then he saw it. The thin hairline crack that ran down the scale he had struck, the clear fluid seeping out. Mattrax's hide was not impenetrable. The dragon could be defeated. All that was needed was time.

Balur brought his war hammer down again. Again. Again. Again. Again. Again. Again. Again. Again.

# 24

## Dragon Slayer

Gripping his axe in both hands, Will crept into the antechamber before Mattrax's cave. His heart sank. He had been hoping that the guard would be asleep, head sinking into his own obscene folds of blubber, soft as a down pillow. Instead, though, the guard was on his feet. Will had had difficulty imagining it before. He just hadn't been able to work out the mechanics of those legs supporting that much bulk. And yet here it was before him.

The guard had his back to Will, was leaning toward the door, head cocked to one side, listening. Despite the thickness of the metal, sounds of utter chaos rang out clearly: roars, screams, howls, the clash of steel, something wet and squelching. The smell of copper was ripe on the air.

All in all, it rather reminded Will of a stag party he'd been to down in The Village. He'd stopped agreeing to go to them after that.

Gods, what was happening down there? He didn't know for sure, only that it was not in any part of what he had once laughingly called a plan. In fact, to the best of his memory the sound of bloody slaughter was the exact thing the plan had been supposed to avoid.

There again, the plan had also meant to keep him out of situations like being alone in a room with one of Mattrax's guards and an axe.

Then Will realized that the guard hadn't even twitched as Will entered the room. He was utterly focused on the door.

The axe felt heavy in Will's hands.

Could he do it? Could he bury a blade in a man when his back was turned?

*Yes*, he decided, *I could*. The gods killed, did they not? Hadn't Lawl himself murdered thousands of men in fits of jealous rage? That said, Lawl had slept with Toil, his own daughter, and then Toil had married Cois, the child, so perhaps the gods didn't always set the best example...

Still, it was the sort of brutally practical thing that he could imagine Lette doing, and he was fairly sure this was a moment for brutal practicality.

His palms slick with sweat, he took a step forward.

"What do you think it is?"

The guard's voice rooted Will to the spot. The guard didn't turn around, didn't look at him. He spoke in a soft, almost conversational way.

"Erm," Will managed. He cleared his throat. What did you say to someone you were planning on murdering? That was a piece of etiquette his mother had never covered with him.

"I thought it was a revolt at first," the guard went on. "Them up top finally had enough and decided to do something about it. Happens every once in a while. Then the boss man, he cleans house. Spring cleaning, I call it." He laughed softly to himself. A low, burbling sound like a spring brook trying to force its way through a block of lard. Then the sound skewed sideways into something less cheerful.

"The thing is," the guard went on, "I don't hear Mattrax. There ain't no roaring. There ain't the crackle of corpses burning." He shook his head. "No. I hear something else." He reached back a stubby arm and beckoned to Will. "Come listen. See what you think."

Will hesitated. He was still holding the axe aloft. Except now that the conversation had started he didn't feel murderous. Instead he felt terribly, terribly awkward.

He let the axe sag, took a tentative step forward. He could get past this man some other way. Hell, he could probably open the flap and be through before the other even reacted. And with his girth, the guard certainly couldn't follow that way.

"Listen," whispered the guard, still not looking at him.

"Erm," said Will, still not entirely sure what to say. He really had no desire to get much closer to the man.

"I said," the guard started, his voice rising in volume, "come here and—" He started to turn. His arm started to swing around. Will caught a glimpse of flashing steel. "Listen!" the guard bellowed.

Will flung himself backward just as the fat guard lunged. The blade swished through the space that was until recently home to his stomach and its assorted bevy of essential organs.

He reeled back, off-balance.

"My house!" the guard screamed. "You bring drugged meat into my house! Feed it to my master! On my watch!"

He was surprisingly fast for such a big man. His arm whipped back and forth, the blade a blur, slicing at Will's stomach. Will backed up as the guard advanced, trying to get the axe in between them.

"You tricked me," spat the guard. His face was transformed, no longer morose, but instead contorted with rage. "It was my job to protect him. To feed him. And you poisoned him. Right in front of me!"

The guard, Will realized, had at some point—sitting all alone in the dark and the heat—gone entirely insane.

"Mattrax is a dragon," he pointed out. "He controls the whole valley. I think he can get by without you."

This, it turned out, was not the right thing to say.

"He needs me!" screamed the guard, and he lunged.

Fast though he might be, the guard's weight betrayed him

in that moment. The lunge was pathetically short. Will, caught flat-footed by the abruptness of the move, felt only the slightest pinprick of the sword's weight as it glanced off his chain mail.

He brought his axe across his body in a short, sharp chopping motion. The blade crashed into the inside of the guard's elbow. There was an ugly crunching sound. The guard screamed. His blade clattered flatly as it bounced on the flagstone floor.

Will stood panting. The guard clutched at his injured arm, sprayed spittle and curses.

Will for his part was quite proud of himself. The fourth fight in his life—the first one involving real weapons—and it had gone significantly better than the first three.

"All right," he said. "Sorry about that. But if you could just step aside so I can go and rob your master blind."

It was, he thought, a rather snappy thing to say. It had … what was the word? Panache. He wished Lette could have seen him in that moment.

With a murderous growl, the guard flung himself upon Will.

Although years of working in the fields had ensured that Will was not an entirely insignificant young man, he stood about as much chance as a reed before a stampeding bull. He was bowled backward, crashing into the room's far wall. His head cracked off hard stone, the world exploded with light, and his balance pirouetted around the confines of his skull.

As his senses returned, he became very aware of the guard's hands around his throat. Just as his vision was starting to clear, it was blurring again.

He was pinned to the floor. He started to thrash back and forth, trying to work himself free, but the guard's weight was implacable and unshakable.

His lungs were burning now, his vision narrowing down to a point that seemed to be mostly taken up by the guard's red, spittle-splattered face.

"He needs me, see?" hissed the guard. "Needs me to protect him from little shits like you."

Will thrashed harder, managed to pry an arm free. He grasped desperately about himself. His palm hit cold metal.

*Cold metal.*

And connected to it... a shaft of cold wood.

With the last of his strength, he smashed the axe handle into the side of the guard's head. There was a satisfying crunch.

For a moment the weight lifted. Will gasped. Air rushed into his burning lungs so fast he almost choked on it.

Then the guard's weight crashed back down on him again. Will thrashed again, but this time with even less success. The axe blade was caught flat between their bodies. Fat fingers closed upon Will's bruised larynx.

Will fought for air, for leverage. He could feel the warm flesh of the guard's exposed gut pressed against his knuckles. The exposed strip of skin where the guard's chain-mail shirt did not reach all the way to his britches. His soft exposed underbelly.

Will twisted desperately, freed one leg. He kicked out, hit the inside of the guard's calves. Achieved nothing. His vision shrank to nothing more than a blurred pinprick.

He bucked, fought for leverage, won it, and brought his whole leg up fast and hard between the guard's legs. The guard gasped in pain. His fingers flew from Will's neck.

In the brief moment that pressure relented, vision still nothing more than a field of winking lights, Will turned the axe blade north. He sliced. He felt flesh give way. He dragged the blade along the great length of the guard's stomach.

Warmth spilled over him. Blood and offal splashing over him with heavy wet thuds. The guard gasped, gurgled, clutched at the spilling ropes of his intestines. And then, quite noisily, and very messily, he collapsed and died on top of Will.

# 25

## Prophecy's Bitch

*Upon further consideration,* Will thought, working himself free from the guard's very literal deadweight, *I'm quite glad Lette wasn't there to see that.*

He emerged from beneath the corpse victorious and covered with blood and offal. He bent and retrieved his axe from beneath the guard's bulk, his boots squelching as he did so.

He felt better with the axe in his hands. He turned it over. It had saved his life. *You should have a name,* he thought. In the legends, heroes' weapons always had a name.

"I shall call you," he said in the empty room, "the Sense of Imminent Disaster." That seemed fitting enough.

Thus armed, he turned his attention to the door.

It was, he soon discovered, not actually a door. There was no handle, and no hinges. It was simply a flap down which meat was poured to fill Mattrax's gullet. He cranked the lever, the flap lifted, the ramp—slick with blood and grease—was revealed.

Sounds of fighting came up to him, curiously muted. He peered down, but a dull flickering light revealed no details. Everything smelled of copper and smoke.

All in all, it was not a tableau that boded well for his future.

Still, Lette could be down there, could be waiting for him. And others who had put their lives in the hands of his plan. Despite his advice that they not do so. And despite that advice, he felt responsible.

Grimacing, he pushed himself through the flap, down into darkness.

He landed heavily. Metal clinked around his feet. He reached down, pulled up a handful of coins.

*Well,* he thought, *I'm rich. Now let's see if I get to stay that way for longer than two minutes.* He wasn't entirely confident of that. Smoke and flickering firelight in a dragon's cave did not suggest a successful attempt at drugging the beast.

Despite the flames, light was minimal. He crept forward slowly, then cracked his nose into a wall that loomed out of the shadows and smacked at him. He stumbled back, tripped over some buried rod or scepter. *Screw you too,* he thought in the general direction of any gods watching him. He crawled forward on hands and knees, reaching out with his axe, trying to feel the way ahead.

He rounded a corner—some rocky outcropping pushing up through the pile of gold, stubbing his fingers—and light bloomed before him. He froze. The sounds of a crowd were louder here. He no longer heard the sound of steel on steel but there was still shouting, sobbing, screams.

The source of the light lay before him on a rolling slope of gold. It was a perfectly round orb—approximately the size of a bull's head—that pushed back the shadows for a full two yards around it to reveal bloodstained coins. Beyond the fringes of its light were only more darkness and screams.

He weighed his options for a moment. A light would allow him to see, and allow for a faster exit, but it would also be much like shouting, "Here I am, come and stab me in my nethers."

That said, whether he had a light or not he was heading toward the voices and whatever crowd they belonged to. He would be seen soon enough either way.

He scrambled forward, grabbed the orb. It was warm to the touch and unfortunately gelatinous. Still the light was steady, and he pushed forward faster now, no longer confined to all fours.

Around him the gold was replaced by a grimmer trove. Bodies lay scattered over the floor, guards and villagers alike. Some were victims of considerable violence—skewered and punctured—others were burned to an almost unrecognizable crisp. Will wasn't entirely sure he wanted to know what had happened here.

He rounded a larger bend in the cave, and suddenly its open mouth was before him.

So was the crowd. They clogged the cave entrance, not screaming or yelling anymore, not caught in life-and-death struggles. Instead they were stumbling about, staring, wild-eyed. Some rubbed stupidly at their faces. Others shielded their eyes from the sudden glare of his light.

Will froze, standing there, bloodied axe in one hand, glowing orb in the other, covered from head to foot in another man's blood.

One by one, it seemed that every single member in the crowd turned to face him, turned to see the sudden source of light.

*Grabbing that,* he thought, *might end up being a mistake after all.*

The crowd stood staring at him, oddly silent. The whole moment felt strangely dreamlike.

"Look—" he started, and found he was rather interested in what would follow that word next out of his mouth.

He never found out. Instead, a voice suddenly rose up from the crowd, loud and clear in the night air.

"The slayer! It is the dragon slayer!"

The crowd shuddered, seeming to push forward and draw back at the same time. The night was alive with murmurs.

Will glanced over his shoulder. Who in all the gods' names were they talking about?

"The Slayer!" shouted another voice.

"As was foretold!" shouted another.

"He fulfills the prophecy!"

Will's brow furrowed. What prophecy? What was everyone talking about?

"Look what he holds in his left hand!"

Instinctively Will looked down at his left hand. In it he held the glowing orb. Nothing else.

Nothing made sense. Everything was darkness and shadow. He hefted the orb higher, trying to make out more clearly what was going on. As he did, it twisted in his hand. And as it twisted, he glimpsed something he hadn't seen before. Some pattern or design painted upon the orb's surface.

He turned it in his hands to get a better look. And then he saw what the crowd had seen.

Not a pattern. Not a design.

A pupil. A pupil in a glowing orange orb.

No. In an eyeball.

In his hand, held up for all to see, he had Mattrax's dead, staring eye.

And the crowd went wild.

# Part 2:
# A Job Done Wrong

# 26

# Morning Worship

Lette could think of no greater sign of how terribly awry things had gone than the fact that she was waking up to the sound of children's laughter.

She stood up from her bed of pine needles, wiped drool from her chin, and tried to put the pieces of the previous evening together.

She had been hidden in the portcullis lock. She had gotten out, killed a guard, found Quirk. Everything had been going well. Then she had opened the portcullis to Mattrax's cave. And that must have been what alerted the guards. Some mechanism she had missed, or more likely, never been in a position to discover. But at the same time the guards came running, so did the villagers. Balur and Firkin must have had something to do with it, but afterward Balur was tight-lipped on the subject. Still, the soldiers and the villagers had clashed in the cave mouth. Then the fight had spilled deeper and deeper into the cave. And then, in those depths, Quirk...

The thaumatobiologist had killed how many? Twenty? Thirty? Enough to make Balur look as if he'd just been handing out love taps all night. The thaumatobiologist had flung fire about like a bartender serving drinks on Barph's feast day, lost in some passion Lette neither understood nor wanted to understand. There had been no way to reason with the woman, and Lette thanked all the gods that Quirk had collapsed eventually. Just keeled over unconscious and dribbling. Though that wasn't before her antics convinced almost everyone in the cave that Mattrax was awake and angry. Even Lette would admit she had felt fear grip her bowels when the first jet of flame had come.

Except Mattrax had been out cold. Hadn't even come conscious as Balur had beaten the brains from him.

Gods, that had been a mess. Balur had been in almost as much of a passion as Quirk. Lette still wasn't sure how she'd managed to drag the lizard man away. Not before he'd gotten himself elbow deep in Mattrax's skull by any reach. Still, she'd managed it. But by then it had become clear to her that the only real option left to them was to get into the crowd and lose themselves. So she'd made Balur grab Quirk, and hidden amongst the villagers, they'd been whole enough, safe enough.

Except then Will had gone and shown up clutching that cursed eyeball...

She looked around her. Women and men were all still gathered around the cave entrance. Campfires burned. People sang and danced. Their half-feral children ran everywhere whooping, and screaming, and—for the love of all that was holy—laughing.

*Where had the children even come from? Gods, if Balur had brought them up to the cave to do murder last night, she was going to kill him.*

There was an atmosphere of celebration in the impromptu camp. And though this barren mountainside was nothing like the packed streets of Essoa, where she had grown up, something in the air reminded her of the city's annual carnivals. All the rules thrown out for a day. The children ruled the households. The dockworkers told the nobles what to do. You went into a store and just took what you wanted from the shelves. Everyone was on the streets, shouting, running, dancing.

The first carnival she remembered, she had gone into a pastry store. It was the one she and her brothers and sisters passed on their weekly sojourn to the temple to pour libations in the hopes that Toil would bless their father's work, and Klink would bless his purse. Everything in the store's window always looked fluffy and delicious, covered in layers of powdered sugar. The store owner had welcomed her with a broad smile, had helped her hold her skirts out so they formed a pouch into which she could sweep armfuls of pastries. And then she had found a quiet rooftop from which she could watch the festivities, while she stuffed her face. It had been glorious. A day of pure gluttony and pleasure.

Then the next day she vomited four times. She felt nauseous for two days more. Every time she passed the pastry store she felt sickness roll through her. And it was not just her. The day after carnival, all of Essoa crawled, a beaten, groaning thing. It was a stinking beast crawling through the filthy aftermath of its own indulgence.

Yes, this reminded her of carnival very much.

They had to get out of here.

Correction, they had to take advantage of the shrinking window of opportunity they had for retrieving as much gold as they could from Mattrax's cave, and then get out of here.

She cracked her neck, pulled a few leaves out of her hair, and set off into the camp. Children ran past her, yelling something about a prophet.

*The prophet...* That could be a problem.

She opened her ears to the voices of the crowd. Situational awareness, she'd heard others in her profession call it. Knowing-where-the-next-knife-is-coming-from was a term that sat better with her.

"Where did he come from?"

"Is he going to stay?"

"Is Mattrax really dead?"

"Must be some avatar of the gods. Ain't no way no mortal man can just be killing a dragon. Probably Klink, I reckon. Dragon keeping all that gold in one place, ain't natural. Money meant to flow. Old Mattrax pissed off Klink and now he's paid the price."

"Like to get my hands on *his* dragon..."

"Oh, you're awful."

"The axe, I reckon. Dug it up from some tomb like as not. Take away that axe and he'd be nothing special."

"A prophet they said. Prophet's talk. Prophesize. Clue's in the name. Mattrax was just the start of it, I tell you. He's come to lead us."

"Didn't look like no prophet. Just looked like some kid. Some farm boy with an axe."

"What in the Hallows did we drink last night?"

They were gathered in small groups. Three men sitting perched on rocks, their heads leaned in. Two women using puddle water to wash the mud from their faces. A young couple leaning against a tree stump, wrapped in each other's arms. A gaggle of teenagers, gathered around a discarded breastplate bearing the tattered heraldry of the Dragon Consortium. And all of them were talking about Will. Every last one.

Yes, the prophet was going to be a problem.

There was a flow to the crowd, she realized. Some faint gravitational pull. She gave in to it, moved with the masses. She felt like a wolf in sheep's clothing. It was a reassuring feeling.

When she found the source of the pull, she thought perhaps she should have known.

Firkin was perched on a rock pressed up against the mountainside. A little stone pulpit. He sat cross-legged upon it, potbelly protruding over his filthy underwear. His beard blew in a morning breeze that sent his words billowing over the small crowd that had gathered at his feet.

"—and verily it was said unto, erm...unto...it was a farmer, I think. Worked in a field anyway. Nice man. Used to buy folk drinks. Very important that. The prophet is always saying that giving someone a free drink is pretty much the height of, erm... being prophetic. Root of all goodness, I think. Wet a man's throat and, erm…verily you shalt be raised up. Thou shalt. Very high. Like really, really way up there."

He was slurring badly, eyes half-closed.

"Anyway, it was said unto this man. It was said verily to him. That erm…to have thine balls back, then thine must follow he who slays the beast. And verily the beast was slain as you saw."

Personally, Lette wanted to slay Firkin very, very badly. But that next knife—it would come from the crowd if she tried it. And while she was good at her job, there were a lot of people here, which would mean a lot of knives.

Instead she limited herself to calling out, "Firkin, what the fuck are you doing?"

Firkin lurched, as if shaken from a trance, or more likely as if he had been nodding off into a drunken stupor. He stared at her blearily, tugged at the tangled mat of his beard, and cast it over one shoulder.

"I am preaching," he said, "profound truths."

A murmur of agreement rose from the crowd.

"You," said Lette with a certain amount of feeling, "are the swill at the bottom of the barrel and you are leaking out and staining all these good people."

Public speaking was not her thing. Still, she was damned if she was going to give ground before a creature as base as Firkin.

The crowd, though, seemed to have other ideas. The murmurs became mutters, an angry tone slipping into the sound.

"Did we not see him?" shouted one. "Holding Mattrax's eye?"

"He came from nowhere!" yelled another.

"The gods sent him!" It was more than one who called that out.

"Probably Barph," said Firkin with a hiccup. "Good god, Barph is. Always my favorite. Got his priorities right."

Lette ground her teeth. "You are listening to the words of a drunkard you would have kicked out of a tavern nine nights out of ten. Your prophet is Will Fallows, a farm boy most of you I imagine have known since birth."

The muttering stuttered.

"Does sort of look like him," said someone nearby.

"I ain't following Will Fallows fucking nowhere," someone replied. Lette smiled.

Then another voice rose up, louder. "Will Fallows is dead."

Silence fell.

"My name's Dunstan Meffit," said a heavyset man with a patchy beard clinging to his rolling chin. "I done worked with Will Fallows since he was a child. Worked for his father before him. And three days ago I went to his farm, and found Mattrax's soldiers there. The barn was burned to the ground, and they told me Will had burned in it. One of the men had his face burned up, said he'd been in the barn and seen it himself." The man suddenly seemed to realize he had the attention of the whole crowd. He tugged at his beard and ducked his head. "Least that's what they told me."

He shuffled back toward anonymity. Lette attempted to find enough expressions of contempt to pour upon the man.

Firkin beat her to it. "He is returned!" he yelled. For a man with such a shrill voice, he could achieve surprising volume. "The gods have returned him to us! They have sent their prophet down into the shell of this Will Fallows! A miracle! Another! He returns from the dead! He kills the dragon!"

"Three nights ago, Will Fallows was looking for his manhood in a cave with me," Lette retorted, but it was too late. The crowd was in a passion. Shouts of "A miracle!" rose up all around her. Firkin leaned back on his rock, smiling beatifically. He closed his eyes and appeared to fall asleep.

If she ground her teeth any harder, Lette realized, she was going to crack a tooth. Still, there was one person who could end this. She pushed out of the crowd and went to look for Will.

\*    \*    \*

She found him siting by himself, leaning up against a trunk at the edge of the tree line. He looked up as she approached. He was a mess. Dried blood formed a flaky beard beneath hangdog eyes. The axe he'd been holding the night before was laid out on the leaves beside him. She didn't think he had slept at all. She grimaced. He grimaced right back.

Finally she asked, "What did you do with the eye?"

He shrugged. "I threw it away."

Lette sighed. "Well thank the gods for small mercies." And then—because if anyone could fill in the gaps, it seemed he could—"What happened?"

He shook his head. "I panicked. They were all praising me, claiming I saved them. Except it was me and my ridiculous excuse for a plan that put them all in danger in the first place. And they were all pressing in. And, gods, I thought they would crush me to death or something." He shuddered. "When I managed to get out of it, I just ran and hid."

Lette took in his hiding place. The edge of an open plain of scree. "You're shit at hiding," she told him.

She grinned at him. After a moment he grinned back. "Thanks," he said. "I think I needed that."

She nodded. "Quite all right." Then, because the answers still weren't all there: "I know you didn't kill Mattrax," she said. "So whose blood is that?" She gestured to the weapon, to his face.

He explained about the guard. When he was done, Lette found she was impressed. She hadn't been sure Will had murder in him. And telling the tale seemed to have calmed him a little.

It was time. "You know Firkin is sitting on a rock," she said, "preaching that you're a prophet, to everyone who will listen to him?"

Will's calm retreated. He curled up on himself. "Please," he said. "You have to go and tell them it's pig's shit," he said.

"No," she told him. "You do."

He looked at her imploringly. "I swear that's all I've said to anyone since I left the cave. They don't listen. Or they listen and get angry. One man called me a fraudulent fuck and I had to take a swing at him with my axe before he'd back off. And once I'd done that, even more people gathered and started screaming at him that he was a heathen." He shook his head. "They want a prophet, but they don't want to bother listening to one."

Lette grimaced. That was simple enough, she supposed. Firkin told them what they wanted to hear, Will didn't.

Which left her original plan.

"We have to get out of here quickly then," she told him. "Firkin's making a mob, and nothing good ever comes from a group of folk most people associate with pitchforks and public burnings. So we find Balur, we find a wagon, we load it up with as much gold as it will carry, and we run like Lawl has opened up the Hallows at our heels."

That, it seemed, was a plan Will could get behind. He stood up, checked to see if anyone was pointing and screaming in an adoring manner. Firkin's sermon, however, was drawing more and more of the crowd away. Which was about the only benefit Lette could ascribe to it.

They found Balur closer to Mattrax's cave, sprawled out on last night's debris, head pointing downhill, mouth open, and snores rumbling out of him that sounded like giant pigs rutting.

Lette kicked him in the side of the head. Balur grunted. So she kicked him again.

"Be leaving it a-fucking-lone, woman," Balur rumbled. Only his jaw moved.

"Woman?" There was no way Lette was going to let that shit lie. She went to kick him again. Balur's arm shot out fast enough that she had trouble tracking it. He caught her ankle.

"It is already feeling like Mattrax was taking a shit in my skull. I would be begging you not to be kicking it anymore. Ours has been being a long and fruitful partnership and it would be being a shame for it to end with me being the one to be tearing your leg off and to be shoving it up your arse."

Lette sneered. "Like to see you try." The truth was, though, that if Balur wanted to, she would see him both try and— assuming she didn't pass out from the pain—succeed.

Balur grunted, let go of her leg, and rolled into a sitting position. He let out a second grunt, somehow deeper and more profound, and put his head in his hands.

"Be reminding me," said Balur, his voice even more gravelly than normal, "to not be drinking any more Fire Root potion."

Lette groaned. So *that* explained it. "You stupid, silly fuck," seemed the best way to summarize that situation.

Balur grunted. "Was killing a dragon."

That, she knew, would in Balur's mind excuse any behavior. Show up at a Batarrian wedding, tear the bride in two, and use both halves of her as a latrine? Okay as long as it resulted in an unimpeachable display of one's might.

"It was an unconscious dragon," she pointed out, for all the good it would do.

"Wasn't seeing you killing it."

Will, Lette realized, was staring and pointing. Both she and Balur turned to look at him. Will's finger wavered at Balur. "You?" he managed.

"Of course him," Lette said. "Who else would get drunk enough to cave in Mattrax's skull."

"So...so..." Will's jaw worked. "Balur's the prophet," he managed. He looked off at where Firkin sat. "They should be worshipping him. Not me."

Now it was Balur's turn to look confused. "They are worshipping you?" He looked from Will to Lette. "Why are they worshipping the farmer?"

Lette couldn't quite resist the short, sharp punch to Balur's pride. "They think Will killed Mattrax," she said.

The transformation was immediate. One moment Balur was a sagging ball of scales and aches, the next he was an eight-foot towering statue built in honor of righteous rage. His arm snapped out, caught Will around the neck.

"You are claiming my kill?" he roared. Brown phlegm flew out of his mouth, spattered Will.

Maybe that particular punch had been a little too short and sharp…

"Balur," Lette said, affecting patience.

Will croaked.

"I am going to be killing you," Balur growled at him. "Or are you going to be claiming that as suicide as well?"

"Balur," she repeated.

"I shall be arranging your intestines so that they shall be reading, 'I claimed the rightful kill of Balur, mightiest of the Analesians.'"

Balur always got far too invested in the whole revenge thing.

"Bal—" she started for the third time, then changed her mind and went for the more direct, "Hey, you, the son of a whore lizard."

Balur snapped his gaze down to her. "What?"

"Let him go, you gargantuan fucking idiot."

Balur curled his lip but did as he was told. Will landed, gasping, pawing at his bruised throat.

"Why?" Balur growled. Whether he was asking for Will's motives or hers, Lette wasn't sure. Maybe Balur wasn't either.

"I didn't claim it," said Will, his voice sounding raw. "All I've done is tell people that it wasn't me. I just found an eye you left on the ground. I was using it as a lantern. I didn't even know what it was."

"The crowd," Lette said, "did what crowds always do. They made a stupid assumption. And then someone did what people always do when crowds make stupid assumptions. They agreed with it, and took advantage of it." That was, as far as Lette understood it, the entire principle of the political system.

"Who?"

Perhaps there was a little Fire Root left in Balur's system. He was never at his best when he was monosyllabic.

"Firkin," she said reluctantly. If she didn't give the name up now, it would just take up more time as Balur badgered her for it.

"Then I am knowing who I must be killing next."

"No!" she snapped with more than a little vehemence. "He is surrounded by a crowd of a hundred or more, all of whom believe him completely."

"Then I will be killing all who are getting in my way," Balur said, already turning.

"No!" There was a shrillness in Lette's voice that she regretted. But it stopped Balur. He turned, looked at her. "No," she said again. "That's not who we are...Not who I am anymore."

Balur stared at her. She saw disbelief. Disappointment. But she wanted to be a better person, not a weaker one. So she held his gaze.

"We are tribe," Balur growled.

"Then our tribe is not killing a hundred innocents today."

Balur curled his lip. For a moment she thought it might come to blows. Analesian dominance patterns died hard. But then Balur shook his head, let his shoulders slump. "You are not being fun anymore."

Lette breathed. "We just need to get the gold and get gone from here," she said.

She flicked her gaze over to Will, checking that he was still on board. He was looking at her with a distinctly nervous expression. She arched an eyebrow.

"I could go and tell them Balur killed Mattrax" he said quietly.

She shook her head. "Shut up," she told him, "and help me get rich."

\*       \*       \*

Lette's nerves tightened like bowstrings as they approached Mattrax's cave. There was another crowd here. Not as big as Firkin's, but big enough to keep her up at night if she had to cut through them to get to the gold.

*I'll let Balur go in first,* said the cold, calculating part of her mind. *Shock and awe. Let him carve a path. They'll start to flee downhill—the path of least resistance. I'll cut them down just as they start to break. Five or six should do it. Women and children if I can. That paralyzes them, gives Balur more time to work. Then they flee backward, toward the mountain. I put a blade in anyone spilling off to the sides. Then we press them up against the rock, finish them. Less than a minute's work.*

She half shook her head, half shuddered. She didn't want to listen to that voice.

*It got you this far,* she whispered back to herself.

"Is that Quirk?" Will had stopped walking and stood squinting.

Lette's stomach did a slow gymnastic routine. Memories of fire and fear. The smell of cooking flesh in her nostrils. She looked over at Balur.

"Wait," she said. "Are you aroused right now?"

Small purple frills had opened up along Balur's neck, narrow vibrant lines of feathery color. Like a fish's gills. Their display was involuntary, and only ever appeared when Balur was contemplating mating rituals.

Balur brushed a hand at his neck, and failed to meet her eye.

"No," he blustered. "It is just being...I am just waking up. This is being the way I am in the morning. It is being nothing to do with nothing." He looked away.

She shook her head. "You sick bastard. You're totally turned on by her body count, aren't you?"

Balur hesitated, then shrugged. "There were being a lot of torched bodies in that cave last night."

Lette grunted her disgust. Still, she was used to Balur's depravities. A lot of his whores liked to share their stories with her. They seemed to think that some battle-scarred bond must now exist between them. She rather wished they wouldn't.

From the poorly stifled sounds of revulsion coming from behind her, it rather sounded like Will didn't want to hear about the depravities either. She wondered what that was like—to still have innocence left to lose.

"If you're so hot and heavy for her," she said to Balur, ignoring Will, "then why don't you go in first, and make sure she's feeling less murderous than last night?"

"Murderous? Body count?" Will, it seemed, had gotten over the mental image Balur had summoned. "What are you talking about? Quirk wouldn't even kill Ethel last night because she's a pacifist. I think she's treating the wounded up there." He pointed. And, Lette saw now, the women and men were almost universally bandaged and hobbling.

Lette turned and smiled. "Ah," she said. "Yes. Well, you know how our thaumatobiologist has given up magic? How she's moved on and made herself a better person?"

Will nodded.

"Yes," Lette said. "So that was horseshit."

"She..." Will started.

"Roasted a score of people alive?" Lette finished. "Yes, she did that."

"Oh fuck."

Balur cut in. "It was being like a firestorm in the night. Ribbons of fire were dancing about her."

"Keep it in your pants," Lette told him. He brushed at his neck.

"She's treating the wounded," Will repeated.

"She probably wounded most of them herself."

"There must have been...I don't know. Some sort of extenuating circumstances."

"Like her being a psychotic, magic-using arsonist and lying to us about it?" Will was cute and all, but it was possible to push the naïve thing too far.

"How about we are going over there and just asking her?" Balur put in.

"I told you to keep it in your pants."

"I think 'just talking' is pretty close to keeping it in your pants," Will put in.

Lette breathed. She had started to calculate whether she could stash Will's body before the crowd noticed. She was *not* going to be that person.

"Fine," she said. "Let's talk."

They pushed through the crowd. Quirk kept her head down as they approached, focused on the stitches she was putting in a young boy's arm. Her fingers made short, precise movements. Strands of pig gut tightened, sealed fleshed together.

"You don't know a... 'better way' to help with that?" Lette asked without preamble. She and Balur loomed over the spot where she sat working. The young boy looked up at them. He was biting on a strap of leather while Quirk worked.

Quirk didn't look up. "I told you," she said. "I'm reformed."

None of them said the word *magic*. None of them mentioned spells. The crowd hadn't put it together yet. There was no need to help them along the way.

"Reformed?" Lette allowed acid to etch the edges of her voice. "You were reformed last night?"

Quirk cinched a stitch tight with a sharp jerk of her wrist. The boy winced, let out a slight moan. Quirk blew out, put a smile on her face.

"Sorry," she said to the boy. "That's the last one, though. You go on to your mother. Tell her how brave you were." She flicked a glance at Will. "As brave as the prophet himself."

The boy's eyes widened along with his smile. He ran off, grinning.

Will was looking about anxiously. "You've heard?" he asked Quirk quietly.

"When it's all someone will talk about despite the fact that you need to amputate his hand, then you work out that it's important to a lot of people."

Will shook his head.

"This is striking me," Balur rumbled, "as being a fairly transparent attempt to change the subject."

The small grin that had graced Quirk's face fled. She looked down at the ground. "I have more people to treat."

"Cauterizing wounds?" It was probable, Lette thought, that antagonizing someone who could cook you in your clothes was unwise, but...gods, she sat there so calmly, trying to pretend it hadn't happened. She had lied, had killed. Lette would not be satisfied until there was some blood in the water.

Yet when Quirk looked up, Lette was afraid she had cut too deep. Something flickered in the mage's eyes. Something bright and dangerous.

"What else would you have me do?" Quirk hissed, with the intensity of a flame. "I caused half these wounds. I cannot go back. I cannot undo them. I slipped. Sometimes I slip. Not often, but last night I did. So I can stand up, and say, Yes, it was me, I did this. And they will string me up and burn me, or something else more inventive but equally vile, and I shall die. Or I could keep my mouth shut and actually do some good healing the hurt."

Lette hesitated. There was some sense to the words.

"That is being all well and good," said Balur, "right up until you are doing it all over again."

Quirk nodded, short and savage. "You're right. I should just end my life. A knife across the wrists is effective, I hear. Maybe I should find a ledge. Just let my past beat me. Just let the person I was win. Or maybe, if I'm going to do that, I should just torch you all. Watch you all burn." She eyed Balur. "The meat would be peeling off your bones before you even got that hammer above your head.

"Part of me wants to do that, you understand? Since I've met you, there's been just a little piece of me that wants to know what you'd smell like if I cooked you." She turned that slow, big-eyed stare on each of them in turn. "But I don't. Because I'm better than that. Because I still have things to offer. Because I am holding on to the dream of who I could be."

Lette honestly felt bad for the woman. Her heart went out to her, in fact. They were alike in many ways. She had forgotten that somewhere along the way. Possibly when her hair was on fire the night before.

However, of more immediate concern was the fact that Quirk's hands were shaking and letting off smoke.

"How close," Will asked, "would you say you were to slipping right now?" He was stepping back as he spoke.

Quirk clenched her fists. "Just let me tend to these people," she said. "Just let me undo a little of the damage I've done."

Lette exchanged a glance with Balur. He shrugged.

"So she is being sorry," he said. "Plenty of murderers are being sorry. It is not stopping us from being the ones who are stringing them up from trees or from being the ones who are then hitting them until they are stopping moving."

Quirk was on her feet in an instant. Lette allowed blades to drop into both her palms even as the curse formed on her lips. Balur was widening his stance. Will was making a round O with his mouth. Firkin's shrill voice was carrying thinly on the wind from where he preached. Sounds of laughter and pain were coming from the crowd, mingling in the air.

"Lawl's breath, it's him! It's really him!"

A girl's cry, breathy and excited, shot into the moment, ricocheted off several walls of inappropriateness, and struck Lette right in the frontal lobes.

"Oh by the gods. Look at him!" Another girl. Just as breathy. Just as excited.

Slowly, keeping her eyes on Quirk for as long as possible, Lette turned her head to look in the direction the voices had come.

Charging, mouths wide, nostrils flared, pupils blazing, with all the energy and ferocity of a pack of wolves hurling themselves straight out of the mouth of the Hallows, two teenage girls flung themselves at Will.

"You're the prophet!" one babbled. "Like the actual prophet."

"Oh gods, he has his axe!" the other girl babbled. She reached out, touched the handle. She was fourteen, perhaps, black curly hair gathered up in two loose buns on either side of her head. She wore a bloodstained smock cut, in Lette's opinion, far too low. Her friend filled out her smock to a lesser extent, but she had eyes the size of saucers, and they were fixed on Will's own.

Will, for his part, looked a lot like he had just stepped in something unpleasant while visiting a much-honored elderly relative—horrified but unsure of whether he could actually say anything.

"Can I...Can I touch you?" said the one with her hair in buns.

Lette watched the refusals form on Will's lips but none of them made it into the audible realm. She glanced back at Quirk. The thaumatobiologist was watching the exchange with a mix of bafflement and disgust.

"For the sake of the gods, Will," Lette said, since obviously someone had to take hold of the moment, "tell her to get gone before her father finds you and accuses you of something indecent."

Too late.

"'Ey up," said a man approaching from farther down the slope of the mountainside. "What the fuck do you think you're doing with my Maisy?" He was large, heavyset. There was fat on his gut, held in place by a tightly cinched apron, but his wrists were thick and his shoulders broad. He wore a flat cap on his head and an ill-advised mustache on his upper lip.

Will flinched away from the girl, arms going wide, palms up. "I didn't. I swear...It wasn't...She...I mean not to suggest that she...Except...Well..."

Lette grit her teeth. She was still holding her daggers. She had been trying so hard to be good. And she knew Balur would be no help. He was grinning too much.

But then the girl's father got a better look at Will. "Oh," he said, and then again, more bashfully. "Oh it's you. I, err, didn't realize, your, erm...prophetness. Didn't mean to get in the way. I mean." He pulled his cap off his head, started to work it in his large hands. "If you've taken a shine to Maisy there, well she's a fine girl. And if you, well...It would be an honor to me and my family if you wanted to...you know...with her."

Will's hands, if anything, got farther apart and farther away from Maisy. The look of horror on his face hadn't left. "She's only fourteen," he said. "Or..." He checked Maisy. "Thereabouts."

"Fourteen exact," said the man, who looked not even slightly abashed. Rather it was a look of admiration on his face. He glanced at Maisy. "See that?" he said to her. "He knew your age right off." He tapped his head, just next to his right eye. "Got the vision, he does. Just like the Voice says he do."

Lette rolled her eyes so hard she almost snapped her head from side to side. The girl couldn't be more fourteen if she tried. That said, at this point neither could the farmer. He was still advancing on Will.

"Would it...erm..." He worked the cap in his hands harder than ever. His broad cheeks blazed red. "Would it be okay if I touched you?"

Will backed up fast, making inarticulate noises.

Lette had had enough. "All right," she said, stepping between Will and his admirers, "that's enough creepy time for today. His prophetness needs a break from all your weird shit. He's decreed you all fuck off for a bit before I shove my foot up your arse."

Beside her, Balur nodded. "Prophetic," he whispered. She ignored him.

The man, his daughter, and her friend all backed away slowly. The man attempted to bow, almost tripped over himself. Lette turned her back on him, put herself between the trio and Will.

"This is only going to get worse," she said, trying to put all the urgency she felt into her words. "Right up until the point when they realize that Firkin is full of shit. And then it's going to get downright terrible. So let me repeat myself: We need to get some gold, get a wagon, and get the fuck out of here."

Quirk looked up from where she was sitting. "You're just going to abandon these people?"

Lette felt her fists clench. Had these people never heard of haste? Balur had his faults, to be sure, but at least he was already moving toward the cave.

"I am not going to just leave them. I am going to actively flee from them, and I am going to discourage anyone who wants to follow using the edge of my sword blade."

"But when the Dragon Consortium finds out what happened here, when they find out they were all here..." Quirk's eyes were wide with shock. "You have accused *me* of killing these people..."

"Yes," Lette said. "Because you did." She had been told tact was not her strong point. Personally she had never seen the need for it. The world was the way it was; you either accepted that or pretended it wasn't until it put the knife in your gut and showed you exactly what color your spleen was. "But I did not lead these people up here last night. I did not even suggest doing it. I did not kill Mattrax. I did not fuck up my part of the plan in any way." The smile on her face felt small, savage, and justified.

"But they'll be killed."

Lette nodded. "More than likely."

Will put a hand on her arm. "Wait. Is that true?"

So pretty. So naïve. "What do you think the Dragon Consortium will do when they find out someone killed one of their members? Shrug, put it down to bad luck, and have another sweetmeat? Or come here raining down fire and vengeance so that nobody ever dares fuck with them again?"

Balur snorted a laugh next to her. They all looked at him. "Sorry," he said. "I am just thinking that there is probably being an underappreciation of sweetmeats among dragons. It is being inappropriate. I am being aware."

"We can't just let this happen," said Will. "We have to do something."

Lette decided to try to take the time to explain it simply once. Maybe then they could just move on to the fleeing bit. "How," she said, "do you think we will manage that? We got incredibly lucky last night. The plan just about worked because we surprised Mattrax in his lair. And still many, many people from your village were hurt." She swept her hand about them, at the injured and bandaged all around them. "Or they were killed," she went on. "So how do you think it will go if one, or two, or three, or four members of the Consortium swoop over our heads, looking for trouble and revenge?"

"Four dragons?" Quirk breathed. "Flying over us? You truly think that could happen?"

"Oh, put it back in your britches," Lette snapped. What was it with her traveling companions and inappropriate arousal?

"We cannot be saving these people," Balur said, finally pitching in to help the cause, his bass rumble adding a sense of finality to his words. "Lette is being right. We can only be saving ourselves."

Quirk shook her head. "This is wrong."

Lette shrugged. "So stay behind, don't get any gold, and get roasted alive by a bunch of pissed-off dragons. What you do here is up to you, but I'm telling you your options."

Quirk and Will looked torn. Lette shrugged. She'd laid it all out. She owed them nothing more. "Come on," she said to Balur, and together the pair walked toward Mattrax's cave.

It was Will who joined her first. Quirk wasn't too far behind. They stood together and just stared at all the gold.

"They say it can't buy you happiness." Will was chewing his lip.

Lette grinned. "Poor people say that. So let's go and get a wagon, and stop being them."

# 27

## Mo' Divinity, Mo' Problems

"You've *got* to talk to them."

Will kept his head down and avoided Lette's gaze.

Quirk's thaumatic cart bounced and jostled beneath him as they made their way down the rutted path. Behind him, the sacks of gold clinked together, providing a musical backdrop to the conversation. Around them, scrubby woods stretched away in every direction. Above, wispy gray clouds looked down judgmentally.

Seven days had passed since they left Mattrax's cave, and this was not the first time Lette had made this argument. The problem was, every time she made it, she was right.

Rapid footsteps saved him from having to admit that. He looked to the wagon's left to see a boy running to catch up with them. He was twelve, perhaps thirteen. Hair painted a thin dark line along his upper lip. His cheeks glowed red with the exertion of running. His eyes were alight.

"Here you go, your, erm... prophetness." He thrust a fistful of papers up at Will as he slowed his pace to match the bouncing wagon. "We found a bunch pinned up all along the road. Pulled them all down, just like you asked."

Will approximated a grateful smile. "Thank you," he said, as cheerfully as he could muster. "I really appreciate it."

If the boy had smiled any wider, Will would have had to get down from the wagon so he could pick the top half of the boy's skull up off the ground. The boy ran off beaming.

"And that sort of shit," Lette went on, "isn't helping."

"Being nice to him?" Will was genuinely confused.

"Yes," Lette spat. "Think about it. Ever since that kid was born, life has shit on him. His parents shit on him. His siblings shit on him. Mattrax shit on him. Possibly literally. This whole fucking valley shit on him. And then he's given this man, this hero to look up to, maybe even worship. And what does that arsehole do?"

As the arsehole in question, Will wasn't sure he liked this line of questioning. "I'm nice to him?" he snapped.

"Yes," Lette snapped back with just as much bite. "The bastard is nice to him. He says please and thank you, and blesses his young stupid head with smiles and platitudes."

"You're right." Will nodded. "I totally am an arsehole." He checked to see if any of his sarcasm had dripped onto his chin.

"You set him up," Lette snapped back. "You ensure the worship. You double down on the crap Firkin has been spouting. And what does that do?"

Will rolled his eyes. He thought it was a trait he had picked up from her. "Makes the best of a bad situation?"

"The crowds are going to kill us, Will." There wasn't the hint of a smile in Lette's eyes. "And we're going to kill them."

Will looked back, over the wagon, over the sacks of Mattrax's gold, over the road of mud and gravel that had been bruising his spine for the last seven days. He looked back at the crowd.

It had all seemed so simple back in Mattrax's cave. The world so full of possibility. Quirk had agreed to fetch her wagon. He had found sacks. And they had filled them full to brimming. A day spent merrily looting. So much gold it took them until dusk to load the wagon up. So much gold they had to reinforce the wagon's axles. So much gold that Balur's purple frills of arousal had become an almost permanent fixture upon his neck.

And then merry and laughing—Lette's hand actually upon his arm—they had left the cave, come blinking into the dying light of the day. And the crowd had been there.

Firkin hadn't been at its head. That was probably what had saved the man's life. But the fire he had lit beneath the crowd was an inferno now. It didn't matter what anyone said to them. It didn't matter that Will wanted to slip away. The decision had been made without him. They would follow him to the ends of the earth.

He'd thought they'd lose interest over time. Give up and slowly drift away. Instead, the crowd had grown, was now perhaps three times the size it had been when they left Mattrax's cave. More flocked to it each day, arriving in greater and greater numbers.

"And if you want proof," Lette said, cutting into the horror of memory with all the sweetness of blunt-force trauma, "just look at those damn papers you're holding."

Will didn't need to look at them. He knew exactly what they were. They were tacked up on trees, all along the major thoroughfares. They clustered at crossroads. They were images of his face, of Lette's, Balur's, Firkin's, and Quirk's. Images and numbers. Lists of the piles of coins that the Consortium would pay for their heads. And those numbers grew faster than the crowd did.

"One of these people," Lette thumbed back over her shoulder, "is going to betray you. Someone—Lawl's black eye, I'd be shocked if it wasn't most of them—is here not because of how nice you are, but because she knows exactly the sort of life our heads could buy her."

Will wanted to argue. He would have loved to argue. But he knew what life was like under the Consortium. He knew how desperate you could get. People could betray loved ones for a little gold. What loyalty did they have for some arsehole sitting on a wagon full of it?

"The bigger this crowd gets," Lette went on, without pity or remorse, "the worse it gets. The more people there are to sabotage us. The more people to get killed when we finally reap what we've sown. You *have* to speak to them. You have to get them to disperse."

Will grimaced. Again, the problem he kept coming back to was that she was right.

"I wonder what the reward is up to now?" He stalled for time, flicking through the posters.

His jaw fell open. He tried to reel it back in before it dislocated.

"Eight thousand gold bulls?" he managed. At its most profitable, his parents' farm had been worth...what? Five *hundred* bulls? Maybe six. And now this. You could have bought half the Village for eight thousand gold bulls.

"What about me?" Lette asked, allowing curiosity to overcome her.

Will was still recovering from the price on his head. He just thrust the papers at her. She flicked through them, put on a sour expression. "I'm still stuck down at two thousand."

"Two thousand?" he said. It was still a staggering amount, of course, but it seemed considerably less than what hung above his head. That didn't seem even vaguely fair. "But you killed so many more people than I did."

"Sexist bullshit is what that is. Quirk is two thousand as well. Then Balur is up at six, and you're eight. Talk about double fucking standards."

"I'm worth more than Balur?" Will's voice was heading toward octaves he thought he'd abandoned along with short trousers.

Lette shrugged. "Well, if you actually grew a pair and told people you weren't a prophet then perhaps you would avoid the problem of being taken for a dangerous ringleader."

Lette, Will thought, was not showing quite as much sympathy as the situation required.

"You might actually want to take the Consortium up on that offer."

Will jerked his head around at the sound of Quirk's voice. She trotted up alongside the wagon, astride a thick-limbed farm horse. Balur strode beside her, long legs allowing him to keep pace easily.

"I am suggesting we turn in Lette," he said. "A good quick cash infusion. We could be spending it on wine and women. The expenditures not necessarily being in that order."

Lette nodded, a little sadly. "Regrettably," she said, "even with all this wealth, we still can't buy Balur class and taste."

Balur opened his mouth for another salvo, but Will flung himself into the breach. "Maybe," he said, "we could take a brief break from sniping at each other and find out what it is Quirk's actually talking about? I'm guessing she doesn't want us to turn on each other for gold just out of boredom."

Of them all, Quirk seemed to have adapted to the situation the best. She spent most of her time away from the wagon and the gold, and in among the crowd. She tended to the wounds of the sick, told stories to the children, led sing-a-longs, and seemed to play an important but poorly defined role in ensuring that everybody was clothed and fed. In fact, in Will's opinion, if the crowd should have been worshipping anyone it was Quirk.

"There's a problem," Quirk said, pulling him back to the present.

"Unless it is being to do with how to spend all this gold, then I am not being particularly interested," Balur told her.

"Well, then I'm glad this matter is gold related," Quirk replied with a slight snap. Will saw Lette checking the other woman's palms, but the leather bridle failed to start to smoke in her hands.

"Oh." Balur sounded slightly chastened.

"The thing is, you see," Quirk went on, slightly more calmly, "we are actually spending the money."

"We are?" Will asked. This was news to him.

"Where are being the whores?" Balur looked around, yellow eyes flashing as sharply as when blades were coming directly at his throat. "Where is being the wine?"

Quirk's expression was growing sourer by the second. Will was beginning to think he understood why she spent so much time with the crowd.

"Over three hundred men, women, and children are following this wagon," Quirk said. "Most of them have lived their entire lives in abject squalor. They have brought nothing with them because everything they ever had has been taken from them by the Consortium. They need feeding, clothing, healing—"

"You be waiting a moment," Balur cut in. "We are paying for that?"

Quirk wheeled on him. "Being astride a horse, her eyeline was for once above Balur's nipples. This seemed to add extra steel to her gaze. "You would rather them starve? Die of diseases?"

Balur threw up his hands. "Yes! How is this even being a question?"

This time when Will looked, there definitely seemed to be a red glow coming from Quirk's hands. "Lette," he said quickly. "You don't want three hundred souls on your hands. We were just talking about—"

Lette's gaze when she turned it on him was no less fiery than Quirk's palms. "We were not talking. I was telling you to talk. And now I am demanding it. Speak to them. End this. Or I shall end you and take my gods-cursed chances with the degenerates following you."

"They are farmers," Quirk snapped, her ire still up, "fishermen, seamstresses. Good, simple working folk."

"According to you they are starving, diseased, and naked," Lette bit back. "That is close enough to a degenerate for me to make no distinction."

This was devolving fast. "Exactly how much are we spending?" Will cut in. Perhaps it was not that much. And against the backdrop of the vast quantity of gold they had taken.

"At the current rate," Quirk said, "we'll run out of gold after eighteen months. But given that the crowds are growing, I think it will be before then."

"Eighteen months?" Will was apparently the only one of them who could speak. He looked at the vast fortune behind them. How could that last only a year and a half? "Mattrax sat on this wealth for years," he spluttered.

"Because he spent almost nothing," Quirk said. "He took. And took. And took." Each time she repeated the phrase it felt more and more like a slap to the face. "He taxed everything and gave nothing. His wealth only accumulated."

"So..." Will started, then realized exactly what he sounded like.

"You want to rule like Mattrax?" Quirk leaned into the cart from atop her horse. He could see the fire licking at the back of her eyes. "That is who you want to be?"

No. No. Gods no. Every reason he had had for starting this— whatever *this* was—was so that he could be exactly the opposite of everything Mattrax stood for.

But... eighteen months.

He turned to look at the gold again, to try to comprehend it. He made it halfway but then his head jerked to a stop. He pulled, but Lette had him by the scruff of his shirt.

"They threaten our lives. They fucking steal from us. Speak to them. Stop this. Before I take whatever passes for your manhood and cram it so far down your throat you end up shitting your own balls."

Dismembering people seemed to have given Lette a comprehensive overview of human anatomy.

"Okay," Will said. He could feel the anger coming off her in waves. "All right. I'll speak to them, see if I can dissuade them. Get them to...disperse or whatever it is."

Lette nodded, short and sharp. It felt less like a sign of approval and more like a kettle letting off steam.

"Just," he went on, "if they start to rip me limb from limb, I'd sort of appreciate it if you could step in and stop that."

He waited for confirmation, for reassurance. Balur shrugged. Quirk didn't meet his eye. He looked to Lette, waited. He waited a long time.

# 28

# Investigating His
# Burgeoning Manhood

"All right then." Will coughed nervously. "Can everybody hear me?"

They had pulled the wagon over to the side of the road against the trees of a small wood. Will stood on its boards, feeling as if he'd been backed up against a wall. Before him more than three hundred faces looked up from a scrubby wheat field, where they were busy trampling the crops. Lette, Balur, and Quirk stood to one side of the wagon, attention divided between him and the crowd. They still did not look particularly ready to leap to his rescue.

He searched the crowd for Firkin, picked him out near the back. The old man was clutching a ceramic jug and swigging deeply. His eyes were red-rimmed, and his beard swung back and forth as he tipped back the jug and swallowed. When he came back up for air, his eyes were on Will. He offered a friendly wave.

He spent almost all his time with the crowd now. Preaching the word of the prophet. Not that he ever spoke to Will to find out what the word actually was. Will was often as surprised to find out his own edicts as anyone. It seemed one of his main ones was to keep Firkin rolling in alcohol.

He wondered if Lette could hit Firkin with a knife from here. Probably. He just wasn't sure she'd do it if he asked her right now.

He still liked her. That was the stupid thing. Lette was in so many ways a terrible human being. Quick to both anger and violence. Focused almost wholly on her own personal gain.

Yet there was something else—almost someone else—lurking behind all that. Someone who was even quicker with a jibe than she was with a knife.

They had been riding together in the wagon, two days after leaving Mattrax's cave. Balur was pacing a quarter mile ahead, still in a fury over the crowd following them. Quirk and Firkin had been back with the flock, both ministering in their separate ways.

"What are you going to do with it?" Will had asked.

"With what?"

He had thumbed back at the gold, and she had pushed loose strands of hair behind her ears, ducking her head while she did it. There had been something strangely unguarded about the moment.

"I don't know," she had said after a second's hesitation.

He hadn't expected that. She seemed so certain of herself in everything else she did. "You haven't ever dreamed of what you'd do?"

She had shrugged, deflected the question. "Have you?"

It had been Will's turn to pause. "I don't know," he had started to say, but that hadn't been entirely true, and it had seemed like they were being very honest then. "I mean I have. But when I did dream about wealth it was always about my parents' farm. I'd put it back into that. Invest it in crops and animals. So it was profitable. Not just a way to get by. A real farm. What my parents always wanted it to be."

"What about now?" Lette had been looking off down the meandering path ahead, at the bumps and ruts, and the eventual blind turn into the unknown.

"I don't know. I haven't really had time to think about it since I lost the farm. I was just focused on taking it away from Mattrax, not really on having it myself."

"I'll take your share if you don't want it." She still hadn't been looking at him, but a smile had played at the corners of her lips.

"You don't know what to do with it either."

She had tossed her head, ponytail flapping. "I'll melt your share down, make statues of myself, and put them up in every town square."

"Classy."

"Oh, they'll be vile things. Big and gaudy and studded with the biggest jewels. But I'll make sure the face is very accurate. So it's recognizably me. And no one will know where they come from, but everyone will assume it's someone very important. And then when I show up in towns they'll all recognize me from the statue."

"Will you be studded with gaudy jewels as well?" He had leaned back, listening to the unexpected pleasure of her rambling.

"Indubitably."

He had almost laughed out loud at that, but he hadn't wanted to break the flow.

"I will have to," she had gone on, "to be sure they recognize me."

"What then?"

"Well, they'll all say to each other, it's that woman from the statues, she must be very important. And they'll do whatever I say, because they don't want to find out what happens when they don't. And they'll bring me whatever I want. And I won't have to spend a penny ever again."

He had started laughing before she did, but only by a second.

Now she stood stony-faced, staring down the crowd. For their part, they all ignored her. They only had eyes for him.

"You can all hear me?" he checked again. None of the people who couldn't hear him heard the question, so there was no response. He hadn't really been expecting one. He was stalling again.

"Erm..." he started. He should have written something down. But he'd put that off too. Until it was too late. Until it was now.

"So, it's come to my attention," he went on. It was how his father had started all his stern lectures.

*So, it has come to my attention that you punted a chicken halfway across the yard.*

*So, it has come to my attention you're unable to tell your arse from your elbow.*

*So, it has come to my attention your mother caught you investigating your burgeoning manhood.*

Yes, that was exactly what he needed to be thinking about...

"So, it has come to my attention"—he tried to strengthen his voice, his resolve—"that some of you are under the impression that I am a prophet. That I killed Mattrax. That—"

His words were lost in a hail of cheering and whooping. People leapt up and down in front of him. They were screaming. He could literally see a man crying. Hands reached out toward him, and the crowd pressed in at the base of the wagon. He took anxious steps back from the edge, stumbling on the sacks of gold. A piece of white cloth sailed out of the crowd and landed on his face. He tugged it off. It was a pair of women's underwear.

"What are you doing?" he asked them. They ignored him completely.

"Stop!" he yelled as loud as he was able. "You have to listen to me."

They did not. They went on for another full five minutes before they calmed enough to hear his cries. He looked at Lette—she had taken a step back behind Balur's protective bulk. She was right. He had left this for far, far too long.

"I said," Will said, his voice hoarse from yelling, "that you thought that I killed Mattrax."

Another wave of whooping broke out through the crowd. Will held up his hands, desperate for silence.

"We don't just think," broke out a voice from the crowd. "We know."

"Why we're here," shouted another.

"Prophet! Prophet! Prophet!" The chant broke out in isolated pockets throughout the crowd. Will hung his head.

"I am not a prophet," Will said as loud as he could, voice full of frustration and disgust. He stared at his own feet. Dust and mud flicked up from the road had spattered his shoes. The wooden boards beneath them were worn and chipped.

Silence fell upon them. He looked up.

Oh, now they chose to bloody hear him.

The gaze of the crowd had changed. It was no longer the stare of a girl gazing into her young lover's eyes; rather it was the gaze of that girl discovering her young lover with his pants down and her sister knelt before him.

Will swallowed hard. In the crowd, a murmur of discontent arose, drifting off into the autumnal sky. It brewed and bubbled, gaining in volume.

Will cleared his throat, and failed to think of something else to say. He checked for escape routes. Surrounded on all sides, they did not appear to be plentiful.

"No," arose a voice from the middle of the crowd. "He ain't no prophet."

The crowd echoed this dissension. The murmur becoming physical, a shudder running through the bodies surrounding him.

"What you say?" A voice from elsewhere. It threatened violence.

"He ain't a prophet," insisted the dissenter.

"Well..." Will started.

"He's a god!" shouted the dissenter.

Will's jaw dropped. He tried to get out the word "no!" but was unable to do it before the crowd erupted.

"No! No!" he screamed too late, but the crowd had gone back

to not listening again. He looked down at Lette. She was shaking her head. Balur was massaging his forehead. Quirk just stared, utterly perplexed.

This time, he thought they would break the cart. It creaked under the pressure of the hysteria. Much like his sanity. He looked out at them, hopeless. "I'm not a god," he said quietly. "I'm just an idiot who got himself arse deep in all of this shit."

A small boy had worked his way to the front of the crowd. He stood at the edge of the cart staring up at Will. And despite the chaos all around him, he alone had caught Will's words. As Will stared down, the boy stared up and their eyes met. Will watched those eyes as all the hope and joy drained away. He saw those eyes fill with horror and despair.

He glanced away, looked to Lette. She was shaking her head, staring at the crowd in disgust.

Will look back at the boy. The child's bottom lip was quivering now. Will forced a smile from somewhere deep in the back of his throat up onto his face.

"No," he breathed and shook his head. "It's okay. I'm a prophet if you need one."

The boy hesitated, then grinned. Will looked away.

# 29

# Aftermath

"Well," said Lette, "that went about as well as sticking your balls in a fire pit."

Will hung his head. It struck him as a fairly accurate description. But… "You saw them," he said. "What was I supposed to do? They're at the point where if I shatter their dreams, they'll shatter me right back."

"You are being fucking deserving of it," rumbled Balur.

They were still all gathered around Quirk's thaumatic cart. The crowd had dispersed, small groups wandering off chatting among themselves. At least they all seemed happy for now. They'd probably go on being happy right up until a dragon shat all over their life expectancy.

"Perhaps it's not such a bad thing."

They all looked at Quirk. She shrugged. "I mean," she said, "what harm can hope do?"

"Well," said Lette, "I suppose it depends on how utterly futile it is, and how many dragons you have chasing you."

"Imagine if it had worked," Quirk said. "Imagine you managed to rip all their hope from them. How much would that really help?"

"Well," Lette said, clearly deciding to ignore Quirk, "now we know that our options are to die at the hands of the dragons, or to die at the hands of an angry mob."

"Dragons," Balur said with a nod. Silence greeted this. Balur looked around, a slightly wounded expression on his face. "That was being the question, was it not?"

This wasn't right. Will just wouldn't accept it. They had killed Mattrax. They had the gold.

"There has to be another option," Will said.

"Why?" Quirk looked genuinely interested.

"Because both of those options are shit."

The smallest smile Lette could make ghosted across her lips. "The farm boy has a point."

Will knew he did. He pressed it. "What could hide us? I mean truly hide us. Get us away from the crowd, the Consortium. Bury us where they would never look."

Balur grunted. "*Bury* is not being the best word, I am thinking."

"Shut up," said Will, who was surprised by his own bravado. Balur must have been too, because instead of removing Will's head from his spine, he did actually shut up.

Lette and Quirk regarded him in equal, skeptical silence.

"I'm serious," he said.

Lette looked at the others, then back at him. She shrugged, quirked a half smile. "Money," she said.

Will threw up his hands. "We have a whole truckload of money."

"A rapidly diminishing truckload of money," said Lette.

"How can we not have enough money?" asked Will. He peered over his shoulder back at the wagon, sack piled upon sack. It was, he felt, a more than legitimate question.

"I don't think you fully conceive the Consortium's resources." Lette had a belligerent, lecturing tone. "You keep complaining that no one knows anything about Kondorra—well there's one thing that everyone outside of Kondorra does know. It's that the dragons are richer than the gods. That volcano you said they hang out in. I swear to you that it must be full to overflowing with gold. They can't just track us to the end of the world. They can afford to build extra worlds to search on."

"We are being so fucked." Balur had apparently decided that it was time for more color commentary, "that a madam would be telling us that we had been earning out at her brothel."

"I'm not sure there's enough money in the world." Lette's face was as open and honest as he had ever seen it. "But if there is, then it's about our only option. Buy ourselves a hole deep enough to hide in." She shrugged sourly.

Silence fell on them. Because what else could you do when the future was that bleak.

And then, despite it all, Balur's face split open with a wide grin. Sharp glinting tooth after sharp glinting tooth put on display in the dying afternoon light.

"What?" Lette asked him.

"More money, you are saying?" he said.

Lette looked at him curiously. "Yes."

Balur's grin widened even farther. He clapped his hands. "We," he said, "are totally going to be killing us another dragon."

# 30

## Never Say Never

"No." Will fought against the rising bile in the back of his throat. He would not do that again. Never. Ever. Again.

Lette stood, paced around the group, a short, tight circle. She looked from Balur to Will, back to Balur. She stopped behind Balur, put a hand on his massive shoulder. "He's right," she said to Will with the slightest of shrugs. Almost an apology. Almost. But not quite.

Will threw up his arms. "How can he be right?" He stood up too, pointed back in the direction they had come. "How can that sort of death toll possibly be right?"

"Actually," said Quirk, "from a purely academic standpoint, I thought the death toll was remarkably low."

"That's because you're trying to assuage your guilt for killing the most of them!" shouted Will. He was reaching his breaking point. "Because Mattrax didn't actually kill anyone! It was just us. Us and our continual fuckups. And now I'm responsible for all of these people. Me. Not you." He pointed at Quirk. "No matter how much you pretend that you are. They're all looking at me. And you're all asking me to lead them to their deaths. At our fucking hands. Well, no. I won't do it. I'm not doing it. You all can fuck right off."

There was a pause. Birds wheeled and called in the sky. Branches rattled in trees. A few people who had not wandered far turned and looked to see what their prophet was raving about. Will didn't care. Screw them too.

Quirk examined her hands. Balur scratched the back of his head. Lette reached up, stretching her arms above her head, staring off into the middle distance.

The time, Will decided, had come to walk away. He turned his back on them.

"You know how to do it, don't you?" Lette said to his back. "You and Firkin talked about that too, didn't you?"

Will walked faster.

# 31

# Shovel Loads of Straw and Shit

It had been the day before Will turned seven years old. He had been mucking out Bessie's sty, flicking glances at Firkin between shovel loads of straw and shit.

"You're being awful quiet there, Will," Firkin said after ten silent minutes.

Will didn't say anything.

"I've been thinking," Firkin went on, "about the problem with drugging the villagers with Fire Root in the morning when we only get the Snag Weed into Mattrax in the evening—"

"My da says your plans go to shit," Will blurted. Suddenly he could keep it in no longer. The pressure of betrayal was too great. And it wasn't exactly how his da had said it, but it's how Firkin would have said it, and it was how Firkin would understand it, so why not just say it that way?

"Ah," said Firkin. Then again. "Ah." He nodded. He scooped up another shovel load and carted it to the wheelbarrow. "You told him then?"

Will just shrugged. That wasn't exactly it. But he didn't want to explain. He wanted Firkin to be the one explaining.

Firkin just went on shoveling. Will had thought he might feel better if he just said it, but now he didn't. The pressure just kept building and building inside him until he thought he was going to break apart with anger and disappointment. He could feel a scream, or a yell building inside him, and he was terrified he was going to cry. He didn't want Firkin to see him cry.

Then Firkin stopped, and leaned on his shovel. "I suppose they do," he said nodding to himself. "I suppose they do."

And then all the pressure was gone, and the sense of deflation and loss was even worse.

"So it was all…" Will tried to find a word for it. "Lies?" he finished, because he did not yet know the vocabulary of betrayal.

Firkin shook his head with vehemence. "No, Will. No. That's not it. And what your da said…"

"My da's no liar," Will said, with a loyalty that surprised him.

Firkin let out a little laugh and reached for his hip flask. "No, Will. That is for sure, and I'd never say he was." He took a deep draft from the flask. "Your da speaks the truth. I've made a lot of plans over the years, and an awful lot of them have gone to nothing but shit. And we are here in a valley ruled by arsehole dragons at least in part because I couldn't come up with a plan that worked well enough. That's true."

"So it's all…all…" Will looked around for a word. His eyes landed on the wheelbarrow. "Straw and shit?"

Firkin laughed. But not his normal laugh. A sad laugh. "I don't know, Will," he said in the end. "I don't know. Some of it probably is. Maybe all of it. I don't know. I've never known with a plan I've made. And, yes, a lot of it has gone to shit. But sometimes there have been successes. Maybe not often. Maybe not even enough to say rarely. But they've been there. And each one has been a beautiful treasure." He took another deep swig. "And some…they've been beautiful failures, you understand, Will? While they've not done what I've planned, they've done other things. Things that I'm proud of. Does that make any sense?"

He looked desperate, there in the shadows of the pigsty. He didn't look like an adult at all. He looked like a worried child. He looked, to Will, like a reflection.

"Maybe," Will said, some of his disappointment and anger

fading. "Perhaps." He wasn't sure if he did, but he wanted to. He didn't want Firkin to be a liar.

"Thank you," Firkin said, and upended his flask. He smacked his lips and tucked it back into his belt.

"So we can rob Mattrax?" Will said just to be sure.

Firkin laughed again, loud in the small sty. "Maybe," he said. "I don't know. But we can *try*, Will. That's the beautiful thing. We can try, and we plan for success, but in the end who knows? Beautiful chaos, Will. Anything could end up happening. Maybe we could even rob them all. I've learned about all of them, Will. Mattrax, and Dathrax, and Kithrax, and the whole cursed lot of them. I can tell you about them all. We can make plans for them all. You can make plans. And then..." He smiled, reached for his flask again. "Beautiful chaos."

# 32

# Where There's a Will . . .

Lette found Will skulking about in a ditch. She watched him from a distance. He had his knees pulled up to his chest, feet firmly planted in the mud. He had plucked a long stalk of grass, was weaving it into a narrow thread.

She was sorry for him, she found. He might be a fool, but he was a good fool. At this very moment as many as forty people were watching him, waiting for the slightest command. But he was oblivious to them. Because he wasn't even looking for people to use. And even if he knew they were there, he wouldn't think to use them. Because that was—infuriatingly—who he was. A good fool. Gods, he could even be her fool if she wanted him to be.

Sometimes she thought she did want that.

But she also wanted to use him.

She shook herself. This should be simple. She should go, talk to him, make him see things her way, and get rich. That's what Balur would tell her to do. And he'd be right to tell her so. She was complicating something simple. Complicated would get her killed. The world was a cruel and harsh place. It demanded cruelty and harshness. And that was why it would kill Will.

It was just that she couldn't help but wish that the world was a place that would keep him safe.

She watched as Will glanced down at the elaborate knot of grass he had woven, placed it on the ground, and plucked another strand.

Lette realized that at some point she had knelt and pulled up a stalk of grass herself. It was a tangled knot in her hands. There was no pattern to its folds, just creases and crumples. She threw it away, stepped toward the farm boy.

"Will," she said. He twitched at the sound of her voice, but didn't turn round. She came closer, placing each foot carefully, as if approaching a rabbit, fearful it would skitter away before she could make it her supper.

"They're going to do it," she told him. "You realize that, don't you? With or without you. Balur has it in his head now. He's going to try to rob Dathrax."

Will turned around at that finally. He looked her in the eyes. *More wounded-puppy bullshit*, she told herself.

"So you're putting this on me," he said. "That's it, right? I have to help you now or it's on my head." His smile was bitter.

She continued her slow approach until she was standing on the edge of the ditch beside him. She felt the urge to reach out to him. She resisted for a moment. Business and pleasure were already at significant risk of getting very confused. But then she let herself give in to it. She rested her hand upon his shoulder. She could feel a fine tremor beneath her palm, as if some current ran through him.

"Come on, Will," she said. "This is a chance for you. Mattrax isn't the only dragon shitting on people's lives. They're all as bad as each other. We have the opportunity to hurt another one. You have the chance to help all the people trailing after us."

"I thought you said they were all dead whatever we did." It was not quite a snarl, but it was closer than he usually got.

She nodded, but did not take the hand off his shoulder. He was a source of warmth on this cold day. "Yes," she acknowledged. "Maybe." She shook her head, almost imperceptibly, but she knew that Will perceived it. "Who knows? If we did enough damage…"

Will laughed again, still cynical, but a little closer to the true feelings she knew lurked within him.

"You think we can take down the whole Dragon Consortium? Honestly?"

"Honestly?" She left a sliver of humor enter her voice. "No." She let that sink in. "But I think we can hurt them. I think, with you, we can make them think twice."

He didn't reply at once, only leaned back. That was a good sign.

"Come on, Will," she said. "You know you can help us. You know you can make a difference. You know you want to." She firmed her grip on his shoulder. "Don't give in to fear."

This was not her first seduction. Far from that. But it was one of the uglier ones all the same. Her heart was not in it, not truly, despite the promised payday, despite Will's hard, flat muscles.

She wasn't sure what was happening to her. Was this what being a better person was like? This weakness?

Will still didn't say anything. She licked her lips. She could feel words lurking at the back of her throat, but none of them stepped up, presented themselves as the right ones. She tried to keep her face warmly neutral, while inside she cursed. She was losing him.

Will looked down at the knot of grass in his hands. It looked impossibly complicated to her. The beginning lost in the end. A continual complex loop.

He followed her gaze. A smile broke through the clouds on his face. "My mother showed me how to make these," he said. "Eternity knots. She made one for my father when he asked her to marry him. He wore it around his neck on their wedding day."

She couldn't tell where this thread was going. She decided to follow it on impulse. "That's sweet." An encouraging smile.

"They rot in the end, though," he said, tossing his away. "The name's bullshit." He looked away from her, down into the brown muddy water of the ditch. "These people, the ones following me, they die whatever we do, don't they?"

The abrupt turn caught her off guard. She hesitated.

"Yeah," Will said. "I thought so."

She closed her eyes. Gods piss on it.

"We run; we're caught. We hide; we're caught. We fight them; we're caught." His voice sank with the utterance of each sad little fact.

She tried to work out how she would explain this setback to Balur.

"So we steal from them."

She looked up. Will was looking at her. His eyes weren't bright exactly, but there was the flicker of that fire in him. A little more heat than she'd seen in days.

"Because it hurts them," he said. "Because maybe it achieves shit all in the long run, but for just a little while, we can piss them off something awful."

# 33

# The Prophet of Profit

"All right," Will said, "this is how it's going to go down."

Quirk didn't know how Lette did what she did, but clearly she was very good at it.

They were all back in the thaumatic cart, on the move again. Will's train of followers stretched off down the road after them, longer than ever now—another thirty souls had joined them while Will vacillated by the side of the road.

She would have to get back to them all soon. She owed them that much at least.

The widows.

The widowers.

The orphans...

She closed her eyes, pushed the creeping thoughts back down.

"First," Will said, "Firkin and I never planned this. He supplied the facts about Dathrax, but we never got as far as an actual plan. So I'm pulling this together based on what he told me."

That sounded like nothing but a recommendation to Quirk.

"Be telling us the plan already," said Balur. "This is being enough with the foreplay." He, at least, seemed to agree with her.

Will sighed, shook his head. "Dathrax," he said, "lives in the center of Athril's Lake. Specifically on an island at its center. Alone. No guards. No castle."

"So he is being a fucking idiot." Balur clapped his hands together. Quirk felt the sound resonate deep in her gut.

"He doesn't have them," Will said, "because he doesn't need them. Athril's Lake is home to the Leviathans."

That got Quirk's attention. She pulled her gaze back from the road and the miniature geography of ruts and puddles. "The Leviathans?" she asked.

Will grinned. "I thought you might like them." He glanced at Lette before he went on. "Monster fish. Nobody is quite sure where they came from. Most say they were regular fish once. Then cast-offs from Dathrax's meals began slipping down into the lake, and the fish grew fatter and fatter living off them. And as they grew bigger, they developed more and more of a taste for flesh."

Quirk quirked an eyebrow. She'd heard enough old wives' tales in her time to recognize one when she heard it. There again, just because Will's etiology of the Leviathans was incorrect did not mean that they did not exist, nor that they held no interest for her. Perhaps she could discover their true origin. Perhaps she could observe the feeding rituals, how they mated and bred. Perhaps she could peel back the mystery of their existence scale by scale, muscle by muscle.

She flashed back to the moment in Mattrax's cave. Her hand outstretched. The scales barely a hair's breadth beyond the reach. Then falling away. Being denied.

The widows.

The widowers.

The orphans...

"Wait." Balur interrupted her introspection. "So the lake is being full of these giant killer fish?"

Will nodded. "The Leviathans. Yes."

"And there is being a fishing village there."

Will nodded again. "Well, a town. But yes."

Balur nodded back. "So, I am wondering, are they replacing the fishermen every day? Is it being where suicidal fishermen are going?"

Will rolled his eyes, though it struck Quirk as a reasonable enough question. "The Leviathans stick to deep water," he explained. They're *big*. As long as the fishermen stick to the shallows, catch small things, everything's fine. It's just when you want to get to the island that you get in trouble."

"So," said Lette, "how do you get to the island?" She was looking up at Will, rapt. It was unlike her to be so unaware of herself, so unguarded.

"Well," said Will, "that's the thing. Dathrax, like all the dragons, is a greedy bastard. He collects exorbitant taxes from everyone who lives around Athril's Lake. And he uses a garrison of troops to do it. But, because he's a dragon, he's also a lazy bastard. Doesn't want to be bothered with these little drabs of gold coming in now and again. Far too much work for a giant sack of scales and shit like him. No, he likes it coming to him all as one big lump sum. So all the gold sits in the garrison in the town of Athril right up until its yearly trek across the lake."

"But what about the Leviathans?" Lette asked. She was leaning forward, chin propped on both hands. Quirk thought that if in that moment, Will had asked her to eat candied bonbons out of his hand, she would've agreed to do so. Was it love? Greed? Infatuation?

Romantic entanglements were not a thing Quirk knew much about, truth be told. Her childhood had not allowed for such things. Nothing soft, or warm, or good had been permitted.

And after that . . . Well, she had been too busy dealing with the aftermath of such a childhood to get romantically involved with anyone, no matter how many students and professors had been intrigued by the rabid young thing the deacon had dragged in.

And now? Well, now she was entrenched in her studies. Her studies gave her focus. Focus gave her control. And she could not afford to be distracted.

Widows.

Widowers.

Orphans...

"The garrison uses a heavily armored boat to take the taxes to Dathrax," Will said, looking at Lette with no less intensity than she possessed when looking at him. "The Leviathans attack, but they can't chew through."

It all sounded so simple, as Will laid it out. So easily put together. Quirk tried to take a step back. She had thought the same the last time she'd heard Will lay out a plan.

But that had not been without its casualties.

The widows...

The—

She shook herself, threw off the litany. She couldn't wallow in self-pity. Would this honestly help all the people following them? She had assumed Lette had promised Will that to get him here. And she believed Will when he said that he cared about the followers. He may not have asked for the responsibility of caring for them, but he seemed decent enough to accept the role. But how far astray would Lette and Balur be willing to lead him?

And what about herself? Did she truly see this as a chance to save these people? Or did she see it just as another chance to see a dragon?

Or, perhaps, instead of worrying about which of those it was, she should think about the risk of experiencing significant stress. Could she be sure that she would be safe to be around? Could she guarantee the safety of the people who followed them?

*Yes,* was the knee-jerk response that flashed through her mind. *Of course.*

Except hadn't events and Mattrax's cave demonstrated that no matter how many times she repeated it, no matter how deep a groove it wore in her mind, her knee-jerk answer was not the whole truth?

Yet if that was not true, then who was she? Was she still that poor rabid girl who had been pulled from the scrub, dragged into civilization?

She shuddered, trying to shake off all the questions rising in her mind.

"Are you all right?"

Quirk became aware that Will was staring at her. She shook again, less violently this time. "I'm fine," she said. "Just a chill, that's all."

They were still all looking at her. Time to put their attention elsewhere.

"So," she said, "a heavily armed garrison is easier to steal from than a dragon?" She supposed that was probably true, though it seemed like a matter of degrees to her.

"Oh no," Will said, "the gold in the garrison is just the yearly stash. The real bulk of the wealth is with Dathrax out in the middle of the lake."

"It is being past the Leviathans?" Balur asked.

"Past the Leviathans," said Will.

"So your plan is involving us crossing a lake full of deadly giant fish?" Balur followed up.

"Yes," Will agreed.

Balur chewed on this. "I know we are not getting into the specifics of this yet," he said, "but so far I am thinking your plan is a bit shit."

Now Quirk was prone to agree. But she would have said any plan that involved getting past a small private army, and a lake filled with monstrous fish, to get to an island populated solely by an enormous fire-breathing lizard was questionable at best.

"Hear the farm boy out," Lette told them all.

But Quirk's mind was off again. She was thinking about the bags of gold. They promised freedom from the Consortium. But that was not all they promised.

Did she want to be rich? The thought had never really crossed her mind before. Money didn't really play a part in her life. The university gave her a stipend that she used for food, and for new clothes if her current ones developed more holes than society seemed willing to put up with. But she didn't have to pay for books. She hadn't needed to pay for the supplies for this trip. The university provided.

But knowledge—that was what she really wanted. And that did lie across the lake, and on that island.

Will was grinning. "Okay," he said, "what one part of our plan with Mattrax actually worked?"

"We got the gold," Lette said, patting a sack beside her.

"Yes," Will said. "But it came with this whole ridiculous crowd problem." He looked about them. Playing up the drama, Quirk supposed. He was far removed from the morose, cursing figure who had stormed off earlier now. "In my opinion," he went on, "the one part of the plan that went off flawlessly was the actual Snag Weed potion. We got it into a cow, and we got the cow inside Mattrax, and he went down so hard, he slept through Balur murdering him."

Balur shifted uncomfortably. "Still counts," he grunted.

"Still completely counts," said Will, with an indulgent nod.

"So we knock out Dathrax," Lette said, as if checking something off on a mental checklist.

"Yes we do." Will nodded some more. "And no need to murder him this time, so we limit the amount of additional heat we pull down from the Dragon Consortium."

A little optimistic, Quirk thought...but it would be another unconscious dragon for her to study. A live one this time.

Despite herself, she started to get excited.

"But how do we get the potion in him?" she asked.

"Okay," said Will. "Bear with me on this one. So, Dathrax, like Mattrax—"

"Wait," Balur interrupted. "Mattrax and Dathrax? That is honestly being their names?"

Will shrugged. "I fantasized about robbing dragons. I couldn't tell you a thing about their naming conventions."

Which was, Quirk thought, rather a shame.

"Right." Will was anxious to get back to his main point. "So what I was going to say is that Dathrax likes to fly around, survey all that he rules over."

"So," said Balur, "we are going to the island while he is flying around and we are stealing the gold then?"

"No." Will didn't even bat an eyelash as he shot the Analesian down. "The time frame doesn't work. Because now we know how long it takes to load a cart with a dragon's gold."

Six hours, Quirk knew. She'd had six glorious hours to examine Mattrax. Could she have longer here? If Dathrax lived alone, how many days would he have to miss his daily flight before his guards came to check on him? If he ruled by fear, as Mattrax had done, it could be a long time. She could brew up enough potions for days...

"Still," Will went on, interrupting her imaginings, "we can use that flight. When Dathrax goes out, he's looking for cows to eat. People to terrorize."

Lette smiled. "He eats cows. So we drug a cow. That makes sense."

"No." Will was authoritative even with Lette. He was starting to enjoy the position of power, Quirk thought. She should be more troubled by that. But the thought of that island, of that uninterrupted time...

"We can't know which cow Dathrax might choose," said Will. "And we can't drug every cow around the lake. It's just not possible. So what is the one thing dragons love more than cows, and power-mongering?"

He reminded Quirk of a professor, one who was really into the swing of a lecture, barreling along on a favorite research topic.

Balur opened his mouth.

"Gold." Will cut Balur off before he could speak, just as Quirk had expected him to do. "They want gold. If he sees gold, he'll go after it like a shot."

Silence met that. And to her surprise, Quirk found herself smiling into that silence, because there was actually some brilliance there. She could see it in Balur's look of horror, in Lette's moment of realization that she had let the reins out a little too loose, in Will's slowly spreading grin. It had cost him to get this far, but it would cost them too, and he knew it. He'd known this would be their reaction.

"We are giving him our gold?" Balur's voice actually sounded timid. Because they were all in on this. They had bet everything on Will.

"We are using our gold as bait." Will was merciless in his calm.

"When a fish is eating the bait," Balur pointed out, "you are not getting it back."

Will was still grinning. "Where will he take the gold? Back to his island. And where are we going?"

Balur perked up. "I am knowing this one," he said.

"But how are we getting there?" Quirk felt this point was still lacking clarity.

"Ah." There was a glint in Will's eye as he looked at her. Then his gaze moved to Lette. "Well, guess who's hidden among all that treasure, armed with Snag Weed poison?"

Balur opened his mouth, then closed it again.

Even Quirk felt her eyebrows rising. "You plan to hide among the gold?" she asked. It wasn't a hard concept to grasp. Just the thought of actually doing it...It was like tying your tooth to a door handle and then slamming the door. Everyone had heard of the concept, but who had actually tried it themselves? "You plan to have Dathrax carry you to his island himself?"

Will had the decency to look a little sheepish at that point. "Well..." he hedged. "Lette and I, actually."

Quirk managed to suppress the eye roll.

"What?" There was a growl in Balur's voice. The seeds of rage. "You are looking to steal another kill from me? You are looking to take my rightful glory?"

"No, no, no." For the first time in a while Will looked wrong-footed. "The reason it's only Lette and I that go...well it's two reasons. First off, she and I are small enough to fit in a treasure chest together. You aren't. And the second is that getting onto the island isn't the hard part."

"It isn't?" Lette seemed to be regretting her trust in Will more and more.

"The hard part," said Will, "is getting off it again." He looked at Balur and smiled. "Which is why I'm going to need you to steal the armored boat from that garrison."

# 34

# Dead Man's Chest

Lette had made many regrettable decisions in life. Asking a bandit prince, "You and whose army?" when she knew full well he commanded ten thousand men. That time she had dated a half-troll. Letting Balur cook. All of these she had put on her mental checklist of things-never-to-be-done-again-even-if-threatened-with-another-of-Balur's-curries. Still, given her chosen lifestyle, she thought she had done a good job of curtailing that list. Many of the people who shared her line of work had, over the years, not been half so prudent, and were now not even half as alive as her.

Yet even with all that experience, even with all the miles she had traveled, she was increasingly worried that this particular endeavor would be the final addition to her list.

The treasure chest rested in the center of a broad clearing. The best word Lette could summon to describe it was *considerable*. A construction of oak boards and iron bands, six feet long and five feet square at the ends. Some farmer had brought it with him, had held all his life's possessions in it. He'd stuck it in the bed of his wagon and almost broken his horse's back making it try to pull the thing. It had an aura of age. It was not so much battered as careworn. Some beloved family possession that could not be left behind. Initials were carved into the wood, rendered unreadable by time. And yet, when Will asked, it was handed over without question. All the farmer's belongings just emptied unceremoniously into the cart. The farmer had actually looked pleased. His wife kept on telling them what an honor it was. And both her son and daughter stood, staring up at Will with big mooncalf eyes.

Will had looked embarrassed by it at least, though not perhaps as much as he might have been a week ago.

Now he was bent over it, lost in his preparations.

"If this kills me," she told him, "I'm totally blaming you."

Will looked up, startled. He hadn't heard her approach. She shook her head. She was a lion among lambs, and yet she was the only one who appeared worried.

"It really shouldn't," said Will, as earnest as the day was long. "I've lined the chest with as thick a layer of cloth as I could get my hands on. It won't protect us from a really long fall, but it will definitely provide some padding. And the oak is at least three inches thick. Dathrax won't crush it when he picks it up. Not by Quirk's calculations. And Dathrax won't want to anyway. Balur and Quirk are going to arrange a bunch of stuff spilling around the edges. Necklaces, things like that."

The chest lay surrounded by their sacks of gold. A few had been opened slightly. Gold glinted in the sun. The sight of it caused Lette almost physical pain. They were going to give this up. Just give it away.

She knew why, of course. Rationally she understood that it was an investment. A way to double their payday. But it still left a deep sting in her soul. It felt like another bad decision.

"And what if someone else comes along?" she asked. "Someone who isn't Dathrax."

"Then Balur discourages them." Will had already turned his attention back to the chest.

Lette arched an eyebrow. She wasn't sure if Will realized exactly what Balur meant when he said "discourage." Part of her—most of her, if she was honest—hoped he didn't. She did not want to have corrupted Will so quickly. Didn't really want to corrupt him at all.

Abruptly she smiled. She had forced Will into the position of cult leader and criminal mastermind, but she didn't want to corrupt him. Gods.

Will had caught her smile. "See," he said, misunderstanding it utterly. "That's the spirit."

Her smile persisted. So adorable in his naïveté. She tried to temper the moment with rationality. "You're sure about leaving Balur and Firkin in charge of the crowd?" she asked. "Because you know how that went last time."

He shrugged. "They'll have Quirk with them this time."

Lette actually laughed at that. "Oh yes, because she's proven herself to be so stable."

Will didn't meet her eye. "I thought it might be best if Dathrax was unconscious before Quirk got on the island."

Perhaps not so naïve after all. Or at least becoming less naïve.

She was saved from following that path of thought further by the arrival of Quirk herself, her thaumatic cart trundling after her. "I think I've got everything you need," the thaumatobiologist said with a cheerful smile.

Cheer made Lette suspicious. In general, people seemed to find that response off-putting about her. But there were only so many leering grins you could see before you started to associate the upturn of lips with the need to separate a man from his manhood.

The thaumatic cart trundled to a stop beside Will. Quirk began to carefully unload glassware.

"What's that?" Lette said. Not that she didn't know the answer. But she was about to clamber into a confined space so that a dragon could toss her through the sky. The idea of adding fragile bottles full of powerful narcotics into the tumbling, eminently breakable mix did not fill her with a happy, buoyant sensation.

Lette followed her gaze. "Snag Weed potion," Quirk said. Then she twigged. "Oh, the glass, yes, I know. Not ideal, but it's what the university gave me."

There was so much nonchalance, Lette thought she might be able to pick it up and use it to throttle Quirk. Instead she restrained herself and said icily, "What if Dathrax drops us?"

"The padding," Will said. But even he didn't sound particularly convinced.

Lette nodded. "Wonderful. So now if I'm not smashed, crushed, or eaten, I also have the chance to be asphyxiated by potion fumes."

Will looked crestfallen. He turned his puppy eyes on her, but she found she just didn't care. Instead she pointed a finger at him. "Get some of your asinine followers to give up some waterskins now."

Quirk bristled. "You can't do that! These are people on the march. We can only get what we can scavenge from the streams we pass. Being able to carry water is critical to everyone's well-being."

Lette found the blade in her hand before she'd even thought Quirk's statement through. And it wasn't the words... It was something in the other woman's tone of voice.

*I've been waiting,* Lette realized. *Waiting for the moment when she snaps.*

And on the heels of that realization, another one. *I'm going to kill her.*

But not now. Quirk was looking at Will, appealing to him. And Lette didn't want to gut Quirk in front of Will. He still had a distance to go before he could accept that level of... practicality.

Will shrugged, kept fiddling with his cursed padding. "I don't really like asking them to give me anything. It feels too close to them paying some sort of homage. I think it enforces this mentality of me as champion."

"You mean the mentality that's stopping them from tearing

you apart as a fraud. Yes, I can completely see why you wouldn't want to reinforce that at every possible moment."

"It's taking advantage."

She tried to take a calming breath. "Your whole plan involves having Firkin use them to attract the attention of heavily armored guards in Athril. It's a little late to worry about exploiting them."

"They'll have Balur," Will protested.

Lette tried not to laugh out loud at that. "I think there's a chance you've misunderstood Balur's interest in keeping anyone but himself alive."

"I'll be there too." Quirk sounded like she couldn't quite decide if she wanted to be offended or not.

"You're going to barbecue their meat for them?" Lette snapped. "Or just them."

Something flashed in Quirk's eyes. Lette for a moment glimpsed real pain. The sort of look a man would give you as you separated the muscles surrounding his lungs and let the air inside him whistle out. And she was very glad in that moment that she had the blade in her hand. Because she was about to have to do exactly the same thing to Quirk. Probably while on fire.

Then Quirk spun on her heel and walked away. A moment later her cart trundled after her, a slightly apologetic manner to its swaying, as if it regretted the whole unfortunate confrontation.

"That was a little cruel," said Will, finally looking up from the chest. He was loading the glassware, she noticed. Did he know he had her on the back foot?

"She cares for that crowd more than she does for us." Becoming a better person or no, Lette was not at all interested in dying for the protection of any greater good.

Will shrugged. "She's only known us a few days longer than she's known any of them, and we can take care of ourselves."

Lette regarded the chest skeptically. She was decreasingly convinced of that.

Will followed her gaze. He grinned. "Come on," he said, "try it out with me." He put a hand on the lip, swung himself over to sit cross-legged.

Lette rolled her eyes, but she followed suit, landing opposite him. The space was not tight exactly, but it was not roomy either. And she was overly aware of the fragile glassware around them, potion trapped behind only the thinnest of barriers.

"Ah," cooed a rumbling voice from above, "be regarding the lovebirds who are snuggling in their nest."

"Balur," Lette said sweetly, "if I thought they were large enough, I would cut off your testicles to use as worry balls."

Balur nodded. "It is being your weird mannish hands. They make even the largest things look small."

Lette wouldn't have minded that insult if she hadn't seen Will snatch a glance at her hands.

"Well," she said, "if anyone is used to a man's hands on their balls..."

She didn't get to finish. Balur leaned over the chest, smiled as sweetly as a jaw full of fangs would allow, and slammed the chest lid down upon them. In the confined space, the sound assaulted them like a blow. Will curled up fetally, hands over his ears.

"It is time to be getting on," Lette heard Balur's muffled voice say. "Dathrax will be taking his afternoon constitutional soon."

The walls of the chest might be three-inch-thick bars of solid oak, but Lette was still convinced that her shout of "Arsehole!" was audible to him.

# 35

## Above It All

High in the sky above Athril's Lake, Dathrax spread his wings and circled. Thermals played like frisking lovers beneath him, bearing him up. The rutting of the winds. Yes, even the wind was base and low in comparison to him. He subjugated it rightfully, ascended it. He rode the wind as if it were his steed, his personal beast of burden.

A bird flapped past, insolently ignoring his superiority. He snapped it out of the air, a barely noticeable morsel. He hated birds. Pretenders to his—

He coughed violently. Sparks danced in the air.

Desperately he flapped higher. Up to the clouds. The clouds were nothing to him. Vapid vapor. He pissed on clouds. He pissed—

He coughed again. The feathers from the gods-hexed bird were caught in his throat, tickling him. With the cough came another flaccid gout of sparks. He twisted his neck, gave a flatulent bark of a cough. Feathers and a small black cloud sprayed from his lips. He flapped away from it furiously, disowning it.

He was not entirely sure when he had lost his flame. It wasn't something he used that often. When he was younger...oh when he was younger. He set afire to everything. When he and the rest of the Consortium had set their sights on the Kondorra valley—they had swept in heralded by a cloud of fire. The world had blazed before them, and they had blazed back. Not a tree had stood. Not a field been unscorched. He had been majestic,

potent, puissant. Sometimes when dignitaries came from neigh-
boring Vinland or Batarra his fire had simply burst out of him.
A great uncontrollable eruption. He had been known for it. His
fire had been the subject of conversations.

But then, somewhere along the way he had just not needed
it anymore. The populace was cowed and subjugated. The gold
flowed into his coffers unfettered, the path greased by fear and
habit. He had sat back upon his island, tossed cows down his
gullet, and enjoyed the simple pleasures of his hoard.

And somewhere in those rolling years of plenty, his fire had
fled from him. Smoke and sparks were all that were left to him.
If any of the others found out...

But they hadn't. They wouldn't. He was above them. Had
nothing to fear from them. They were nothing to him. He was
Dathrax. Flame was just a tiny facet of his armamentarium. His
teeth were like razors. His claws were gilded with the gold of
his enemies, and could unseam steel plate as if it were paper. A
single blow from his tail could crush a house. He was impregnable, unstoppable, undefeatable. He was Dathrax.

He coughed again. Another cloud of feathers came out. Bile
burned at the back of his throat. Nothing else did.

And so he went on, though truly all he wanted to do was to
go back to his island, and bury his head beneath a thousand
crowns.

And then he saw below him...

Could it be...?

Surely not...

And yet, spread out below him was...What was it? What
could it be? Some merchant's stash? The start of some robber's
hoard?

Whatever it was, it glinted like gold.

And whatever it was, it was his now.

He closed his wings, plummeted down from the heavens,
and went to investigate.

# 36

# Liftoff

"Sorry," said Will for what Lette was pretty sure was the four hundredth time.

"Look," she said, "I understand your desire to play the gentlemanly card as much as possible, it's a good look for you, but if you're going to apologize every time your foot brushes the glassware, I think it could get tired pretty fast."

*Could. Ha.*

"Erm..." said Will. "Sorry?"

"Oh shut up." Lette was glad it was dark inside the chest. She couldn't quite help the irresponsible smile that crept up onto her lips.

"You're smiling," Will told her.

Bastard.

"Only at the thought of the noises you'll make as I feed you your fingers."

If eyebrows made a noise when they were raised, Lette imagined she would hear that now. But all there was was silence. Silence, darkness, and heat. And the increasing awareness of Will's body close by.

"I've got to say," Will said then, "the angry and violent look is pretty good on you."

She let that lie there. Almost ignored it, because she didn't trust herself to respond to it. He was bold in the dark, was Will. She shifted her weight, brushed a foot against something.

"Sorry," she blurted.

Will laughed. Too late she realized that she had grazed the glassware.

"Shut up," she told him again, but couldn't quite muster her usual bite. She cursed again, more to herself than to him. He just kept on laughing, a low, steady chuckle.

It wasn't helping that it was so gods-cursedly hot in this chest. She shouldn't have put on her mail. Though the thought of lying in wait for Dathrax completely unprotected lacked any appeal whatsoever.

She shifted her weight again, felt her foot brush against something else, managed to hold her tongue.

"Actually," said Will, "that *was* me."

"Well, actually," said Lette, "I'm not sorry."

"I think I'd be sorry if you were."

Cois's hex on his balls, he was flirting with her. She was waiting to be plucked from the earth by a fire-breathing, death-dealing lizard, and he picked now as the appropriate time to finally find his confidence and start flirting with her.

She wasn't sure if it was guile, luck, or some innate savant tactical genius that allowed him to pick the perfect moment when her defenses were down. She closed her eyes. It made no difference. She was sitting in the bloody dark. She opened them again.

This was ridiculous. She was a mercenary, for crying out loud. She was the veteran of a hundred battles. She had killed far more than a thousand men. She had left a bloody trail through three countries on her way to this gods-hexed valley. Stories were told in hushed whispers of the destruction she had wreaked. If she wanted something, she took it.

Will made a sound, the beginning of some verbalization. He never got to finish it.

She uncoiled out of her cramped, cross-legged pose, unfolded past the glassware, to him, on top of him. Her lips pressed against his. They were soft, and his skin was rough, his stubble pricking her cheeks. She pressed up against him harder, swallowing his gasp.

Then, for a moment, her heart sank, as he lay there, momentarily stunned beneath. She was not worried that he wouldn't respond, simply that this was as breath-stealing as his response would be.

Then he rallied with force, his large, rough hands finding purchase on the back of her neck, in the small of her back. Her tongue snaked between his lips.

She had gotten his shirt unbuttoned—feeling the rough tautness of his chest, the hard nubs of his nipples—when something heavy slammed into the chest. The whole world rocked. Glassware shuddered. Gravity clutched loosely at her, and her gut flipped.

Will sucked in a breath.

"If you make a single comment," she said, "about the earth moving then this is all over."

He was silent as the chest rocked rhythmically. Could she hear wings flapping?

"I wasn't going to say that," Will said, sounding disappointingly nervous. "Though," and suddenly there was some life in his voice again, "I was going to introduce you to my dragon."

Lette decided she was going to enjoy this more if she shut him up with a kiss.

# 37

# Rabble-Rousing

It was being, Balur thought, a good day to die. It was being an even better day, though, for other people to do it.

He strode easily down the road, feeling the weight of his war hammer bounce against his back. The autumn sun was high above him, the fresh smell of Athril's Lake was in the air, and the promise of violence was before him.

The only grit in the oyster of his life was the crowd of three hundred peasants marching at his back. They kicked up dust. They muttered to themselves. And they detracted considerably from the clean smell blowing off the lake.

He looked over at Quirk. "I am knowing that Will is the mastermind, and all," he said, "but are you thinking that we could be doing all of this without this lot?" He jerked his head back in the direction of the followers.

Quirk didn't exactly grimace, but she didn't exactly smile either. "I'm not sure," she said, "that we get a say."

Balur grunted. He did not like that answer. "Will has been gaining power," he said, "very quickly, and without experience. Perhaps we should not be respecting his opinion." It was perhaps more than he should share with Quirk. Not that he had many others to share the insight with. And Quirk struck him as the practical sort, especially after what she had done in Mattrax's cave.

"I'm honestly not sure," she said, "that Will gets much of a say either. You know as well as I that he'd rather be rid of the crowd."

Not for the first time in his life, Balur wished he had an eyebrow to arch. What Quirk said was true. It was just not a very comforting fact.

Quirk seemed to get the idea anyway. "If they listen to anyone," she said, "they seem to listen to Firkin."

Balur chewed on that. "But Will is going to Firkin," he said, "and is telling him what to do. And then Firkin is being doing what Will asked him to do." Command, whether direct or by proxy, was command as far as Balur was concerned.

"Just because what Will wants and what Firkin wants are the same thing," said Quirk, "doesn't mean that Firkin is doing it *because* it's what Will wants." She let that sink in before adding the kicker. "The question is, what *does* Firkin want?"

Balur was liking that even less. Quirk was making it sound like a problem that could not be solved simply through the application of a flat metal surface to a curved bone one. Though perhaps if the curved bone surface happened to be beneath the skin of Firkin's forehead . . .

On the other hand, that would mess with Will's plan, and messing with Will's plan had not been entirely beneficial the last time around. In fact, Firkin not following Will's plan was largely what had led them to the point of having followers to be concerned about. So perhaps a little creative thinking on his part was not what the situation required at this moment.

In the end, Balur decided, he didn't really like any of the options before him, and so he reconsidered his attitude. Perhaps, after all, this was not a good day to die. It was just a very, very good one for killing people.

Athril was a large and bustling town. The lake stood at the confluence of several rivers, and if one skirted its edge, and avoided the territory of the Leviathans, then it was an entirely navigable stretch of water. Certainly the taxes imposed by Dathrax were obscenely high, but the taxes everywhere were obscenely high. And compared to Will's louse-ridden armpit of a village, Athril appeared positively metropolis-like.

The walls of the buildings were painted as often as they were whitewashed. People bustled through the streets too busy to pay attention to each other. Store owners called from the doors of shops—solid and with glass in their windows—rather than from rag-covered stalls. The occasional crowd of guards walked down the street, eyes watchful for all the mischief a cowed populace could summon.

Fishing vessels clustered on the shoreline, enjoying the safety of the shallows. Their owners sat in small groups mending nets and exchanging exaggerated stories. A crowded market square filled the air with a thrumming noise that was audible from the town center to the stockade wall, where at that moment three rather nonplussed guards were regarding Firkin, Balur, Quirk, and several hundred of their closest friends.

"You want to come in?" said one of the guards, as if he had never heard of such a thing, and as if his proximity to a gate were something entirely coincidental. He looked to his colleagues.

"I don't know," said one. "Dathrax never said nothing about no big crowds."

"He said not to let in no one suspicious," said the first. "I'm finding a crowd like this somewhat suspicious."

"You can't be generalizing just like that," piped up the third guard. "For example," he said, "that bloke over there is looking dead suspicious. But those two are just kids. I don't think no kids are suspicious."

"What if they're dwarves?" said the second. "I'm reckoning dwarves are suspicious."

"Now that's just open racism that is," said the third. "You can't just go saying that all dwarves are suspicious. Very diverse people. Lot of different outlooks on the world. Some are arse-holes to be sure, but some are lovely."

"He's into that short one over at the brothel," said the second.

"So what if I am?" said the third. "I have diverse tastes, I have. I'm a man of the world. Should try yourself a short arse, and see what you're missing."

Beside him, Balur noted, Quirk was clamping her lips together with considerable force.

"The problem is," said the second, "no one ever said what the definition of *suspicious* was. Open to too much subjectivity."

"No it's fucking not," said the first guard. "Subjectivity is the whole fucking point. You're a guard. A professional. You are paid to have a discerning eye in this arena. If you don't, you're not a guard, you're a fucking bystander."

"Now hang on, Joel," said the third guard. "That's a bit strong"

"I'm not sure it's strong enough," said Joel.

The second guard looked miserable. He fell back against the stockade wall, kicking at the dirt.

Balur opened his mouth to make a suggestion. That was as far as he got.

"So you're suggesting," said Joel to the third, "that we divide them up into two groups, one suspicious and one not suspicious?"

"I think we have to judge them as individuals," said the third. "It's the only fair way."

"That's just not practical, Frederick," said Joel.

Balur opened his mouth to contribute but once more they ignored him.

"In this case," said Joel, "I think you have to judge the crowd as a single unit. It's the only practical way."

"I," said Frederick, puffing out his chest, "am a man of princi-ple. And that principle supersedes practicality."

"Well," said Frederick, "I think we know then why I'm a captain and you're not."

"It's a corrupt system," opined Frederick.

"Not corrupt," said Joel, shaking his head. "Just an imperfect system in an imperfect world."

It was at this point that Balur punched all three guards in the head. One, two, three. They slumped to the ground one after the other, stacking up like logs for the fire. Balur leaned forward and pushed the gates to Athril open. He then stepped aside and let Firkin lead the crowd into the town.

Quirk looked at him. "Very gentlemanly," she said.

"Don't have to be being civilized to be civil," replied Balur, still looking down at the guards. Quirk's smile pleased him.

# 38

# The Worst-Laid Plans

A lot of people, Dathrax knew, envied dragons for their ability to fly. It had never made much sense to him.

Breathing fire? Yes, of course. There was majesty to that destruction. The long, savage claws? The sharp, inescapable teeth? Of course Dathrax could see the appeal of being able to rend one's foes limb from limb, and of fearing very little in return. Also, the long, sinuous body. That seemed an appealing trait. To not be bound down by the bulk of other large animals. The dragon's natural grace? Surely that was to be envied?

But flight? Dragging his majestic arse across the sky, slow painful wing beat by slow painful wing beat? All the running to take off, all the planning to land, the painful stretch of the muscles between his shoulder blades? No, Dathrax had never truly seen the appeal of that.

There was the gold, of course. People envied dragons for that as well. And Dathrax could see the appeal of that. Gold was beautiful. Gold glistened. Gold soothed the soul. Gold held him tight as he slept at night. It wrapped its caring arms around him and fed his soul as he faced all the trials and tribulations this life brought him.

If only gold wasn't so cursedly heavy.

Dathrax flew, and Dathrax was carrying a chest full of the gold he loved, but he increasingly wished that he wasn't.

All of which went to explain why Dathrax—when only

halfway to his island, but above his garrison of troops—let go of the large chest of gold and jewels he had been dragging home. It would, he decided, come to him along with the rest of his taxes at the month's end. He had enough to tide him over until then.

And so he flew on unencumbered, the chest plummeting down in his uncaring wake.

# 39

# A Sinking Feeling

Lette momentarily broke from Will's lips when she felt a lurch in her stomach. Was it, she wondered, her conscience finally kicking in? Her rational mind? She stared around, but of course saw nothing but blackness.

Will snaked his hand back behind her head, his fingers tangling with her hair. "Come back," he said.

"I'm fairly sure we're plummeting toward the ground," she said. She thought she should probably be panicking.

"A dragon's holding us," Will pointed out. "He's not going to crash. He'll just pull up." He attempted to distract her by sliding his hands down onto her arse. To be fair, it was rather distracting.

It was at that moment that the chest crashed down into the Athril's Lake garrison. Will and Lette survived thanks to the thick cloth padding that Will had painstakingly stitched to the inside of the chest. Quirk's vials of Snag Weed potion, however, did not.

Almost instantly, the chest was filled with glass, fluid, and fumes. Lette had only the opportunity to say, "Oh shit," before the fog filled her lungs, and she knew no more.

# 40

# Waiting for Gods

Balur did not like to think of what he was doing as lurking exactly. Biding his time perhaps. A tactical pause in activities... maybe. If one was feeling fancy. An opportunity to drink far too much... Well, that went without saying.

Through the window of the tavern, he saw that the sun had dipped down to meet the surface of Athril's Lake. Murky brown water was transformed to blazing fire.

It was not the only fire alight in Athril that night.

Balur had first ascribed Firkin's success as an orator to the fact that the citizens of the Village receiving his message had been completely out of their skulls. His subsequent success as a preacher on the road... well, perhaps that was being because of the serious trauma that affected those accompanying them. Witnessing the murder of your lord and master, even an abusive lord and master... That could mess with a man's head. Balur could be seeing that. And those who chose to flock to Will, and to listen to Firkin... Well, they had clearly been abused by the Dragon Consortium. Balur could see them not being of a mind to listen to reason, and perhaps preferring Firkin's particular brand of insanity. But Athril was different.

Athril was, for the Kondorra valley, affluent. Athril was bustling. Athril, he thought while knocking back the second half of his pint, had pretty good beer. And unless his mark was very much off its aim, those three women over by the bar making eyes at him represented a well-established red-light district. What in the name of the Hallows the people of Athril had to complain about, he could not see. And yet they flocked to Firkin like flies to shit.

It had started almost as soon as they were through the gate. Firkin had begun to work himself up into a lather. There had been deep breathing, the beating of his pigeon chest.

"Citizens!" Firkin had shrieked. "Countrymen! Fellow oppressed people! I bring you the word of the prophet!"

For their part, the populace of Athril had shown a surprising willingness to listen to this twaddle. They had laid down their daily wares and left the comfort of their homes and shops and come out to listen, muttering in what sounded a lot like assent.

Balur had immediately put some distance between himself and Firkin. Quirk, he had been pleased to see, had stuck close to him.

He was well aware of everything he had said about keeping an eye on Firkin, about the promises he had made assuring Will that things wouldn't get out of hand. But there was keeping your word, and there was sticking your neck out and asking for a sword to fall upon it.

Balur wanted to get rich, no doubt. He particularly wanted to get rich through minimal effort, and the thieving of gold from Dathrax. However, he did not see that goal as being mutually exclusive with the long-term survival of Firkin and the populace of Athril. If they wanted to get themselves all worked up, and all stabbed by a bunch of guards, well, that was fine with him. In fact, the more of the populace the guards were busy stabbing, the less likely they were to be stabbing him as he broke into their garrison.

That particular chain of events had not, it seemed, percolated into the consciousnesses of Athril's populace. To be fair, they didn't know Will and Balur were using them as a distraction to break into the garrison, but they still showed remarkably little concern about abandoning their daily lives and throwing themselves into full-blooded rebellion.

Balur had not been entirely sure what he thought of that. On the one hand, it was good that the plan was proceeding so easily. But what such behavior promised beyond the short term... Balur was not entirely sure about that.

Balur did not like the long term. Thinking about the long term generally seemed to involve not doing what one wanted to do in the short term. Thinking of tomorrow's hangover took the joy out of tonight's drinking. Thinking of tomorrow's itchy red rash took all the fun out of tonight's whoring.

Balur was a creature of action, and the long term often seemed to demand inaction. Therefore, Balur was of the general opinion that the long term could go fuck itself. But Firkin and Will—and the fervor they both seemed to generate—were forcing him to think about it.

To ease his discomfort, Balur slammed his fist down upon the bar. "Beer!" he bellowed. And then, in case that had been unclear, he added, "Beer!"

"Wouldn't it be easier," said Quirk from the seat beside him at the bar, "to go into this clearheaded?"

"Clearheaded?" asked Balur. He looked around the tavern. He cocked his head to one side. He could hear at least four conversations that included the word *prophet* going on at this moment. "If I was clearheaded, then I would be the only one in this town."

Quirk graced him with a slight smile. "Yes," she acknowledged, "but sardonic bravado aside, wouldn't be it be easier to break into the garrison if you were sober?"

"Sober?" asked Balur. The mental effort of trying to process that caused his face to scrunch up, eyes and nose swarming together. From Quirk's expression, he guessed she thought he was making light of her. But the idea had genuinely never occurred to him.

Liquid of any sort was precious in the Analesian desert. What liquids were available were rationed out in a manner largely determined by merit. Warriors merited fluid. And most of the fluids that the Analesians possessed were alcoholic.

Now, confronted with this new concept, Balur attempted to match his idea of sobriety to his idea of combat. The results were not appealing.

"No." He shook his head violently. "No." He said it again, hopefully this time with the emphasis he felt the words deserved. Just in case, he said it a third time. "No!" He shuddered. "You would do that sort of thing sober?" He looked at Quirk with horror. "You are being barbaric."

Quirk looked at him quizzically, then shook her head. Balur started to make significant inroads into his next pint. He cast another look to the tavern window. A man was running by. It took Balur a moment to realize that he did not have flaming red hair.

His head was on fire. He was pinwheeling his arms, and screaming as he ran past.

Balur narrowed his eyes. He had not been to Athril before, and the ways of humans were still, even after all this time, somewhat foreign to him. However, in his experience, setting fire to your own head and then shrieking in horror at the experience was not the sort of thing humans tended to do for fun.

The man disappeared out of sight leaving only a trail of dissipating smoke. Still, if Balur cocked his head to one side he could make out distant sounds of shrieking, and of large, important pieces of architecture breaking.

He switched his narrowed gaze to Quirk. "Are you hearing this?"

"I was rather hoping," said Quirk to the glass of white wine she had been nursing for the past hour, "that I might be imagining it."

Balur set his many teeth into a savage grimace. There was but one explanation. And when Balur found him he was going to kill him.

# 41

## Talking His Way into Trouble

Firkin was having fun. In fact, he had been having fun ever since they dosed the bread in the village. Truly it was difficult for him to remember the last time he had had this much fun. To be fair, he had difficulty remembering quite a lot of things. Including, from time to time, his own name. But he was fairly certain that his reduced circumstances had not allowed for this much fun in many a year. But here, now, praise be to all the whoreson gods in their mighty Pantheon, he was having so much fun he just might shit himself.

"Brothers!" he called. "Sisters! Very close cousins! Fathers! Mothers! Those who confuse the boundaries between them! The prophet has come!"

The thing he found utterly insane, beyond all possible reason, was that they listened to him. He could say pretty much anything that came into his head and they listened to him. All he had to do was tell them that the prophet had said it, or that the prophet was going to in a second, or that the prophet might say it someday soon, or that the prophet definitely hadn't said it but wanted it known all the same—and they listened.

"Tear down the old world! Toss out the old! Reclaim your truth!" They loved that one. He sometimes—often when being tended upon by young and nubile things—wondered what they imagined it to mean. Still, he thought as he watched a gaggle of teenage boys smash the windows in several stores and snatch goods into their pockets, there was little enough harm done. And the citizens, just like him, seemed to be having so much fun.

"Burn your wasted years! Set fire to the ashes of your history!" That one, he knew, definitely didn't make sense. You couldn't set fire to ashes. They'd already been set on fire. But nobody called him on it. No one told him to stop gibbering. Nobody called him an idiot. If he'd told them the prophet had said they should drown him in alcohol they would have complied. It was fucking brilliant.

"To the heavens! Mount to the skies!" That was a new one. He wasn't sure what they would make of it. It was fun to mix it up sometimes.

To the west, the dying light of the sun was being replaced by a new light as houses went up in flames. The heat rolled out across the streets toward him.

"Be reborn and usher in the new! Remake yourself in the prophet's image!" Across the street, at that very moment, he could see a man dousing himself in oil. He set a torch to his clothes and ran off screaming down the street, arms flailing, smashing into buildings, leaving a wake of fiery destruction behind him.

Firkin smiled. Yes, he was definitely having a tremendous amount of fun.

# 42

## Inferno Rodeo

Balur watched as guards poured out of the garrison. The light of burning buildings fought off the encroaching night.

"You have to admit," said Quirk at his side, "that he is very good at his job."

Job. Balur considered that word. It implied a level of professionalism. A certain mindset and dedication to one's cause. He would not have wanted to consider Firkin as a professional anything. The best that could truly be said for him was that he was an enthusiastic amateur.

That said, there was no denying that he was effective. It was just, Balur thought, that his enthusiasm seemed to also make him side-effective. And it was those side effects—side effects like men setting themselves on fire and running screaming through the streets—that had pushed him out onto the streets. Yet he was effective enough that Balur would yet again have to delay killing the old man.

He had no doubt that his regrets would be both plentiful and profound.

Still, with Firkin's distraction fully under way, Balur knew that he and Quirk were now to break into the garrison, steal the armored ship, and sail out to meet Lette and Will on Dathrax's island. What was more, the stream of guards leaving the garrison had slowed to a trickle. Balur could still see a few armored men standing behind the wooden walls of the garrison, but now they seemed pitiable and few.

"It is being time," he said to Quirk, hoisting his war hammer down from its clasp on his back. Quirk licked her lips.

"How many lives do you think have bought us this opportunity?" She was looking down at her hands. "It seemed so simple when Will said it. So clean and clinical. A distraction. Such a small, simple word. But what distraction really means is guards hacking down men and women in the street."

Balur nodded. Personally, he had thought that that bit was obvious.

"This," he said, "is seeming incongruous with your levity of a moment before?"

Quirk cocked her head to one side. "Incongruous?"

Balur fixed her with the same stare he liked to use on particularly cocky combatants. "Just because I am having a predilection for crushing skulls, is not meaning that I have not been having the time to improve my vocabulary."

Quirk shook her head. "I think it's a syntax thing."

Balur didn't let up on his gaze. "This is being another incongruity thing."

Quirk's answering smile lacked mirth. "Haven't you ever heard of putting a brave face on things?"

Balur shrugged. A man bleeding profusely from a gash on his forehead ran past bellowing.

"There is no need to be being brave," Balur said. "I am being confident in my ability to carve a path to the ship."

Quirk couldn't even muster a smile anymore. "That's what I'm putting a brave face on about, Balur. I'm a pacifist. My childhood was a fucked-up nightmare of murder and bloodshed. And I put that away. I became a new person. I became someone better. Just an academic. And now, just so I can go and pursue that new passion, just so I can escape my past...everything around me is turning into a nightmare of murder and bloodshed."

Mostly, Balur thought, it was low-grade vandalism and rioting, but he got her point. "Okay," he conceded, "that is being a bit fucked up."

Quirk let out a noise that might have been called a chuckle had it not sounded quite so much as if it had murdered all the other chuckles to ensure it was the one to escape. "No," she said. "What's really fucked up is that I'm okay with it. This doesn't bother me. Not the way it should. Just this..." She hesitated, screwed up her face, as if trying to force some expression to the surface. "...mild regret. Nothing sufficient for..." She swept her hand at the town. Yells echoed out, screams. At the far end of the street, three silhouetted figures were beating a guard to the ground. "...this. It's chaos. It's madness."

Balur nodded, feeling the grin spread across his face all of its own accord. "There is being something of a magnificence to it."

"Magnificence?" Quirk blanched. "Gods, you better be drunk."

Balur's grin stayed in place. "I am not believing that you have ever been seeing me wholly sober."

That shook her out of it, for just a moment at least. She blinked several times very rapidly. "I don't know if I find that comforting, or that I'm just more upset that I find that comforting."

At the end of the street, the figures finished beating the guard and moved on. Balur stepped out of the shadows he had been waiting in, and swung his hammer experimentally. "How about I am going and caving some heads in, and you are thinking about it."

Quirk looked away from him, then back, down at her own hands. She closed them, but clenched them only loosely. Then she shrugged. "I guess that's as good as it's going to get."

That was enough for Balur. He started to pace down the street toward the garrison. He swung the hammer as he went, letting its momentum transfer into him, its pendulum weight winding up the clockwork of his rage. He felt muscles loosen in his shoulders, the white rush of adrenaline in his veins, the sharpening of his vision. He licked the air, tasted blood, and sweat, and fear.

"Doesn't this…? Isn't there something about this…?" Quirk scampered along behind him. "There's something odd about this, right? I know things got out of hand back in the Village, but we were using the potions back then. Here…we haven't…I haven't…" She shook her head, plainly troubled. "Why are they acting like this?"

And, yes, it was a little odd. Balur had been thinking about just that. The people of Athril had leapt to violence with surprising alacrity. Had it been too quickly? Or was the populace's animosity toward the Dragon Consortium so great that it took but a single match to set the whole place aflame?

But only part of him was wondering that. A part of him knew that could wait until later. That could wait until his business with the town guard was done. The gates to the garrison were before him, and he was closing on them fast.

He let his war hammer knock for him. Boom, boom, splinter, crash. The gates flew wide. Guards wheeled around. Swords were drawn. But Balur was already upon them. His hammer descended. A skull cracked. A man fell.

"Kerunch," Balur muttered to himself.

A guard ducked inside the circle of Balur's hammer head. He had a short sword drawn. Three scars made horizontal bars across his face. He thrust the point of his blade at Balur's ribs. Balur shifted his grip, brought the hammer's head up, the handle down. His hammer's hilt smashed into the guard's nose. The man careened back, collided with one of his fellows. They went down in a tangle of limbs. Balur's hammer chased them down.

"Twofer," Balur said to the bloody mess at his feet.

Three guards circled nervously. Behind them, the rest of the garrison's numbers were thin. Reinforcements hung back, nervous about rioters finding other points of egress. Balur feinted one way. The guards fell back, nervous glances jumping between them like fleas. He swung experimentally with his hammer. Two guards fell back again, but one darted forward. Balur let go of his hammer with one hand and slammed his fist out, caught the guard around the neck. He hoisted the man aloft, hurled him at his fellows. Their retreat turned into a stumble. He showed them no mercy.

That was when the first arrow struck him.

It caught him in the shoulder, arcing in from the left. The point did not skitter off his scales, instead finding a soft spot at the juncture of three plates of his natural mail. He stumbled under the impact. Even over the cries and screams of the rioting, he still heard Quirk's inhalation of breath.

He turned, looked for the offending archer.

Arrows fell like rain. He cursed. Three archers at least. Perhaps four, or even five. He hesitated for a second, just long enough to take stock. Just long enough for them to pull new arrows from their quivers.

"Come on!" he yelled at Quirk, then dove for cover, running on all fours like a beast. He crashed into a wall, felt it sag under his weight. Arrows smashed into its far side. Quirk came running and screaming, crashed to earth at his feet.

"Knole's holy tits!" she screamed. "I thought we were meant to be sneaking in!"

"Well, now is being a good time to begin sneaking, I am thinking." Balur was aware of an irritated snap to his tone but didn't really care about it. "Or," he said, possibly a little vindictively, "maybe now is being a good time for you to be losing your shit and roasting all of those bastards alive."

Too far. A glance at her eyes told him it was too far. Not far enough to push her into rage, to push her into setting *his* arse on fire, but too deep to avoid hurt. Deep, base hurt.

"Fuck you," was all she muttered. But she was retreating, drawing in on herself, when she needed to be aware of the world, of everything, of all the pointy metal flying toward her head.

He took stock. The wall they were being behind would hold off the arrows, but it wouldn't be stopping the archers from circling around. They had to be moving, keeping their momentum. He poked his head up above the edge of the wall, got a quick sense of the lay of the land, ducked back down to avoid the three arrows racing toward his skull.

The garrison was built on the edge of the lake. Beyond them the ground sloped down and away toward a dock. Numerous low buildings were scattered between. Barracks, armory, canteen, storage huts. He could make out a few extra boats moored up at the dock.

He risked another look, felt an arrow glance off the top of his skull, score through a scale there, but he saw what he was looking for.

The heavily armored tax boat was surrounded by its own low stockade wall, spiked wooden pillars jutting up into the air. The boat beyond rose imperiously above them, an attitude mismatched to its pitted, rusted iron sides. Its prow was slung forward like an underbite, its cabin hunched low as if afflicted by some terrible curvature of the spine. The cloth of the sales looked greasy and stained.

Balur felt a strange affinity for it. It'd been built for power, and nothing else. It had a single purpose, a single focus. It would get its job done, beautiful or no.

Now all he had to do was steal it.

# 43

# A Burning Desire

The sound of arrows smacking into wood. The scent of burning flesh on the wind. The screams of women and children. Quirk closed her eyes and tried not to think of her childhood.

She had been seven when they came for her. Men on horses. Thick-limbed and savage. Their blond hair tied back in plaited ropes.

Those had been years of war, she had learned later. Hers was not an uncommon story. Many villages had been slaughtered. Many war bands vied for control of Tamathia's outer reaches as civil war ripped through the capital.

None of that knowledge made any of what happened to her any better.

They had killed her parents. Killed her friends. They had been about to kill her. She hadn't known telling them about her magic would save her. It was her habit not to tell people. Only her brother Andatte had known of it. Andatte—sweet, kind, beautiful Andatte. Two years older than she, so determined to protect her, to keep her safe from all the world. And it was he who had saved her from the horsemen's blades. It was he who had told them about the magic.

She still thought it would've been better if he had just let them kill her then.

She and Andatte had been cowering back against the wall of

the hut in which their mother and father had been killed. She could still remember the feel of the hot blood on her cheek. The coppery taste of it on her lips. She could still remember the way the stench of the horse's sweat had cut through the smell of the slaughter. The man leering down at them. Andatte throwing himself down upon his knees.

"She's been touched!" he had screamed. "The gods have touched her!"

The blade has hesitated in the air above him for a moment. The man's leer had switched from Andatte to her.

There had not been belief in his eyes.

"Show him." Andatte had turned to her, begging. "Show him or he'll kill us."

She had been scared of the magic even then. She had not understood it. What did it mean to be touched by a god? Why her? She had not wanted to show the man. She had never shown anyone. Had kept it hidden away. Her secret, her shame. Andatte only knew because he had spied. But she had not blamed him, because he spied only because he cared. And he cared now.

And so she had shown the horseman.

His shrieks had quickly drawn the others. They had found him, a living pyre atop a screaming horse. Quirk's palms had still smoked. The horsemen had drawn their swords, but approached more slowly, more hesitantly. When Andatte had pled her case to them, they had believed him then.

They were dragged to meet Hethren, the monster in charge of this slaughter. He was eight feet tall, covered in muscles and scars. A corona of divine power blazed around his head. A demigod. Some half-divine brat come to tantrum through her world. And there covered in gore, and mud, and the ash of the first man she killed, they were introduced. Scared as she was, she had lashed out with her fire. He had laughed as it washed over his skin, leaving blisters that burst and disappeared. He had clapped his hands at her, and put a knife to Andatte's neck, and made her kill another of his men. That was the beginning of the pattern.

Hethren had taken them both from that place, and he had broken them. When she killed his men, when she tried to break free, he rewarded her, and he punished Andatte. He had broken their will, broken their moral code, broken their humanity—torn it free from their guts.

She had trouble now remembering Andatte, as he had been. When he was kind and beautiful. Always the rabid horror of what he had become tore up through her memories. How Hethren had loved him. And he had loved to put the blade to Andatte's neck, so he could tell her to burn the world. But long before some farmer had driven a pitchfork through Andatte's stomach and torn the life and guts from him, she had not needed that encouragement.

She made Hethren strong. She had stopped trying to burn him, burn his people. She had made his whole tribe strong. She made them grow. She made the people cower in fear. She made them burn instead.

And then eventually, because of her, Hethren had burned too bright. It had been ten years. The civil war was long since over. Order was being returned to Tamathia. And Hethren had grown too large to be ignored.

He was hard to kill. A demigod of the grassy waste. A creature who healed faster than anyone could hurt him. But Tamathia did not send just one. They sent a troop of five hundred, and he could not pick the arrows out of himself fast enough. They had found him, a twitching mass surrounded by dying men, and they had hacked off his half-divine head. There was no healing that.

All told, the whole thing was a slaughter. She was supposed to have been killed along with the rest. But a mage, even a rabid, mindless mage such as her, had been too precious to waste. Instead they had bound her hands in smother rags, kept her in a barrel of water, and flung her in the back of a cart to drag back to the capital.

Six years it had been before they had taken the smother rags off her. Before they were sure she wouldn't try to burn them all alive. She remembered learning to use her hands again. The weakness in her fingers. Trying to grip her food. They still wouldn't give her a knife. It was another two years before they gave her that.

Eight years. Eight years to find her way back to herself. Eight years of quiet cajoling, of unwarranted kindness, of endless patience. Eight years of putting up with her violence, her tantrums, her rage, her unquenchable fear. It had taken eight years, but she had found herself. She had made her way back. And at the age of twenty-five she had been admitted to the Tamathian University.

Quirk blinked and was back in the present. *It would be so easy,* she thought, *to watch everything burn. To reach out and touch fire, the way the gods had reached out and touched her. These people were weak, and she was strong. In all rights she should burn them. That was what the world demanded, in the end. The sacrifice of the weak to the strong. That was what these dragons understood, creatures of fire that they were. They oppressed, because that was what the world demanded of them. And it demanded no less of her.*

That was what Hethren would say.

She thought she had silenced him, drowned him in the years and the academia. But she heard him now, his voice low and throaty, hovering somewhere between seduction and threat.

And he was right. It would be so easy. She could feel the flame tickling the backs of her palms, begging to be let loose. The flame spoke with Hethren's voice.

Which is why she took such pleasure in denying it. She would be better than that voice. Better than she had been. She was a professor at the Tamathian University. She was an ambassador of knowledge, and culture. And she would not retaliate. She would not escalate this madness. Instead she would indulge in her gods-given right to freak the fuck out.

"Shiiiiit!" she shrieked as she hurtled between the covering wall and a barracks ten yards away. Arrows thrummed through the air around her. She could hear them clicking off Balur's scales.

He crashed against the wooden wall beside her. Planks cracked and splintered. She spared him a glance. Not all the arrows had skittered off. Arrows peppered his shoulders and one protruded from his chest.

Her glance registered with him. He shrugged. The shafts of the arrows rippled. "Not deep," was all he said.

All of this. All of this so she could see a dragon.

And yet even as she tried to question her motives, a thrill of excitement ran through her. He would be out there now, the dragon, the beast. The fumes of her Snag Weed potion would have conquered his flames, laid him out. He would be lying there, waiting for her. Like a virgin on his wedding night.

This was her fire now. This was what she would bring to the world. Intellects would ignite, not bodies.

*And what if the world burns so you can get that knowledge?* Hethren whispered in her ear. *Better to cauterize the wound now. Staunch the flow.*

That had been one of his favorite games. He would slice Andatte's neck—not deeply, but just deep enough—and have her cauterize the wound.

"That's all you are doing," he would tell her just before he sent her stumbling into the heart of a village. "Just cauterizing a wound; stemming the flood of chaos. We are control, you and I. We are saviors."

But she never just cauterized. It was always a lie.

"Go!" Balur bellowed beside her. "Move!"

His arm sent her flying forward, catapulted down a muddy

track between low buildings. She tried to hunker down, but there was not enough cover in all the world. She could hear Balur grunting as the arrows struck him.

"We are still not sneaking!" she screamed.

Then he was shoving her sideways, back into cover.

"We are getting to that," he said, panting and bleeding.

She reached out, tentatively. "You can't keep on like this." She wanted to do something. To bind those wounds.

Like she had bound the wounds of the people she had then marched to this death trap.

Something was wrong with her. Very, very wrong. Something was still wrong.

"Am being okay," Balur grunted.

She tried to grin. "Just a flesh wound?"

He shook his head. "Being muscle mostly. Being painful, but not be doing much actual damage in the long term."

She opened her mouth, processed that. Just painful. He had to have at least twenty arrows protruding from him. "Oh," she said at last.

"Pain is being the thing that gets in the way of what we are needing to do. Pain is being up here." He tapped the side of his head. "What we are needing to do is being out here." He swept his arm at the shit storm of a garrison. "This is not being a time for being in one's own head. Now is a time for being out in the world. The time for being in one's own head will be coming later."

It was the most she thought she had heard him ever speak at once. Considering what was going on, it seemed an odd moment for him to choose.

He shrugged. "That is being all warrior code and bullshit. Analesians who cannot be killing enough people are talking too much. I am thinking it will be helping you now. Personally, though, I am not being bothered with the being in my head bit at all, and I am doing fine."

Quirk blinked twice. There was actually good advice in there. Perhaps now—with shouts pursuing them and arrows falling about their heads—was not the best time to plumb the shadows of her soul. Perhaps now was a better time to haul arse and try to stay alive long enough to contemplate her navel later.

"All right," she said nodding. Then, "Does this mean we can sneak now?"

"Yes," said Balur gruffly. "We are beginning to be sneaky now."

# 44

## God of War

Firkin sat back and took a moment to enjoy a job well done. The bleeding town guard he happened to be sitting back on groaned slightly. Firkin cracked a looted wine bottle on the back of the man's skull and he lay still. Firkin held the leaking bottle over his face, and let the wine trickle over his mouth and chin. It tasted good.

He was satisfied. "Go and preach my name in Athril," Will had told him, and preached he had.

"The prophet!" people screamed. In every street. In every town square. "In the name of the prophet!" The cry was borne forth from every corner of the town, carried on the billows of smoke from a hundred fires.

And the people shouting it even seemed to be winning. He hadn't really put much faith in the town rabble at the beginning of the fight. Not nearly as much as they had put in him. But over the course of the past few hours they had slowly made a believer out of him.

He knew the people were angry. He had heard every iteration of their story. Stolen livelihoods. Stolen lives. He had heard every nuance of their rage. But he had not seen how that could overcome actual training and sharp steel.

In the end, though, it was simple. The Dragon Consortium had ensured the subjugation of these people by making sure they had nothing to live for. But now, with the idea of the prophet burning bright in their minds, they had something to die for.

They hurled themselves at the guards. They blunted blades with their bodies. They swarmed and overwhelmed. They attacked with a ferocity that not even Dathrax with all his wealth could afford to buy.

Firkin had watched a tavern cook throttle a guard with her own braid, even as he hacked at her arms with a short sword. He had seen six men kick a heavily armored guard to death, and only one had been able to walk away. He had watched men set themselves on fire and charge into guard towers never to emerge.

For the prophet.

Not for Will. No. No one screamed Will's name. It was for the prophet.

He felt the shift in the city, the change in the power balance. The guards felt it too.

"Retreat!" shouted their commanders. "Fall back! To the garrison!"

And suddenly the town's citizens were standing in empty streets. Were pushing forward with no resistance.

For a moment, he felt them stumble, and he felt them hesitate. He stood up, started running, started shrieking.

"Forward!" he screamed. "The prophet commands it! He commands you to take this town! He compels you to strike down your enemy!"

And they did it. Not for Will. But because it was the word of the prophet. Because the voice of the prophet told them so.

And, running through the streets, potbelly swaying with the weight of the wine in it, Firkin smiled.

# 45

## What's in the Box?

Everything was chaos. Everything was confusion. Guards were running every which way that they could, shouting, desperately calling out for information. Smoke was everywhere. Those who had ventured into the town seemed to be retreating, but no one inside the garrison knew from what.

This sort of thing totally gave Balur a hard-on.

He stroked at the frills of his neck self-consciously, and hoped Quirk was too focused on avoiding imminent death to notice.

They crouched in the shadow of the armored tax boat. A guard ran past, did a double take, opened his mouth, and died as Balur jammed the claw of his thumb through the man's Adam's apple.

"Almost there," he whispered.

Quirk nodded. She seemed to have pulled herself together a bit since he had given her his little pep talk. Motivational speaker—Lette had never suggested that career path for him. That was showing a lack of foresight on her part. Still, if she had, he might not have been ending up here, about to line his pockets with the gold of two dragons.

He wondered what she was doing now. Hauling sacks of gold down to the island's coast, he hoped. Not getting too preoccupied with the bulge in Will's britches.

Though perhaps a good tumble in the grass next to an unconscious dragon would get her head straight again. Off all this "better life" crap, and back on track with the good thing they had going. Get back to being each other's tribe.

He took that anger and put it into launching himself onto the armored boat with a roar. He caught the rail, heaved himself up one-handed, feet clearing the boat's sides with ease. They smashed down on the wooden deck with the crack of splinters.

A ballista was mounted upon the deck's boards next to the spot where Balur had landed. A lone guard stood there, pointing it off over the surrounding garrison. He started, squeaked, then began to haul the massive siege crossbow around to face Balur.

"Do you really think that's going to work?" Quirk asked the guard, as she bodily heaved herself up behind Balur. "I mean really?" She pivoted herself over the edge of the boat, half-tumbled to the floor. She looked at the guard from where she sat. "He's got to walk about two paces before he drives you down to the harbor floor with his hammer. Just jump overboard and try to survive till the morning."

Balur turned round and furrowed his brow at her. She was spoiling his fun.

Fortunately the guard—a skinny redheaded fellow, whose face was spattered with freckles like bloodstains—seemed to take this as an invitation to haul once more on the ballista.

Balur took three steps—not two—and backhanded the guard into oblivion. His limp rag of a body sailed over the ship's rail and landed with a wet crack.

Quirk grunted. "Well, at least I tried to save one."

Balur nodded. "I am thinking we can call your conscience spotless."

Quirk stared at him for a moment. "I can never tell if you're being sarcastic," she said.

Balur didn't bother to let her know; instead he turned and set off to find the mooring ropes.

He was happily experiencing great success in this task when

Quirk took it upon herself to interrupt him with a shout of "Knole's tits!"

Considering that the goddess of knowledge was generally considered an asexual creature and that nobody was currently trying to kill them, this exclamation gave Balur pause. First he double-checked his assumptions. No—Knole had not descended from the heavens to earth and proceeded to get busy with anyone. Neither had any of the guards appeared to have noticed their presence yet. Instead the garrison's defenders were still largely preoccupied by the mass of deranged rioters trying to claw their hearts from their bodies.

These eventualities accounted for, Balur went to investigate. It did not take long and concluded with him barely managing to breathe out the words, "Knole's sweet apple arse."

Next to the pilot's cabin was a set of stairs down into the hold. And at the base of those steps was Gold. Not just gold, but *Gold*. Sacks upon sacks of it. Sacks stuffed so full that they ripped and coins burst eagerly forth. Coins so deep a man could wade through them. Coins that filled the full length of the boat's not inconsiderable hold.

"The hoard?" he breathed. "Here?"

Quirk shook her head. "No. It can't be. If the hoard was here, then Dathrax would be here. Dragons sleep with their hoard."

That exhausted the depth of Balur's guesses. "So…?" He tried to turn to her, but had trouble taking his eyes off the gold.

"It's the taxes," Quirk said. "This is just one year's taxes. Dathrax lets it collect here all year before the guards take it to his island."

Balur felt his eyes growing wider. Wider. "This is being just one year's worth?"

Quirk nodded.

"And the Dragon Consortium are being in power for how long?"

"Thirty years at least."

Balur let his tongue taste the air. Let the flavor of all that gold wash through him. He felt his neck frills extend almost painfully. He did not care.

"Oh," said Quirk, looking at his neck. "I didn't know you could do that. They're pretty." Which, all in all, did not help. Balur buried his face in the one sack, inhaled deeply.

Something caught at the back of his throat. Something familiar. He cocked his head to one side, sniffed the sack again, scenting deeply.

"Quirk?" he said finally.

"Yes?" She had wandered deeper into the hold.

"Why is this sack of gold smelling of Lette?"

Quirk's finger had been tracing the latticework of a large chest half-buried in the center of the room. "Because..." she started, then trailed off. "Are you sure?"

"Lette is being my tribe," he said with impatience. "I am thinking that I would be recognizing her scent."

"Are..." Quirk started, then stopped. "Couldn't..." She looked around them, as if expecting to see Lette leap out from one of the chests and shout, "Surprise!" She scratched at her short brown hair. "Might one of us have brought the smell in? We hang around with her."

Balur shook his head. He could smell the way Lette's scent mixed with his own, with Quirk's. This was not that. This was distinctly and definitively Lette.

He looked around, trying to figure it out. But she was not here.

"Oh fuck." Quirk said.

"What?"

"It's our gold," Quirk said. "It smells of Lette because it's *our* gold." She sat down heavily on the large chest whose scrollwork she had been tracing. "Because Dathrax didn't bring it to his island. He was too lazy a bastard, and he brought it here to his garrison so they could bring it over for him. That's why the boat's so full. Because it's full of Mattrax's gold. Not just his year's taxes. Oh shit. Oh god fuck."

Balur looked around, all his happiness hemorrhaging away, and bleeding out around his feet.

"Then…" he said, trying to put it all together. "What about Lette and Will? How were they getting to the island to knock out Dathrax?"

"Ohhh…" Quirk dragged out the word, adding horror in increasing waves to the sound. "Ohhhhhhh…"

She stood up, stared in horror at the chest she was sitting on.

"What?" Balur asked. The tension was killing him.

"The chest," she said. "Inside the chest."

Still it eluded him. "What?" he asked. "What's in the chest?"

# 46

# Open Your Eyes

Will had been having a rather pleasant dream. It involved him, Lette, and a fairly promiscuous cheddar.

Being slapped awake made for a rather disappointing finale.

"Uh?" he said groggily to the blurry figure holding him by the scruff of his neck. "We there yet?"

"No!" bellowed Slappy Slap-Pants, and Will found he'd been hit in the face again.

Balur came into sharp focus. He dropped Will. Will landed hard. His mouth felt like it was full of blood, and his head full of bear shit. He groaned, spat, and took hold of his temples.

He said, "What's going on?" Except it sounded like, "Wha-suh-guhn?"

Balur provided no answers. He had moved on, was holding someone else aloft, was slapping them.

Lette. It was Lette.

Will tried to put the pieces back together. There had been a plan. There had been a plan because they had been planning something. Something...

Gold. Stealing from Dathrax. Stealing his hoard.

He became aware that he was sitting on a pile of gold. Which suggested that must be going fairly well.

He tried talking again. "What's going on?" It came clearer now.

Quirk looked at him. "Why in Knole's holy name do I listen to you?" she asked. It seemed rhetorical, which was lucky because

Will really wasn't up to answering her. "We're still on the boat, Will," she said when he failed to respond. "The fucking boat!"

A boat. That meant his plan had involved a boat...

Lette landed with a thud beside him. Balur stood over her looking mildly disgusted. She rolled a sleepy head bearing a bewildered expression in Will's direction. "Wha-suh-guhn?" she asked him.

And then it came back to him. All of it. The whole plan. The idea that he should be on an island with a drugged dragon right now. That he should not have been heavily sedated. That Quirk and Balur should be on this boat alone, piloting through monster-infested water to him. To gold.

He stood up, adrenaline burning the last of his stupefaction. "Are we on the lake?" he asked. "Did you get out of the town?"

"No!" Quirk almost shrieked. "We only just got on board and found you and all our gold here."

*Their* gold. Will tried to fit that to the known facts.

"Oh fuck," he said, as the pieces slotted home. "That lazy fucking dragon." Dathrax hadn't taken them across the lake. He'd dropped the gold off at the garrison for them to transport.

Dathrax.

"Oh shit." He looked up, stared at the others' faces.

"What?" Lette asked, apparently having failed to develop telepathy while she was unconscious.

"Dathrax," he said. "He's still conscious."

Lette shrugged. "So? We haven't done anything to attract his high and mighty bullshit attention." She yawned.

But Will was looking at the glance Balur and Quirk were exchanging. Lette followed the direction of his gaze. "What?" she asked. Then again into the awkward silence, "*What?*"

"So..." Quirked resumed her nervous pacing. "About that..."

# 47

## Where There's Smoke...

Lying, replete, upon his island, Dathrax raised his head. There was a strange smell upon the air. He was having trouble placing it.

He had been thinking about Mattrax, about what had happened to him. Dathrax had never liked Mattrax. He wouldn't have called him a rival exactly—that would have acknowledged that he and Mattrax existed in the same league as each other—but of the other members of the Consortium, Mattrax was the one with whom he had interacted the most often, and the most acrimoniously.

In many ways he should be celebrating Mattrax's death. They had had a number of competing trade agreements with Vinland and Batarra. And Dathrax's highly profitable grape trade route had been consistently, even suspiciously, plagued with bandits where it had run through Mattrax's territory.

The problem was the manner of Mattrax's death. If he had choked on an ox bone, or found some particularly inventive way to die of gout, if he had been crushed by the weight of his own stash of gold...well the merchant guilds of Vinland and Batarra could have understood that, respected it even. Death by indulgence was something they all secretly wished for as an epitaph. But Mattrax had not had the decency to die that way. As he had been in life, Mattrax was an insolent son of an iguana slut lizard.

A popular uprising. It was almost enough to make Dathrax spit fire.

Almost...

This prophet. This popular fucking hero. They kept raising the price on his head. By the Hallows it was almost so high that he would consider hunting down the human stain himself...

Dathrax snorted at his own joke. Two pathetic wisps of smoke rose from his nostrils, withered in the evening breeze.

Smoke...

That was what he could smell.

And smoke meant...

But he couldn't...Well...he could. He just...He had a sore throat, probably. He would be breathing fire in no time.

Dathrax was up on his feet. Sniffing the air, trying to trace the scent. Had one of the others in the Consortium found out about his *temporary* problem? Were they all holed up in the Hallows' Mouth volcano mocking him?

He scrabbled up one slope of the earthen bowl that contained his hoard. Coins and crowns shifted beneath his feet, making the going hard. He spread his wings, beat once, rose up into the air, scanned the horizon.

And there, a red smudge on the horizon, in opposition to the setting of the sun: Athril itself. His stronghold. The seat of his power, his garrison, the home of all his gods-fucking-cursed taxes.

His town burned. Its smoke drifting to him across the water.

Curling his lip, Dathrax beat his wings, and went to rain down hell on whoever dared to disturb his evening's repose.

# 48

## Far, Far Too Late

Will emerged from the ship's hold into a world of flame and chaos.

"Gods' hex," he whispered. "What did you do?"

Athril was a burning shell of a town. Ash, smoke, and screams rose in equal measure. All around the garrison, guards and townspeople were twisted in thrashing, bleeding bundles of struggling limbs.

"It was Firkin," Quirk mumbled.

"You were meant to be in charge!" Blame and horror were probably not the most helpful things to add to the situation, but Will couldn't contain them. He just couldn't. He couldn't believe this situation.

*Again.* Again everything had gone to shit. What had he been thinking? How had he allowed Lette to talk him into this?

He looked at her. He saw his own look of horror in her eyes. Her lips made a small round O of shock.

Those lips...

That distracted him from his bewilderment for a moment. And no, he could not blame Lette. Not even if she did deserve some of it. He had known he didn't know what he was doing. But he had gone ahead and laid out his plan anyway. Even knowing how many lives were on the line.

Gods...How many bodies lined Athril's streets tonight? How many deaths was he responsible for?

"This isn't a town," he whispered. "This is a fucking funeral pyre."

Beside him, Lette shook her head. "No. It's worse," she said. "It's a signal beacon to Dathrax that someone is screwing with his turf. We have to get out of here before he notices. Before he comes and roasts us alive."

Gods, yes. She was right, Will knew. But he couldn't move. He was paralyzed by the enormity of this disaster.

"Come on." Lette grabbed his arm. "We have to move before it's too late.

"Hrm," Balur rumbled. "About that..."

# 49

# Dragons Come Home to Roost

"Oh," Quirk breathed. "Oh." A sigh. An exhalation of breath to make room for her expanding wonder.

She watched as Dathrax swept in over the waters of Athril's Lake.

He was majestic. He was a piece of the heavens peeled away from the sky and brought to life. His wingspan was as wide as a palace. His scales were the color of warming coals—charred black brushed with a deep burning red. His claws were the gray of polished steel, his teeth the yellow of old parchment. He rode the thermals over the lake like a king rode his charger to war. His sinuous tail lashed the air. Scales rose like the dorsal fins of a fish along his back. His head was massive, the size of an oxcart, the vast jaw occupying almost all of its length.

And his eyes. His burning bright eyes.

For a moment she believed their gazes met. Across the distance and the waters. Like lovers at their first dance. She felt his gaze boring into her, peeling away the layers, the carefully constructed armor of academia, of morality, of humanity, until she was just a flame dancing in the mote of his eye.

But she was not alone in this nakedness of the soul. She saw him too. He shared his nature with her, in that brief but oh-so-eternal moment. She saw the fire in him as well. The bestiality, yes, but the majesty too. He ruled this valley because that was what he was. He was a ruler, a king, the apex of creation.

And then he roared.

She couldn't breathe. She gasped. There was no room in her left for oxygen.

The sound thrummed through her. Every part of her was alive to it. His roar was the unheard music of her soul.

She tried to capture everything, commit every tiny detail to memory. The number of his teeth. Their estimated length, diameter. The breadth of his wingspan. The bones in each one. How they articulated against his back. The shape of the muscles working as he reared up at the shoreline, as he hung suspended in the air for a moment. How the fat deposits hung from the space below his rib cage. Even the dragon's paunch was magnificent. Its size. Its audacity. Its grandeur.

She tried to catalog these moments. To capture them now as she would capture them later.

Around her she could hear people screaming, people dying. People she had cared for, had struggled to keep happy and healthy on their journey to this place. And she did not care. Everything was eclipsed by this moment.

"Beautiful," she breathed. "He's absolutely beautiful."

Dathrax crashed down on the outer wall of the garrison, rear claws pulverizing the wood that he grasped. The wall struggled, sagged, collapsed.

Dathrax landed heavily on all fours.

"Meh," said Balur, standing almost forgotten at her side. "He is a fat fucking lizard, and he is going to die."

# 50

# Taking Flight

*Well,* thought Will, *this is it. This is how I'm going to die.*

Dathrax roared again. Guards and citizens quailed. A circle of desolate ground opened up, as if blasted clear by the force of the dragon's rage. People tripping in their haste to flee. Dathrax, bent, shoveled them up into his massive jaws. He bit down. Bodies exploded beneath his teeth. Organs were forced out between bones by the strength of the bite, flying through the crowd like bloody shrapnel.

And then, still, madly persistent in the wake of Dathrax's roar, voices rising up. "The prophet! The prophet!"

*Shut up,* Will thought desperately. *Stop saying my name.*

Dathrax advanced through the decimated garrison. People fled. He barked, and snapped, and roared. He bit through the corners of barracks. Blades shattered beneath his teeth.

*Why doesn't he just set us on fire?* Will wondered. He kept waiting for Dathrax to rear back, to see the light at the back of his throat. He was braced for a fireball that just wasn't coming.

They had to do something. Attack was futile. There was nowhere to hide. That left running.

"A boat!" he shouted. "We're on a boat!"

"Yes." Balur nodded calmly next to him. "That is being correct."

Will turned and punched him. His fist collided with something that felt like a cliff face. He bit back on his grunt of pain in order to bellow, "Cast off you, fucker!" instead. "Get us out of here. Out on the water."

Balur creased his brow. "Why?" He sounded genuinely confused.

"Oh," Will said through clenched teeth, "I don't know. It just, you know, seemed absolutely fucking essential to the bit where we run away with all the money and don't fucking die!"

Balur look hurt in a way that Will's punch had failed to achieve. "But I am wanting to kill it." He pointed at Dathrax.

Will nodded. "Okay, you stay here and do that while the rest of us run away." He looked to Quirk and Lette. "Sound like a plan?"

"Absolutely." Lette was already moving toward one of the mooring ropes.

Quirk just stood staring at Dathrax. Panic, Will assumed, had robbed her of her senses.

"Hey!" Balur still looked hurt. But Will was too busy moving away from the pilot's cabin and toward the mooring ropes to pay that much heed. He reached the first one, started to uncoil it from around the mooring post. A moment later Lette was there. She hacked through it with her short sword. The rope fell away.

"Here." She held the sword out to him. "Take this."

It was Will's brows' turn to furrow. "Why?"

Lette cuffed him lightly. "All the obvious fucking reasons."

Dathrax was closing the distance. Whether he had truly spotted them, or if the gods were just pissing on Will from all the way up in the heavens, he wasn't sure, but the end result was the same. They would die very soon unless they got the boat moving.

He used Lette's short sword to hack through another mooring rope. Lette was on the other side of the boat using her broadsword to set them loose.

Will hacked at another line. It severed with an audible snap. The boat lurched beneath him, settling more firmly on the launch ramp. It began to slide toward the water. Slowly at first, picking up speed. The pitted steel hull screamed against the rough stone.

And then with a crash of spraying water, they hit the lake, were free of the ramp, and were sliding through the water. Above Will, sails suddenly snapped taught. He looked up, saw Lette flinging herself through the rigging, snapping lines tight, looping knots.

He breathed fully for the first time since standing upon the deck of the boat. They were getting away. They had a hold full of gold, and they were getting away.

Gods, they were even getting away from Firkin and the crowds of worshippers.

It might not have worked perfectly, not by any stretch of the imagination, but it had worked enough.

Balur strode up to him. "I am still objecting to this fleeing nonsense. I am not liking to be turning and running."

Will just shrugged. He was not giving a shit what Balur liked.

"Oh," said Quirk, still standing at the edge of the boat, still staring back at the shoreline. "I wouldn't worry about that."

Will turned, blanched.

A roar reached out to them across the water.

Dathrax, wings spread, was rising up from the ruins of Athril, and giving chase across the lake.

# 51

## Totally Fucked

*Okay,* Will thought to himself. *This time we are definitely going to die.*

"Ballista!" The scream came from above. Will looked up again. Lette was descending through the rigging as fast as it was possible to do without just calling it "falling."

"Get to the fucking ballista!" she yelled, and even managed to point, though Will couldn't work out how that was possible unless she'd had a third arm all along and just failed to mention the thing.

He decided to hold that question for later.

Instead he spun, saw the series of three ballistas lined up along the side of the boat. One even had a bolt loaded, a thick rope stretched taut behind it, ready to fling the spear-size bolt into the heavens.

Or potentially into the underbelly of the enormous flying death-beast that was chasing them down.

He scrambled toward the war machine, took hold of the massive stock. It was mounted on a steel column, able to pivot both vertically and horizontally. In a calmer moment, Will might have taken the time to be impressed by the workmanship and ingenuity. Or possibly to be disgusted by the fact that Dathrax would shell out top coin for something to defend his tax barge, but would leave the citizens beholden to him squatting in squalor. But things were not calm. So instead he screamed, "Fuck you!" and loosed a bolt at the beast.

The whole ballista lurched in his grip. A great thrumming spasm that ran up his hands and made his teeth click. His feet skittered across the deck.

The ballista bolt flew, arcing up into the night. Firelight glinted off its steel tip.

It fell twenty feet short of Dathrax. The dragon screamed, swooped up, heading out of range, preparing for a plunge.

"What is it you are doing?" growled a voice in Will's ear.

"I'm sorry," Will babbled. "I didn't know the range. Lette was saying... I thought she meant—"

He was cut off by Balur's powerful hand slamming into his chest, sending him to the floor.

"You are trying to steal my kill!" Balur roared.

Will's head sang ribbons of light and pain through his skull from where it had hit the deck, but he still had the wherewithal to think, *Oh for fuck's sake.*

"We are meeting the beast on the deck. Like men," Balur growled. "We are seeing then whose mettle is being a match for it. Then I shall be seeing if you can truly back up the claims of your followers."

"I never said I killed the dragon!" Will screamed, intimately aware that he was moments away from being killed *by* a dragon. "I tried to explain that to them very clearly. They won't listen."

"Dathrax is being my kill!" Balur roared. "You are not to be stealing it from me."

Beside them there was another cracking twang as a second ballista bolt shot into the heavens. Will and Balur snapped their heads to stare.

High above, Dathrax screamed.

Lette stood there, cranking the rope back into place while Quirk fit another bolt back into the groove of the barrel.

"Here's a suggestion," Lette said, without looking at them. "How about you two put your dicks back in your britches and actually help out."

Will felt his eyes go wide. *"My* dick. I didn't..."

Dathrax screamed again. And then the sound of beating wings dropped away. And then Will had more important things to do than protest his innocence.

Dathrax dropped like a piece of flaming midnight. Rage, and claws, and jaws that opened like the gates of the Hallows. The pilot's cabin exploded into splinters. Dathrax slammed through it, claws outstretched.

*Piloting,* thought Will. *One of us should have been doing that.*

He would have loved to have followed that up by thinking it was the first time their incompetence had saved them.

Dathrax shot off, launching himself back up into the night. Within moments his massive bulk was just a shadow in a night sky.

Will stared in horror. The devastation had been so absolute and so abrupt.

"He's trying to cripple the boat," Lette called. She was leaning back on the stock of the ballista, angling it up as steeply as it would go, hunting the heavens. "Kill our maneuverability. Someone get us to open water. Somewhere we can move."

"Let him be coming!" Balur bellowed. "Let him be tasting my hammer in his throat."

"Shut the fuck up and steer!" Lette yelled.

"I'll do it." Quirk went to dart away.

Balur caught her by the shoulder. "No," he growled. "Burn him. Set him alight in the dark."

This was a double standard slightly too far for Will. "She's allowed to try and shoot at him in the sky, but I get punched to the floor?" His ribs still ached from where Balur had pushed him.

No one seemed interested in joining him in his outrage.

"No," Quirk said. She was staring at the ruined pilothouse. "I won't do it. That's not who I am anymore."

"We need to see," Lette said from behind her. "We're blind. We need to know where he is so we can shoot him."

Quirk still stared into space. She muttered something.

"What?" Lette said.

But Will had heard her. She had said, "He's majestic." He wished he hadn't heard it, but he had.

He was saved from working out what to truly think about that utterance and its implications by the dragon himself.

Dathrax dropped, shrieking out of the night. He smashed into the front mast. The massive pillar of oak shattered like so much kindling beneath his claws. Rigging snapped, whipped the air. Sails flapped like writhing bodies. And then the mast was smashing down onto the deck, flipping end over end toward them.

Balur bellowed, released Quirk, sent her flailing toward the edge of the boat, as he flung himself backward, sprawling back down the steps leading to the hold.

"Cois's syphilitic cock!" Lette screamed.

Will stared as the shattered mast plunged down the deck toward them, digging a furrow through the decking. A ballista was flung away into the waters. The air was full of shrapnel.

He dived toward Lette. She was hauling another of the ballistas, trying to line up a shot. A tangle of wood and rope was barreling toward her head.

Will collided with her just as she fired. The ballista bucked. Will's shoulder crunched into her midriff, sent her skidding. Wood smashed against the cross arm of the ballista, leapt up into the air. Will and Lette landed with a crunch. The bolt arced into the heavens. Ropes slashed the air above their heads.

Dathrax screamed. Not rage this time, but genuine pain.

Beneath Will, with satisfaction in her voice, Lette said, "Up your fucking arse."

Will pushed to his feet, reached down a hand toward Lette, but she was already halfway up, ignoring it.

The ship was a mess of tattered cloth and limp ropes. The second mast bent at an odd angle.

"Shit," Will said. "We'll just be sitting here." He could see Dathrax in his mind's eye, lining up a run on their blind side. Circling above, picking out their positions. While they sat there and waited.

"All right, all right. I be fucking going to steer." Balur's feet pounded toward the ship's wheel. It stood solitary and sullen in the tangled mess that had once been the pilot's cabin.

"Help me load another bolt!" Lette was already cranking back on the ballista. Bolts lay scattered on the ground. The war machine itself was still tangled in the detritus of the shattered mast.

Quirk stood silent, still, staring.

There wasn't time to snap her out of it. Will lunged for one of the ballista bolts, seized it up. He tried to fit it into the groove along the war engine's barrel, but too much half-smashed wood was in the way. He clawed at it, clumsily, off-balance as he tried to grapple with the weight of the bolt. It was as thick as his arm, over four feet in length.

"Come on!" Lette snapped. She was searching the skies. Will glanced up.

"Where is he?"

Quirk mumbled something else behind him. He had neither the time nor the inclination to decipher it this time.

"I can't see him." Lette was panning the ballista back and forth, as Will desperately tried to set the bolt in the barrel.

"Come on," he muttered to himself. "Come on."

A single solitary flap of wings. The muffled clap of giant leathery sheets of skin. Nothing else, but distinctive enough to focus all of Will's attention.

The sound did not come from above them.

Will and Lette whirled around. Lette heaved on the ballista, but it was heavy, and the bearings rusted by years of spray from the lake.

Dathrax swept in low over the surface of the lake, wings spread, their trailing edges flapping in the night air.

He must have circled high then dived when out of sight. Reflected moonlight glimmering off the surface of the lake made the burnt charcoal scales of his underbelly seem to crackle with cold fire.

He opened his jaws. It seemed to go on for days. A great cavernous revealing of teeth. That jaw seemed to eclipse everything for Will. It swallowed the night, the boat, promises. Everything narrowing down to that ever-encroaching gullet. That single point of darkness, becoming the whole world.

And then light. Brilliant, blinding, as vast as that mouth. Flame that lit up the sky like a new sun. Consuming. Hungry. Deadly.

Will braced for that last painful moment. The one where he felt the skin and muscle peel back from his bones, the sharp scream of every fiber in his body, followed by—

And then it was over. The flame and the light faded. Dathrax was pulling up and away screaming. Will was alive.

And Quirk was standing beside him, arm outstretched, palm smoking.

# 52

# Hot-Tempered

Once, back at the Tamathian University, a young mage very interested in sight had informed Quirk that he had created a set of lenses that perceived the thaumatic world. They could, he had told her, see the invisible strands of power that the gods had used to stitch together reality. He wanted her to try them on and tell him what she saw. Later she realized that the mage had been making a clumsy pass at her, but she hadn't realized it at the time, and had simply been interested in the science.

She had sat in a wooden chair while the young mage perched a vast contraption upon her head. He had adjusted levers and fitted small round pieces of colored glass into slots in front of her eyes.

"Do you see it now?" he kept asking. "What does it look like now?"

"A bit purple," she had told him. Then, "Just like your office except mauve," another time.

He had grown increasingly frustrated, had appeared to be on the verge of saying it was all her fault, his nascent romantic intentions be damned, when all of a sudden, everything had aligned. He dropped a piece of what looked like perfectly clear glass before her right eye, and the world changed.

She had seen not just things, but the relationship between things. She had seen how one piece fit with another, and with the space between them. She had glimpsed, for just a second, the whole interconnected design of the world.

Then the machine had overheated, detonated, and set her hair on fire.

Quirk had very much the same experience as Dathrax swept down on the tax boat.

She had stood paralyzed by the glory of the beast. By the memories of fire. She had seen him in his entirety. She had not seen each interlocking piece of the puzzle. Not the muscle or the sinew or the blood vessel. Not the flight pattern, nor the physiognomy of his wings. Rather, she had seen it all. The whole perfect beast.

She had seen how its presence connected with the other thoughts chattering and skittering in the background of her mind. How the arc of its claws intersected with her fear for the citizens of Athril. How the arch of its neck encompassed her concerns for her own culpability in their collective demise.

And as Dathrax swept down upon them, she had realized that all the conflicting, nonsensical, potentially insane thoughts swirling in her head actually added up to one bright, clear, shining image.

She was afraid. She was piss-her-britches terrified.

She didn't know what she was doing. Not out in the field, away from her university. Not in this boat, taking part in what could optimistically be described as a crime. Not in this fight. She had no answers.

And she was very clearly about to die.

And when the world was reduced down to that moment, to that single truth, everything became very simple.

That fucker had to burn.

# 53

## Insult to Injury

Fire? Fucking fire? They were trying to set fire to him now?

Dathrax screamed his rage. *How dare they? How dare they even conceive of such a thing? That was just...just...*

*Gods' piss on it. It was embarrassing was what it was. If he had to explain a burn to the other dragons at the next Consortium meeting... Well, if he had to do that, it was going to be with this hexed prophet's skull lodged between his teeth. Gods curse it.*

He swept up into the sky, using his speed to put out the smoldering fires on his shoulders. With one claw, he pulled the ballista bolt out of his chest. He tried to make his scream sound more like the bellow of rage it ought to have been.

Dammit, he was out of practice at this. Thirty years ago, this sort of thing had been second nature to him. Now it all seemed distant and somewhat beneath him.

They were on a boat. He cast his mind back. Someone else in the Consortium...Kithrax perhaps...had always had a rule about boats. But was it to always land on them and devastate the troops or to never land...?

Why would you never land?

Fuck it. Dathrax had had enough of them taking potshots at him with those damn ballistas. *They were* his *ballistas! They protected* his *gold. His gold, which these bastards were stealing.*

He folded his wings close to his body. He was taking the fight to these fucking thieves. And he was going to eat every last one of them alive.

# 54

# We're Going to Need a Bigger Boat

"Starboard!" Will yelled.

Lette glanced at the direction he was pointing. "That's port," she said.

Quirk sent a jet of fire up into the sky. There was a flashing glimpse of scales, then it whipped out of sight, into the dark of the night.

Another blast of flame arced up. There was another glimpse of Dathrax on the other side of the boat. Lette hauled on her ballista, but she was too slow, Dathrax too quick.

Will finally forced the ballista bolt through the mess of netting and wood to sit flush in the war machine's barrel. His palms were drenched with sweat. His knees were shaking.

Then Dathrax came, dropping out of the sky like a meteor. He screamed toward the heart of the boat. He would tear the thing apart just with the force of his landing.

Beside him, Lette grit her teeth, sighted. "Got you," she said. Given that there was about two seconds before Dathrax smashed into them, Will wasn't sure that taking the time to try to sound intimidating was really well advised.

Lette fired. The bolt thundered skyward. But it did not fly free. Instead it snagged with the mess of ropes still twisted around the ballista. It wasn't a bolt they flung at Dathrax's heart, but instead a sprawling mess of tangled wood, and sails, and cord.

The bundle sagged through the air, missed Dathrax's skull

by inches. It smacked into his right wing, near the massive knot of muscle that joined it to his oversize frame. The bundle flew open like an exploding bedsheet. Ropes and sails wrapped around Dathrax's body, tangling and snagging.

Dathrax screamed, knocked off course at the last moment. He spun out of control. His body crashed into the edge of the boat. The ship lurched sideways, kicked up a vast wave. Dathrax's tail lashed out. It slammed into the second mast. Wood splintered, gave way.

The mast came crashing down. More ragged cloth and rope slashed the air. Will dived for cover, ballista bolts forgotten. Shrapnel exploded around him.

Dathrax bounced off the boat, flapped dizzily through water. He limped upward.

Quirk sent fire chasing after him, great gouts thrusting out of her palms, blooming in the night. Flames raced over the deck of the boat.

Not everything, it turned out, was soaking wet.

Fire mixed with the chaos on board the boat.

Will picked himself up. Something massive was pounding across the deck. He braced for a grisly reptilian death.

The grisly reptilian in question, however, was Balur. "Be coming back!" he yelled at Dathrax's retreating form. He spun his hammer above his head. "Be coming back and be fighting me like a man!"

Will blinked, tried to get his bearings. If Balur was over there... He turned to look at the wheel standing in the shattered pilot's cabin. It was alone again. And on fire.

The boat was by now about halfway between the shoreline and Dathrax's island. With both its masts gone, and its wheel on fire, it seemed inclined to stay there.

Something large smashed into the boat. The flames that increasingly coated the deck flickered as the deck rocked back and forth.

"The water!" Lette yelled. "Dathrax is in the water!" She was pulling herself to her feet using what was left of the ballista. It wasn't very much of the ballista, truth be told. Just the stump of its pivoting mount. The other siege machines were in similar states of disarray.

Will was halfway to the ship's rail before he realized Dathrax couldn't be in the water if he was flapping awkwardly in the air above them. He could hear the dragon's angry roaring.

Something hit the hull again. Hard. The boat rocked. Will staggered. The hull was struck again, and again. Will pitched forward. The rail struck his midriff. He sagged over it, stared down into the water, felt his breath tumble away from him to be swallowed by the churning water.

*Why*, he found himself thinking, *does Dathrax need state-of-the-art ballistas mounted on his tax boat anyway?*

The answer leapt out of the water and tried to bite his face off.

Lette, whom Will was, at that moment, willing to sanctify as the patron saint of just-in-fucking-time, caught him by the back of his collar and heaved him away from the rail.

The Leviathan—one of the mutant fish grown fat and wrong on the bloody runoff from Dathrax's diet—was ten feet long from nose to tail. At least six feet of that length appeared to be taken up by its mouth. Its jaw was a prodigious unwieldy thing that lent the creature a blunt, squat appearance despite its length. Teeth jutted from it at angles that suggested whatever god was responsible for its creation had been at the end of a long shift and had just jammed a fistful of the things in to be done with it so he could go home for a cup of tea and a bit of a kip. Its scales had the rainbow glisten of a moldering corpse, and its fins resembled tumors far more than any physiological adaptation to an aquatic lifestyle.

The Leviathan rocketed past Will's face, stinking and snapping, stunted body thrashing furiously. For a moment Will was eye-to-eye with it, staring into a gelatinous orb the size of his head, and brim full of insane hatred. Then gravity claimed it and it smashed back down into black water.

Blows to the ship's hull were coming from all sides now. The ship didn't so much rock as it did quiver. Suddenly the ballistas made so much more sense.

In the prow of the boat, Balur was still calling challenges to Dathrax.

"Your mother was thinking you were a shit stain on the floor!" he bellowed. "She was being impregnated by iguanas! If she could be holding her liquor you would not be existing!"

A Leviathan fish leapt up out of the water at him, for a moment hung in the air above his head. It opened its jaws.

Grabbing his hammer, Balur smashed the Leviathan in the side of its head.

"You are having the genitals of a field mouse!" he went on without pausing as the Leviathan sagged back to the water.

Quirk was running, and screaming, aiming streams of fire at the water, sending up clouds of scalding steam all around them.

And above, Dathrax was circling around, and coming back for more.

# 55

## Free Fall

With a final deafening roar, Dathrax plunged out of the sky and smashed into the boat. This, though, Will had time to recognize, was not the lightning raid of claws and teeth that had come before. This was not deft destruction. The knot of sails and rigging had worked itself even more completely around Dathrax's body. His right wing was hopelessly tangled with his back leg, and his neck was being pulled brutally to the left. He came at the boat sideways, almost skidding through the air.

Balur still stood in the prow, hammer raised high above his head, mouth pulled back in a monstrous grin, howling in joy.

Dathrax struck him full force. The front of the boat disintegrated, so much wood pulp and flotsam. Balur sailed through the air, his flight actually gaining momentum from the hammer still clutched in his hand. The Analesian cleared the full length of the hold, came down on the ruins of the wheel, and lay there quite still.

Will had all of half a second to take that in before Dathrax claimed his attention once more. The vast dragon was writhing on the deck, trying to right itself. As it did so, the boat dipped violently, the smashed prow sinking toward the waterline.

Shattered planking, bits of broken mast, knots of ropes, rolling ballista bolts, actual ballistas—all went tumbling down the length of the boat, toward Dathrax. Desperately, Will flung himself sideways to escape a deluge of barrels crashing past him, rolling toward the dragon.

Dathrax flailed again, snagging more of the ruined ship around his limbs. He tried to get a foot steady beneath him, but with his weight, and the ship's impaired structural integrity, the limb shot through the deck, to be mired in the hold below.

The boat was tilting even farther now. Balur's body was sliding back toward the prow. Will, lying prone, started to slide as well. He managed to brace his foot, caught hold of one of the ship's rails that was still intact.

The thing he was bracing his foot on yelled. It turned out to be Lette's face. She was hanging grimly to the ship's rail directly below him. Quirk was another yard farther down. The wooden rail she was holding on to was smoking.

Beyond Dathrax's increasingly desperate flailing, he could see the water churning as the boat sank deeper and deeper below the waterline. Vast aquatic bodies writhed. Fins sliced the water's surface into finer and finer froth.

"Balur!" yelled Lette. "You have to get Balur!"

The lizard man was almost parallel with Will, and picking up speed.

*Isn't he your partner?* Will almost said, but didn't. *The things I do for infatuation.*

He planted his legs against the rail and before he could think about it much, he leapt. Whether he traveled horizontally or vertically he was no longer sure. He smashed through tumbling piles of detritus, closed the distance between himself and Balur.

He crashed back onto the deck, landing woefully short. He scrabbled for a handhold, found none. He plunged down, slipping and sliding. On the plus side, he was careening toward Balur on a pretty decent intercept trajectory. On the more negative side of the equation, Dathrax's jaws—stretched wide in a scream of frustration—were waiting for them both just beyond that.

Will could see panic in Dathrax's fiery eyes now. The dragon lunged his massive jaws at the stump of a mast, bit down, searching for any purchase it could get. The mast splintered and shattered. Dathrax spat a mouthful of splinters and smoke, let out a bellow of despair.

Something in Will—no matter that he was falling down the deck of a near-vertical ship, no matter that he could see his imminent death waiting for him—took flight at Dathrax's plight. He might be about to die, but so would this tyrant, this despot, this *arsehole*.

In the abrupt warmth of this hope, a plan flashed into Will's mind. Suicidal. Idiotic. Foolish beyond imagining. But the same could be said of all his plans so far, and they'd gotten him this far.

If he'd had time, he would have laughed at that.

But there was no time. He simply reacted. He bunched his legs and kicked off from the surface of the deck. He flew out into space. Then he was in pure free fall. No safety net beneath him. No deck. Only the writhing, snapping head of Dathrax the dragon.

He slammed bodily against the dragon's skull. He felt scales rip at his skin. But there was no time for pain. Even as he skidded over the dragon's brow, even as he felt the raw heat of Dathrax's breath blasting up at him from outraged nostrils, even as he planted one foot in one of Dathrax's yellow eyes, he reached out a hand for Balur just as the lizard man plunged toward the dragon's jaws.

And caught him.

*That was,* he thought, *pretty fucking magnificent.*

Then the pendulum weight of Balur tore through Will's precarious balance, pivoted them like ballerinas, Will's heel slip-sliding over Dathrax's eye, both of them flailing in the air. Then, hand in hand they went tumbling toward the water below.

# 56

## Reaction Shot

*Okay,* Lette thought, *that was pretty impressive. Incredibly stupid. But impressive.*

# 57

# Splashdown

The only thing that saved Will was that just before he hit the water, Dathrax did.

The dragon finally lost his fight with the disintegrating surface of the boat, and fell, flailing and tangled into the waters below.

Will struck one half-stretched wing, felt a lot of important organs slam into each other, tasted his spleen, felt Balur's weight tear his arm out of its socket, and was sent flying out across the lake.

The dragon, at the mercy of momentum as it had been at the mercy of few other things during its long and repulsive life, went straight down and landed in the dark waters of the lake.

The Leviathans lost their shit entirely.

Even as Will fought to stay above the surface of the water, the dragon's screams made him shudder.

Suddenly a powerful hand caught him by the neck, hoisted him upward. He yelled, but then found he was staring into Balur's face. The lizard man was floating on his back, legs kicking powerfully, tail wriggling sinuously. He seemed to be staying afloat effortlessly. Despite this, his slit eyes were crossed and he was bleeding from a considerable gash in his forehead.

"We are being in the water," he said thickly. "How are we getting in the water?"

"Oh," said Will, still getting his own bearings. "Usual way.

Attacked by a dragon. Had our boat torn apart. Were sent flying into a lake populated by giant mutant fish."

Balur's eyes focused a little at that. He managed to fix Will with a narrow stare. "Dragon?" he said. "I must be killing it."

Another scream tore through the night.

"Sorry," said Will. "I think the Leviathans have beaten you to it."

Dathrax was still struggling, but more in the way that a well-flayed steak struggles when repeatedly beaten with a large machete, than in any sort of coordinated, I-might-survive-this kind of way. The boat was a rapidly diminishing pyramid of wood.

"Fucker of whores!" Balur yelled. "That is being my kill! Those fish are stealing it from me!"

Will, however, was more concerned with other issues.

"Lette," he said. Lette had still been aboard that boat. She had no flailing dragon to knock her free. She was there, in that mess of jaws and death.

"What about her?" Balur had caught the tone in his voice. The bloodlust momentarily drained away. He pawed at the blood trickling down in his face and into his eyes.

Will wasn't sure how to put it. Lette and Balur were... Close didn't seem to be the exact word. It held implications of intimacy that didn't fit. Integral fit the bill perhaps. They were lopsided halves of some indivisible unit. And they had just been divided.

However he put it, it would need to be delicate.

"She's dead," he said.

Balur went totally still. His legs did not kick. His tail did not slide from side to side. Slowly they began to sink.

"Quirk too," Will added as an afterthought.

Water lapped higher.

"She is being dead?" Balur's growl was so deep that Will barely caught it.

He opened his mouth to reply.

"Who's dead?" said someone behind him. They sounded rather curious.

Will twisted in Balur's grip, felt his jaw go slightly slack. "You are," he said.

Lette, treading water, managed to give a small shrug. "I've had worse," she said.

"Fuck all of you." Quirk, paddling to catch up with Lette, seemed to be taking things with less calm.

"If you are ever telling me she is being dead again," Balur said to Will, "then I will be seeing how hard I am having to squeeze to make you vomit up your intestines."

That, Will found, took a lot of the wind out of his sails. His thoughts turned to darker territory.

"How come we aren't being eaten alive?" he asked.

"The Leviathans," Lette said, "seem more preoccupied with Dathrax. Guess he's tastier. Or just bigger." Her breath was punctuated by a slight panting as she kept up her strokes.

"How about," Will suggested, "we head to shore before they finish him off and go looking for dessert."

"Sounds good," Lette said.

"Fuck all of you," Quirk said again.

And so they swam through the dark waters back toward the burning town of Athril, as behind them, the bloody remains of the dragon Dathrax sank beneath the waves.

# PART 3:
# A JOB WORTH
# DOING WELL

# 58

## Love and War

Exhausted, limbs shaking from exertion, Lette dragged herself up onto the dock of Athril's Lake. She flopped onto her back, tried to get her breath back, failed, waited to gather the energy necessary to try again.

Balur came next, rising, dripping out of the water like some protean beast leftover from a mythic age. He dragged Quirk in one hand, Will in the other. He dumped them unceremoniously. They collapsed, shivering and gasping, on the cold cobblestones. They had almost drowned a hundred yards from shore and Balur had dragged them bodily through the water from there. The lizard man managed to keep his feet, but even he was hunched over, breathing hard. The gash in his forehead was still dripping blood onto the edge of the dock.

They were miserable, they were exhausted, but they were alive. The attention of the Leviathan fish had been wholly focused on Dathrax's bloated corpse. They had been left unmolested in the waters.

Lette's mind went back to those final moments. The pivoting boat, everything collapsing, tumbling away. Balur pitching down toward death and dismemberment. And then Will. Why had she asked him to help? Why hadn't she done it herself?

She remembered again how it had felt to be hanging there. Dathrax and the Leviathan fish below her. Everything burning.

Being able to smell the smoke as the rails burned in Quirk's grip, only a few feet away.

She had been afraid. She had asked Will because she had been struck with a moment of weakness. There was no other way to put it.

Lette did not like that memory. She was a warrior, a rogue, a scoundrel, a pirate. She had a gods-hexed reputation to maintain.

But Will had not hesitated. He had leapt out, had careened toward death. And he had done it for Balur.

What was Balur to Will? The lizard man was tribe to her. Family. Partner. Home in some messed-up kind of way. But to Will? To Will he was probably just some giant, some barbarian. Which, she supposed, was what Balur was. He was a simple creature. A war hammer smashing without apology into the face of life.

Who would risk their life for that?

In the end, of course, the answer was simple, but she waited for a while before she faced it. Will had saved Balur because of what the lizard man meant to her.

It was an act of... what? Love? A shudder mixed with the shivering. She was not someone to love. Not unless love meant a bottle of spirits and a tavern bed rented by the hour. And yet replacing the word with *lust* left something hollow in her gut.

*Infatuation* perhaps? She thought she could live with that word.

Such a fucking stupid thing to do. And yet impressive in its boldness. In the grandiosity of its dumbness. *I will be this stupid for you*, it said. And there was something very flattering in that.

She dragged herself that much closer to Will, reached out and squeezed his hand. He looked over at her. A smile started to form. Then it turned into a gagging sound. He turned away just in time to miss her.

"The sound of victory?" she managed.

He looked up at her, grinned queasily, wiped his chin with the back of his free arm. *There have,* Lette thought, *been more romantic moments charted in the annals of history.*

"Well," he said, "we're alive. I guess that counts for something."

She nodded. "Something."

He hesitated. "I quite want to kiss you again," he said. "But I just..." He nodded in the vague direction of the vomit.

"We can hold hands," she said.

"Could you just, please..." Quirk's voice was no stronger than Will's. "Shut up," she said. "I'm begging you."

Lette looked at the woman. Part of her was still calculating the angle to drive the blade into Quirk's ribs, so the thaumatobiologist's heart would empty its contents into her lungs. But bedraggled and exhausted, Quirk didn't look much like a threat. She looked instead like the mast of the boat that now lay at the bottom of the lake. Shattered and broken.

"I am being with Quirk on this one." Balur nodded.

"You too," Quirk told Balur. The academic seemed to have drowned much of her stoic calm in the lake.

It was a sign of his exhaustion that Balur complied. They all just drooped there, panting, waiting for someone else to break the moment, to force them into the next decision, into the next step of whatever fresh hell they had just created. Lette just didn't have the energy to focus on anything other than the next moment.

She should have predicted that Will wouldn't have the good sense to keep his mouth shut.

"Wasn't there fighting going on when we left here?" he said. "Where is everybody?"

Reluctantly Lette raised her head. The stubborn fragment of her will to live refused to give in. The city was quiet. Dying fires still crackled. The occasional bit of building frontage collapsed. But no one was mounting anyone else's head on a pike. It made for a much quieter scene compared to her last visit to Athril.

"Should probably check it out," Will said.

"How hard did you get hit on the head?" she asked him. "The last thing we should be doing is seeking out other people." She pulled her hand out of his. "What we should be doing is running quietly into the night before anyone notices we're here. We just killed *another* member of the Consortium."

"And buried every coin we had at the bottom of that lake," Quirk added.

The silence that followed that statement was briefer than the one before, but so much more profound. When Lette broke it, there was an almost tangible sensation of rending.

"We did what?" Her voice reached for an octave it couldn't reach and scraped along its breaking point.

But she knew. Of course she knew. She just hadn't allowed the information to make it to shore with her. But now it came clambering out of the lake like a dragon's diseased zombie corpse come to pursue her forever.

Dathrax had taken the bait, their wealth, and he had put it on his tax boat. And they had put his tax boat at the bottom of a lake.

A lake infested with giant mutant fish who would soon be very hungry indeed.

"No," she said to herself. "No. No."

They were back to square one. Except now square one held an entire Consortium of incredibly powerful, incredibly motivated dragons all looking to kill her.

She looked at Will.

This was him. His fault. It had been his plan. And she had... Gods...

He was the only way out of this she could think of.

"What do we do?" She hated herself for asking it. Hated him for holding the only hope she had.

"Run," he said, echoing her own advice back to her. "We have to run."

"Too late." There was fatalism in Balur's voice. "I am hearing footsteps. Many of them." He stood straight, reached back, hesitated as his hand closed on nothing.

"Where the fuck is being my hammer?" he said quietly.

Oh shit. As if they didn't have enough problems.

Will wouldn't know a warning sign if it chatted him up at a tavern, took him up to its room, drugged him, and robbed him blind. "The bottom of the lake," he said.

Lette watched as reality ruptured somewhere in Balur's stomach and all the bile and hatred of the Hallows poured into him, puffing him up. He towered over Will, apocalyptic.

The serendipitous arrival of a large crowd broke the moment. Balur didn't deflate but he was frozen as, from a cross street at the top of the docks, Firkin appeared. He was at the head of a much battered, bleeding, bedraggled, but undeniably triumphant crowd.

"Prophet!" Firkin cried.

Will winced.

"Lord! Master! Utterer of the words that fall upon the ears of the people who have ears! We have come to utter words to you! To deliver to your ears the words of the people with ears! Words and ears are very much involved. They are being of critical importance! Thus you have spaken, and thus I spake again. And thus it was spaked."

Firkin seemed to be struggling with his oratory. He tugged angrily at his beard.

"Firkin," Will said wearily. "I don't—"

"Prophet!" Firkin screamed over him. "The people of Athril come bearing you a great gift."

A great cheer arose at this. Firkin beamed. Lette didn't see why. Unless they were giving Will a crap ton of sweat and grime, they had come remarkably empty-handed.

"I don't want—" Will started again, just as ineffectually as before.

"The people of Athril," Firkin screeched on. "The people with words and ears for your ears. Except for the ears part. Their ears. Your ears are still definitely a part of this. They come with a great gift for your ears." Here he hesitated. "And eyes. And legs. Pretty much all of your body." He hesitated again. "Definitely all of your body. The people of Athril bring you a great gift for your body, even the bits of it that might cause you shame, and you generally find unappealing to the eyes of others. Because we do not care about their eyes. Just their mouths. And their words. And the gift that the people of Athril have for you. In their hands. So their hands too. Except the hands are metaphorical."

There was a rumbling behind Firkin. He finally, finally seemed to be losing the crowd. Lette settled back. After a long evening, watching Firkin torn limb from limb by an angry mob might make for quite a pleasant distraction.

And then Will went and saved him by asking, "What is it?"

Lette clawed at her face.

Firkin smiled as the crowd cheered once more.

"The people of Athril," he said, still grinning, "present to you: Athril!"

# 59

## Of All He Surveys

The sun seemed reluctant to rise over the devastation that had once been the town of Athril. When it did so, it stared down sullenly upon events, half-hidden by a slowly dissipating scrim of smoke.

*Judgmental bastard,* thought Will.

He had found a building that was at least two-thirds intact. Its stairs had let him up to a third floor. The roof had collapsed into the street below, and torn away a good chunk of the wall along with it, affording him a good view of the city and the fields beyond.

He could see the crowds coming.

The sun was barely up and already the crowds came; came to see what the prophet had done.

And when they found out? He had no idea. He would need to tell them something probably. Have some words of wisdom.

"Hello, everybody," he rehearsed in his head. "Welcome to what used to be a bustling, functional town. Don't mind the dead bodies. That's just because of everybody going insane once my name was mentioned. And don't worry about the shit storm of dragons that is almost certainly descending upon this place. From what I've seen so far, the ensuing death, while violent, is pretty quick. There's not much of that flailing around in agony involved. You may shit yourself in terror, of course, but everyone else will be dead in a few moments so there won't be much for you to be embarrassed about. Any questions?"

*No. That probably wouldn't do.* Still, he was hard-pressed to think of anything else to tell them. He missed the days when his biggest problem was whether or not to kill his father's old pig.

What had happened to Bessie? He hoped she had escaped the guards. She likely had. She was a wily old thing. Smarter than he was, that was for sure. Lette, Balur, Quirk, even Firkin—they'd have done better if they'd had her lead their merry band. Maybe they should track Bessie down, find out if she would lead them to safety.

Except Bessie was probably smart enough to turn the offer down at face value.

He chuckled to himself.

"Oh," said a voice behind him. "You're here."

He flinched around. Quirk was standing at the top of the stairs that had brought him up here. He hadn't heard her approach.

"Sorry." Will found himself apologizing.

Quirk shook her head. She had found a clean dress from somewhere. Something silvery-white, made of linen. She looked almost priestly. "I was just looking for somewhere quiet," she mumbled. "Away from it all."

Will let a smile ghost across his face. "So was I," he said. "It doesn't help as much as you'd think."

"You were laughing," Quirk said. She looked suspicious. It was a very different look from the one she had worn when she had wandered into a cave in the middle of a rainy night. Will had the impression that the events of the past two weeks had cracked the veneer of professional reserve. Something more feral was peeking through those cracks.

"You know who sits alone, laughing to themselves?" Will asked her.

Quirk nodded slowly. "You have a point."

"I think I'd like company," he told her. It seemed a sensible step considering how solitude was working out.

Quirk considered that. "I'm not sure I do."

He shrugged. "If it doesn't work for you, I'll clear off. I'm not making much progress up here."

"Progress on what?" She seemed to regret the question almost as soon as it was out of her mouth. But he wasn't willing to let the opening go.

"What to do next."

At first he thought she was smiling. But perhaps, upon closer inspection, it was more just a baring of teeth. "Trying to come up with a plan?"

He shook his head. "Trying to come up with whether I should come up with a plan."

Some of the tension seemed to go out of Quirk's shoulders. She sagged a little, stepped off the stairs, and walked toward him. She sat down on the creaking wooden floorboards. This place had been an attic once, he thought. Battered old possessions—the sort that nobody actually wanted, but didn't want to throw away either; the ambivalent detritus of living—were scattered about them. Poorly executed oil paintings of people with buck teeth and mismatching eyes. Religious texts everyone owned but that no one read. Chests of clothes that were providing a good home for moths.

"They've really got you all twisted up, haven't they?" she said.

"Who?"

"Lette." Quirk looked at him flatly. "Balur too. And Firkin. All of them."

He wasn't sure how he felt about that. Balur and Firkin didn't seem like the most adept schemers. He wasn't sure how he felt about being called their patsy. And as for Lette...

"What about you?" he said, a touch defensively. "You have no interest in what I do next?"

The look she gave him was utterly unguarded. Utterly desolate. "Fuck you," she said, and abruptly stood up.

Will didn't know what had just happened. He stared up at her. "What?" he asked. "What happened? What in the name of the Hallows did I just say?"

"What happened? What *happened*?" Quirk's eyes were wild as she looked down at him. The wind wafting through the town made her long dress billow around her. Her mouth became a rictus, not quite a smile, not quite a cry of anguish. "I chose, Will," she said. "I made a decision."

Will remembered the events of the night before once more. Quirk standing there, just staring at Dathrax. The words "he's magnificent" on her lips.

"A good one?" he asked hopefully.

He didn't really feel hopeful.

"A long time ago," Quirk said, "I told myself I wouldn't use my magic anymore. I had been used by a...He was called Hethren. He was...a bandit. Worse, I suppose. But he looked at me and all he saw was my magic. And when he looked at my magic, all he saw was a weapon. So that's what he made me into: his weapon. He made me hurt a lot of people. He made me like to hurt people. With my magic.

"But I was rescued, Will. I was saved. Not by any of the gods. Not by Lawl, sitting on high. Not by absent Barph, dancing and drinking his way in merriment. Not by Cois, fucking her way through immortality. Not by Knole, even though all the other academics I know worship her for her learning. Not by Klink, with all his wealth and treasure. Not by Toil, bringing life to our fields. Not even by Betra, mother to us all, who promises to hold us to her bosom even as Lawl judges us, each and every one. None of them took an interest in me.

"No, it was a few good women and men. It was people who looked at me and didn't see a weapon, who didn't see my magic at all. It was people who just saw a damaged child. And they helped me find my way to be a better person. They helped me reach a point where I could promise to myself, 'No more. I'm done with magic.'"

She had a far-off look in her eyes. The wind billowed.

"I loved being that person. I loved how happy it made them.

My discoveries. My theories. I wanted to be the best thauma-tobiologist in all the world. For them. And I had come so far. I hadn't lost control in so long. So I came out here into the world. To achieve that dream. And, you know what?"

She finally looked at him. There was a genuine smile on her face. He didn't dare answer, dare break whatever spell this was.

"I was awful," she said. "I couldn't even find a dragon. I didn't really even know what I was looking for. But then I met you. And Lette. And Balur. And even Firkin. And stealing from a dragon wasn't exactly what I'd had in mind, but I thought it would get me close. And it did. I got so close. Close enough to touch a dragon."

She shook her head. "But I lost control. It had happened before. But this time I hurt so many people. And I was so upset with myself. With all of you. For putting me in that situation. But at least it was an accident. It just slipped out. An old trauma rising to the surface. I can understand that. I can excuse that."

All the mirth was falling away now—just more junk in the room. "But last night…Last night I chose. I made a decision. I didn't panic. I had control. And I reached for my magic anyway. I…I…" She was struggling to get the words out now. "I chose to set fire to the world." She shook her head. Let her eyes settle on him. They were as heavy as Balur's war hammer.

"You want to know what I think you should do next?" she asked. "I think you should go fuck yourself, Willett Fallows, and you should leave me alone to work out what to do with all the pieces of the person I thought I was."

She sat back down. Both of them stared off into space. The crowds were drawing closer, Will could see. Some were almost at the town gates now. The fact that they hung askew on their hinges didn't seem to be dissuading anyone.

"Sorry," Quirk said after a while. "That probably wasn't fair."

Will shrugged. "No," he said, "I think it was."

Quirk nodded. "I know, but I was trying to be nice."

"Given how many people are dead because of me," he said, "I'm not sure there's much need to be nice to me."

She nodded again. Will had rather been hoping that she wouldn't.

"Do you worship the gods, Will?" she said apropos of nothing.

"Erm," he said, caught off guard. Then he said, "Yes," because that was what you said. Then, "I mean, not religiously..." but that wasn't right either. "Well, yes, religiously. Obviously. Sort of the definition of worshipping them. But, well, I don't follow all their dictates to the letter. No one does really. Well, not many people anyway. I celebrate the major feast days. I offer up a few libations now and again. That sort of thing. Regular worship, I suppose."

Something in her look made him feel like he needed to defend himself, though he wasn't sure why. "I mean," he said, "they're up there, aren't they? Unless they're down here, screwing your wife anyway." That seemed to be most of what the gods did when they involved themselves with their creations. Quite often when disguised as an animal, which, he now thought, was a rather weird kink to be shared across the entire Pantheon. But he was wandering off topic. "It doesn't seem to be worth pissing them off," he finished. Not, perhaps, the most theocratically sound argument, but it was one that worked for him.

"And how," asked Quirk, "is all that worship working out for you?"

The stink of blood and ash was thick in Will's nostrils. "It's had its ups and downs," he said. Then a thought occurred to him. "Don't you worship the gods?" That she might not seemed absurd. Dangerous in fact. Could all that have happened to him be because he'd fallen in with a heathen that the gods wished to smite?

But Quirk said, "Yes, I do. Knole mostly. Goddess of wisdom, and all of that. She's important to the university. There are a lot of statues of her saints watching over the libraries and

laboratories. There's a lot of beautiful architecture back there."
For a moment she had a wistful look on her face. "But that's not
really why I asked."

"So why?" Will was unsure about this whole line of
questioning.

"You're a god," Quirk said to him.

Will considered that. "Perhaps you should lie down," he said.

A small exhalation of amusement escaped her nostrils. "Not
literally. I don't mean that. Because I have not literally gone
insane. I mean you're a god to these people." She nodded her
head toward the open wall space before them; the ruined city
and its ruined population beyond. "They think of you just the
same way they think of their gods."

"Erm," said Will. He was back to monosyllables.

"When you pray to Lawl," Quirk said, "when you pour a libation to Cois or Barph before a night down at the tavern, do you
truly expect them to step down out of the heavens and intercede? Do you expect them to manifest at your beck and call? Do
you expect them to truly consider you and your needs? Do they
ever? Or do they come and go as they please, at their own selfish
whims?"

"Well," Will said. This seemed like it was skirting very close
to heresy and he had pissed off enough incredibly powerful
beings that he didn't feel the need to add the entire Pantheon to
the list.

"You don't expect them to answer," she answered for him.
"You just hope. You just think, *Well, maybe that will nudge them in
the direction of doing something that will work out for me.*"

Will hesitated, then grudgingly nodded. That was, he supposed, completely accurate.

"It's the same with you," Quirk said. "To them, you are a force
in the world. Someone who can change things. And they are
desperate for change. They don't believe they can truly influ-
ence you, but they hope that when you change things it will

work out in their favor. They're desperate. It seems to them that any change at all will help them."

When he heard things like that, it was very hard for Will to regret the deaths of Mattrax and Dathrax, imminent death of his own or no.

"So you're saying," he said, finally putting it all together, "that I'm like you. I have to make a decision." Though he wasn't sure if he knew what he was meant to be deciding anymore.

Quirk was looking at him as if he had started to become blurry and had to be held in the clarity of sanity.

"You're not saying that?" Will checked.

"There's nothing even vaguely similar about our situations," she said. "I'm having a moral and existential crisis. You're trying to work out a way to dodge feeling responsible for the murder of thousands."

Well, when she put it like that... All the nascent hope that had been building in his chest went out of him in a single sighing breath.

He put his head in his hands. "I just...I need to work it out. But you're right, I'm a god. I can push them how I need them. I can...do...something..."

He looked up at Quirk's scoffing sound. "What?" he asked.

She shook her head sadly. "You're not a god," she said, as if addressing a toddler trying to pick up his father's sword and shouting that he was Lawl's son upon the earth.

"But you said..." Will protested. Because she really had.

Quirk rolled her eyes. "You wouldn't have lasted a day at Tamathia," she said.

"I'm not trying to survive a day in Tamathia," Will snapped. "I'm trying to survive a whole bunch of them right here in Kondorra."

"I said they see you as a god. They think of you that way."

"You said I was an agent of change," he said, and he sounded petty even to his own ears.

"How many times has that change been the one you wanted?" Quirk asked.

She had a point there.

He met Quirk's eye. "How many times," she asked him, "have they done what Firkin asked?"

That was not math that Will enjoyed doing. But then a grim sense of satisfaction fell upon him. He had purpose once more. "So now," he said, "I go find Firkin and tell him what to god-damn do."

Quirk let out her small chuffing laugh again. "You really don't get it, do you?"

Will's sense of satisfaction ebbed away, joined Quirk's earlier mirth, and the household junk on the attic floor. "So what do I do?" he asked plaintively.

"You go to Firkin," Quirk said, "and you find out what he wants you to do, and then you pray you survive it."

# 60

# The Hand Inside the Puppet

"Firkin," Will said, "we've got to talk."

Firkin was sitting in a font in the middle of a burned-out temple to Lawl. The king of the gods was attempting to look down sternly upon them, but his statue had taken several serious blows, and looked a little cross-eyed. Above them, a crew of men were hard at work, stripping the lead tiles from the frame of the roof above. Dust, splinters, and nails rained down about them in small eddying showers.

"Lip flappery!" Firkin announced to the empty room. "Tongue-smacking witchcraft. You come to weave it into my mind with your sound words. Get your thinking into my brain with your lexical magic-ery."

He grinned broadly at Will. "Won't work," he said with a grin. He turned the side of his head toward Will, pushed back the wild tangle of hair, and revealed a blackened chewed-up thing that could, possibly, be described as his ear. He had plugged it with something yellow and revolting.

"Keeps out that word tomfoolery," Firkin said with a knowing wink to Will.

"But," Will protested, "you can hear me."

Firkin's grin disappeared like a cockroach scuttling for the shadows. "Prototype," he grunted, then stared sullenly at his feet.

Several pounds of lead crashed to the floor in the corner of the church. The tile floor cracked. "Sorry," someone yelled half-heartedly from up above. Considering people had flocked to this place in his name, Will might have expected a little more regret.

He took a breath. Tried to regain control of the conversation.

"This prophet thing," he said, shoving his hands in his pockets and starting to pace. "It's really getting out of hand."

"Not hands," said Firkin, leaning forward. There was still some water left in the font. It splashed over the sides. Firkin tapped the side of his head. "In heads, it is. Words put ideas in heads. Like little burrowing beetles. Yes." He nodded to himself three times. "Words are burrowing beetles with idea seeds. And seeds grow. Grow in brains. And burst out of mouths." He pantomimed vomiting. "Become words. Propagation that is. Big long word with lots of syllables. I know it. You know it. Because of the seeds." Firkin's eyes rolled. "In our brains."

"Right," said Will, struggling through the analogy. "But I think that perhaps some pruning of this particular idea could be in order."

"What idea?"

For just a moment, Firkin looked perfectly lucid. And perfectly confused. It was one of the most unsettling things Will had ever seen.

"This idea that I'm a prophet," he said, trying to find his footing.

"You're not a prophet?" asked Firkin, still looking perplexed.

"No," said Will. He wasn't sure what was going on, but it seemed like Firkin was actually receptive to outside input for a moment. He needed to take as much advantage as he could.

"Who said you were?" asked Firkin. He looked interested now.

"You did," Will pointed out.

"Quite the bold statement on my part," Firkin commented.

"But false." Will wanted to be clear on that point.

"Well," said Firkin, "I should clear that up then."

Will smiled. All of a sudden, this was going astonishingly well. Firkin stood up, looked around. His gaze fell upon the workers above him. "Oy!" he yelled at the top of his lungs.

Several of the group stopped, looked down. "What's it?" yelled one.

"This guy!" Firkin screeched back. He pointed at Will just to be clear. "He's not the prophet."

There was a distinct pause at this. Will felt like he'd somehow been blindsided, even though this was exactly what he'd asked for.

"Erm, okay then," called back one of the workers. "Good to know."

Firkin beamed. He turned to Will. "Well," he said, "that seems to have cleared that up."

Which didn't explain why Will felt more confused.

"Hey," called the talkative man from above. "Where do you want all this lead then?"

"In the central square!" Firkin snapped back, a bark of authority suddenly slipping into his screeching voice. "The prophet compels you!"

"All hail the prophet!" the men called back as one.

Will stood and stared at Firkin. "I thought we just talked about this," he said.

"About what?" Firkin was all innocence and confusion again.

"About this prophet stuff. The prophet doesn't compel anyone to do anything."

Firkin's face twisted through a variety of expressions Will could not entirely place. It seemed to settle on something between disgust and indignation. "How the fuck would you know?" asked Firkin. "You just told me. You're not him."

# 61

# A Tribe Called Dysfunctional

Elsewhere, Lette found Balur leaning against Athril's broken town gates. The heads of a few city guards had been mounted on makeshift spikes. She arched an eyebrow at him.

"I am getting fidgety when I am not having much to do," he said by way of explanation.

Next to them, a slow but steady stream of people was making its way into Athril. Farmers for the most part, Lette would say. Some alone, some dragging their families in their wake. A spattering of merchants in among them. More would follow. It would take a little longer to dislodge the more comfortable ones from their city homes. But they would come. From all over Kondorra. Eventually the weight of this human tide would force them out of their comfortable homes, make them wash up here at Will's feet.

Balur's eye skipped over each and every one.

"You're keeping Will safe," she said with a sudden smile. "You big softy."

"I am not knowing what you are talking about," said Balur, not meeting her eye.

"You're worried about him," said Lette. "You're worried about spies from the Consortium. So you're standing here and keeping an eye out for them. Because you care. Because beneath that tough grizzly exterior, you have the soft, squishy heart of a six-year-old girl."

"He was losing my hammer," Balur grunted, with a vehemence that made the travelers on the road into town look up and shy away. "He is being lucky that I have not ripped his intestines out of his arsehole and throttled him with them."

Currently Balur appeared to be armed with a savage piece of iron, which had perhaps once been a fence post.

"But you are guarding him," said Lette. "You're doing it anyway."

Balur grunted, used his scanning of the crowd as an excuse to not meet her eye. Lette thought. "Not for Will's sakes then." The pieces fell into place.

"For mine," she said.

Balur ground his teeth. Finally he just said, "We are being tribe."

Lette, though, felt anger rising. "So," she said. "You're not protecting him. You're protecting me." It was not a question, but she expected an answer all the same.

Balur just stared at the crowd.

"That one," he said. "Concealing a sword under his cloak."

"He's come to fight," Lette snapped. "For Will. For what he represents. And you are deflecting. You say we're tribe. And I know what you mean by tribe. I know the importance of that word to you. But if we're tribe, the only member of it that needs protecting is you before I unseam you and piss on your guts."

She closed on him, didn't take her eyes off his face, daring him to test her.

He glanced at her, knew it for a mistake, looked away fast, but not fast enough.

"I don't need your fucking protection!" she snapped.

The crowd definitely heard that one. They paused, started to bunch. "Keep fucking moving," she snapped, not sparing them a look. "Before I chop your balls from your bodies and send you all chasing after them."

That seemed to do the trick.

Balur, though, still wasn't meeting her eye.

"I *don't*—" she started to repeat.

"Old Lette didn't need protection," Balur said.

That put a stumble in the step of her argument. "What do you mean, 'old Lette'?" she asked.

Balur shrugged. It looked like two continents trying to get it on with each other. "I am meaning the Lette who we left behind in Vinland. The Lette who was pocketing a sack full of gold, and spitting in a god's eye. I am *not* meaning the Lette who is making puppy eyes at some fool of a farm boy. I am *not* meaning the Lette who is hesitating before she is planting the blade hilt deep. I am *not* meaning the Lette who is worrying about a herd of fools"—he nodded savagely at the crowds—"before she is worrying about herself. I am meaning the Lette who I was working with, and was living with for ten years, who I was trusting my life with. I am meaning the Lette I am waiting to see return."

He ground his teeth hard. The metal of his fence post was groaning under the pressure of his grip.

Lette felt herself thrumming, like a bowstring after the arrow is loosed. But she had yet to work out where the arrow had been aimed.

"So," she said. "I am not supposed to have ambition? I am not supposed to have goals? That's what people do, Balur. They live. They desire. They strive to change. I am trying to make myself better."

"Better at what?" Balur snapped. His voice was full of contempt. "Better at being one of these cattle?"

"Better at being someone who can sleep at night," she spat back, not giving him an inch. "Better at being someone who can look her reflection in the eye."

"Oh," Balur scoffed. "So you are having a conscience now?"

Lette hesitated. That was a little close to the bone. "No," she said. "But I'm trying to grow one."

Balur looked at her. Yellow slit eyes boring into her. "Truly?" he said. He sounded as hurt as she felt. "You are truly wanting to be more like them?" Again he swept a hand at the passing crowds. They were shying away from them, pressing into the far wall of the archway, looking straight ahead, refusing to make eye contact.

"Well..." she said. "Not exactly like them. Like them with balls. And brains."

Balur laid a hand on her shoulder. Her knees asked politely if that could never happen again, please.

"We are having that," Balur said. "We are having balls. We are having brains. And we are having fun. We are having success. That is why we are being tribe."

Lette looked at him. The big, brutal psychopath, more loyal to her than she ever had any right to deserve. And she said something she knew would cut him to the core.

"They're my tribe too."

Balur was eight feet tall. He was covered with armor thicker and stronger than any steel plate. He could wield a two-handed war hammer like it was a child's plaything. He had a mouthful of teeth like knives. He weighed more than half a ton.

And she had just taken all the fight out of him.

He took his hand off her shoulder, stepped back, almost a stumble.

"We're tribe, Balur," she said. "But I'm human too." She shrugged. "Always will be. Can't shake it."

A ghost of a smile passed over Balur's face. It looked like the smile had enjoyed a particularly grisly death.

"Was always knowing there was being something funny about you."

It was her time to lay a hand on him. His forearm was thick and heavy beneath her palm. "This isn't the end, Balur," she said. "You know that, right?"

He nodded. "Just the beginning of the end."

She looked away. More words wouldn't help. Balur wasn't really a words sort of person. Unless she spelled it out for him in a message made of body parts, perhaps. But, ultimately, that was the sort of thing she was trying to avoid these days.

"At least," she said, "I'm not the one going about armed with a fence post."

"It is not being a fence post." Lette knew they were through the worst of it because Balur was willing to sound offended. "It is being the hand of a temple clock."

She sighed. And he questioned her desire to change. "You defaced a god's temple for a weapon?" she said.

Balur shrugged. "Well at this point it is being clear that we have pissed off every deity in the heavens above. I am figuring, at this point, fuck it."

She tightened her grip on his arm. "Yeah," she said. "Fuck it all."

# 62

# Planning for the Funeral

They all met back at the garrison. Even Firkin. Will wasn't sure how they all knew to go there. They'd not spoken about it. They'd made no plans. And yet, as he wandered in, kicking at stumps of charred wood, and the hoops of shattered barrels, there were Lette and Balur coming in through the remains of the fort's western gate; Quirk was already squatting on what was left of one of the barracks buildings, and Firkin—alone for once—was coming in from along the shore of the lake.

Was it some sort of bond? Something they had forged back in that cave near his farm? Did it tie them all together, keep them in the same orbit? Or was it just that this was the epicenter of today's disaster, and its gravity simply pulled them irresistibly in?

He watched Lette as she approached. Watched her watch him. He wasn't sure where they stood. She had taken the loss of all their coin badly, had stormed off shortly after Firkin had presented him with the sacked city. Their nascent romance seemed like it was going to have trouble surviving.

But as they all closed in on Quirk, Lette stepped away from Balur slightly toward him. Not much more than a step. But enough for his hopes to raise their head up off the bar and take a look around.

Quirk watched them all approach. "What are you doing here?" She was still having trouble finding her calm, it seemed.

Will almost laughed. "I don't think any of us have a clue," he said. "Not the slightest idea."

"I am having a clue," said Balur. He sounded slightly offended. "I am looking for a better weapon than a clock hand and then I am getting the fuck out of here."

"To be fair," Lette chimed in, "that is the best plan I've heard in a while."

"Ah," Quirk nodded. "The abandon-everyone-and-try-to-save-yourself plan. How noble."

Balur shrugged. "I am never professing to be noble. And I am not sure you are being full of altruism, based on what it was you said last night."

Quirk's jaw clenched. "I am *being* conflicted, all right?"

"And judgmental," Lette added.

*That,* Will thought, *probably wasn't helping.* Still, just standing there and not saying anything wasn't contributing much either.

"I don't know if we can just run from this," he said. "I don't think anyone's going to let us. Not the Dragon Consortium. Not the crowds here."

"Maybe you cannot be escaping here," said Balur. "But I am not being any prophet. No one is wanting me to stay."

"I'm not a prophet either," Will snapped. "But that doesn't seem to be helping me out."

"Debating whether you are a prophet or not doesn't make much difference if everyone believes you're the prophet." Lette sounded tired, he thought. Though perhaps that shouldn't be surprising. They all looked tired. All except Firkin, at least. He looked pretty much like he always did. Like he'd been founded marinating at the bottom of a beer barrel just around the point when unnameable things had started to grow on him.

"They don't believe I'm the prophet," Will protested.

This was met with a narrowing of eyes. And so he told them of visiting Firkin, of what had transpired.

Narrowed eyes switched their attention to Firkin. Firkin drew himself up, stuck out his pigeon chest, and attempted to look at them haughtily. The overall impression was that of a man suffering the last bitter extremes of constipation.

"The people come!" he said in a declarative voice. "They come not for me. They come not for you. They come not for Will. Nor Balur. Not Lette."

"You will be telling me who they are coming for," Balur informed him. "Or I will be showing you what your intestines taste like."

"They are coming for the prophet," Firkin told them. As if they were idiots. As if he hadn't already pissed Balur off way too much.

"Will is the prophet," Quirk pointed out.

"He told me he wasn't," said Firkin, looking wounded.

"I'm not!" Will thought this point bore repeating until everyone knew it.

"Then why is your flap trap clitter-clapping like someone took a piss in it?" said Firkin shrilly.

"So they don't care who's the prophet?" Lette look confused.

"And you do?" Quirk asked Will.

"What?" He threw open his hands. "You have the sole right to being conflicted right now?"

It was Balur's turn to look confused. "I am not understanding this word. Conflicted?"

Lette sighed. "Imagine there was a whore you really wanted, but she'll only sleep with you if you kill the troll. But if you kill the troll you also kill the whore. That's conflicted."

Which taught Will that teaching should not be in Lette's future.

"Why is the whore dying?" Balur looked offended by the sheer concept. "That is making no sense."

Lette shook her head. "It's just the principle. I'm trying to illustrate it for you."

Balur shook his head. "Well on principle I am lying to the whore about the troll, bedding her, then killing them both later."

Lette rolled her eyes. "Of course you are."

From her expression, Quirk's opinion of them all didn't seem to be improving.

But Will's mind was moving down a different track. "Wait," he said. "Maybe there's something in that."

"Signs of a very toxic childhood environment?" Quirk hazarded a guess.

"What if I lie to the crowd and tell them I'm the prophet now, and then just bail on them later?" Will said.

"Then you'll have the moral compass of a weasel," Quirk commented, but Will wasn't paying any attention to her anymore.

"Why would you even do that?" Lette looked at him as if he was publicly shitting his britches.

"So the crowd will listen to me when I tell them to get the hell out of here. So they're not sitting ducks for the Consortium when they come raining fire down upon our heads."

Lette weighed that. "We do need to leave here."

"Wait," said Balur. He even raised a finger.

"What?" snapped Lette, which Will thought was uncalled for.

"Is conflict always involving whores?" asked Balur. "Because if so…"

"Shut up," Lette told him.

*Okay,* thought Will, *maybe it was called for.*

"And then what?" Quirk spoke as if the mercenaries hadn't. "When you get far enough from here, you betray their trust, reveal you have no clue what you're doing, and take cover in their numbers, hoping the dragons kill them and pass you by?"

Will deflated slightly. "It sounds bad when you put it like that."

"Trust me," Quirk told him, "it sounds bad however you put it."

"I am thinking," Balur rumbled on, "that some whores may have been conflicted about me."

"I swear," Lette told him, "I will remove your guts and fashion them into a timepiece for that hexed clock hand…"

"Words!" Firkin suddenly screamed. "Round and round and round like a cat held by the tail. Screaming, and scratching, and biting, and pissing words. But never releasing them to go sailing headfirst into the wall." He turned on Will, thrust out a bony finger. "You!" he screeched. "Are you this fucking prophet or not?"

"There is no prophet." Lette made a final bid for sanity. "You made him up. Then people thought it was Will. And everything went to shit."

"It went to shit waaaaay before that."

For the first time Will wondered whether Quirk had been drinking.

Balur was shaking his head. "I have lost track completely. Is there being a prophet or not?"

Everyone, Will realized, was looking at him. He didn't understand how this kept happening. He didn't have any answers. And his guesses seemed to have a pretty consistent history of being wildly off base. And yet here they were again.

He tried to lay out the facts for himself. The undeniable, unavoidable truths of the situation. Dathrax was dead. Word was spreading. Had spread. People were already flocking to Athril. The Consortium would therefore know soon enough. Then the Consortium would descend upon them all and kill them. That last step would be particularly easy if they all stayed in one place. He could slip away and abandon everybody here, but if he did he would have an unconscionable number of lives on his hands. And there was no real guarantee that he would survive much longer than the crowd. He could instead assume the role of the prophet, and drag the crowd with him. And all that would achieve would be delaying the inevitable.

It was, he was forced to conclude, a shitty list of facts.

Still, delaying the inevitable was the option that seemed to keep him alive the longest. And that's what life was anyway, wasn't it? Staving off the inevitable for as long as possible. If he could delay the inevitable for another fifty years, then he'd probably be ready to be killed by dragons by then.

Of course if he could delay the inevitable by five minutes he would, at this point, call himself impressed.

"Yes," he said to them all. "I am the prophet."

Lette looked at the ground. Quirk looked like she couldn't care less. Balur looked like his mind was back on whores.

"Well," said Firkin, "I wish you'd mentioned this earlier. It makes for a very confusing ecclesiastical message."

Will couldn't give less of a shit about that. He plowed on. "Okay, first things first. I decree we need to leave the city. Get on the road."

Firkin looked at him hard, mouth working. "*You* say?" he said.

"Yes," said Will.

"What about the prophet?" Firkin looked deeply suspicious.

"I *am* the prophet," Will insisted. "Everything I say, the prophet says."

"Everything you say?" Firkin checked.

"Yes."

"Well," Firkin said, shaking his head, "I am the high priest of the prophet, his spicy mouth upon this bland and flavorless world, and he didn't say shit to me about that."

"I just said it!" Will protested.

"You weren't the prophet then," Firkin said, a sly look in the corners of his eyes. "When you were the prophet you said you weren't."

"Well, I am now, and I'm saying I am."

"You weren't the prophet," Firkin countered. "So you can't say you're the prophet. Only the mouth of the prophet can decree the word of the prophet. Only I, the utterer of his sumptuous words, can say—"

He cut off abruptly as Balur slammed the flat of the clock hand into the back of his skull. He dropped bonelessly to the floor.

"Hmm." Balur examined his improvised weapon. "I suppose I could be getting used to this."

# 63

# Making Like a Hooker and Blowing This Joint

Eventually, after what Balur referred to as "some light encouragement," Firkin got up in front of the crowd and announced that the prophet "in his wisdom of prodigious length and most satisfying girth" had decreed that they "abandon the sight of this most holy battle and sally forth, questing for fresh combat."

It was a little off script, and Lette had to spend five minutes restraining Balur from killing the filthy old man. They were moving, she told him, and that was enough for her.

Still, as she stood upon one of the remaining garrison walls to oversee the exodus, Lette couldn't help but feel that it was all too little, too late.

There were just so many of them. It was a crowd that no longer numbered in the hundreds but in the thousands. Every single man, woman, or child who had fallen in Athril seemed to have been replaced by at least ten newcomers. People had uprooted their entire lives. Herds of cattle, sheep, and goats all followed the crowd out of the town. People sat upon wagons loaded with chickens, turkeys, and other poultry that Lette would only have been able to discern by taste. Minstrels wandered, singing songs of the prophet, of his great feats, and of the dragons he had struck low. Soothsayers stood, causing eddies in the crowd, as they cast stones and predicted the downfall of the Consortium. Priests for all the various gods were scattered about, laying claim to the prophet. That Lawl had inspired him, or Toil, or that he was the herald of Barph's long-awaited return. Fistfights broke out between religious factions. They'd even picked up more than one string of whores, and there was one woman with a cart loaded with work shirts onto which she had crudely stitched the word "Profit." From the looks of things, the one she was making was considerable.

The thing was, it was all so infectious. There was an air of revolution in the air. Watching them all, it would have been simple to buy into their hope, to relax and let confidence wash through her.

*How many spies are already in the ranks?* the cold voice in the back of her head asked. *How many will sell you out as soon as the Consortium adds another zero to your Wanted poster? How many zeroes will they have to add before you sell Will out yourself? You're penniless now. All the gold is gone. There is no new life anymore. If you're the first to bail, there's a greater chance you'll survive.*

She shook her head. There was no way she was surviving this.

And if that was true... What was there truly to consider? Simply how to spend the time remaining to her. What sort of legacy would she leave behind? How would she be remembered? Who would look back on her memory fondly?

Balur? Will? Maybe—but only for the seven or eight seconds before they joined her in the swirling guts of whatever dragon had consumed them all.

So if no one would remember, what then? She knew what Balur would say. It was carte blanche. Life without consequences. They could do what they wanted, when they wanted, as they wanted. There need be no fear of the consequences. They were already as dire as they could be.

*What about the gods?*

*Fuck the gods,* came back Balur's voice. *If they are getting their heads out of their cups for longer than a second it's only so they can be burying them in the lap of the nearest partner. This is being a world that was being created by horrible degenerates.*

All of which was true enough. But there was another voice too. One it took her longer to identify. And when she did, she wondered how it had got there.

*Well, maybe no one will remember you for what you've done so far,* said Will's voice, *but what if you did something memorable before the end?*

How had he managed to get so deep beneath her skin? He and she hadn't even...

She considered that. Maybe *that* was the real problem. And well...If one had limited time, there were worse ways to spend it...

# 64

## The Sappy Romance Chapter

At first, Will thought he was under attack. He tried to scream for help, was smothered. His limbs were pinned. His assailant was everywhere.

By the time he finally figured out what Lette was doing, he was reduced to just hanging on for dear life.

# 65

## Fiery Indignation

Deep inside the Hallows' Mouth volcano, the dragon Kithrax drew in his breath and snorted out a perfect smoke ring. It drifted away, perfectly symmetrical, glistening almost silver in the light.

He blew the ring for several reasons. Partly because he was very good at it, and he enjoyed the simple narcissistic pleasure of watching it float away. Partly because he was bored out of his considerable mind and at this point pretty much anything was a welcome distraction. But mostly, he did it because it really pissed Horrax off.

Horrax. That dirty, fetid, shit stain of a dragon. He squatted opposite Kithrax, brown plump body looking like something a swamp hawked up in revulsion. He scratched idly at himself with a long yellow claw, then stuck the tip in his broad flat jaw and slurped away.

"I think," Horrax burbled, his voice such a wretched croak that at first Kithrax was convinced he was belching, "that I don't give a shit."

Kithrax blew another smoke ring at him. It was a way to signify his rage, but he very much doubted that Horrax had the mental capacity to pick up on such a nuance. Of course, he could announce his rage in a more obvious way, something that even Horrax would understand—clawing out his throat, for example—but he simply refused to expend that much energy on something as worthless as the brown dragon.

"You don't care? *You don't care?*" Quirrax was working herself into a lather again. Lithe and green, Quirrax pawed at the ground with one forepaw and polished one of her golden horns with the other.

"Don't give a *shit.*" Even enunciating clearly, Horrax sounded like he was soiling himself.

Kithrax hated these meetings of the Dragon Consortium.

"The people of the valley are rising up against us and you don't care?" Quirrax spun on about, scattering golden coins in great flurries all around them. She scratched at the air. "This whole endeavor has been a disaster from beginning to end and now this. This! And you sit there and you don't care!"

Fire shrieked out of her mouth at the last, boiling to blue with the heat of her exasperation.

"Don't give a shit," Horrax burbled again.

"Horrax has a point," Bruthrax cut in. "This is simple. We crush them."

Kithrax could appreciate Bruthrax. The massive red dragon was a blunt instrument. He was the hammer that saw every problem as a nail. He knew it. He didn't care. But if he was told to wait then he would bide his time. He acknowledged Kithrax's superiority without question.

"We fly out there, like we should have done a week ago," Bruthrax went on, "and we devour them whole. And then we drop their rotting remains on anyone who thinks to try it again. We send a message."

"Mmmm," Horrax burbled in agreement. "You tasted good." The sound of his laughter brought bile to the back of Kithrax's throat.

"And what about their taxes?" asked Quirrax. "What about their gold? What about our income streams? That's ten thousand people no longer lining our coffers."

"Humans breed," Horrax burbled, licking his lips lasciviously.

Kithrax blew another smoke ring directly at him.

"And you would do what, Quirrax?" Scourrax raised her sinuous yellow head from where it was resting on Kithrax's jet-black flank. She slithered forward. "You would talk them out of their madness?" She made a scoffing sound. "You would stand before them, and bend your head down to them, and plead oh so nicely that they understand you? That they see things from your point of view?"

Fire shot from Quirrax's mouth, shooting harmlessly over their heads. Scourrax laughed and the others joined in.

Kithrax permitted himself a momentary smile. Ever the voice of reason was Scourrax. Right up until her patience ran short and she clawed out your eyes. He felt his loins stir, and immediately the smile vanished. This fucking prophet forcing this absurd meeting of the Consortium. He'd been trying to wean the other dragons off this need to meet. He thought he had at least another year before he had to watch Horrax...exist in front of him.

The audacity of these people. These humans. To defy the Consortium. To defy *him*. He had come to this valley and blessed it with order. He had put humans in their rightful place, had shown them that they were nothing more than educated cattle. They should be grateful to have the responsibility of leadership—something they never had the capacity to truly deal with—lifted from their shoulders. And now they rose up, and shook their fists like angry children.

"This talking is wasting fucking time," Bruthrax said. He shifted his weight on a pile of coins, gold reflecting against his red scales. "We go there and we raze them to the ground. We leave ash and bone. We make a grave that no one will ever forget. We make a desolation of their hopes, their dreams."

"Don't need all of us to do that," Horrax burbled, and then yawned massively at them all, as he lay down his fat head. Kithrax could never work out why he had been sent to the valley with the rest of them.

"We are here to rule," Quirrax said tremulously. "We need people to rule. If we kill them all—"

"Shut up!" Kithrax roared. He could take it no longer. Curse them all for making him stir to life. He rose up, shaking Scourrax off his flanks once more, towering over them. "This pathetic bickering."

He spat flame. It landed at Quirrax's feet, turned coins to golden slag. She shied back, hissing.

"We are here to rule. To show the viability of our rulership. And this act of defiance sets you to whimpering like children? You are unfit to rule." He looked specifically at Horrax while he said this.

Burthrax was smiling. "So we—" he started.

"No," Kithrax snapped. "*We* do nothing. This prophet, these people—they are beneath us. They are nothing to us. They are not worthy of our attention."

"You just—" Quirrax started.

"Shut up," Scourrax snapped at her, preening slightly, the way she always did when he took charge.

"The human rebels must die," Kithrax went on. "But we will not sully ourselves with their deaths. We will not stoop to such things. *We are the Dragon Consortium*." He ran his claws through the coins that sat all around them. "We have resources beyond their imagining."

He lowered his head, looked at them each and every one. "We send an army and"—he permitted himself a savage smile—"we make the humans kill each other."

# 66

# The Dripping Jaws of the Future

Several days after their departure from Athril, Will found himself sitting down on a soft grassy slope, surrounded by a crowd of his own worshippers, watching Firkin preach.

"We stand upon the precipice!" the old man shrieked. "The edge! The lip—if it were a cup. That bit of the cliff your mother was always on about you not stepping upon, even though she did concede it would be one less mouth to feed, and if she'd known how much corn children consumed, she would have kept her legs together more often when she was younger."

They had found a natural bowl in the landscape to make their camp in that night. A small rocky escarpment made a semicircle describing half the bowl. On the other side, the land sloped down to its base. A natural amphitheater. Alcohol may have robbed Firkin of many of the important parts of his mind, but it hadn't robbed him of his sense of drama. He stood on a barrel, letting his shrill voice bounce off the rock wall to the gathered masses. There must have been two or three thousand of them, sitting there listening, rapt.

"We stand and we stare at the future. We see it eyeballing us from across the room. And at first we are not sure if it wants to fuck us or fight us. And maybe we are scared. That little rumble in our guts that makes us squeeze our cheeks tightly and worry just a little about how we shall be explaining the state of our britches to our wives later. Or maybe we are a little bit excited and we want to give it a wink or two. But then there is a cursed missus again, and we have explaining to do again. Gods piss on it!"

The crowd murmured. As it didn't sound like a collective "What in the name of the gods is he talking about, and what are we doing here?" Will honestly couldn't think what they were saying.

"But what if the future is not unknown?" Firkin went on. "What if it is not some bloody dripping dragon's maw, our balls caught in the vise of its teeth? What if the future is the prophet, and our balls are cupped softly and protectively?"

Will shook his head. They had left Athril three days ago now, and every day the crowds had grown. Lette estimated their number was between five or six thousand by this point. She said that at the current rate of growth they'd be ten thousand in a day or two.

That was when she was talking, at any rate. But she didn't seem that interested in doing that with him these days.

Not that he was complaining.

A smile crept across his lips.

"The prophet caresses our future. He massages it gently. He treats it with the love and respect it deserves. He does that-thing-that-girl-from-the-edge-of-town-did-that-one-time to it."

Will had started coming down to watch Firkin preach the night after they left the scene of Dathrax's death. Lette had been lying, snoring in his makeshift tent, and he had been staring up at the stained canvas, trying to figure out what he was supposed to do, how he was supposed to lead these people to anything but imminent death. And then he'd heard Firkin's preaching, and thought that maybe instead of figuring out what he should do for himself, he should just go and listen, find out, and then report back.

"Bathed in dragon's blood and dragon's gold, the prophet

comes!" Firkin shrieked. "Smoking from their fire that does not touch him. And we welcome him into our lives, and he is considerate enough to bathe and change his clothes before he comes in!"

The trouble was, Will reflected, that Firkin's sermons were remarkably low on detail. There was no path to the future he described. It just happened, springing out of Firkin's mouth fully formed, with none of the intervening messy middle parts. Still, it was comforting to hear about a future where he succeeded, where whatever he did, he pulled off. And so he kept coming back, night after night. No one seemed to recognize him in the gloom. It was peaceful, meditative.

Still, it was getting on to be time to leave. No one had recognized him yet, but he made sure he left before the main assembly. He didn't want cries of "the prophet!" to lead to him being trampled to death by his own congregation.

So head down, he stood and slipped away. No one called out. No one hailed the divinely chosen man who walked among them. Well, all except for a middle-aged woman in a floral pattern dress who hissed at him to stop blocking her view.

When he was younger, his ma had told him stories of kings and sultans who would go out into their cities in disguise, to walk among their people. Typically, they would get themselves into trouble, learn great wisdom from simple people, reveal themselves to the great wonderment of all, and then return to be even more fabulous kings or sultans. In Will's experience, anonymity was pretty much identical to every other day of his life: He wandered around, felt slightly bored and impotent, learned no great wisdom, and returned to his tent the same useless arsehole he had been when he left it.

And yet, as he returned to his tent, he found he was still smiling.

The tents might be one of the best things that had happened to him since he'd lost his farm. A merchant had given them to him, bowing, and murmured a request that he "place them into the holy hands of the prophet," which he still found amusing. There were three of them, vast and palatial. They were pitched at the center of the camp. Little flags blew from canvas crenellations around the rim: red on Balur's tent, green on Quirk's, and purple on the one he shared with Lette.

It was that last fact that truly had him smiling. In fact, if he was left alone with anyone for longer than ten seconds he liked to tell them that he shared his tent with Lette. Regardless of how many times he had told them before.

For her part, Lette seemed to be dealing with the encroaching disaster better than he was. Not that she talked about it much, but he assumed she was because most of her time was spent either using him for his body or sleeping.

Will cracked his knuckles, and kept on smiling.

A shape wrapped in white detached itself from the shadowy shape of the tent. From the dark skin he could tell it wasn't Lette. His smile faltered.

"I've been waiting for you," said Quirk. "Where were you?"

"Sorry," said Will. He didn't feel it, but he wanted to explain about Firkin's speeches even less. "If I'd known you wanted to talk then I'd have stayed here."

"I didn't know," said Quirk. She didn't snap, but she came as close as she could to the precipice of doing so without falling over. "But at least I was here to receive the news when it came in."

"What news?" Will felt like this conversation was taking place out of order.

The flap of his tent pulled back, to reveal Lette, backlit by candles, wrapped only in a bedsheet. She rubbed at her eyes sleepily. "News?" she said, stifling a yawn.

"The news I was too busy not knowing about to stay here and receive," said Will, a little testily. His peaceful mood was evaporating.

"Is it about the looting?" Lette said, rolling her neck from side to side, releasing a cascading roll of pops and clicks. "Because I think we established we don't give a shit."

"The looting is an important issue," Quirk snapped. "We have enough problems, without people who profess to worship Will looting actual gods' temples. Surviving is hard enough as it is without us prompting some deity to come down here and fling thunderbolts at us all."

Will shook his head. This again. "I still don't understand why people keep taking the roofs off temples. It makes no sense."

Quirk smacked her forehead in frustration. "How many times do I have to tell you? It's the gods-hexed lead."

"Surely it's not gods-hexed if it's from a temple," said Lette. Apparently she never grew tired of baiting Quirk.

Will held out a hand, trying to quiet her. *Because that's bound to work*, he thought. "Lead," he tried to explain to Quirk, "isn't an explanation."

"It's a soft metal."

"You're a soft metal." That, he knew for a fact, was childish. But how many times would they talk about this?

"A soft metal is one they can work on the road. We need so many things. Bowls, spoons, knives. You can fix pottery with it. It's something they can use on the road."

"So let them take it!" Will said for the umpteenth time.

"The wrath of the gods," Quirk snapped back.

"Be fucking the gods."

They had woken Balur, it seemed.

The lizard man stumbled out of his tent. They all took a moment to take in the sight of him. Someone had started the rumor that small donations of gold and jewelry could curry favor with the prophet. Balur—probably the source of the rumors—had immediately set himself up as the person to whom all such donations should be given. Which went partway to explain the purple robe draped over his shoulders, the reams of necklaces around his neck, the bangles and baubles at each of his wrists, and the seven tiaras perched upon his broad, flat head. He looked like a cross between a king, a whoremonger, and a dragon's midden heap.

"The gods have been fucking with us, and been showing us no favors," he said. "Why should we be showing any to them?"

"Oh, I don't know," Quirk said with a shrug, "perhaps because of the *vast* power differential?"

"Two dragons are being down," Balur said with a cocky grin. "And I am still standing."

"One was unconscious while you bludgeoned it to death," Quirk pointed out. "The other was eaten by mutant fish, and you only survived because Will saved you."

Balur didn't actually redden—his scales were too thick for that—but there was a definite stiffening to his posture and a glare of outrage that seemed to suggest reddening would go on if it could.

"I will be looting some lead, and will be cramming it up your arse," Balur spat back.

"Look," said Will, throwing up his hands. "We've had this conversation thirty times so far, and every time we just insult each other, posture, and then realize that even if we did want to do something we couldn't because we're outnumbered almost a thousand to one. So," he concluded, turning to Quirk, "if it's all the same to you, I'm going to go to bed."

He stepped toward Lette's welcoming smile.

"Wait," said Quirk with disappointing insistence. "That isn't the news."

"It's not?" said Will, hoping he'd heard wrong.

"No," said Quirk, from three feet away, and very clear indeed. "It's not."

"Then why are we arguing about it?" Balur asked, not unreasonably.

"Because your *partner*—" Quirk said, acid on her tongue.

Will held up his hands. "Can't we just pretend we all argued for five more minutes and feel shitty about ourselves so we can skip to the bit where Quirk gives us the actual news?"

After much surreptitious glancing, the other three finally nodded. Will sighed.

"Quirk," he said, "please, what is your news?"

She pushed both hands through her close-cropped curls. "So," she said, "the Dragon Consortium is pulling together an army to destroy us."

She delivered it like a tired waitress would deliver a mug of stout to a man who had ordered the same thing a thousand times before. Her tone was so flat it took a moment for the size of the news to sink into Will. And then he realized the news was so large that only the tip of it had soaked into him. The rest of it was still poised above his head, waiting to drown him completely.

"A fucking army?" He tried to double take but the moment had passed. He resorted to staring wildly around as if somehow the army would appear from nowhere, stand there, and let him gawp incredulously at it. "An actual army?"

*For him? The Dragon Consortium was raising an army for him?* In a truly messed-up way, that was almost flattering.

"They're dragons," Lette said. She was holding up her bed-sheet with both hands now. Clearly she had not dressed for such a protracted discussion. "They're massive, fire-breathing lizards that could obliterate us as soon as look at us. Why in the name of the gods do they need an army?"

And then it hit Will.

"We've killed two of them," he said quietly. *"They're scared of us."*

"Yeah," said Quirk. "That's great. You've scared them so much that now they won't be satisfied by just killing us, but only by raising an army to kill everyone whoever came within a one-mile radius of us all. That's brilliant. Very good job." She spat onto the ground.

"How many dragons are there being left on the council?" Balur asked, staring off into the night. "I am always meaning to be asking that and I am never getting around to it."

"Is now really the time?" said Quirk, at the same moment as Will said, "Five."

Balur gave his iron clock hand an assessing look. "Their time has come...?" he said, tentatively.

"I will fucking gut you right here and right now," Lette told him.

Balur shrugged. "That is being fair."

Quirk grabbed her forehead. "Why in Knole's holy name did I even bother telling you? What did I expect? Why would an army marching down upon us be in any way galvanizing? Let's just sit around scratching our crotches for another few days. The imminent death of everyone here shouldn't be any cause for concern!" She spat again.

Will liked Quirk. She was smart and had a good moral compass that he could grab hold of at times when Balur and Lette were ganging up on him. But he had had enough of her right now. "Did you ever consider for a moment that the imminent death of everybody here might be what is causing some of the paralysis?" he barked. "That a little added pressure might not be exactly what is needed?"

Quirk actually hesitated there. Apparently she had not considered that.

"Look," Will said to Quirk, "you want a plan, we stick to the one we've got. We keep running away. They're a big army, we're a small group. We can move faster and we're more agile than they are. We can outrun them indefinitely."

Quirk made a contemptuous sound. "Agile?" she said. "Our followers number in the thousands, and not a single one of them is a well-trained, well-paid, professional soldier. They're going to slaughter us."

"Keep your mouth shut," Lette hissed. "Morale at the camp

is going to be bad enough when this news hits without your words of encouragement."

"Can't Will be coming up with a plan?" Balur suggested.

"No!" Will said before anyone else could jump in and argue in his favor. "My past two plans have got us in this mess by killing two dragons."

"Exactly," said Balur, nodding. "That is what I am thinking. You come up with five more plans and we have nothing to worry about."

Will shook his head. "No," he said. "No more plans. We stick to what we're doing. We just keep running away. Eventually they'll give up."

"The average dragon," Quirk told him, "lives for about two thousand years. I'm not sure you'll wait them out."

Will shrugged. "I don't care. No more plans. Not one more. I'm done."

# 67

# One More Plan

Seven more days passed. News of the Dragon Consortium's army continued to percolate into their camp. Estimates of its size came in. Fifteen thousand men and horses. Thirty thousand. Forty. Fifty. There was talk of siege engines, war wizards, griffin riders, a contingent of troll mercenaries.

Their own numbers grew, Lette's prediction playing out as the ragtag group hit and surpassed ten thousand souls. But their growth rate never outpaced the rumors of the Consortium's army. No matter how many empty fields they passed, how many abandoned villages, there never seemed to be enough of them to make a stand.

Will lay inside his tent, Lette's arm curled around him, her head resting on his chest. He could feel the soft gusting of her breath steady and slow across his skin. His fingers tangled with her red hair. She smelled of the road, of sweat, and dust, and sex. There was the dull throbbing of exertion in his crotch.

It was funny, he thought—they didn't even talk about the gold anymore. None of them. Not even Quirk, who had insisted it was so critical for keeping their followers housed and fed. They seemed to have hit a critical mass of bodies and goodwill. People came to them loaded with corn, bread, milk, livestock. Several makeshift canteens had evolved, which doled out food to the masses. Usually he found some left outside the tent. Somewhere along the way they had picked up some pretty good cooks.

Outside the sun was rising, beginning to lighten the walls of the tent. The camp would be breaking soon. Every day they pushed on fifteen or twenty more miles. An aimless wandering flight, not quite sure of the location of the army they were fleeing from, not quite sure what safe harbor they were heading to.

*Maybe this will last forever,* Will thought. *Eternally fleeing. Never resting, but never having to stop and face things either. Maybe we can just drag this out without end.* Lying there with Lette's sleepy weight pinning him to the cot, he thought there were worse ways life could play out.

A noise at his tent flap drew his attention away from theoretical futures to the very practical present. Quirk was sticking her head into his tent.

"Will," she said in a soft tone, "you need to come and see this."

He wanted to ignore her. While the edge on Quirk's anger at all of them had blunted somewhat of late, being with her was still like carrying a hive of bees around with you—constantly concerned you were going to drop it on the floor and unleash rage.

Still, he carefully extricated himself from beneath Lette. She moaned slightly, rolled in her sleep. Will loved these unguarded moments. The softness in her, normally so well hidden, momentarily exposed. He kissed his fingers, brushed them through her hair, then pulled on his shirt and went to face the day.

"What is it?" he asked. Quirk was pacing back and forth in front of his tent.

"Come with me," she said and turned away from him, forcing a path into the stumbling crowds camped around them.

The journey was not a brief one. The camp was vast now, stretching off for half a mile in almost every direction. Livestock milled down the narrow aisles between tents and carts, stomping past the campfires where bowls of porridge and corn steamed and bubbled, and slices of toast were being burned. The cooking smells mixed with the stink of privy holes, the musky funk of unwashed bodies, the scent of churned-up earth.

They had camped between the edge of a forest and the rise of a small hill, one of the gentle folds in the land near the floor of the Kondorra valley. Quirk led him up the slope of the hill to where a small knot of men was waiting.

"Cattak," she said as they drew closer, and one of the men tugged at a forelock and bobbed his head.

"Quirk, ma'am," he said back to her. He was a man of about forty, thick-limbed and hard-featured. A scar carved its way across one eye, down into a thick thatch of stubble. His jet-black hair was swept back from his tan face. His hands, Will noticed, were heavy and callused. A workingman, but what work, Will wasn't sure he wanted to know.

"Cattak," said Quirk, finally turning to face Will, "was one of our camp's most prodigious looters. He and his men here could strip a church of all its valuables in two hours flat."

"Healthy work ethic," said Cattak, tugging at his forelock again. The men at his back, all of whom seemed to have been cast in the same mold, nodded their heads and mumbled agreement.

"I approached him," Quirk went on, "because I thought I could put that work ethic to less sacrilegious use."

"Only too happy to find another way to oblige," said Cattak. "Anything we can do to help the prophet."

Will gave an embarrassed smile. "Thanks," he said.

Cattak looked up at that, a darker spark shining through his humble demeanor. "You one of them that know him then?" he said.

"Erm..." said Will, not sure how to respond.

"Cattak," said Quirk, "this is Will."

"Oh," said Cattak with absolutely no spark of recognition. "Nice to meet you then, Will." He stuck out a hand. Will took it, shook. He had the distinct impression that if Cattak wanted to break every bone in his palm then he could.

"Cattak," said Quirk once more, "show Will what you showed me."

"All right then." Cattak nodded, turned to Will. "Keep your head down," he said. "Don't want them spotting us." He promptly dropped to his belly in the long grass that covered the hilltop. A second later, Will was the only one on his feet.

Feeling slightly self-conscious, he got down onto his belly, and found himself staring at Cattak's retreating feet, as the man wormed his way toward the crest of the hill. Hurriedly he worked his way after him.

Quirk dropped back to be level with him. She was wearing a dull brown dress today, he noticed. Had she chosen it as being better to hide the grass stains?

"What's going on?" he asked, without a tremendous amount of hope that she'd actually let him know.

"I've had Cattak and his men acting as outriders," she said. "I've been trying to redirect the energies of the looters, and the gods knew we needed scouts of some sort. We were running blind from an army, Will. It was absurd."

*Were? Was?* Will wasn't sure he liked the use of the past tense there. But then they were at the crest of the hill, and he was looking down into the valley beyond.

The land flowed down in a straight run to the river Kon. It was a sweep of patchwork fields, green and yellow dotted with the red of poppy and the blue of lavender, the whole thing punctuated by copses of trees scattered like emeralds. The river lay beyond, reflecting the sun like a line of liquid silver strung through the world.

It was a beautiful sight, and Will didn't pay it the slightest heed, because sprawled all over it was the Dragon Consortium's army.

He felt the air go out of him, tried to get it back, couldn't. His mouth fell open, stayed that way. He tried to take it all in, couldn't.

All the rumors had been true. *All* of them.

Fifty thousand men. A contingent of griffin riders, their beasts massive and majestic, tugging at leashes, stretching vast wings in the rising morning heat. War wizards, their tents crackling with lines of violet puissance. A contingent of troll mercenaries lolling against the siege weaponry. One massive brute scratched his back against a trebuchet; another picked at his teeth with a ballista bolt.

Finally Will managed to put everything into words. "Fuck," he breathed.

"Pretty much," said Cattak by his side. He sounded sanguine about it.

Will turned to Quirk, seeking someone less stoic about staring death in the eye. "We're fucked," he said to her, expanding on his theme.

"Yes," she said, still a little too matter-of-factly for Will's tastes, though he could hear the buried panic beneath her words. "We *need* a plan, Will," she said. The panic was clearer there.

"We run," he said. "We run like fuck."

"We're already running," she pointed out.

"Okay then." He nodded. "New plan. We run faster."

So they ran.

News of the Consortium's army spread through the camp like wildfire. Panicked cries were rapidly hushed, the smarter, steadier heads knocking sense and quiet into those more prone to alerting vast armies to the presence of their enemies. As quickly and as quietly as possible goods were thrown into carts, animals were herded, dirt was kicked into privy holes, ashes scattered onto fires, and tents were bundled into squares of stained fabric. There was no time to truly disguise that the camp had been there, but Will was glad that at least a token effort was being made. It showed that people had the right attitude at least.

All the while, runners came back and forth from Cattak giving updates on the Consortium army's maneuvers. Will stood beside Quirk listening in.

Lette mostly involved herself in stopping Balur from leading a charge on their enemies. For once the lizard man and Firkin were united on an issue.

"We should smite them!" Firkin had squealed upon hearing the news. "With our"—he had stared at the ends of his arms—"smitey bits."

"Fists?" Will had suggested.

"Good enough!"

"Look," Lette had interjected, "I know deranged cults are all about the suicide thing, especially when it's on a grand scale, but I for one am going to use your intestines as a skipping rope should you attempt to rabble-rouse on this one."

That had given Firkin pause. Unfortunately Balur was more than willing to crack Firkin in order to make an omelet. Especially a bloody omelet of war.

"Do not be listening to her," he had said. "It is being your divine duty to unleash the wrath of the heavens upon this army. You are being the pointer finger of the prophet or some such bullshit. You are knowing you want to."

"He is not knowing shit, Balur." Lette's voice brooked no argument. "He's a violent drunk."

"He is being a right-minded holy warrior. You are being pussy." Balur was apparently in a brooking-argument kind of mood.

Lette had opted for a long-suffering look. "Not wanting to commit violent suicide is not the same as cowardice."

Balur shook his head. "I am not understanding humans."

Lette didn't seem to care about that. Even now, though, a good hour and a bucket of Will's fear-sweat later, Balur was still pacing around the camp demanding they go "cut the head off the beast."

"No, Balur," Lette said yet again.

"How about just the genitals."

"Sit down and shut up, Balur."

Another of Cattak's runners approached. Will tuned out the bickering. "They seem to be organizing their scouts."

"Shit," said Will. "How close are we to departure?"

So far, it seemed, the Consortium forces were ignorant of how close their prey was. Will wanted to keep it that way for as long as possible.

"We can leave anytime you want," said Cattak's runner. He was another hard-faced man, eyes lost in a network of sun-stained wrinkles. "Just a case of how much you want to leave behind."

"What if we ran now?"

The man squinted as he descended into thought, hiding his eyes even deeper than Will had imagined possible. "Depends," he said eventually.

"On what?" Will snapped, because apparently he was the only one with a sense of urgency around here.

"Well," said the man, "if we run now it will be hard going. Have to leave a lot of the wagons and the livestock behind."

"And if we stay."

"Probably harder going," said the man, "considering how their outriders will be finding us and we'll be busy fighting a battle we can't hope to win." He cracked a grin at Will. Most of his teeth were missing. Will suppressed the urge to knock out a few more.

"Give the signal and let's get the hell out of here."

"What signal?" asked the man.

"Don't we have a signal?" Will looked to Quirk. She seemed like she was vaguely in charge of these sorts of things.

Quirk shrugged. It was at least a very official-seeming shrug.

In the end they settled on the signal being somebody telling people to leave, and telling them to tell everyone else. It was surprisingly effective. A few minutes later they were all heading for the forest that they'd kept at their back. The going would be slow, but Will prayed it would be slower for the people who had to drag a bunch of trebuchets after them.

*     *     *

It was almost midnight when they all staggered to a stop. There was no sermon from Firkin. There were no campfire songs. There were no campfires. Women, men, children—they simply collapsed to the ground, pulled up blankets if they had the energy, and fell asleep.

It had not taken the Consortium outriders long to find the remains of their camp. It had taken them even less to figure out what it meant and where their enemies were going.

Fortunately mobilizing fifty thousand troops took a considerable while, even if some of them did ride griffins. And the woods had worked as Will had hoped. Still, in the end Will's troops were a bunch of farmers, merchants, and craftsmen, who had spent their lives being worked to the bone, beaten down by fear and exhaustion. Their pursuers were trained soldiers, well paid and well equipped. Will's followers had maintained their lead over the course of the day, but not by much.

Somewhat to Will's embarrassment, he found that someone had taken the time to erect the prophet's tent. It felt like an undeserved privilege. All he had done was lead these people into this trap. All he could do now was drag them around the countryside until finally they were too exhausted to do even that, dropped to the ground, and were put to the sword.

Lette, though, was of another mind. "Get your arse in there," she told him.

"What?" he said. "No. Please. I'm too tired."

Lette rolled her eyes. "Not that, you pervert. I'm knackered and I want to sleep."

"Oh." Will wasn't sure why he felt mildly offended. Still, he allowed Lette to push him into the tent. He was just about to remove his shirt when Quirk joined them.

"Hey!" he said.

"What do you want?" asked Lette.

"A rational fucking plan," Quirk said, without the slightest hesitation.

Will wondered if just tearing his hair out and flinging it at her would get her to let it go. *There was no plan.*

Balur shoved into the tent after Quirk. "What is going on?" he asked. "Is it that we are all going to sleep in here?"

"No," said Lette. "It is definitely not. It is being that you and Quirk are getting the hell out so I can sleep, wake up early, and abuse Will's body."

"Hey," said Will, then wondered what he was objecting to.

"A plan!" Quirk almost shrieked. She was, Will realized, genuinely furious. She quivered from rage. Smoke slowly drifted up from her palms.

Beside him, Lette went very still. All softness forgotten, as if it had never existed. Balur shifted his weight slightly.

"There are," Quirk hissed, "ten thousand men, women, and children here. They are for some un-fucking-known reason paying attention to what you say, and specifically to what you badger Firkin into saying. Now when it comes to robberies, to getting all these people into this horrifying bloody mess, you are willing to sit all night figuring everything out. But, here, now, when it finally actually fucking matters, when lives are actually at fucking stake, you dodge the whole fucking question. And I will not have it any longer. You will think. You will make a plan. You will execute it. And knowing you bunch of half-witted morons you will almost certainly fuck it up, but at least, as I die in a painful and pathetic bloody mess, I will know that I kicked your arses into just fucking trying. To giving these people the leadership they are asking for, even if you are fundamentally incapable of providing the leadership they truly deserve."

She stood panting slightly, staring at them each in turn, daring them to speak against her. A dull red light was shining from her palms.

The moment hung, absolutely silent.

Will tried. He truly did. He wanted so badly to have a plan.

For there to be a way to fix this. But he hadn't spent years fantasizing about this. He had never spent his idle hours wondering what he would do if he were the head of a cult being chased by an opposing army sponsored by rich, murderous dragons. It was, he realized, a critical flaw in his imagination.

"I want to tell you I have something," he said. "I truly do."

"Not good enough!" Quirk yelled, shoving her hand out at him.

Will saw red. Bright, burning red, pointing straight at him. He flinched away, squealing in embarrassing fright.

Lette moved, lunging forward, a dark shadow in the gloom of the tent, the blade in her hand reflecting the red light of Quirk's palms. Even stumbling back, Will made out Quirk's surprised yell. A gout of yellow fire flared over his head. He yelled again, tripped on something. Balur yelled. There was another yell he couldn't place. Then he couldn't place much because he was on his arse, feet in the air, head buried in the sheets of his cot. He twisted, tangled further, sat up, head wreathed in sheets.

Everyone around him was yelling, shouting. Too many voices. A scuffle. Something slammed into his legs. He yelled, clawed at the blankets.

When he finally got himself free, Lette, Balur, and Quirk were standing in a semicircle before him. Quirk had her palm held out in front of her, a yellow flame dancing in her hand, casting a flickering light about the scene.

There was a tear in the tent wall. A chest lay, overturned, its contents spilling out. And lying on the floor, with Balur's not-inconsiderable foot planted in his back, was a young man.

Will stared at the man and tried to figure out where he had come from.

Through the tear in the tent wall, he supposed.

Lette was holding her short sword. It was pointed at the tiny part of the young man's neck that was visible between Balur's taloned toes.

He remembered her leaping between him and Quirk. Between him and magical fire. "You saved me," he said, somewhat bewildered, but deeply touched.

"What?" said Lette, looking up at him confused. "No I didn't."

Which was not exactly the tender message of love Will had been hoping for. "But..." he floundered. "You leapt. At the fire. Between me and it."

"No I didn't," Lette said again. "Quirk lit up the tent, I saw this tool's shadow through the fabric." She indicated the young man on the ground. "So I slit the tent flap and grabbed him."

"But..." Will kept coming back to that word. He looked at Quirk. The fire...

"She leapt at me!" Quirk protested. "It was self-defense!"

"I didn't leap at you!" Lette looked outraged by the very suggestion.

"Well, two of us clearly thought you did." Quirk put her free hand on her hip.

"Well, two of you are clearly idiots."

This had gotten very far away from tender messages of love. Will found he didn't have much left to say.

"Can I get up?" the young man on the floor said into the silence. His voice was muffled by the mouthful of dirt Balur was forcing him to eat.

"No, you cannot get up," said Lette, her voice full of disgust. "We just caught you spying on us. What do you think we are, idiots?"

The spy said nothing.

"Well," said Balur after a moment. "He is having a point."

"Shut up," Lette told him. She poked her short sword into the nape of the spy's neck. "Now talk. What are you doing here?"

More silence. Lette pressed harder with the sword. The young man yelped. "Spying!" he shouted. "What do you think?"

"Why is it you were spying?" Balur rumbled. He leaned forward slightly, adding pressure to his foot.

The spy's yelp was even more muffled this time. "You know the prophet," he managed.

"We know the prophet." Will rolled his eyes. "Well obviously…" Then a thought brought him up short. He considered it, tossed it away, and it bounced off an imaginary wall and hit him in the side of the head. He winced. "Wait," he said. "Who do you think the prophet is?"

The spy spasmed on the floor. It took Will a moment to realize he was trying to shrug beneath Balur's crushing weight. "What I was trying to find out, weren't it?" he managed between mouthfuls of sod.

"Wait," said Lette, prodding the man with her sword again. "You don't know who the prophet is?"

"You fancy telling me?" asked the spy hopefully.

"No," said Lette, "because we're not—"

"Me," Will shouted. "It's bloody me!" He couldn't believe this.

"—idiots," Lette finished.

And perhaps, on second thought, Will could believe it. Firkin telling the looters in Athril that he wasn't the prophet. Their nonresponse. His ability to wander to Firkin's speeches unmolested. Cattak's nonchalance at his name. The man telling him to give the tent to the prophet…

The crowds had grown so fast, had amassed so many people who not been there that night at Mattrax's cave, that he had become lost in the crowd.

"Nobody knows who I am," he whispered.

"What?" said the spy, trying to twist on the floor to get a better look at Will. "That guy? Are you serious?"

Lette reached out a hand, touched Will on the arm. "I know who you are," she said softly.

And there it was, that tender message of love. So unexpected in this moment, and all the sweeter for it. But for Will it barely even registered. He was already miles away, staring into space, feeling the fireworks explode against the confines of his skull, a chain reaction of destruction and insight, everything suddenly falling into place.

"Oh shit," he said. "Oh no. Oh Betra's sagging gut."

Lette removed her hand.

"What is it?" Quirk asked.

"Oh, we are so screwed," Will said.

"What?" Quirk pressed.

He looked up at her, despair in his eyes. "I'm so sorry," he said. "I have another plan."

# 68

## According to Plan

The effect, Will thought, would have been much the same had he, at that moment, torn off all his clothes and started to whirl his member in a circle while shouting "Look at me, I'm a windmill!"

Quirk took a step back. "What?" she said. Despite it being everything she'd been asking for, she seemed totally unprepared for the eventuality.

Lette cocked her head to one side, contemplating, calculating. "What?" she asked, not surprised, though, just asking for detail.

Balur simply nodded.

"What?" echoed the spy from the floor. He sounded hopeful.

Balur applied pressure. The spy gurgled. There was a wet cracking sound. The spy spasmed and lay still.

"Gods!" Will shouted, stepping back from the sudden spray of blood that spattered his legs.

"Knole's knockers," Quirk swore, wiping as blood spatter hissed in the heat of her flame.

"What?" Balur's face was the picture of innocence. At least, it was as innocent as a giant, blood-spattered lizard man's face can look while it's smiling at you with a mouth of razor-sharp teeth.

"The plan!" Lette snapped. "Focus on the fucking plan."

"He just killed someone," Will pointed out. Not unreasonably, he thought. "All over my feet."

"He does that sort of thing all the time," Lette said, and from her tone it sounded like this was indeed not the first time Balur had forced a man's intestines out of his anus in front of her. "It's like leaving a dog near a tree. Eventually something's going to get sprayed. We'll clean it up later. Now tell us what the plan is."

"Well, I'm distracted now." Again, Will was confident he hadn't wandered into the realm of unreasonableness.

"Look," said Lette, mimicking a reasonable tone in much the same way that a shapeshifter would mimic a man before gutting him and stealing his family, "I have grown very fond of you these past weeks on the road, and I very much enjoy your, erm, swordsmanship. However, if you don't tell me this plan I will carve the tendons from your arms and use them to hang you from the nearest tree. Am I clear?"

Will swallowed very hard. "Yes," he muttered. "Totally clear."

"Good."

"I don't know," Balur rumbled. "Maybe we should be clearing it up now. Folk are always smelling a bit of shit when they are dying this way."

"Well, whose fault is that?" Lette said.

Balur shrugged ruefully. Still he bent down, peeled what was left of the body off the floor, and threw it out of the hole Lette had cut in the tent wall.

That, Will supposed, was as close as he was going to get to a cleanup job.

"Okay." He sat down on the edge of the cot. "Let me think this through."

"Talk it through." Lette was insistent. Beside her Quirk nodded.

"Okay." Will nodded. "So I'm thinking... spies. It's obviously easy for them to get spies into our camps." He looked off through the now bloodstained slit in the tent wall and grimaced. Lette nodded in agreement. "That's not really a surprise," he went on. "There's ten thousand of us. That's an impossible number to really keep track of. But," he said, feeling the first edge of a smile grace his lips, "the Consortium army has five times that number."

"I'm having trouble seeing that as a positive," Quirk said.

"My point is," Will said, "is it would be easy to get people into *their* camp."

"So your idea is we slowly slip ten thousand people into their army and hope they don't notice?" Quirk looked more than a little dubious.

"No!" Will was a little disappointed that that was the response. Certainly his plans had had flaws, but...*Screw it*. He tried a different tack. "Look, why does anyone work for the Dragon Consortium?"

"Because they are being actual men, who know that life is only being lived to the fullest when your blade is sunk into the chest of another man, and his blood is spilling over your hands and onto your feet?" Balur hazarded.

"No," Will told him categorically. "The Consortium is in fact incredibly stable. Nobody really wants to attack a nation run by dragons, and the dragons sweeten that pot by being fantastic merchants."

"Then they are signing up because they are being lazy cowards?" Balur tried again.

"They're bullies," Quirk put in.

Will had to concede those two points. "Well, okay, yes, those are good reasons. But not the ones I was thinking of."

"This is a being a guessing game now?" Balur said. "We are going to be irritating the Consortium army with brain teasers until they go home?"

"Money," Will said irritably. "Money and fear. That's why you work for the Dragon Consortium. Because it's about the only way to make real cash in this stupid, bloody valley, and because you're scared that if you don't work for them you'll end up on the wrong end of a three-foot-long canine."

"I am still saying it is because of the cowardice," said Balur.

"I just said fear," Will said. "Like just now."

Balur grunted.

"If this goes any slower," Lette told him, "I'm removing a few tendons on principle."

"Gods," Will swore. Why did everyone think additional pressure was helpful? "Okay, listen. They rule with fear and coin. So what if we take those away from them?"

"Then we'd be killed in the attempt because of the army of fifty thousand heavily armed troops we're facing?" Quirk suggested. "This is seeming recursive."

"Just listen," Will said.

"Stop asking us questions then," Quirk snapped back.

Lette started dragging the flat of a knife's blade back and forth along the leg of her britches.

"Okay, fine then." Will took a breath. "We don't have to actually take the gold and the fear away. We just have to make the troops think that they're gone."

"How are we—" Balur started.

"I'm getting to that," Will almost shouted. He pushed hair away from his forehead. It was slick with perspiration. "They already think we're led by a powerful dragon slayer. But there's a difference between having heard that, and actually seeing it. For decades, no one in Kondorra has truly believed, deep down, that the dragons can be killed. That's part of the Consortium's strength: our despair. Anyone who's bought into the idea that a dragon really can be killed—they're with us now. The people who need more proof—we're fighting them."

"What proof?" Lette asked. She was more caught up in it now. "We left the bodies weeks back on the road."

Will smiled. "Well...maybe we're not entirely honest about what we show them." He looked at Quirk. "You've studied Mattrax and Dathrax enough to know what a dragon skull might look like. I figure, we kill a few cows, mash their carcasses together, and parade our decapitated dragon's head around in front of them. We make them see what we've done."

"We have not been decapitating a dragon, though," Balur said.

"I know." Will reached out and patted Balur's arm. Despite his exhaustion, he was caught up in this now. "But we trick them."

Balur narrowed his eyes. "Trickery," he said as if the word left a bad taste.

"Think of it like sneaking up on them then," Will said. "We're sneaking up on the enemy so we can stick our blade in his back."

Balur thought about that. "So we can be feeling his blood on our hands?"

"Attaboy." Will smiled. Halfway there.

"What has any of this got to do with spies?" Lette was definitely hooked, but she was yet to be netted as well.

"Well," said Will, "we've taken care of the fear, at least as much as we can. So now we take care of the gold."

Quirk chewed her lip as she listened.

"We need to infiltrate the Consortium army's camp. We need to start spreading rumors. We tell them that the Dragon's wealth is a lie. That they're actually out of gold and have been hiding it."

"Who would believe that? How would that happen?" Lette was still skeptical.

Will's mind whirred. And then the final pieces clicked into place. But he was careful to keep the smile off his face. "It doesn't really matter," he says. "We just need to put the thought in their heads. We tell them…" And then, as if it had just occurred to them, which he supposed it really had, "…that dragon's fire turns gold into lead. That's why they keep taxing people for more of it, why they seem unable to ever have enough."

Lette still looked dubious.

"Then," Will said, letting his smile out a little, "a wagon arrives. It's a merchant. Except not really a merchant. It's another of our spies. They say that they're there to demand payment. That the Consortium hasn't been good on its payments."

"But why would a merchant come all the way out here?" Lette asked. "It doesn't make sense."

"They wouldn't," Will agreed. "But Hallows' Mouth is only three days from here."

"Hallows' what?" Balur looked at him askance.

"Hallows' Mouth," Will repeated. "The volcano where the Consortium all meet. And if they've put an army together to hunt us down, you can be sure they've met."

"Oh." Balur nodded sagely.

"Remind me," Lette said, "why they meet in a pissing volcano?"

"Because they are having style," Balur said before Will could answer. In the end, he supposed that was pretty much the answer.

"And explain to me," Lette went on, "why in all the Hallows you would want to do this on their doorstep?"

Will had done it. He had finally found something that made Lette go up an octave. Her demeanor of professional detachment shattered and spilled to the floor, in tiny shards of disdain and ennui. She stared at him incredulous.

He held firm. *This would work,* a voice inside told him. Because it had to work. It had to be flawless. Or they would all die.

"We have to do it there," he said as calmly as he was able. "We have to appear fearless. That's how we undermine our enemy's fear of the Consortium, by not having it ourselves. By appearing utterly, unshakably confident."

"But we are not being that," said Balur. Even he seemed dubious about this level of audacity.

"Of course we're not," Will said. "But it's a con. This whole thing is a con. If we don't sell it, we don't get the gold."

And just like he knew it would, that drew them up short.

Balur cocked his head on one side. "We are getting the gold?"

Will grinned. "All the goddam gold."

Balur looked at Lette. "Okay," he said. "I am not knowing about you, but I am being willing to hear out the rest of the plan."

Lette was looking at Will the same way a cat would look at a mouse that suddenly revealed it was brandishing a broadsword.

"So," Will said. "That's the scene. We're parading about right before the Hallows' Mouth, marching into their stronghold, bearing the decapitated head of one of their own at the front of our hugely outnumbered army. We officially don't give a fuck. We are fearless. Why are we fearless? Is there nothing to fear?

"Meanwhile they're hearing these rumors that all the gold is gone. A merchant even showed up demanding payment. The rumors are everywhere—"

"Stop painting the gods-cursed scene and tell us about the gold, Will." But despite her tone, Lette was leaning forward. She wanted him to convince her.

"Suddenly the prophet's line bulges," he said. "Shouts go up. The tension has been unbearable. Everyone's attention is drawn. I don't care how disciplined a soldier you are. You look.

"But in the end it's nothing. Just a feint, or night maneuvers. So you go back to what you were doing. But in the morning, all the gold in their pay wagons is gone."

Balur clapped. "We are stealing the gold."

Will nodded. "Right under their noses. Right during that feint, we take it and we run. And they find all their gold is gone in the morning. And there's chaos. Because there's no fear. There's no gold. So there's no army. There's rioting."

"And then," Lette said, with a sour expression, "the dragons, who are right there, because we walked right into their laps, burst out and kill everyone."

Will let himself smile one last time. "Well…" he said. "They come out certainly. They come out, and they face sixty thousand humans. All of us. My followers. Their own. And, yes, the dragons are powerful. But we really have seen they can be killed. We really have seen them die. We *could* have one of their heads at the front of our army if we wanted it. They take us on, and they lose."

Silence. He waited. Waited for them to take it in. Waited for the challenges. He felt an odd sense of calm, sitting there in the flickering light of Quirk's single flame. He was ready for this.

"Who are we sending?" Balur rumbled at last. "Who do we send to spy and steal? Who do we trust?"

"We trust no one," Will said simply. "But remember, *they don't know what we look like.* That spy didn't even know I'm meant to be the stupid prophet in the first place. *We* can go." He pointed. "Lette and I. *We* infiltrate. *We* spread the rumors. *We* steal the gold. Quirk"—he smiled at her—"shows up as the merchant. It's low risk. Low violence. Just needs a trustworthy face." He tried to read her expression, but despite the flame in her hand, she managed to keep to the shadows.

"And you." Will nodded to Balur. "You stay here. Pretend you're the prophet's general. Or the prophet himself. I'm not sure. That might be more believable to most people here than it being me. You organize the feint, the distraction. You provide cover for Lette and myself to steal the gold. Simple."

There was another pause. "Simple?" Lette asked.

Will considered. "Well, maybe not. But it's about the only way I can figure that we might get out of this. We're out of options. It's all or nothing now. The dragons have to die. Or you're right, they'll hound us to the ends of the world."

Lette and Balur exchanged a look. The lizard man shrugged. "I am liking the bit where I get disgustingly rich and kill dragons."

Will for a moment worried that the reason all of his plans had gone so poorly was that they had been selected more for their optimism than their workability.

Lette shrugged back at Balur. "It's not great, but considering the other option is to be chased until we're exhausted and can be slaughtered like newborn lambs, then I'm willing to try it."

Will tried to mask his relief. It was all about confidence now. All of it. He had two out of three. Which just left… "Quirk?"

Another pause. Quirk's shadowy form staring back at him. Only her palm truly visible, the flame dancing there.

Then she closed her fist. "You're kidding, right?" she said.

Crap sticks.

"No," he said.

"Drag these people into a fight?" she said. And she did not sound happy when she spoke. "That's your plan? Abandon them so you can play at thieving again, which, gods, you have proven yourself oh so adept at." She would be scoffing, Will thought, had she not been so clearly choking on her own rage. "And assuming you don't fuck that up, and leave them all alone to be slaughtered, then the whole idea is to pick a fight?"

"Well," Will started. But he had to concede, "Yes."

"Who do you think will survive that fight, Will?" She shook her head. "I mean, suppose you're right and eventually we might be able to bring the dragons down. The casualties will be horrific. Utterly, unspeakably awful. And when you're tallying up those casualties, who do you think will die first? The heavily armored knights and soldiers chasing us down in this disaster? Or do you think it will be the unarmored, unarmed farmers and merchants who have given their all to the belief that you can help them?"

There were a lot of answers to that. He hadn't asked anyone to follow him. They hadn't even really followed him, just the idea of a man that had overlapped with him for a brief moment. That without his plan, they would die in exactly the same way, a worse way perhaps, cowering and on their knees. That at least his plan gave them a few more days of hope and a chance to die standing on their feet.

But he didn't say any of that. Because Quirk wasn't interested in hearing that. She was smart enough to have evaluated it all and found it wanting.

So instead he just said, "Yes, that's the plan."

And this was it. This was the moment when things would hold fast or break apart.

"Fuck you," Quirk whispered. "Fuck all of you." She shook her head. "I should burn you all."

She turned, and walked out of the tent, leaving the fabric flapping in a cold breeze.

"Shit," Lette swore.

"We are not needing her," Balur said. "We can have someone else be a merchant. That is being the easy part."

"Shit," Lette swore again.

But Will was smiling. Not for them. To just himself this time. Because everything was going according to plan.

# 69

## Running on Empty

Lette watched Will work the next day. Watched him walk through the camp.

"The prophet has a plan," he would say, touching a man's shoulder, a woman's arm. "He's seen a way forward. He's seen a way for us to win." Or he would pick up a young child, grin at them, and say, "The prophet is taking us to a field of victory." He sang songs—silly tavern ditties that poked fun at the dragons. They brought smiles to the worried, harassed crowds. The smiles spread, little spots of warmth kindling through the crowd. Trudging footsteps gained a bounce to their strides. Chins were lifted a little higher.

Here and there he would meet with men. Hard men, by her professional assessment. And he would put his head close to theirs and whisper. And then they too would go off through the crowd, smiling, whistling, singing. By the afternoon the march felt less like desperate flight and more like a vigorous bit of exercise. They were not a baying, confident army yet but they were far more upbeat than they had any right to be.

For her own part, Lette had a harder time finding her confidence. All she had to do was look over her shoulder to receive a reminder of how close their pursuers were. Griffins were silhouetted against the skyline. Dust clouds kicked up by fifty thousand feet blurred the horizon.

All she had to do was look ahead and see the smudge of smoke rising from Hallows' Mouth.

It was an insane plan Will had conjured up. If she was honest about it, it was borderline delusional. She could almost believe he had cracked under the strain.

But she was going along with it. She saw—and this was almost laughable—no better alternative.

If there was one thing that could be said for it, though—it was a plan that was, in the end, based on hope. Dangerous, irrational hope. But not greed. Not fear. Not anger. Hope. And it was a long time since she'd been motivated by anything that felt like that.

When they came to the crest of a hill she looked down, saw most of the crowd stretched out before her, and felt the old coldness rise within her. She could imagine where she would send her griffins if she were in charge of the Consortium's forces. *Diving into the weak spots, where the women and children were clustered around wagons. Where they would cause the most damage. Then when they had done their work, I would start up the trebuchets. I wouldn't aim at anything in particular. Use loose shot, something that would maim more than kill. Until the screaming made the air ring. By then the trolls would have had time to maneuver, be ready for their charge. I would have them slam into the flank for maximum damage. Shock troops. Leave Will's followers reeling, easy pickings for the rest of—*

But then she was able to stop it, step away from that coldness. She was able to see something different. She was able to see not a disorganized rabble, but something else. Something motivated, angry, hopeful. She was able to see people who wouldn't need to fight. People that Will would save.

That she would save.

That left another question, though. She had started sleeping with Will because it was better than descending into utter hopelessness. If she was to use this plan as a balm for her pessimism instead, then where did that leave her and Will? Did she need him anymore? And if she did, and it wasn't simply that she needed him for a good lay, or as a place to drown her fears... then what did that say about who she was? About how she felt about him?

But rather than answer that question, she stayed back, and she watched.

The crowd marched on. They lost their lead little by little. And then as night fell, as they pushed on hard toward midnight, she saw the lead open back up once more. Not quite what it had been but enough for them to survive another day.

*Two more,* she reminded herself. *Will said it to me himself. Three days to Hallows' Mouth.*

Could they make it that far? She honestly couldn't tell.

She met him back at their tent as night fell.

"How are you?" she asked, peeling her travel-stained shirt from her body.

"Tired." He wrapped thick arms around her. She resisted the urge to sink into them, to rest her head against his chest, and breathe in the heady musk of his scent.

"What about Quirk?" she said. She sounded more anxious than she would have liked.

His brow furrowed. The crease between his brows was adorable. She tried to murder the thought, scowled at him desperately.

"Are we all right without her on board with the plan?" she pressed.

"Oh." Will shook his head. "That's all right. I spoke to her, sorted everything out. It's all okay. She'll do it. Under a bit of duress, admittedly, but she'll do it and that's the main thing."

He had? She did? Lette hadn't had her eyes on Will all day, but this was a fairly major event for her to have missed.

"What did you say to her?" she asked. "She seemed pretty adamant last night."

"Oh." Will flapped a hand. "Some stuff about seeing how the

dragons governed their armies and their troops up close. A different societal viewpoint other than oppressed peasants like me. That sort of thing. Just wore her down."

Lette wished the light was better in the tent. She couldn't tell how honest he was being with her.

Not that she could really complain about him finally developing a little guile. She just wished it wasn't directed at her.

There was a knock on a pole near the tent's entrance flap. She whipped around, a knife finding its way from her boot to her hand in the blink of an eye.

But it was not an assassin come in the night. Instead it was one of those hard men she had seen Will talking to in the crowd earlier.

"Begging your pardon," he said.

Will released Lette from his embrace. "Sorry," he said to her, and he genuinely sounded like he was. "This will only take a minute."

She hesitated. Did she go to the tent flap and listen? Her instinct was to do so. She could not help but feel that Will was hiding something, after all. But was it as simple as self-preservation? Or was the impulse coming from the fact that she was, despite herself, increasingly attached to him?

She did not want to be one of those shrill waiflike women who clung to their man begging to know every detail. That horseshit was for people other than Lette. So in the end, she stayed by the cot, got undressed, and when he came back in simply raised an eyebrow and asked, "And?"

Will started, eyes still adjusting to the darkness. "And what?"

"And who was that?"

"Oh." Will blustered a little. "That was Cattak."

"Cattak?" She ratcheted her eyebrow up another notch. She wasn't entirely sure what effect it would have in the dark, but it felt right.

"He's, erm..." Will shuffled his feet. "He's a friend of Quirk's I suppose. Very efficient man."

She waited for more. It did not come. "And?"

"And what?" asked Will, sounding about as innocent as a man elbow deep in another man's intestines.

"And why the fuck is he knocking on my tent pole at midnight, Willet?" She wielded his full name like a bludgeon.

"Oh, he's been..." Will hesitated, stepped forward, and whispered to her. "He's in charge of creating the fake dragon head. He's working with Quirk to get it right."

"Why are you whispering?" she said out loud.

Will pulled back, gave her an injured look. "Spies," he said, still in hushed tones. One was out there yesterday, there might be one again tonight.

It was, she supposed, a fair explanation. It did cover everything from his circumspect behavior to his whispered tones. After another moment, she decided to let it slide.

"You're an idiot," she said and ruffled his hair. "Now come and get into bed."

The dragon's head was revealed the next morning, and Lette had to concede she was quite impressed. While it wouldn't hold up to close inspection, from a few yards away it gave a fairly good impression of a moldering, monumental skull. Bones and horns were knit together with white cotton. She wondered how many cattle had been slaughtered to create it.

As the morning sun rose, Firkin stood at the head of the camp beside the creation, and sold it all to the crowd.

"Behold!" he screeched. "The bit of our enemy that sits above the neck! Where all the thinky parts go! Except his thinky parts are gone! Rotted away! Because the prophet rotted them! By chopping them off his neck! And that's what happens when you chop someone's thinky parts off. You might think that the thinky parts would go on thinking and you could keep them with you, in a little jar or something, and pull them out when you were feeling a little lonely, or just needed someone to say,

'It's all going to be all right, you'll find a new bottle of that whiskey somewhere else,' but it turns out you can't, and you'll just stay lonely, and people will avoid you because of the head you're carrying about in a jar. Such is the fate of all enemies of the prophet!"

Lette wasn't entirely sure why, but the crowd pretty much lost its collective shit over that.

The tone of the crowd was different that day. Instead of tavern shanties, battle hymns rose up into the blue skies. Old songs, sung on feast days. Choruses from the epics, about divine champions spearing great beasts, tearing other armies limb from limb. Slowly the journey was transitioning from chase to charge.

The Kondorra valley spread out as they made their way southward, the rolling hills that edged the river Kon transitioning into stretching grassland. Wild horses ran alongside them as they marched. Herds of cattle watched from a distance. And Hallows' Mouth presided over it all.

The volcano squatted, solitary in the center of the plains, rising abruptly from the flatland, like some wart grown out of all proportion. Smoke streamed from its crater, smudging the sky to the south and west. Trees and shrubs seemed to avoid its shade. Its walls were a stark, craggy black. Occasionally she thought she could make out long, sinuous shapes flitting through the air above it.

She caught sight of Quirk, riding a horse slowly through the crowd. She hurried up beside her.

"Is that...?" she said, pointing to the flying shapes.

"The Consortium?" Quirk didn't look down. "Yes."

Lette tried to calculate the distance, to allow her eyes to accommodate for the distance.

"They're fucking huge," she said eventually.

"Yes," said Quirk. "Yes, they are."

She did not, Lette thought, sound like a woman at peace with herself.

"Will says you've changed your mind about his plan. That you're going to play the merchant for us."

Quirk rode on for a few more steps. The horse she sat astride was a gray mare, flecks of white dappling its sides. Its footfalls were slow and steady, pushing through the long grass of the plains.

"I wouldn't say I changed my mind. But I will play the part of the merchant for you all."

Not exactly the answer Lette had expected. Not, she thought, really the answer she had wanted either.

"If you don't sell this..." she said. She tried to make it sound like a threat, but the truth was, if Quirk didn't sell it, Lette would most likely be put to the sword and be unable to wreak any revenge whatsoever.

"I'll do my part." There was steel in the thaumatobiologist's voice. "This, I have come to realize, is important to me. Not for the same reasons it's important to you. But it is important. Gods, it's about the only thing I've got left now." She finally looked down at Lette. Gave her a hollow smile. "All the compromises I've made."

Lette didn't really give much of a shit about the compromises Quirk had made. The thaumatobiologist had a rod shoved up her arse and it would take several strong men and a barrel of grease to work it out, and Lette was shit out of grease. Still, motivations did concern her. If Quirk was only going through with this because she saw it as a way to save her own skin, to sell them all out for some gold and a ticket back to Tamathia, well, then that was something she needed to know about.

"So why is it important?" she asked.

"Did Will tell you about my past?" she asked. "Did I make for good pillow talk?"

Lette didn't rise to the bait. "Yes," she said. "He did. Hethren. Banditry. Mass murder." She didn't say she was sorry for it. She wasn't. Quirk had made it out alive. There were plenty of people who hadn't.

"Yes," Quirk said. "Banditry. Mass murder. And then redemption. Good people took me in when no one should have done. They made me into someone new. They made me into a person who could become Quirk the thaumatobiologist. A woman who could lose herself in books. A woman who could—and I'm sorry if this sounds like bragging—but a woman who could excel in her field. And I have become that for one reason, and one reason alone. To express my gratitude. To say thank you for being given the chance to be someone new. And I told myself a lot of things about who I'd become. I told myself I was reformed. I told myself I'd left magic behind. I told myself I was a good person now. That I was kind. And a lot of those things have been stripped away from me. I am not good. I am not kind. I am still that scared little girl who wants to make all her fears burn away. But the thing that remains, the one thing that lasts while everything else collapses into ash...I am still a grateful woman. That's still who I am. And I made those good people a promise. I promised them I would come out here, and that I would come back with knowledge about dragons that no one else had. That no one else had ever dared to have. That was how I would repay my debt. Because they truly and honestly care about the wealth of human knowledge. They are good people. They are kind people. And I will honor that. I will do anything and everything I can do to honor that. And if that means pretending to be some fucking merchant so that you can put the lives of ten thousand men, women, and children at risk, and try to steal gold you don't deserve, then I have found that I can live with that. And I'm not proud of it, and I'm not going to repeat it again, or explain it any more than this ever again. I'm going to shut it away, and try to ignore it. And if I get out of this alive, I will act as if I am the good, kind person they have tried to make me. Because that will be a form of thanks too. Even if it is a lie."

She looked down at Lette. "Does that answer your question?"

Lette considered. On the whole, she found she believed Quirk.

The woman simply wasn't that good a liar. She had her demons, but so did everyone. It was just that Quirk seemed to take hers so very seriously.

Also there was the fact that Quirk's reins appeared to be on fire.

"Yes," she told Quirk. "That answers it. But there is one other question."

Quirk ground her teeth.

"Cattak," Lette said. "Who is he? What's he to Will?"

"Cattak?" Quirk sounded surprised. "He's a looter. He was acting as a scout for me. But now that we can see the Consortium's forces on our heels, there doesn't seem much need for him. I didn't know he and Will were still in contact."

Which was another answer Lette hadn't wanted.

"So," she said, "Cattak didn't help you build the dragon skull?"

Quirk twisted her head onto one side. "Some men did. Maybe they report back to Cattak. I don't know."

"But he wasn't there personally?" Lette pushed.

"I didn't see him."

"A looter?"

"Yes," Quirk nodded. "That seems to have started back up again. I've seen three temples with their roofs missing since this morning. Lawl alone knows what use they think all the lead will be now."

Lette nodded slowly. What use indeed?

# 70

# Hubris Is a Dish Best Served Charbroiled

In the depths of Hallows' Mouth, Kithrax raised his head. Gold coins tumbled from it. Below him, magma bubbled and rumbled. And yet, the sound of rumbling geological rage was still not quite enough to drown out the sound of Horrax's flatulent snoring. The squat brown dragon was oozing over the edge of one of the ledges that lined the volcano's central vent, drool spilling from his mouth to hiss and spit in the molten rock below.

He could kick Horrax, push him over the edge. Maybe he'd recover before he hit the magma, maybe he wouldn't. Kithrax wasn't worried about the consequences should Horrax survive the fall—he'd been itching for an excuse to rip out Horrax's throat for the best part of a century now. No, it was that he might subsequently be expected to administer Horrax's swampland territory to the west. Gods, the less he had to do to sully his life by interacting with humans the better.

Rather than sit there and wait for the murderous rage to overwhelm his senses, he shrugged fully from his nest of gold and pushed off into space, launching himself toward the open crater of the volcano, riding the thermals out through the volcano's rocky mouth, and drifting silently up into the night sky.

It was all spread out below him. The whole absurd pageant.

The prophet's pathetic forces. The Consortium's own over-whelming army.

Why did they bother? Why did they struggle? What did they imagine they would accomplish? Did they imagine that there was some glory in dying this way? That when they arrived in the Hallows below, that Lawl would be down there waiting to shake them all personally by the hand?

*"Well that was futile, but jolly good show all the same."*

Lawl was a lecherous, anarchic imbecile, and so were all the other gods. They had done nothing to save these morons when Kithrax and the rest of the Consortium had rolled into Kon-dorra, and they would do nothing now. His was the face of the future. This pathetic flailing below him was the last gasp of the past.

"Should eat them now."

The face of the future gave a decidedly unbecoming gasp of surprise.

Bruthrax laughed as he swept past over Kithrax's right shoul-der. Considering the size of the massive red brute, he could be surprisingly quiet.

"Should just go down there," Bruthrax said. "End it now."

Kithrax could not quite restrain himself from snapping at Bruthrax in anger.

"I'd enjoy eating some of them," Bruthrax went on, ignoring Kithrax. "Always fight on an empty stomach, that's what I say."

Kithrax got himself under control. He flapped up to fly par-allel with Bruthrax, a sleek shadow to Bruthrax's crimson bulk. "That," he hissed over the wind, "is because you're a fucking moron."

Bruthrax laughed easily. "Without a doubt."

Kithrax grit his teeth, and tried to explain using very small words. "We are above them. We are like gods to them. They are puny. They do not concern us. If, for a moment, they start to think they do, then this sort of shit"—he snorted fire at the masses below—"will become the norm. They can hiss and spit, and fuss like little infants, but we will ignore them."

"Like you ignore Horrax?" Bruthrax laughed again, like thunder in the sky.

Kithrax ground his teeth again, harder this time. "I have my limits. Do you wish to find them?"

Bruthrax executed a lazy, carefree barrel roll. "You think you're above all of us," he said. "I get that. It's okay." A shrug rolled the length of his sinuous body. "But you're not. You're down in the shit with Horrax. Just like all of us." He swooped down toward the gathered troops. "Shit like this will keep on happening. They'll keep on fighting. It's stupid and pointless, but so is life. It's probably especially stupid and pointless for the people living under your rule."

He rolled away.

Kithrax knew he should abstain from sniping and bickering. It was below him. But he was tired, and offended by Horrax, and Bruthrax, and the poxy little prophet below him. "I'll gnaw the resistance out of their guts," he snapped.

Bruthrax cast a glance back over his shoulder, circled Kithrax once in a slow circle. "Then you'll end up having to kill them all, and you'll rule over nobody. Though perhaps you'd prefer that."

And with that he flapped away.

# 71

# The Third Day

Will was already getting dressed when Lette woke in their cot the next morning. He was dressed as plainly as ever, a rough work shirt, dull brown britches, leather boots that had seen better days. A farmer. A young farmer even. In his early twenties. And he was about to lead ten thousand men into battle. And they didn't even know it.

"Good morning," she slurred through the last vestiges of sleep.

He turned, looked at her, smiled. "Good morning," he said. "At least, well... I suppose the morning is all right. But by midday we should be in position. Which means a lot of maneuvering to make sure everyone is where we need them to be. And it'll take the Consortium army time to get organized. So I suppose it will be a little after midday when we enroll in their army. So I guess the morning—"

"Will?" She cut him off. He was adorable still, but his nervous rambling was too much.

"Yes?" He pulled himself back from the brink of mental chaos.

"Where were you last night?" The tent had been empty when she had come to bed close to midnight. And she had fallen asleep before he came back.

"Oh," he said. "Talking to Cattak. He was coordinating. Getting Quirk's merchant's wagon ready. You wouldn't know it to look at him, but he is a surprisingly crafty man. Heart of an artist."

"Hmm." She nodded. "Will?" she said again.

He had bent to pull on his second boot. He looked up at her. "Yes?"

"Why would anyone need lead from the roofs of three temples two days before a battle?"

She watched him carefully. The way his brow furrowed. The way he looked away from her, down at his boot. He tugged it on hard and sharp.

"No idea," he said. "Why?"

"Because that was what was looted the night before last."

"Oh." He stared off at the tent flap. "No idea." He shrugged. "Hope perhaps. Or belief. Planning for a day after today." He smiled. "That would be nice."

Despite herself, she smiled as well. That would indeed be nice. The idea of a future. Of quiet times. Of days that weren't full of marching and fear.

But those thoughts were a trap.

"Cattak was a looter," she said, leaning back on the bed, stretching broadly.

He didn't start. Didn't jerk around. No sign of surprise at all.

"Yeah," he said. "That's what Quirk told me. But he's reformed now."

*That's what Quirk told me.*

So he assumed she had gone to Quirk. Which of course she had. And if he had expected that, he could have expected this question. Which could explain the lack of reaction to her questions.

It could...

She decided to push it, show her hand completely. What would she be losing at this point? A few hours of companionship?

"Quirk said she didn't see Cattak when she was working on the dragon skull."

He did move at that. A grim certainty set in. *The fucking liar.* She prepared to beat the truth out of him.

"Shhhh!" he hissed at her. He stepped toward where she was lying.

Lette hesitated, caught off-balance. What was he—

"Don't talk about the skull," he whispered, bending down to place lips so close to her ear that his breath tickled. "We don't know who's listening. And no, she wouldn't have seen him. She was putting all the bones together. He was off slaughtering and stripping cows down to the bone."

An explanation for everything. Simple and neat.

Too neat?

Maybe, but it seemed a step beyond Will to have planned that far. And what could he hope to gain from deception anyway?

*Sell one of us out to save his own skin. They don't know who the prophet is. They don't know it's supposed to be him. He could go over there, sell out Balur. Sell out me. He'd have me surrounded by the enemy. A lot of gold would go his way...*

She pushed the voice away. If Will's plan was betrayal, if the plan died, if they didn't try the plan...all the outcomes were the same.

So whatever the plan was, whether it was what he said it was or not, she might as well go forward anyway.

Will sat up, tousled her hair. "Stop worrying," he said. "We're totally going to see five dragons die today. It'll be great." And with that, he slipped away.

The morning passed much as Will had predicted. He had let Firkin loose among the crowd, and the old man was in fine fettle, screeching out words of praise as he staggered through their numbers, a wineskin swinging from his hand.

"Say they can rain down fire on us, do these dragons. Didn't see Dathrax raining anything down. Just saw him raining down. In little pieces. All chopped up by the prophet he was." Even Firkin's hiccups and belches rang out over the crowd's noise.

"Bunch of fat liars!" he screeched. "Bet their fire is a lie! Couldn't roast a sausage if their lives depended on it. And they'll depend on more than sausages tonight! Will depend on us! And we're not dependable! Can only depend on us to go stabby-stab-stab." He thrust his wineskin at the heavens. Wine slopped down onto him. He licked at it as it dripped down his chin and into his beard.

"Liberation! Reparation! Inebriation!" Voices rose with his, chanting. Lette wondered if the crowd knew what they were saying.

A man elbowed her. "Why ain't you singing."

"Because I'm not a fucking idiot," she told him, and as his face curdled, put a fist into it.

She went to find Balur instead.

He was perched on the back of Quirk's thaumatic cart, searching through piles of armor and jewelry as it trundled along. The whole crowd was wheeling around to the east, to put the river Kon at their backs. It was a poor defensive position, truth be told, but Will's hope was that it would provoke the Consortium army into forming up to the west. And as there was no plan to actually fight, the poor defensive position didn't really matter. It just provided a buffer zone to exist between the armies while they put their plan into action.

Balur plucked a bejeweled helmet from the back of the cart and held it up to her. "It is being some farmer's family heirloom," he said. "The old man had been hiding it from the dragons for thirty years. Then he was hearing about a prophet, and was getting some hope, and was giving it up like it was his redheaded stepchild." He perched it on top of his head. "Is it making me look prophetic?"

"It's making you look like a bit of a dick," Lette offered up.

"A prophetic dick?" Balur asked.

"What are you doing up there?" She couldn't help but smile as she asked.

"Is being theater," he said, mock-wounded. "I am having to sell myself as a prophet to fifty thousand armed men across a battlefield. I am needing to look the part."

"Balur," she said, "you're an eight-foot-tall slab of scaled muscle. I think that sells the idea."

She reached up, patted his tree trunk of a leg. Though he would never admit it, he was nervous.

"I," she said, "am going to be over there telling everyone within earshot about what a horrifying, murderous, merciless arsehole of an Analesian is leading these rebels. About how he crushes men's skulls in his bare fists. I am going to make them piss themselves at the sound of your name."

He looked down at her, smiled fondly. "You are being very sweet."

She looked up. "Still tribe?" And she would never admit it, but she was nervous too.

"Still tribe," Balur said. "Even if you are being a total pussy now."

"I just made a grown man cry," she offered up.

"Did you do it by feeding him his testicles?"

She sighed. "No."

"New Lette is still a pussy."

They grinned at each other.

"Last one to kill a dragon," she said. "That one is the real pussy."

He knelt down, put one massive hand over hers. "Deal," he said.

"Deal."

It was as good a way to say goodbye as any she knew.

The crowd was finding its final position when she eventually found Will. He had been harder to locate than she thought, just another face in the crowd.

"Ready?" she asked.

"Erm..." He studied his hands. They were shaking slightly. "Let me see. My pretend army is in position. The fake merchant wagons are prepared." He nodded at two farmer's carts that had been outfitted with wooden frames and brightly painted cloth so that they resembled merchant's wagons. "I haven't shit myself yet. So I think this is as ready as I'm going to get."

"Quirk knows what to do?" she asked. The plan seemed like a flimsy thing now that she was about to execute it. As pathetic as a wooden sword held up to defend yourself from the widening jaws of a dragon.

"She says she does. She's the one driving that wagon." He pointed. Lette did a double take. She hadn't recognized the woman. Instead of one of her simple, plain dresses, she was wearing an outfit of billowing silks that boasted more colors than a Salerian whore's painted face.

"Where did you find that outfit?"

"Oh." Will found a smile from some deep reserve. "It turns out we have a traveling circus that joined a few days back. We cut up a couple of their tents."

She shook her head, put an arm around him. "Are you sure," she said, "that this is really the first time you've tried to con a bunch of dragons out of their kingdom and their fortune?"

He shrugged. "If it wasn't, I think I'd have better control of my bladder."

She carefully removed her arm from around his waist. "Come on," she said, "let's go and put the fear of you into our enemies."

The journey took longer than either of them would have liked. The grasslands of the Kondorra valley offered little in the way of cover, and they had to cross half a league of it to reach the opposing army without being spotted.

Hallows' Mouth stared down at them as they crept around the northern edge of the battlefield, trying to keep hidden among the tall grasses, dashing from bush to bush. The volcano

provided a hard, harsh edge to the field's southern border, jutting abruptly up from the ground. Craggy cliffs of brown rock
tore up through the earth, belching smoke and emitting ominous roars from their guts.

The Consortium dragons remained conspicuously absent, as
if they were trying to tell the world how little they thought of
this upstart prophet and his upstart army.

To be fair, they had good reason to think little of them. Their
own vast army was arrayed before them, and it both outnumbered and outmaneuvered their opponents.

The Consortium army had no problem with making itself as
conspicuous as possible. They spread out like a tidal wave. Figures in gray armor, massing, spreading, staining the valley, as
the smoke gathered overhead. Griffins rose into the air, roaring
and calling, wings beating at the still air. The trolls sang war
songs in deep baritones, full of grunts and howls. Trumpets and
horns rang out. The sound of fifty thousand pairs of feet marching in time, the jingle of chain mail, the clank of swords, halberds being set. The rhythmic thud of tent poles being erected.
The neighing of their cavalry's horses. The growling of their
war dogs. They dominated the plains, the sound of them, the
stench, the sheer unfolding volume of them.

Lette felt a heaviness in her chest. "How in all the Hallows are
we going to spread word through all of them? It's not possible."

But Will just looked at her. "The night we fought Dathrax.
The night we didn't kill him, and he almost killed us. The next
morning thousands of people showed up in Athril. I wasn't
even sure what had happened and people from leagues away
were coming to tell me all about it. Word spreads around here,
and it spreads fast. And you and I will talk about it with everyone we see."

It was horseshit, she knew, but it was reassuring horseshit, so
she let it slide.

As they drew closer to the Consortium army, Balur and Firkin started to get the prophet's army worked up. The fake dragon skull was visible across the plain. A group of men were dragging it back and forth through the dirt, whooping and screaming. Cheers and boos rose up in equal measure. Catcalls were hurled into the air, the details lost but the tone unmistakable. The tavern songs started up again, lewd and loud, and accompanied by gestures that were disparaging even from this distance.

"Okay," said Lette, "I know I haven't been in the Kondorra valley that long, but I have traveled a fair amount. And the people here are fucking insane. Do they have any idea what's about to happen to them if a fight actually starts? They're going to be slaughtered."

Will shrugged. "You oppress a people for long enough, it starts to get to them, I suppose."

"Or you just breed them weird." Lette had seen oppressed people before. To her the "breed them weird" argument seemed like it held more water.

"Where are you from, by the way?" Will asked suddenly. "I can't believe I don't know that."

Lette could. She never found herself to be a particularly interesting subject. Still, Will had probably earned the information, and given their prospects of survival, he would likely be taking it to his grave.

"Salera," she said. "The capital. Essoa. My father was a fishermen, and my mother a seamstress." She dropped as much of a curtsy as she was able to, crouched behind a scrubby bush. "I was to sew dresses for fine ladies, thank you kindly."

She watch Will try to process that. "A seamstress?" he said. "Had they met you?"

"I was a child, Will," she pointed out. "I hadn't had much of a chance to kill anyone at that point."

"Now you're making up for lost time?"

She shrugged. "Being a seamstress didn't stick."

He nodded; that seemed to make sense to him at least. "How

does one go from being a seamstress to, erm"—he gesticulated stabby motions with his hands—"doing what you do?"

"I ran away at thirteen. High jinks ensued."

She saw him doing the mental math.

"Don't ask how old I am," she warned him. Still it was fun to watch him match the woman he knew to the girl she described.

"Did you..." He struggled with the wording. "Did you leave anyone behind?"

She nodded. "My parents. Four brothers. Two sisters. Six aunts. Five uncles. Twenty-seven first cousins. Couple of second cousins. I didn't keep track of all of them."

She saw Will's eyes go wide, searching her for hurt. But there wasn't any. It was fifteen years gone since she had said farewell to them, and she had long had time to make peace with the decision.

"You miss them?" he said.

"I think their lives are more peaceful without me, and mine is less peaceful without them, which is how I like it."

He nodded slowly. "I miss my parents every day."

She rested a hand on his shoulder. "I chose to leave mine. That makes a difference."

He nodded.

"Enough of this sharing, emotional bullshit," she told him. "Let's go raise some hell."

"The fuck you want to do?"

Lette forced herself to not grit her teeth. For "raising hell," this was a poor start.

She and Will had managed to circle around to the back of the Consortium's army forces. Now they stood outside a bloodred tent, trying to look earnest, while a large sergeant at arms strode back and forth in front of them, succeeding mightily in looking like an arsehole.

"To enlist," said Lette. She held her hands clasped in front of her. She made puppy eyes.

"Why the fuck I want to enlist two undisciplined shits like you on the eve of battle?" said the sergeant. He scratched at stubble, disturbing several flies that were sunning themselves on his pockmarked cheeks. "We outnumber those bastards five to one."

"Well," said Lette, as innocently as she could, "does it help that I can do this?"

She gave the sergeant credit that he managed to get his hand onto the hilt of his sword before she had him on the ground with a dagger at his throat. His Adam's apple bobbed painfully against the edge of the blade.

A few nearby soldiers whooped and hollered. None bothered to raise a finger.

"Erm." The sergeant beneath her swallowed. "Sure. Yeah. That would probably... Yeah, we could use you." She slowly stood up from where she had been straddling his chest, ghosted the blade back up her sleeve. The sergeant massaged his throat. He glanced over at Will, a little nervously. "What about you?" he said. "Can you...?"

"Me?" Will scoffed. "I was the one who taught her to do that."

"Oh." The sergeant considered that, and whether he wanted another demonstration of the skill. He decided against it. Lette tried to keep her sigh of relief inaudible.

The sergeant pointed. "Green tent, five rows that way. Tell them Gurn sent you. They'll kit you up." He rubbed his throat. "Then just find somewhere useful to be at the front. We'll be setting up for the rest of the day. Take care of those bastards tomorrow morning, be roasting meat over their corpse fires by lunchtime." He nodded. They were dismissed.

Keeping her smile tight and demure, Lette walked away, following a step behind Will.

*He taught her how to do that.* She was going to kick his arse for that.

"Oh," said the sergeant to their backs, and she went still.

*Dagger to his throat, three more into the crowd at random. Sow confusion, then run. Use the tents as cover...*

"One more thing," the sergeant went on. "Stay out of the way of the trolls. Those wankers are fucking mental."

# 72

## Pressure Building

Balur had never been a huge fan of deception. If you were wanting a fight, you were going up to a man and you were punching him in the face. You did not point one way, hope he turned, and sucker him in the kidneys. That was not a fight. That was not a test of your mettle. That was a way to show that you kept your balls in a little purse and had forgotten what you were meant to do with them.

And, this—what he was doing now. This posturing and pretense. It had sounded like a good way to stay alive. But now that it came to it, it was just deception and horse dung.

He stood astride Quirk's thaumatic cart. Jewels and furs were draped around his shoulders. Firkin stood at the foot of the cart, screeching and yelling. The thronging crowd pressed toward him, reaching up, trying to touch him.

He was their prophet. They adored him. They worshipped him. They would do whatever he said...

Before him, the dragon's skull—the deceptive, horse dung skull—made another pass of the crowd. The crowd screamed hate and adoration in equal measure.

Balur knew that many lives depended upon him sticking to the plan, upon him only playing the part of the aggressor, and never actually following through. But part of him yearned to give the order, to lead the charge forward, to immolate himself in the thrust and cut of combat. How many could he be taking with him? What was the size of the path he could be carving through their forces?

His willpower wavered. He felt the bellow building in his chest, the red starting to occlude his vision.

But Lette was over there. She was depending on him to hold the line.

He let the breath out.

On the plus side, at least he could spend his afternoon taking out his frustration by hurling the vilest insults he knew at the enemy.

# 73

# Lying Liars and the Lies They Tell

Lette had to admit, the uniforms the Dragon Consortium supplied were damned fine. She had, over the years, been attached to a number of armies, controlled by a number of different men and women. City garrisons defending against barbarians, as well as rioting citizens. Bandit horse lords battling against members of their own extended families. Dukes and earls looking to expand their territory. She had even joined one army so that she could spend a year being promoted until she was in proximity to her assassination target.

In her experience, all armies, no matter their purpose or financial backing, had one thing in common: their universally shitty uniforms. They scratched, itched, hung wrong on your frame, bunched in inexplicable places, and generally only served to make you feel like an idiot.

The Dragon Consortium, however, seemed to exist at a greater tier of wealth than any she had previously been exposed to. The uniforms—black cotton with two batlike wings in gray stretched over the breast—fit neatly over the chain-mail shirt with which she had been provided. The helmet was well padded and snug. Even the boiled-leather boots fit her well.

Will clanked after her, moving as if wrapped in thick bundles of cloth.

"How do people fight in this stuff?" he whispered to her as they left the green supply tent and headed out into the army proper. "You might as well fight with a baby pig tied to each arm."

Lette sometimes worried that being a farmer had damaged Will's analogies.

"How about," she suggested, "you take off all your armor, I'll hit you with my sword, and then when you've finished scooping your entrails off the floor, you hit me with your sword, and we'll see who comes out better?"

Will kept his grumbling inaudible after that.

"So," he said finally. "This is your territory. Where do we start with the lying?"

"One of the important things to remember about being a soldier," she told him, "is that it's boring as shit. Bored people talk about anything they can. So we just need to find a gathering. Dice games. Cards."

They found what they were looking for in less than a minute. A large group of soldiers gathered in a circle. Eight sat facing each other, one shaking a dice cup. Another thirty or so were all standing around, catcalling and placing bets.

Lette dug an elbow into his ribs. "Put everything you have on me."

She enjoyed his bewildered stare as she stepped up to the circle.

"Any of you pussies got balls big enough to take on a girl?" she said with a grin, as she wedged her way between two large men.

They looked at her in much the way they would look at a turd that had fallen from the sky and landed between them.

"Closed game," said one, cracking his knuckles.

She reached to her belt, detached a purse, and tossed it into the center of the dice circle. It landed with a heavy clink. As long as no one opened it and discovered it was full of copper sheks, then everything should go fine. And Lette had no intention of letting anyone get close to the coppers.

The other eight dice players were all staring at the purse.

After a moment the knuckle-cracker nodded. "Room for one more," he grunted.

She took stock of the opponents quickly. Three others the same size, stature, and intelligence level as the knuckle cracker. A woman who looked angry that she was no longer the only person with a set of tits at the circle, and two men, built on more slender frames, but with no signs of any greater intellect to balance out the loss of muscle weight. Only one other man, who was watching her carefully. There was at least a flicker of intellect behind his eyes. Unsurprisingly, the largest pile of coins was in front of him. But he had also been careful not to take so much as to actually piss off those of a knuckle-cracking disposition.

She let her first roll of the dice fly randomly. But she judged their weight and bounce as she shook the cup. She watched how the dice rolled, how they landed in the dirt. A lord and two swords. Not a terrible roll. Not enough to win the round. She saw the other woman smile. Lette picked the dice up, rolled them in her palm, felt the weight, the imperfections in their sides.

The round concluded. She pulled the only gold bull left in her purse out, tossed it to the knuckle-dragger who had lucked into throwing three queens.

It took her three more rounds to be certain she could roll pretty much anything she wanted. None of them had eyes as quick as her hands, and while the other woman had a larger chest, Lette had undone a few more buttons.

She glanced up at Will. He was staring at her instead of betting. He had infiltrated an army raised entirely to crush him and everything he stood for, and he was still distracted by a bit of skin. Men were all idiots. She arched her eyebrows at him, picked up two of the silver drachs she had won, and rubbed them together slightly.

Will came back to life, leaned over to the man beside him, and started talking.

Lette didn't win much at first. Just enough. She played slowly, and methodically.

Then the opening came. The other woman couldn't bluff for shit, was grinning at her dice, and throwing gold bulls at the pot as if they were going out of style. Lette rolled, put her cup facedown, went all in.

A hush fell.

The other woman stared at her with hate.

She felt bad for the woman in a way. In other circumstances they might have had a lot in common. It was not easy to be a woman in this line of work. It required more skill, more dedication, and more strength of will than it required in men. As a rule, she generally liked women of the blade. But today she didn't need a friend. She needed all eyes on her.

The others ducked out of the hand. The woman pushed her stash of coin into the center of the ring with a curl of her lip. She lifted her cup. Three kings. A good roll.

Lette allowed her face to fall, picked up her cup.

Silence. Absolute and utter.

An emperor. A king. A queen.

The woman's specific accusation was lost in her scream of anger. The generalities were very clear, however. Lette was a cheat, and a whore, and had to die.

She had a knife out, was lunging across the circle. Dice, pots, and coins went flying.

Lette waited calmly. As the woman was about to strike she flowed to the left, caught the arm holding the blade by the wrist, twisted hard. The woman pivoted through the air, landed hard on her back. The snap of her wrist was audible to all. So was her scream.

Lette allowed the woman to scramble away, then calmly she took her seat and gathered her winnings.

All in absolute silence.

Then the man beside her clapped her on the back so hard her

teeth snapped together. "That," he said, "is how you play a fucking dice game."

Laughter, cheers, someone passed her a drink. And now, now she had them.

As other soldiers gathered, brought there by the commotion, she started to talk.

"Good thing I found this game," she said, taking a swig from her ale. "Not so many anymore. Folk getting worried."

The man with quick eyes looked at her sharply, but didn't say anything. Another man took the bait, though.

"What you talking about?" he said. "Can't piss in this place without it landing in a dicing circle."

She looked at them all, painting her face with confusion. "Ain't you boys heard?" she asked.

"Heard what?" rumbled one of the men beside her.

She shrugged. "Here I was thinking I was playing with some proper, hard-core gamblers, and instead I'm just playing with a bunch of deaf bastards."

"Heard what?" the man rumbled again. The bass was deeper, and the goodwill was draining out.

She took a sip from her ale, dragged it out.

"Pay ain't coming," she said, as if it was the most obvious thing in the world.

"The fuck you say?"

A chorus of questions, expletives, and denials broke out at her statement. She took another sip, waited for them to die down. She could see what Firkin liked about having an audience.

When the general hysteria had softened to a dull murmur, she rolled her dice, tossed in a few silver drachs. She was planning on losing this hand.

The man next to her caught her arm in his giant mitt of a hand. "What are you talking about?" he said.

She shrugged. "All everyone's talking about over on the east side of camp. The Consortium. They're almost out of coin. We're getting stiffed next payday."

"The dragons are bloody minted," said another soldier.

There was enthusiastic agreement.

The next part made no sense to her, but Will had been insistent she make this detail very clear. She was tempted not to include it just to punish him for being a cryptic bastard, but the stakes were too high for pettiness now.

"You don't know?" she said looking round, incredulous. "You didn't hear?" And of course they hadn't. There was nothing for them to hear. "You know what happens when a dragon breathes fire onto gold?"

Shrugs, laughter, confusion.

"You get hot fucking gold," said one man.

She shook her head, as if saddened by his naïveté. "Lead," she said, dropping the word like the metal itself. "It all turns to lead. Worthless shit." She shook her head as if disgusted. "And they try not to do it, but they're fucking dragons. They breathe fire in their sleep the same way we snore." She was embellishing now, but they seemed to need more convincing. "And so it's taken a while, but now it's all lead. Why do you think they need to collect more of it each year?"

The volume of the murmuring dropped down a note at that. People shifting their gaze. Reconsidering their bets. And perhaps, just perhaps, reconsidering what the hell they were doing here.

And right on cue—

"You see that bloody great dragon's head they were parading about?" Will's voice rang out clearly in the crowd. "Didn't even know you could kill a dragon. Let alone chop its bleeding head off."

The murmur was back twice as hard and fast as before.

"You can't kill a dragon."

"Why the fuck we here then, if that prophet bloke didn't kill one?"

"Killed two, I heard."

"Three, I heard."

"Three?"

"I can't go without pay for another week. I already owe those fucking whores more than a month's worth. They'll chop my hand off."

"They'll chop off worse than that."

"Gold to lead. That's alchemy. That bitch is talking shit."

"Alchemy is lead to gold. Gold to lead is all fucked is what it is."

"The dragons have got to be good for it. Always are."

"Always said we couldn't kill them, but look what's happened here."

"Come on, ladies!" Lette bellowed through the crowd's confusion. "We playing dice here or what?"

But they weren't playing dice anymore. They were questioning everything. She took them all in the next two rounds, pocketed her winnings, and headed off to find the next set of dice players.

By early evening they were hearing the story back themselves. The pay wagons were full of lead, the dragons were full of shit, and the prophet and his band of nutcases were going to chop the balls off the Consortium dragons tomorrow.

"You know what?" said Will, leaning down to whisper in her ear. "I don't think Firkin could have done better than this."

They had discussed bringing the old man over, but it hadn't seemed worth it from a number of angles. He was unpredictable at the best of times, even if he was curiously efficacious. And he was needed back with Balur to help keep the crowds in line and inspired. Plus not having him here meant they could avoid seeing, smelling, or hearing him.

"That is," Lette told him, "honestly the only time I will ever allow myself to be compared to Firkin."

Will grinned. "You're amazing. Where did you learn to roll dice like that?"

She smiled back. "A lot of people can roll like that," she told him. "It's just not many who can roll like that and never get caught."

"You were cheating?" He looked genuinely shocked.

"No, Will," she deadpanned. "My life might be a shit show of death threats and madness right now, suggesting that all the gods in heaven hate me and everything I stand for, but actually I have been blessed by lady luck."

His smile faltered. "Oh," he said.

She patted him on the back. Given the scale and audacity of what they were trying to pull off, things were indeed going surprisingly well. Certainly people had told them they were full of shit, but nothing had come to blows yet. The plan to steal the gold would be looking considerably harder if they had been slapped in irons and were being pelted with rotting food matter.

Not insurmountable, but harder, to be sure.

"Quirk should be here shortly," she said, glancing at the sun in the sky.

"Which is why," Will said, "we are here." They rounded a corner, leaving one row of tents for another, and saw a substantial crowd gathered about a hundred yards away.

"Oh by the gods," Will breathed. "It's working even better than I thought it would."

The crowd, from what Lette could tell, did not look like a happy one.

"What is that?" she asked.

"That," he said, with a look of distinct satisfaction, "is a bunch of pissed-off people all around the pay wagons."

"What?" Lette's eyebrows went up. She liked, at this point in her career, to think that she had more than a little experience in the fine art of purloining shit. And in her not inconsiderable experience, surrounding the aforementioned shit with an angry mob was not a great way to set yourself up for success. She explained this to Will using a significantly larger selection of curse words.

"Don't worry," he said. "We need this crowd. Quirk has to have an audience. Balur's distraction will pull them away. He's been milking that skull all day."

Lette tried to look confident. The feint. Except, now that it came down to it, she couldn't help but think that Balur was not really the feinting sort. He was more the full frontal bludgeon to your face sort. Perhaps though, if he wasn't drinking, he would resist.

*If he wasn't drinking...*

Gods. They were so screwed.

And then beyond the crowd, two brightly colored wagons rolled into sight.

# 74

# Money Makes the World Go Mad

The first thought to enter Quirk's head as she rounded the bend in the road and found herself staring into a crowd of belligerent, shouting soldiers was *I have made a terrible mistake.*

Cattak had scouted ahead, told her the route to take. Now he sat at the reins of the wagon behind her. He was posing as her guard, he had told her. Will had organized everything.

And apparently Will had instructed Cattak to point her at the biggest shit show in the camp and send her on her way.

She heaved on the reins of the horse that was pulling her wagon, felt the wheels trundle toward a stop yet never quite reach it, the cart still carried forward inch by inch by momentum. In the back of her head, she heard an unwelcome voice spurring her forward—*There's nothing you can do except go forward now. You're in too deep.*

Was that true? Was this the only way?

Maybe it didn't even matter. Maybe it would be easier to just surrender to the gravity of fate. Walk in the direction she'd been pointed, find out what waited along that path. Other directions...she'd have to figure things out for herself. Have to face the consequences.

What would her friends at the university think if they could see her now? What would they tell her to do?

Their voices seemed very far away.

"What's going on?" Cattak had rolled to a stop beside her.

"You know something," she said. "Some plan of Will's I'm not privy to." He hadn't told them everything. That much was obvious. But why not? Paranoia? That had never plagued him in the past. Though Balur had never had to kill a spy at his feet in the past either...

Was coming to the Consortium's camp—embedding himself in the enemy—the *only* way to win? She couldn't believe that it was. But she didn't have any other plans.

"I have my instructions," Cattak said. "But I have no fucking clue what he's up to."

She looked at Cattak. A hard man devoid of romance. That's what she'd liked about him. A man with an entirely practical imagination. If she wanted an answer grounded in reality, he seemed like the person to provide it. "So," she said to him, "why in the names of all the gods are you here?"

Cattak shrugged. "Well, Will's the prophet, isn't he?"

Quirk honestly didn't have much of a comeback to that. "If this works?" she said. "Then maybe. Just maybe."

She flicked the reins, felt the horse gain speed.

"Just be loud," Cattak said beside her. "Boisterous. Like you're the most important person in the world. They won't like you, but they'll believe you."

The twitch of Quirk's lips was very far from a smile.

"Ho!" she yelled as she drew closer. "Ho! Who here speaks for the Dragons of Kondorra?" She dropped her voice an octave or so, tried to insert an arrogant swagger into it. She might not like Cattak's advice, but it did seem likely to keep her alive.

A harassed-looking man in his mid-forties and drenched in sweat pushed through the crowd toward her.

"Where are you going?" called more than one voice in the crowd.

"Come back!" demanded more.

"Pay us!" became a popular refrain.

The man caught the bridle of her horses. "I don't give Lawl's left nut for who you are, get you and your wagons the fuck out of here."

Quirk felt her resolve quaver. This was an ugly crowd. She didn't know what hornet's nest Lette and Will had stirred up, but she was not excited about jamming her hand into it.

Cattak drew his wagon up beside her. Why hadn't Will asked him to do this ridiculous task?

She glanced over at him. Saw the steel fully exposed in his gaze. And she knew. They would never have believed Cattak. He was too obviously a spy. She...She was the worst person for the job, and that made her the best.

"I'm not going anywhere until I get my pay!" she yelled. *Just stick to the script.* The words Will had given her became a plank to hold on to in the rapidly switching currents of her fear. "I sold the dragons good hard steel and I expect to be paid. Four gods-hexed months I've been waiting for my pay, and I ain't waiting anymore."

Her words dropped into the crowd like stones into water. Silence splashed through it, rippled out slowly, stilling every tongue, bringing every pair of eyes to bear on her.

She felt the sweat rolling down the back of her neck in a thick sheet. The guard holding her horses released them so that he could claw his hands down his face.

"Someone"—Quirk raised her voice, which to her only seemed to emphasize the tremor in it—"get me to those gods-hexed dragons so I can get paid before that prophet fucker opens all their bellies and defrauds me of good coin."

"You fucking—" the man started, but the end of the insult was lost in the eruption from the crowd. They surged forward. Quirk flinched backward, scrambling toward her wagon bed, feeling the brightly colored silk flapping at her back. But the crowd was not aimed at her. Instead they lunged at two black, heavily barred wagons parked at the edge of the crowds. Horses stood tethered, whinnying as the crowd encroached. One reared, kicked large gray feet into the air.

Very large men in very large black armor, wielding very large maces, surrounded each cart. As the crowd rushed them they set about themselves. Black steel rose and fell, and red painted the air. Shouts of rage turned to howls of pain and fear. The soldiers beat back the crowd.

"You!" spat the man, who was back hanging on to her horses for support. "You keep your fucking gob shut!" Froth sprayed from his mouth. He turned on the crowd. "You'll get your fucking pay!" he bellowed. "I don't know what piss-hexed beer put this stupid fucking idea in your head, but there's gold. And you'll get paid end of the week. Same as fucking always. So fuck off and go back to having whores poxing your cocks before I have my boys kill more of you than that prophet wanker will ever manage."

"Ain't no gold!" shouted some anonymous body in the crowd. "Them dragons all gone turned it to lead."

*Lead?* Quirk was forced to admit that she still didn't know much about dragons, but she did know a lot about alchemy and more than she would like to know about magic. There was no way she was aware of to turn gold into lead.

But she kept her mouth shut.

"You're a stupid fucker, aren't you?" the man by her horses yelled back into the crowd. "Those wagons are full of the shiny stuff, and if you ever want to see any of it, you'll keep your mouth shut, and fuck off, and do your job."

"Show us!" yelled a woman's voice. It sounded familiar to Quirk's ear. *Lette?*

"I ain't showing you shit, because I don't have to show you shit," the man told them.

"He ain't got it!" yelled another familiar voice close to where maybe-Lette's voice had come from. *Will?*

"Who said that?" yelled the man. "Show yourself, so I can

carve your heart right out of your chest, you fucking coward." He was a big man, and his hand was on a short sword in his belt.

Whoever the speaker was—Will or no—he wisely kept himself hidden.

Quirk knew she had to speak, but she was still staring at that hand on that sword. She did not want to speak, did not want to commit to the next step. Surely enough had been done, enough had been asked of her.

Next to her, Cattak cleared his throat.

She closed her eyes. She had come this far.

"Shut up, you fat fuck," she said, every word feeling wooden in her mouth, every one of them sounding like her own death sentence. "Take me to the dragons. You're going to be one of the first the prophet kills, and I don't want to be stuck trying to talk some sense into your bloated corpse."

Gods, the man wasn't even fat. It was all muscle. Quirk could tell because everything in the man had suddenly gone tense.

The crowd was laughing now. But it was an ugly laugh. Soldiers near the black pay wagons were still on the ground, bleeding, weeping, groaning. The tethered horses whickered, and stamped, trying to get away from the stink of blood.

The man turned on her slowly. He cocked his head to one side. "You want to see the dragons?" he asked her. His voice was low and dangerous.

It took every ounce of willpower Quirk had to keep from shaking her head desperately. The fire buried in her heart had never felt so far away. Her palms were icy with fear.

The man moved with a sudden speed that belied the bulk of his muscles. He leapt up, bounced off the wooden tongue between her wagon's two horses, landed on the toe board, and towered over her. He reached down, grabbed her by the scruff of the neck.

A moment later she was lying in the dirt, trying to focus, tailbone, back, and jaw aching from the force of her impact on the ground. The man jumped down, dragged her to her feet.

"Well," he said, with a savage smile. "Now you get to meet the fucking dragons."

She shot a glance at Cattak as her captor started to haul her away from the crowd, and from the army's camp, and toward Hallows' Mouth. But six of the men in black armor had pulled crossbows from their backs and he sat quite still, arms raised.

"Merchant, my arse," said the guard as he pulled her stumbling through the fields. "You're a spy. And I'm going to enjoy watching everything the Consortium does to you."

# 75

## Impatience

Meanwhile, back in the prophet's camp, Firkin was getting sick of being Balur's whipping boy. *Do this,* Balur would say, and because Firkin didn't want to taste the lizard man's fist at the back of his throat, he did it. *Say this,* Balur would tell him, and he would say it.

It was taking all the fun out of being the voice of a nonexistent prophet.

Under different circumstances, he thought he would have quite enjoyed Balur's company. The lizard man had the right priorities in life: fighting, drinking, and women. Firkin might not have put them in that order, but at least Balur had picked the right top three. Not like those others. Will with all his concerns about the right thing to do, and his head being stuck in Lette's britches. Quirk with her conflicts, and her desire to learn shit. What did learning shit ever do but fill up space in your head that could be taken up with little black circles of swirling beer? Lette...well, Lette could have been fun except she seemed far too preoccupied with Will's head and her britches these days.

The whole thing was a gods-hexed shame. There was an army at his back, a dragon's skull being paraded before him, another army to attack. He should be up there, preaching, yelling, baying for blood to be spilled. It could all have been so fucking beautiful.

But no. No. Will had told Balur, and Balur had told him, don't flap your trap. Keep your tongue still and be a good little priest.

Well, if he'd known he'd have to be good, Firkin would never have become a priest in the first place.

And who was Will anyway? He'd told Firkin he wasn't the prophet. And then that he was. Or that he wasn't but he said that he was. Firkin was very unclear on the whole issue.

All he knew was that he wanted to watch a really big fight through the gentle glaze of blind drunkenness and he wasn't.

But Balur was a reasonable lizard. A god-fearing lizard. So maybe if a prophet went to have a word in his ear...

Balur was standing in Quirk's thaumatic cart, occasionally striking his chest, and turning to give various elements of the assembled crowd a view of his best side.

"You!" Firkin shouted. He had decided to play it gently. He didn't want to piss Balur off. Balur was, after all, very large. "You don't have any balls!"

Balur looked down at him. Firkin did his best to focus.

"Great big lizard." Firkin hiccupped. "Great big fists. All that..." He waved his hands vaguely, forgot what point he was trying to make, hiccupped again. "And where do you have your fists?" he asked.

"They are about to be being around your throat," Balur told him.

"Jammed right up your arse!" Firkin told him, as if he hadn't spoken. "Because little old Will told you to put them there. Takes your...your woman...your little Lette, and then he tells you to stick your hands right up your arse and you do it."

"You better be watching your tongue," Balur growled. "I have been killing holy men before."

"Go ahead!" Firkin spat. "Least be better than you..." He lost his train of thought again, fought to find it again, grabbed on to the slippery little bastard with both hands. "Be better than watching you parade about like a peacock with no cock."

That he thought was clever. A well-landed blow. He thought it for all the time it took for Balur to punch him hard in the face.

# 76

# Hallows' Mouth

Quirk stumbled yet again, scraped her knees yet again, was dragged to her feet yet again. The man from the pay wagons was unrelenting. His arm was a steel bar, his fist a vise that held her, heaved her inexorably upward. She had clawed at both hand and arm and achieved nothing. She had pushed the man too far, well beyond his breaking point, and she could not pull him back.

Fear thrummed through her. Her legs shook uncontrollably, threatened to send her tumbling again. She tried to breathe, tried to find her center.

They spiraled up. The path wove its way around Hallows' Mouth, twisting through arches of heat-scorched stone, narrowing to thin precipices, weaving around vents that bubbled and belched foul sulfurous smoke. She tried to keep her free hand pressed to the side of the volcano, but as their elevation increased, the stone became too hot to touch. Above her, the sky grew darker.

She had a good view of the battlefield now, could see how paltry Will's forces looked against those of the Consortium. Any tiny flaw in the plan and they would be utterly obliterated. And there were so many flaws.

Right now, Quirk felt like she was the largest one.

Eventually, the path twisted through an archway leading into the craggy cliff face. They were halfway up the volcano's side. By Quirk's estimate she had been climbing for almost two hours. Her breath was ragged, her legs shook. She was having trouble distinguishing terror from exhaustion.

The tunnel closed over her like a clenching fist.

"Like I explained, I'm completely willing to take an IOU," she said between gasps, but the man had long since stopped paying attention to her.

The heat rose. Sweat stuck her colorful robes to her body. She felt too exposed. She should have argued with Will for the role of a soldier. At least she would have gotten some armor that way.

The tunnel sank deeper into the rock. The walls took on a twisted, jagged look, as if the path had been forced into the volcano against the rock's will. Torches gave off a smoky red light.

A pair of doors emerged from the gloom. They were massive, painted the same black as the pay wagons. A single leathery wing carved into the surface of each. She was dragged unceremoniously to their foot. They towered over her. Doors for giants. For gods. For dragons.

The man banged hard on the door, the steel knuckles of his gauntlet booming off the wood. The sound echoed down the empty stone corridor.

There were no guards here. She supposed she knew why. She supposed she knew exactly what was behind those doors. You didn't need guards when anyone smarter than a particularly blunt rock knew to stay away.

The man dropped her to the ground. She cried out as she struck the unforgiving stone once more. But this time he didn't pull her to her feet. This time he walked away.

She watched him leave, too exhausted to beg anymore. This wasn't how it had all been meant to happen. Not at all.

Behind her, the door creaked open.

She tried to take stock, to get a grip on herself. She knew what was behind that door. She knew *who* was behind it. They were why she had gone on this stupid gods-hexed escapade in the first place. Just two days ago she had been explaining how seeing them was one of the few important things left to her in the world. And now she couldn't move.

She was surrounded by fire. She could feel it pulsing through the mountain. She could feel creatures defined by it waiting for her. She tried to take strength from that.

*I should be as at home here as they are.*

Which was great, and everything, but even if she was as at home as they were, they still outnumbered and outweighed her to a laughable degree.

"Enter." The single word boomed out. More of a growl or a roar than a word. She felt her sternum vibrate with the force of it.

Her fear. The heat. The power of that voice. Her desire to immolate herself against the flame of a dragon, a real true dragon...It all twisted inside of her. It all came together and made that voice utterly compelling, utterly irresistible. She knew she could run, yet she found herself clambering to shaking feet, leaning on the black door for support as she pushed her way into the room.

She had to see. She had to.

The chamber beyond was vast in the same way that a mountain is vast. Quite possibly because the chamber occupied almost all of a mountain. Its ceiling arced up to the crater far above. Its walls tumbled down toward the smoking pit of lava far below. Heat clogged the room, pressed against Quirk like a physical force. She had to push through it to get into the room. She blinked her suddenly dry eyes, tried to take everything in.

Around a central column of smoke that plumed toward the distant crater, the central crags of Hallows' Mouth had been cut into flat tiers.

Each and every one dripped with absurd wealth.

She scrubbed at her eyes several times waiting for the heat-induced mirage to fade away, but it did not. It stayed resolutely, stubbornly there. And for the first time, Quirk truly understood why Lette and Balur would go to such great lengths to try to steal this wealth.

In Tamathia, the university was considered one of the wealthiest institutions in the country. It had an endowment that would last it generations under even the worst financial climates. It owned significant parts of large cities, and counted as the largest landowner shy of the emperor.

All of the university's wealth would perhaps have counted for one of the tiers she could make out now.

As she watched, a small cascade of coins tumbled from the edge of one tier. They crashed and clattered down onto the one below, dislodged a small mountain of necklaces. They went spilling down toward the edge. Enough gold to feed a midsize village for a year spilled into the volcano's burning magma.

Quirk tore her eyes away from the obscene waste of wealth and back to the movement that had started it all. Slowly, uncoiling at a leisurely pace, the dragon emerged.

It was sixty yards long from nose to tail. Its body was jet black, sinuous. Golden eyes glittered in a fine-boned, elegant head. Nostrils flared red, then yellow, then blue. Flames jetted out as it stretched wings like silken expanses of midnight. It opened its mouth slightly and a bright red, forked tongue tasted the air.

Quirk was frozen. Mattrax and Dathrax both had been majestic, titans of the air, but this creature, this was . . . was . . .

"Beautiful," she whispered.

It beat its wings once, twice. The swirling thermals from the volcano caught it and bore it up easily. As it rose into the air, other dragons appeared. A bloodred beast with a white underbelly, wings disproportionately short against the vast tube of its frame. A sinuous yellow dragon that moved in writhing coils through the air, barking and yipping in a curiously canine manner. A majestic green creature with golden horns that preened its way through the air. And finally a squat, dirty brown crea-ture who appeared as ungainly and uncomfortable in the air.

One by one they landed, the black coming down last of all, circling twice about the column of smoke above the heads of all the others before deigning to grace the earth with his presence.

Quirk would have staggered back if she could. Would have dropped her jaw open. But she could do nothing. She was par-alyzed, overcome by the enormity of the moment. They were so close to her, so massive. Fear and desire tore at her in equal measure.

She could touch them.

They could kill her.

She could ask them everything she could think of.

They would roast her alive long before they gave an answer.

But what it would be to die that way, to be immolated in the purity of their fires.

She shook her head. She was the enemy of these creatures. They were selfish and brutish. They wanted to kill everyone.

She was a scientist, a thaumatobiologist. This was everything she had ever dreamed of.

They were killers.

She was here to deceive them.

And if they discovered that deception…then their nature would take over and they would kill her.

Her thoughts turned to every other thaumatobiologist who had left the safety of their academic towers to study the beasts of which they dreamed. She thought of their corpses. Of the plaques in the hall of remembrance listing out their demises.

*Edmondel Allaband—Speared by Unicorn*

*Carped Metheril—Trodden upon by Giant*

*Robart Pondra—Head mounted upon wall by Wyld Huntsman*

*Fettrick Battar—Wished away by Djinn*

She didn't want to be another memory, another failure.

"So," said the black dragon in the same titanic voice that had brought her into the room. It was the voice she imagined Lawl used to call dead warriors from the Hallows into battle. It crashed through her, left her body feeling scoured clean. "You are the spy the prophet has dared to send. His saboteur."

She and Will had talked about this. There were things she was meant to say in this scenario.

*Quirkelle Bal Tehrin—Hubris and dragons*

Gods, as selfish and ugly as it was, she wanted to live. She wanted to write of this moment, of all the moments and scraps of information she had gathered. She wanted to teach all the world of these creatures. And she wanted to see the world learn from her.

Ten thousand lives had been placed on her shoulders.

Will's life. Firkin's. Balur's. Lette's. All the rest.

She knew what she was supposed to say.

She made a decision.

"Yes," she said. "Yes, I am, and I want to tell you everything I know."

# 77

# The Center Cannot Hold

If you had asked Lette the day before what she might change about Will, and if she could change just one thing, she would have been tempted to reply that it was his professionalism. There might have been a few more base, physical improvements to contend with, but professionalism would have definitely been in the mix. He was too easily swayed by his emotions. He had not found the calm, quiet place it was necessary to visit when circumstances called for hard decisions and clear thought. She would have wished for him to have a still place to visit, an inner core of peace to lend him strength in what was to come.

Today she would like to rip Will's inner core right out and use it to beat him to death.

Quirk had been arrested and was now—mostly likely—being merrily tortured to death, while giving up every intimate detail about them and their plan. Their descriptions would be disseminated quietly and efficiently throughout the army, and just before the battle broke out, they would be seized, and stripped, and then their flayed corpses would be displayed for everyone to see.

There was, of course, the chance of escape, but even if that happened, how far would they truly get? Without Quirk to rile them up any further, the Consortium troops were back to looking for just the sort of distraction two renegade soldiers would provide. Their concerns about pay had ebbed to a belligerent murmur. Lette had tried to kindle the flames with a few more incendiary dice games, but all she had to tell them was yesterday's news.

Now she and Will were no better off than they had been a few days ago. In fact they were worse off, because all the opportunities to survive, to truly get away, had fled with them.

They should have sent Firkin and his followers off to Hallows' Mouth as a sacrificial tribute while the rest of them headed for the coast. They should have stuck with enlisting in the Consortium army, and lived out their days as well-paid soldiers. But instead they had run headlong into this dead end. It was inescapable.

And did any of this bother Will? Did any of it seem to put a single concern in his head? Did his guts quiver, his bowels loosen, and his food rebel in his stomach?

No. Not for a single fucking second. He just sat there with mooncalf eyes, waiting for the world to come crashing down on them.

"We should leave," she told him. "Just leave now. Get as much of a head start as we can. Forget the gold. It'll just slow us down and we'll never have a chance to spend it anyway. If we're lucky—stupidly, insanely lucky—we might make it to the coast, and we can sign up for some navy, and die of scurvy on an ocean somewhere. At least that'll give us a few more months."

He patted her on the shoulder. "Have a little faith. Please."

"Faith?" If she ground her teeth any harder she was going to be left with blunt stumps in her mouth. "You're going to pull the religious leader now? You know where I'm going to shove your fucking faith?"

He put his arms around her. "Don't worry," he said. "The plan is going to work."

"Was it working when Quirk was carried away?"

They were still at the back of the Consortium camp, the stretch of dirty grass between the black pay wagons and Quirk's brightly colored ones. The angry mob of soldiers was reduced to a few belligerent souls, probably more interested in being in the army's rear ranks than they were in ensuring fair pay for all their fellows.

"Balur will make his feint soon. Quirk will find a way out. Everything will work."

Perhaps, she thought, it was a coping mechanism. A way of dealing with the stress. Absurd blind faith was the only way he could keep putting one foot in front of the other. He couldn't face the dream crumbling around him, couldn't take the tastes of the ashes in his mouth.

She put his head in both her hands, pulled him gently toward her, until their faces were level. "We *have* to go, Will," she whispered, trying to drive the words into his head, so that he would see the truth. See reality. "We *have* to leave."

"Trust—" he started.

She head-butted him. Hard.

"Ow!" he yelled, as he fell down hard. "Fuck!" He grabbed his nose. Blood streamed down his chin. "Has Barph got your brains? What the fuck did you do that for?"

He clambered to his feet, blood still flowing from his nose.

"Are you fucking listening to me, Willett Fallows?" she asked him. "Because I am saying this only once more. I am fucking going. I am escaping this rattrap of a future. And I am running out of fucks to give about whether you accompany me or not. So either start moving your arse toward the horizon, or I shall leave you here to burn along with the rest of your Barph-addled dreams."

"No." Will shook his head. Blood flew from his injured nose. "Lette, please. Just a little more time. You'll see."

"You're fucking mad," she told him. And she turned away. It hurt. It hurt more than she expected it to, and she could see in her mind's eye the wounded, pleading expression he would be wearing at this exact moment. But she did not turn back to him.

She just took a step away. And the step hurt too, but she kept on moving.

The roar, though—that stopped her dead in her tracks.

At first she thought it was the dragons, finally roused from their nest in Hallows' Mouth, coming down to see to them personally. She could see them clearly in her mind's eye as well, rising from the crater, the greatest force of destruction that volcano could ever spew, arcing down, wings spread, lungs full of fire…

But then it came again, and it was a sound she knew, a sound she was intimate with, that could lull her to sleep in times of trouble. It was the sound of men mobilizing for war.

Men yelled, trumpets blared, feet drummed against the ground, armor shook, weapons rattled, dogs barked, griffins cawed, trolls roared, captains called for order, and none came.

Someone put a hand on her shoulder and she spun, knife already in her hand, pressing it to the jugular.

*Step back to avoid the spray. Don't be blinded.*

But it was Will. Just Will.

"Balur," he said.

But she looked at the chaos, and the way the whole of the camp pulsed with sudden energy, the way it surged, like a hound that has finally torn through its leash. "No," she said. "This isn't a feint. This is more."

She fought the knowledge for a moment, but in the end she knew Balur. He wouldn't…simply couldn't just feint.

Will saw it on her face, and before she could stop him he was taking off through the camp, running toward the front line.

"No!" she tried to call, but her shout was lost in all the other shouts of soldiers readying for war.

"The pay wagons," she muttered to herself. "The fucking pay wagons." For now was the time to strike, to steal, and to run, and to hide, and to maybe have a celebratory quickie in a copse of trees for at least getting that far before the inevitable capture, torture, and death.

She could run at that moment, she thought. She could just turn tail and run for herself, try to save her skin.

But was that who she was anymore? That was certainly the woman she had been when she entered the Kondorra valley. A survivor. Self-interested, perhaps. Uncaring, perhaps. Vicious, definitely. But a survivor.

Hadn't she wanted to leave that woman behind, though? Hadn't she wanted to be a better person? Someone who didn't just survive, but lived?

She hesitated. Then, suddenly she was running after Will, pushing through bustling men and women. A sergeant yelled at her to stop. She almost forgot herself and planted a dagger in his skull. The blade was in her palm, then she remembered how she hadn't been killing people here, because that was the definition of suicide. So she ran on, ignoring his increasingly angry yells. Will had a good fifty yards on her. Had his head down, was barreling forward.

"The prophet!" people yelled all around her. "The prophet is coming! The mad bastard is attacking."

*Mad bastard?* Yes, that seemed appropriate.

*I could probably catch Will with a dagger in his calf, even at this distance, at this pace. Probably. Bring him down, drag him away. People would think the kicking and screaming was the injury.*

Griffins were taking to the air, screaming. Their riders yelled to each other, bronze spears gripped tight. The trolls were bellowing, beating on their war drums, a solid bass line of anger and rage starting to build under the chaos of the camp. Starting to give it direction. More and more soldiers were running to the front. She was losing Will in the crowd.

She pressed closer, faster, closed the distance. She could outrun some gods-hexed farm boy. The blade still in her hand called out to her to be thrown. Just enough to spin him around, slow him down. A flesh wound.

*Just a little closer. Just to be sure.*

And then suddenly Will ground to a halt. Her hand was cocked but she never threw. She stumbled up to him, panting hard. And there was no more crowd. She and Will stood at the front of the camp. Squares of women and men were forming to their left and right, but the plain ahead of them was utterly empty.

And across the field, they saw Balur and his army march to war.

# 78

# Conflict

The sound of war filled Balur's vision. The sound of *his* army. *His* to command. Their adoration had grown with each pass of the fake dragon skull. Their ardor for *his* words. He was their prophet now.

A feint. To stall and to feint. That was what Will had asked him in that tent, that night. And he had stalled. He had burned with frustration. Until Will was nothing but a distant memory to these people.

And now he unleashed his rage.

# 79

## Good, Honest Thievery

Lette pulled desperately at Will's shoulder.

"We have to go," she implored him. "Now."

He pulled away from her, stared. "They're really marching," he said. "All of them. Against the dragons. They really believe they can win."

"Yes," Lette agreed. "And they're fucking idiots. Can we go now?"

He turned to her. Finally. And his eyes were shining.

"We made that," he said. "We made that belief. We made all of that hope."

"Yes," she said again. "We deceived a whole shitload of people and now their deaths will be on our consciences for the next seven or eight minutes before we die ourselves. Now let's get the fuck out of here so we can let that reality sink in for a bit. Oh, and yes, steal the fucking gold, as that's the one tattered remnant of this plan that is still standing."

She seized his wrist, pulled him. He came stumbling, a man in a daze. And yes, she supposed, there was some glory to it all. A crushed people, rising up, rediscovering their will, refusing to take the oppression anymore. Even if it was a futile gesture, there was a certain grace to it. But honestly, she would much rather wait until the threat of death was just a little less imminent before she sat back and appreciated it.

The going was harder this time. They were fighting the tide of the crowd. Soldiers yelled at them to get out of the way.

Someone called out, "Deserter!" She threw her dagger that time, and he ate the blade. There was no time to retrieve it. She would miss that dagger. She had won it in a knife-throwing contest in Batarra against a drunken minotaur. Oh well.

The troll's war drums picked up tempo. The lighter snare of human drummer boys picked up the beat, sent battalions out into flanking maneuvers. The griffins formed up in the sky, wings beating the air hard. The numbers were absurd. The Consortium's army would swallow the prophet's. It was going to be a massacre. The sergeants and lieutenants were shouting out the orders to form up with relish.

Above them, Hallows' Mouth boomed and roared. Black smoke obliterated the burgeoning night. No stars would shine down on this slaughter.

Then they were at the rear of the camp. She pitched left, course-correcting toward Quirk's colorful wagons. Beyond those, the guards had pulled the pay wagons farther back, the black-painted walls receding into the darkness. The soldiers who had been guarding them were gone, called away to war.

Because all concerns about gold, about lead, about bankrupt dragons...all that was gone now. All this army cared about was the slaughter to come. Will's plan had been a nice dream, a good last-ditch attempt, but they had failed.

She crossed the final fifty yards to the pay wagons at a flat sprint. Her legs ached, lungs burned. There was nothing left to do now. Just run, and run until they could run no more, and pray that was enough.

Quirk had been right, they should have left the lead on the temple roofs. They needed all the divine luck they could get.

That thought almost made her laugh, as she leapt into the seat, flicked the reins at the still-tethered horses. Behind her, she heard Will scrambling up into the second wagon. *This at least,* she thought, *is some good honest thievery. No deception. No deceit. Simply taking what I want and then fleeing into the night.*

# 80

## Sellout

Quirk just wished the trembling would subside. She was alive, wasn't she? She was not stuck between any creature's teeth. They were listening.

"Will," she said, the quaver evident in just that single syllable. "That's his name. The prophet's Willett Fallows. From the north of the valley." She looked from massive leering head to massive leering head. "That's what you want to know about, right? Who he is? How he did this?"

The black dragon—sinuous, beautiful, deadly—lowered its enormous head until she was eye-to-eye with it. She could drown in those eyes, she knew. Their gold was the only wealth she desired.

"You will tell us everything, little spy," it said. The force of the words blew her back. She staggered under their impact. "You will give up everyone and everything. And then as we devour you, you will thank us."

She dropped to her knees. She felt bruised from the impact of his breath.

And yet there was so much majesty in him. So much she wanted to study. If only she could measure, observe, so much more.

But they were not creatures of patience, she knew.

"He's not a prophet," she said. "That's just bullshit. Some lie that was told, and took hold, and became...well, not useful, really. But the people wanted it to be true. I don't think he ever did. Will that is. But others did. There's this man, Firkin, you see."

She was gabbling, she realized, but she could hardly think straight. Not here and now. There was too much fear. Too much excitement. *To be this close to them.* It was madness. It was divine.

"But it's a lie he used in the end. Will did. To come here. To try to kill you. That's what he really wants. He hates you, you see. He thinks you're just... well, he calls you fat, lazy lizards. That's what he tells people. That you just lie around getting fat on the backs of other people's work, that you're like a plague. He has nothing but hatred for you. I think, if you peel back everything else that he is, that's what remains. That hatred."

Her words, she could see, were having a poor effect on the dragons. The black's lips were peeling back from its teeth.

*A completely different jaw structure from the other two,* one part of her mind said. *Though the teeth look the same. Could it be some subspecies? The result of interbreeding? Or just a natural variation?*

A different part of her mind just said, *Oh shit, oh shit, oh shit, oh shit, oh shit.*

The red dragon leaned down, snuffed at her. Even kneeling she was almost bowled over.

"Pathetic," it said.

"Yes." Quirk nodded. "That's exactly what he says about you."

The dragon roared.

And roared.

And roared.

The world around Quirk became a liquid oozing thing, running out of focus into a messy slop in the back of her quivering mind. It took a while for it to stop. Her nose was bleeding, she realized. There was a high-pitched ringing in her ears.

"He insults us," said the black. Every word made Quirk's skull ring with pain.

"Yes." She nodded, wished she hadn't. "The whole fat, lazy, ugly, diseased, diminutive genitalia thing—"

"Enough!" bellowed the dragon.

Quirk clutched her head and fought the urge to vomit.

"We do not need to know his history," hissed the squat brown dragon. Mercifully, its voice was quieter than the other's. "We do not need to hear his crimes. We do not need to know his plans. We need nothing but one thing. So you will tell us where he is if you have any desire to see the sun again."

Quirk nodded desperately. Fear held her as strongly as their claws. It was ice, stifling her fire. She looked up, toward the distant crater, the distant sky, toward the false promise of escape. She would love to see the stars one last time. But there was only smoke, leaving everything gray and obscure.

And then, drifting down from that distant window on the world, filtering in between the ringing in her ears, and the hot huffing of the dragon's breath, and the clinking of their claws on the coins at her feet, she heard the sound of drums, and the call of trumpets, as an army mobilized for war.

And despite herself, she smiled.

"Where is the prophet?" she said. "Well, right now, I think he's stealing your army's gold."

# 81

## The Midnight Ride of
## Lettera Therren

Lette rode. She rode like she had never ridden before. Like the gates to the Hallows had opened up and spewed forth the spawn of her nightmares, setting them upon her tail, screaming for her life, and baying to bury their jaws in her guts.

And then they truly did.

Her horses streaked across the plains, over the rolling hills. The pay wagon smashed up and down, thrashing over the grasslands behind it. How she had not broken an axle, she had no idea, but she praised whichever misanthropic deity had decided to spit in the eye of all the others and keep her whole and hale this far.

Then the roar rose up behind her, and killed all her hope dead.

She glanced back. She shouldn't. She knew that. All she would see back there would be all her possible futures narrowing down to the one that led to the Hallows and an eternity as Lawl's puppet in that bleak underworld. But she still glanced back. She wanted to see that future rushing toward her on a dragon's wings. She probably did it, she thought, because she was stupid. She had been, after all, stupid enough to get herself into this situation.

One by one, the dragons emerged from the cloud of smoke that wreathed Hallows' Mouth. Five of them, wings spread, necks stretched out, spouting geysers of fire into the night air. Then, one by one, they dropped down, and plunged toward her.

At least, she thought, her death would be pretty fucking epic. Five dragons to take her down. They might sing a song about that.

Fire filled the world behind her. She heard it, a rushing, roaring crackle that turned grass to ash and split stones in half. She felt its heat licking at her even through the thickness of the wagon at her back. She felt it closing in.

She glanced over to where Will leaned forward in the seat of his wagon, desperately thrashing the reins, urging more speed from his panicking horses. But they had nothing left to give.

Then the heat was gone. A black shape roared over them. She felt the downdraft from its wings buffet her. It streaked up into the sky. Two more dragons raced past on either side. A sinuous yellow monster on the left, a red behemoth on the right.

All three wheeled in the air before her. They were going to come back round. She and Will were sitting ducks.

Will responded first, hauling on his reins. His wagon began to turn. She heaved the leather strips in her own hands to avoid crashing. He was turning them both away from the attack.

And then a vast green beast landed directly in their path. Her horses screamed, tried to run in different directions. The strain on the reins almost flung her from her seat. She yelled, heaved, forced the horses under control, tightened her turn. The wagon rose up on two wheels. She felt the heavy mass of gold in the wagon shift behind her.

"Fuck all the gods!" she screamed. "Fuck all of you!"

The cart crashed down, straightened. The roaring, snapping mouth of the dragon rushed past in her peripheral vision. She heard the clash of its teeth closing behind her.

She risked a look at Will. He was still there, still hanging desperately on.

Flame. Flame lighting up the world. It raced past to her left.

Then to her right. And then a fresh stream, crossing directly in front of her, filling the world. Unavoidable.

She closed her eyes, felt the horses leap. The wheels smashed into a rise in the field, the wagon bucked into the air. Unbearable heat embraced her.

Then the moment was over. And she was still alive, still moving. She could smell her own smoldering hair. Dark shapes raced in the air above her.

She was pointed back at the Consortium army now. Back into the bulk of their enemies. She sought for a way to turn, hauled left.

A dragon—brown, broad, and ugly as a whore's arsehole—tore through the night toward her. She pulled the horses up as short as she could. They reared. The wagon bucked again. Steel-gray claws raked the air in front of the horses' noses. A frustrated roar filled the world around her.

Then the horses were running again, out of control now, dragging her along behind her. Smashing back the way she had tried to turn away from.

She could hear crackling from behind her, could smell burning wood. She risked another glance back.

The roof of her wagon was on fire.

"Oh fuck Lawl right in the arse."

Another glimpse at Will. He was directly ahead of her, almost upon the Consortium camp now.

She saw the dragon the moment before it opened its jaws. She opened her own mouth to call out wordlessly, pointlessly as it dropped out of the sky, as fire filled its mouth.

She saw Will lost in flame.

And then, miraculously, incomprehensibly, he emerged from the jet of fire. He tore off his flaming jacket, and rode on, crashing through tents and smoldering fire pits, his wagon flaming along with hers, twin beacons in the night.

"Gods," she breathed. And then she too was plunging into the chaos.

# 82

# What the Lizard Man Saw

Balur watched in horror as the dragons emerged from Hallows' Mouth. That had most definitely not been meant to happen yet. The massively superior army baying for their blood. Yes. That he remembered. He was prepared for that. Tooth and claw, blood and steel, man versus man. But the dragons...

And not just one dragon. Not even two. But five. Five dragons. No, that he was entirely unprepared for.

Balur was aware that he could be a prideful creature. It was not his finest quality. And if he was honest—truly honest with himself in a way that made him feel distinctly uncomfortable— he knew that he had not killed a dragon. What was more, he *could* not kill a dragon. Not truly. Yes, he had been caving in Mattrax's skull but that was not being full-blooded combat. No one was being red of tooth and claw in that encounter. He had just been committing murder. Very slowly. And his arms had ached at the end of killing Mattrax. If the dragon had not been drugged into oblivion then he would not have stood a chance.

One dragon was beyond him.

And five...

A pox upon the cocks of all the gods.

What was more, Balur saw, he was not alone in his doubts. The charge of the prophet's army, his ten thousand women and men, fueled by rage and holy ardor, stumbled and stopped.

They stood hesitating, wondering if they still held on to their courage.

Even the Consortium army stopped, stood, and stared. Even though these were the dragons they fought for. Even though these were their lords and masters. Balur thought he tasted their fear upon the air.

These dragons were not mere mortals. They might not be gods, but they were surely halfway there.

Balur looked at the fake skull held aloft at the head of his army. It seemed such an absurd thing now. Such a ridiculous pretense.

And then, for a reason he could not fathom, the dragons turned away. Everyone watched as they flew *behind* their own army, as their flame fell upon the ground in great obliterating sheets. For a moment the whole Consortium army had their back to the prophet's forces. And no one moved to take advantage. The thought didn't even enter Balur's mind.

Then the dragons were racing back toward their own army. They roared, screamed, fell from the heavens, raked the ground with claws and fire. For a mad moment Balur thought the Consortium was going to tear apart the very men and women committed to defending them. Perhaps they were done with humanity entirely, were going to raze every creature from that place and live free from the irritations of lesser beings.

Then shouts came from the Consortium army, yells. Confusion and panic joined the tastes on Balur's tongue. It tasted of battle, yet robbed of the blood. And still Balur did not understand.

And then he saw, and he did.

Two wagons, both streaming fire, tore through the Consortium forces. Soldiers danced out of the way. The wagons' horses screamed as they fought desperately to escape, rearing, kicking, stamping forward.

But more than that, Balur understood the significance of those wagons. He knew who drove them.

They were the Consortium army's pay wagons. A week's worth of gold for fifty thousand soldiers. The pay that was supposed to disappear. The pay they were meant to steal.

Lette sat at the head of one of those wagons.

Balur's heart seemed to seize in his chest. And yes, yes, he had understood the risks. And yes, he had known their chances this day. And yes, he had been fully aware. And yet he had never truly believed that Lette could die. That idea could never truly take root in him. Because she was his tribe. He was hers. They were inseparable halves of a single whole. They would die together. Back-to-back in the thick of bodies and blood.

He leapt clear of Quirk's thaumatic cart, forced his way through the ranks of troops. He swept his broken clock hand back and forth, cleared a path with the flat of the blade. People fell back. He ignored them. They were nothing to him. He just had to get to Lette. He had to die with Lette.

In the chaos and the dark he couldn't make out which wagon she drove. He could just see the wagons' flaming outlines thrashing through the enemy forces. He saw a troll take a swing at one cart with a club, lost sight before the beast made contact. He swore aloud as he broke free of his own ranks. He started to run.

The dragons circled above, five vast beasts hanging in the night sky. They dived and roared, but they held their flame. While the wagons were mired in their own troops, they did not set the night on fire. They screamed and slashed the sky, but the wagons plunged on.

For a moment, Balur dared to hope. Somehow the moment would be drawn out. The flipped coin landing on its edge and staying, spinning forever.

Then the wagons were bursting free of their lines, heading into the quarter mile of grass between the two opposing lines of troops. A last, mad, impossible, stupid dash for the cover of their own troops. As if that would somehow stop these dragons, as if that would somehow not herald the beginning of the slaughter.

Balur redoubled his pace. He would get to Lette. He would—

He would do no such thing.

With the wagons finally exposed, the dragons dropped from the sky as one. A writhing tumor of scales and wings. And as one, they unleashed their fire.

Balur threw up a hand, blocked his eyes. Afterimages flashed against his eyelids. Two wagons standing in the exact spot where a new sun crashed upon the earth.

He stood alone, between the two armies, scraping at his eyes.

When he could see again, he howled.

Two wagons stood still in the center of the plains.

Two wagons wreathed in flame.

Two pyres.

Two graves.

# 83

# The Inevitable
# Cliffhanger Chapter

Inside Hallows' Mouth, it took Quirk a while to realize that the dragons were simply not coming back. She had told them that Will was stealing their gold, and their collective roars of rage had knocked much of the sense out of her for a while. But she remembered them taking off, remembered them wheeling away toward the crater.

And they had left her here all alone inside the volcano.

And she was, somehow, against all the odds, still alive.

She stood up. She took stock. And a realization fell upon her. This was her chance to study a dragon's lair. This was her chance to examine their most intimate abode. Who knew what traces they left beneath the gold. Scales? Picked-over meals? Scat?

She could take the risk. She could learn so much.

After careful consideration, she reached down, grabbed as much gold as she could shove into her pockets, and legged it as fast as she could out the door.

# 84

# Financial Collapse

Balur stared. He felt the skin of his face stretching, muscles in his cheeks and forehead tightening, his slit eyeballs dilating. He felt his eyes pushing forward, testing the limits of their sockets, all in an attempt to express the depth of his horror.

Before him, one by one, the Dragon Consortium landed on the dull burnt grass of the plain. Beneath his feet, the ground shook with each impact. They stood in a circle around the flaming ruins of the pay wagons.

Around the ruins of Will and Lette.

There was a great tearing inside him, an agonizing ripping of self; pain and sorrow and hate all fracturing in his guts. He wanted to drop to his knees, to scream at the night. He wanted to charge forward, to smash into those dragons, to bore into their hearts and drink their blood. He wanted to be immolated in their fire, a blazing signal fire for Lette's memory.

Slowly, piece by piece, the wagons fell apart. A slab of paneling fell away. A wheel collapsed. An axle finally, inevitably shattered. A wagon dropped to the ground. Its roof caved in, slumped away. The blazing walls collapsed.

The fire was bright, a crackling yellow and white, hard to look at in the smothering darkness of the night and the clouds of Hallows' Mouth. The dragons were brightly lit, their bellies glistening, their snaking necks shimmering. The scene was perfectly clear.

And so it was that everyone saw when the walls of the pay wagon collapsed, not golden coins spilling out into the night, not wages ready to be paid, not jewels sparkling in the gloom.

Instead they saw nothing but dull chunks of lead scattering across the landscape.

A great inhalation of breath. A gasp so great, so collective, that the wind actually caused the flames to flicker. Even the dragons seemed to gasp in that moment.

Quietly, ignorant of the attention placed upon it, the second wagon collapsed.

Dull chunks of lead rolled loose.

Balur didn't understand. It made no sense to him. Why were the dragons paying their troops in lead?

But only a tiny piece of him cared. And it was too easily obliterated by the war raging in him between grief and hatred.

Murmurs arose from the Consortium army. A few shouts. Then cries of outrage. Anger.

"It was true!" cried out a voice, carried on the night's wind.

Inside Balur, hatred won the war.

He let out a howl of rage, the purest, greatest battle cry of his life. A scream that ripped up through his gut and left him hollow. Then all that space filled with fire, with bile, with bloodlust. He charged. He charged still screaming, still doomed, not giving a single fuck. He was going to die, but he was going to die maiming the fuck out of some dragons.

One beast turned to look at him. An arrogant sneer on its face, marred only by the disbelief that something this insignificant, this profane should dare to challenge it. It sucked in its breath. Fire sparked at the back of its throat.

And then, falling out of nowhere, as inexplicable as a thunderbolt from the gods, a bronze spear sailed out of the air, and smashed into the scales above the dragon's golden, glittering eye. A spark flared in the night where it struck. The spear sailed harmlessly away, glancing off the thick scale. But the dragon jerked its head. The storm of fire aimed at Balur became a stuttering, sparking cough, billowing harmlessly into the night.

Above the dragon a griffin rider wheeled his beast around. He was shaking his fist. His beast screamed. He seized another bronze spear, hurled it. It slashed down the dragon's side, tearing a ragged hole in its wing.

The dragon screamed. A sound of shock. A sound of pain.

Balur stumbled to a halt. A Consortium soldier was attacking his masters. Balur didn't understand what was happening.

Neither, it seemed, did much of the Consortium army. They all stared at the skies. And then there was another griffin rider beside the first. She swooped around the dragons. Her spear flashed through the air. A spark flared just above the dragon's eye where it struck. The dragon roared again.

Then an arrow loosed suddenly out of the crowd, borne aloft by shouts of rage and anger. It punched a tiny hole in the wing of a black dragon. And while it couldn't have felt like more than a gnat's sting, that dragon too roared. Almost as much outrage as pain.

And then more arrows. Like the start of a rainstorm—those few drizzling drops. And then a lightning bolt, flung by one of the Consortium mages. And shouts of outrage and anger were the booming thunder that followed.

And the dragons roared, and twisted, and seemed to try to understand what was happening.

And then, suddenly, like a cresting wave breaking, the Consortium troops surged forward. There was no discipline to the charge. There was no cry from the sergeants, no long blast on the trumpet. And yet, as one, the entire Consortium army put their heads down and hurled themselves forward.

For a moment the dragons stood stunned. They did not—could not, perhaps—understand what was happening. For thirty years they had reigned with absolute power. Their citizens had been absolutely cowed, controlled through poverty and fear. For thirty years they had been untouchable. Monarchs. Despots. Gods.

And now they were not.

Around Balur, a cry arose. "For the prophet!" seemed to echo from every lung. A wave of sound smashing around Balur. And then the sound of feet. Ten thousand pairs of feet. His army swarmed around him, charged for the dragons.

Bronze spears flew through the air, punctured wings. Griffin's smashed down against dragons' backs, claws slashing. Lightning bolts crackled down, charring and hissing

But the Consortium's hesitation lasted only a moment. The Dragons of Kondorra had not won this valley through backdoor deals, through mergers, or through buying out their competition. They had fought for this place. They had ripped it free of its formers owners. And they would not go down now without a fight.

Flames dug a trench through the oncoming troops. The red dragon opened its mouth and spewed an obscenity of roaring death that left crumbling black bodies in its wake, filling the air with the scent of roasting meat. The green dragon sprayed a wide arc of flame. Soldiers, unable to halt their charge, piled into the wall of fire. Nothing but ash emerged from the other side. The brown dragon vomited up great smoking balls of greasy fire that it hawked across the field of battle like catapult stones. They crashed down flinging burning bodies about like children's toys.

Not all were killed outright. Some took a few moments, lying gasping as their skin sloughed off, melted anatomy exposed. Balur could see one woman reeling back, her forearm seared off, the wound neatly cauterized at the elbow. He couldn't hear her screams over the cacophony of the battle.

He tried to work it all out. Everything that had happened. Everything that had led to here. The dragon's wealth had been revealed as a lie. Every soldier in their army had seen it. They had seen it after a day of seeing the skull of a dead dragon paraded before him.

Gold and fear. Both removed. Just like Will said. The Consortium troops rising up against their masters. *Just like Will had said.*

And then it struck him. Really struck him. Like a punch to the solar plexus. *No. Not as Will had said.*

*As Will had prophesized.*

"Holy shit," he said to himself.

And then he threw himself into the battle. With a smile on his face. With his teeth bared. With the broken arm of a clock raised high above his head. For the memory of Lette. For the promise he had made her that he would end a dragon. And ripping, and tearing, and snarling, he lost his perspective on the battle, became only a raging, ripping participant.

The fighting had intensified around the brown dragon. Its bloated body shortened the range of its sweeping claws. Its fire, lobbed away, let the soldiers get close. Plus it was an ugly motherfucker, squat body the color of excrement, with a sickly white underbelly. Balur tore toward it.

A griffin smashed into the back of the brown dragon's head. Its beak slashed at one of the dragon's massive eyes. Blood bloomed in the socket. Then the dragon clawed the creature free, disemboweled it with one long slash of its claws.

The brown dragon spread its wings, shrieked a roar so loud that men nearby dropped to the ground and clutched their helmets. Then a storm of spears fell. A contingent of soldiers cheered until the black dragon fell about them, ripping and tearing, gathering mouthfuls of them, scattering chunks around the battlefield.

But it was too late for the brown one. Its wings were a ruin. It beat the air with ragged flaps of flesh, and went nowhere. Troops were already climbing over each other to mount its back. They hacked at its flesh with swords, pikes, axes.

The brown howled, rolled over, crushed lives with its bulk.

Armor was flattened. The men inside simply burst, a mush of muscle, bone, and blood squirting between the seams of plate mail. But the dragon's white belly was exposed now, and men, undeterred climbed up, hacking, sawing.

The dragon's flesh ruptured massively. It contained an ocean of blood, a mile of spilling slippery guts. Its screams sounded like the sky tearing. Flame gushed out of its mouth, spilled out the spreading seam in its stomach. Its bowels burst into crackling fire. Men fell to the floor screaming, covering in flaming shit. The brown dragon writhed, its death throes ending yet more lives.

And then suddenly it was still. Suddenly it was dead.

For a moment the whole battlefield seemed to quake with the impact of the moment. The dragons—mouths full of flame and blood, claws in the guts of their foes; the soldiers—spears poised ready for launch, blades caught in scales; they hesitated for a moment. Battle cries and roars died away.

It had happened. The unthinkable, the impossible.

The people of Kondorra had risen up and killed a dragon. They could all see it. They all knew it. Man and dragon alike. It could be done.

Balur felt it like electricity. A tremble in his legs, his guts. He could feel the blood pulsing faster in his veins, racing toward some crescendo. Some howl of rage, and fear, and joy.

Then the battle was rejoined, harder and faster, and more ferocious than before. The dragons battling for their lives, the men fighting for lives they thought they'd already lost.

Flame lit the night. Claws rent the air. The heavens spat lightning. The trolls made it to the circle of battle, closed around the yellow dragon. Their massive clubs fell, smashing through pale scales, making black blood spit up from ruptures in the flesh. The dragon rose spitting and yipping, letting out curiously canine barks. It hissed out flame in white-hot, scorching streaks, fire that ate through flesh and bone, slicing through bodies like a blade six feet wide.

It took to the air, the yellow dragon, rising on broad wings, shrieking in outrage and pain, black blood streaking down its pale sides, falling like rain on the troops below. A few men still clung to its sides, still hacking away, futile and mad. One by one they lost their grip, fell to the ground like bombs full of meat.

Fire lanced down, scribbled murder on the battlefield. Soldiers flung spears. They fell harmlessly short. The dragon bellowed victory.

The catapult stone caught it completely unawares. Launched recklessly out of darkness and into darkness, the vast chunk of stone sailed through the air, then smashed into the neck of the beast, ripping through scale, muscle, bone, tearing a great gaping hole in its throat.

The writhing dragon went limp instantly. Blood poured in great gouts, steaming and spitting, a waterfall bursting forth from the night sky. Below, the weight of it smashed men to the ground, turned earth to mud.

And then it fell. All its glory and grace gone. A sack of meat and shit—the dragon smashed into the ground. Dirt and mud and the broken bodies of soldiers flew, all caught in its collapse. A great tidal wave of its own blood sprayed in all directions.

And then it simply lay there, dead on the ground.

A great cheer arose from the lung of every man, woman, and child still able to breathe upon that battlefield. The sound swallowed Balur, chewed him, and spat him out, reeling from the magnitude of what was happening.

What was happening?

They were winning.

Were they winning?

The dead lay around like felled wheat. Everything was fire and blood. Two dragons were down but three remained. Shock and awe was slipping away through blood-slick fingers. The tide of battle teetered on a blade's edge, on the point of a dragon's claw.

The red dragon burst free of a gnarled knot of soldiers swarming over it. It caught women and men beneath its massive paws, trampled them to the ground. It rose up, roaring, belching fire, launched itself into the air, to take the place of the yellow.

Catapult stones went flying, but the red was wise to that now. It twisted out of the way of the first, the second. They crashed down into the human army, obliterating life, smearing it across the mud. The dragon caught the third stone, spun with the weight of it, hurled it down to the ground. Screams rose from frail human lungs.

The green dragon arched up out of the battlefield, swept up in an arc, dripping blood and bodies. It streaked low across the field of battle, arrows clattering off its thick scales. Fire lashed out of its mouth, swallowing the fringe of the battlefield. First one catapult went up in flame, then a second, and another. It left a line of five pyres at the edge of the field.

The black stayed on the ground, pacing in a circle. The wall of flame rose around it, a perfect circle, growing higher and higher. Spears, and arrows, and men were all immolated.

The red came crashing down to land, using its own body as a battering ram. Lines of soldiers tried to break, to turn, to run. Bloodthirsty comrades pushed them forward. Both groups died messy deaths. The red dragon kicked off for the sky once more.

The head of the black dragon lashed out through its circle of fire, dragged mouthfuls of screaming soldiers back.

The green swept back and forth, breathing fire the whole while, like a child erasing chalk from a board.

Then the griffins fell upon it. There were fewer of them now. Perhaps half of the force that had started the battle. But they were still a black clot of feathers, rage, and claws that swept out of the night and landed en masse on the dragon's back. Their beaks rose and fell. Their claws peeled back great skeins of scale and flesh. The green dragon screamed, roared, immolated its own body in great gasping streams of fire, but it fell to the ground before all the griffins did, nothing more than a chunk of meat.

# 85

## Flights of Fancy

This couldn't happen.

This wasn't happening.

Kithrax denied it utterly. It was some gods-hexed hallucination brought about by inhaling fumes from the volcano.

Then a bronze spear landed in a gash already scored in his side, and the pain was so much it made the world shimmer before his eyes. He screamed. Pain, and rage.

This couldn't happen.

It was.

It had all seemed so simple. Their armies poised to smash everything and everyone. One final day of relaxing, and flirting with Scourrax left to him, and then he could leave them all behind for another year. And they'd had the prophet's pathetic, obvious spy brought before them, and it had been so much fun to watch her quake.

And then...then she had said the prophet was stealing all their gold. And she had just been...insulting them. Insulting him. And it had just been too much. That, and Horrax's foul halitosis washing over him. And so he had gone to rain down death. He had gone to put the fear of everything he and his fellows were into every human in this gods-hexed valley. He had risen to raze the world of this cursed, poxing prophet.

And he had done it. He had killed the little shit stain of a being.

And... And...

Gods, they had had the audacity to attack. Attack *him*.

At first he had almost laughed. Watching them throw themselves at him. Like so many moths drawn to his flame. But then Horrax had gone and died. And some part of his mind was cackling with glee, because it was Horrax. Fucking Horrax. That unpleasant turd of a dragon, so long a thorn in his side, had been killed by... these *people*, these *peasants*, these *unworthies* that died so easily in front of him. But as part of him cackled, another part of him screamed that something was very wrong here, that this should not be happening, that these people could not do this.

Part of him had been afraid.

But fear was laughable, was ridiculous, was beneath him. He could not be frightened. That would be like the lion fearing the lamb. So he bit, and he chewed, and he roared, and he spat fire, and killed, and killed, and killed so that they would see his dominance. So that they would understood how paltry and fleeting this sensation of victory was.

And then Scourrax fell, her sleek, twisting body falling limp to the ground. Her yellow body a massive, twisting monument to this violation of the natural order of things.

And it was not as if he had loved her. That was not it at all. There had been no dependence of that sort. At least not on his part. She, he could believe, had needed him quite desperately, but that had been a one-sided affair. But in that moment he had experienced a pain he had not expected, a tearing in his chest utterly different from and utterly dwarfing the pain in his flanks and wings.

And that had been two of them dead. Not just Horrax. Suddenly this was not some hideous aberration in the fabric of reality. Suddenly this was a groundswell of change. Suddenly the world was in free fall, a helter-skelter, pell-mell slide into madness. And he roared again, bit again, slashed again; he painted the world red with fire and blood. He smashed back against this abrupt change in the momentum of the world.

And somehow, against all he could believe, it was not enough. And now Quirrax lay dead. And now he and Bruthrax were the only dragons alive in Kondorra. They were an endangered species.

And this could not be.

But it was.

He reared up on his hind legs, spread his wings, let them see the size of him, the majesty, the glory. He made them see who it was they attacked. A god, or close enough. They had him before them. They did not need this absurd false prophet. Why did they not see?

*Why did they not see?*

There was a great jagged pain in his guts, and his roar of defiance became a scream of pain.

Lightning slashed out of the sky in a brilliant white flare and scoured a second line of pain down his chest. A third came. A fourth. He flailed backward, muscles convulsing. He fought for control of his jackknifing body. Another blast of lightning crashed into his cheek. He could smell the skin cooking, scales peeling away. Disfigured. His body defiled.

It was his magicians. The ones he had hired, had paid for with his own coin. They were doing this to him.

"Traitors!" he screamed. "Ingrates!" But the words burbled out of his ruined face, an ugly grunt. And he realized he sounded just like Horrax. And in his pain, and his horror, he wept. After all he had done for this valley, after he had shaped it into everything it was. He was their fucking lord. Their master.

He collapsed under the onslaught of lightning bolts, lay twitching on the ground. And as the soldiers closed in around him, he was unable to defend himself.

# 86

# Red of Tooth and Claw

Balur watched as the black dragon was finally taken down in a spectacular display by the Consortium mages. Only the red was left now—a massive brute, seventy yards of knotted muscle, scales so thick that they bore scratches but almost none of the creature's own black blood. It laid down wave after wave of fire, scorching the fields, leaving swaths of charred corpses.

Balur's frustration was almost overwhelming. Red fringed his vision. Every time he was almost upon a dragon, was almost on the point of burying his steel in its guts, some other fucker was getting there first. There were just too many people. He had seen the griffin take the brown creature's eye, and had tried to force his way through the scrum of howling soldiers, but they were simply packed too tight. A few people scrambled over their fellows, but they were small and light. When Balur tried to do it, he just squashed people. Stupid frail people.

"I am being the fucking prophet!" he bellowed. "Be letting me through so I can be wreaking my holy vengeance!" But no one could hear him over the roar of the battle. And so he had struck out toward the nearby yellow dragon, now fighting against the tide of the battle. And just as he had raised the clock hand above his head to hack deeply into her side, she had taken to the skies, and not come down until those cowardly fucking catapults hiding at the back of the battlefield had killed her. He had almost cheered when the green dragon had set them on fire.

And then the green had turned back to the battle. It had turned back toward him. As if it saw him standing there. He had raised his clock hand, pointed between its two eyes.

"Be coming at me, you fucker." He had whispered it. Words impossible to hear in the clamor and press of the fight. But it had known. He had known it had known. There was no need to push against the crowd now. The fight was coming to him on bright green wings. His moment of glory. The moment that would be written down and passed along in stories for years to come. The battle that parents would tell their children about. The story that would drown him in women.

And then those motherfucking griffins. A gods' hex on whichever horny, cursed eagle lost to the mists of time had given in to the desire to shove itself inside a lion. And may Betra spit on the memory of that slut whore lion nursing her fucking brood all so that now, centuries later, they could all shit on his dreams.

The green dragon had dropped to the ground dead.

He wasn't even fucking surprised when the wizards took down the black dragon. Of course they did. Whores, all of them.

And so there was just the red. A titanic beast. The army charged and broke itself against him again, again. Walls of the dead formed around him. He came smashing through them, spraying corpses and flame.

Paltry lightning flashed, but the wizards had spent their power. The red beast shrugged off the attack. The few remaining griffin riders marshaled their steeds and flew at him. He took to the skies, and their corpses fell like so much rain. Spears glanced off him. Arrows lay at his feet, snapped in two.

And finally the human army seemed about to grind to a halt. They had almost nothing left, and what they did have seemed paltry in the face of this titanic beast.

And finally, watching the slaughter, watching the cursed griffins fall, Balur felt the finger of destiny pressing down on him.

*This is it,* he knew. *This is being my moment.*

And almost as if one of the gods had reached down from the heavens and pushed them apart, the soldiers opened up a path from Balur to that red dragon.

He put his head down, raised his clock hand, and charged.

# 87

# Living the Dream

It rose before him. A mountain of flesh. A cliff face of rage. It roared and slashed. It breathed gouts of flame into its attackers. It sent a score to their graves with each exhalation. A few soldiers clung to its back, hacking desperately at the thick scales.

Balur put his head down, doubled his pace. Every part of him thrummed with the certainty of his movements. Every part of him moved with absolute alignment to his purpose.

Above him the dragon jerked its head, sighted on him, inhaled.

Balur threw himself to the right, rolled. Fire engulfed the world behind him. Heat tore at him. But he was on his feet, running.

"Come on!" he roared. "Be coming on, you fat motherfucker. You small-pricked excuse for an iguana!"

There was no way for the dragon to hear him above the press of battle, above the screams of dying men, the army desperately trying to press in. But he knew: The dragon heard him.

He ran into a roar like a solid wall of sound. It was not the first wall he had smashed through. He kept running. He kept his grip upon the clock arm.

The dragon lowered its head, roared, opened its jaws to greet him.

Lette was dead.

Dragons were dead.

And Balur did not give one single fuck.

It slashed a claw at him. He rolled, jabbed with the clock hand, felt it lodge between two scales. He was hoisted off his feet by the brutal force of the dragon's blow. His body snapped like a whip in the air, but he didn't loosen his grip on the lodged clock hand.

He crashed to earth, was dragged with violence through mud and muck and half-baked bodies. Still he held on, feeling the blade tremble and shake, still wedged in between the toes of the massive dragon, slowly working its way deeper. The dragon raised its foot. Balur dangled from it, pistoning his body, wrenching the clock hand from side to side, trying to saw his way deeper, to the meat of this beast. It would know his name.

The dragon prepared to stomp.

With a snap the clock hand tore through the scales and bit deep into the flesh of the dragon. It squealed, jerked its foot instinctively away from the ground. Balur's body flipped like a top. He twisted on the blade desperately, trying to wedge it deeper, but then it came free, and he was sailing, somersaulting through the air.

He landed upside down, feeling his jaw snap tight, tasting blood, feeling his spine creak and groan.

The dragon's severed toe landed beside him.

Together, both Balur and the dragon roared.

The dragon opened its mouth and the world filled with fire.

Balur rolled backward, desperate, almost hopeless. There was nowhere to go. The churned, blood-soaked mud of the battlefield saved him. He was coated in the sodden stuff, it caked onto him as he rolled, not fully absorbing the furnace heat of the dragon's flame, but taking the lethal edge from it. He was left half-baked in a hard shell of earth.

He burst free, snarling in pain and rage. That it would try to cook him. As if he were being nothing more than some sacrificial meal brought before it. As if he had not sawed flesh from flesh. As if for all its days it would not remember him at every step. Now there would be being no days for remembering. Now there would be no mercy. He would rip its heart out with his teeth even if he had to claw his way down its gullet to do so.

The dragon hesitated, startled at Balur's survival, his ferocity. If not dead, he should be a shuddering mass of wretched wounds, not this whirling dervish of hate. Balur took full advantage, ran flat out, hurled himself at the dragon's injured leg, held defensively beneath its body. The dragon jerked back, but Balur launched himself into the air, sank a hand into the exposed meat of the injury. The dragon screamed, flailed, but Balur, brimming over with hatred, clung on. Desperately he hauled himself up. He clutched the dragon's ankle. It kicked. He still held on.

All around, men and women of the human army were starting to stare. Their attacks faltered. Everything was coming down to this absurd, outmatched battle. They stared at the severed toe in the dirt, a totem of the impossible ferocity of Balur, and the impossibility of his task. He simply could not hack the beast apart into piecemeal chunks.

Could he?

Neither combatant seemed to care. Balur had managed to find purchase, braced against the talons and ankle of the dragon, and was hacking determinedly away at its calf. Sparks flared off the dragon's scales with each blow. The dragon scratched and clawed, and flailed, but Balur wormed his way deeper, out of range.

With a howl, the dragon shook its whole body and launched itself into the air. Balur felt the ground dropping away as an abstract thing. He was too focused on his task. He would be ending this monster. It would be knowing his name. Everyone would be knowing his name. Even the gods. Just as soon as he hacked its cursed leg off.

The creature jackknifed beneath him, and for a horrifying moment he felt his grip loosen. Freed from the need of supporting its own weight, the dragon no longer held its foot in a way that braced Balur so tightly. He clutched desperately at the limb, the blood haze of battle fighting against his deeply ingrained desire for self-preservation. He satisfied himself by biting at the wound he had been gashing in the dragon's leg. He would gnaw his way through this tree trunk of flesh if he had to.

The world spun around him as the dragon lurched and flailed. Balur's legs shook free from their perch, flapped in the air. He redoubled the strength of his grip. He dug his jaws deeper, felt a scale crack beneath the pressure of his teeth.

Blood burst into his mouth, hot, stinging. He gagged and spat. Fucking dragon even tasted like piss. He licked at the air whirling about his head, but all he could taste was gore. Grimacing he took another bite. He would not be forgotten.

The contorted dragon finally managed to fold itself almost in half in the sky. It scrabbled at Balur with its hind legs. He felt its claw score a deep gash down his back. His arms spasmed and for a moment he was in free fall before he caught himself, clinging desperately to the dragon's ankle.

The battlefield whirled beneath him, a dizzying blur of faces. An arrow lanced past his ear, clattered off a scale near his arm.

"Be stopping your shooting at your prophet, you imbeciles!" he yelled into the whirling wind. He doubted it had much effect.

He strained to pull himself higher against the bucking whirling of the dragon. His fingers were slipping, arms finally tiring. He should let the clock hand go, use the hand to get a better grip, and yet if he did, then what was the point of being up here? He needed the sharpened slap of metal to ram into the dragon's skull and scramble its brains. So he held stubbornly on, fighting to get a leg up, to gain a foothold.

Which is why, finally, he lost his grip, and was sent tumbling into the night sky.

# 88

## We All Fall Down

Balur tumbled, arse over elbow, through the night. *So this is being it,* he thought, and he had no regrets. This was a good way to die. Soaked to the bone in his enemy's blood. The taste of his enemy upon his tongue. There was glory in this. He would be in the Hallows with Lette soon, and together they would kick the arses of all the dead for all eternity.

Then a roar swallowed him, and jaws filled his vision.

The red dragon had looped back through the air, was coming up below him, jaws wide, to snatch its prize from the air.

Balur's resignation fled him. This fight was still his to be won.

He pulled his knees to his chest, folded his head down, made a cannonball of his massive body. Then as the jaws were about to embrace him, he flung himself wide, pistoning out arms and legs into a violently spread eagle.

His fist slammed into the dragon's nose, his foot into its lower lips. Jaws snapped shut beneath his stomach. Its snout punched him in the balls. He folded over the dragon's muzzle in a howl of agony. The dragon snorted in surprise and anger, a blast of hot air, that sent him flipping upward. Desperately, Balur clung to the upper lip of the dragon with his spare hand, feeling saliva working at his grip.

He dangled from the dragon's nose as it lanced straight up into the sky. It snapped its jaws beneath him, but he was out of reach. He felt the bellows of its lungs fill with air. Fire shot up into the night sky. Liquid flame streamed past his fingertips. He could feel the skin blistering. He screamed, fighting to keep his grip. But it was too much. The dragon bucked and again he was sent flying into free fall.

This time there was no chance to recover as the jaws closed around him.

# 89

# Apotheosis

Incisors clashed shut, the enameled bars of a hot black jail. Somehow Balur was still whole inside the dragon's mouth. It did not care for chewing. It would swallow him in his entirety, feel him flail in the bath of its stomach acid.

Desperately Balur fought for purchase. His claws scrabbled against slick teeth. The tongue pulsed beneath him, pushing him toward the gaping gullet, just visible in the gloom of the mouth.

With his free hand, Balur snagged a chunk of gum, hung by a single aching arm while the tongue lashed and curled about him. The sharpened clock hand was a deadweight pulling him down. *Gods why did he still have...*

*Gods!* He was still having his clock hand!

The dragon's tongue curled around him. A great muscular wave sent him flying toward the back of the dragon's throat.

Balur slashed wildly. Hacked at the tongue, at the roof of the mouth.

The dragon screamed in pain, the whole mouth convulsing around Balur. In its confines the sheer volume of the howl almost scrambled his brains, sent him reeling toward the dragon's throat. The teeth parted. Light flooded in. He could see the battlefield below, the massive bulk of the Hallows' Mouth volcano rising before them, a fist of rock smashing up, heavy and black in the midnight blue of the sky. Blood rained down upon him.

Fighting against the rising slickness of the mouth, Balur braced himself on the dragon's tonsils. He thrust down, speared the creature's tongue. It roared once more. The dangling uvula thrashed back and forth like a mace, crashing into his ankles. The convulsions of the tongue finally tore the clock hand free from Balur's hands, and suddenly he was in as much peril as the dragon's orthodontics. The tongue flailed about, slamming the heavy spear of iron back and forth scoring deep trenches in the fleshy walls.

Balur held on for his life. The pulsing throat of the beast beckoned him to his doom. The dragon roared again. They were feet away from the volcano now, rushing straight up its vertical slides. He heard a clatter as its wing smashed into rock, and the jolt made him lose his footing.

One of his whirling fists struck the thrashing clock hand, still buried deep in the dragon's tongue. The blade bit deeply into his palm, but still he held on, fighting through the pain. The throat closed around on of his feet, pulled violently at him. Bellowing, Balur reached up with his other hand, seized the hilt of his clock-hand blade. Bracing his feet against a blood-slick something, he wrenched the makeshift sword sideways and felt muscle tear as he sliced the creature's tongue almost in half.

"Balur!" he screamed into the mad chamber of the dragon's mouth. "My name is being, Balur! Are you knowing me now?"

Another howl, of rage, and pain and hate. The world whirled in the glimpses he caught between its teeth. Blue night, black rock, and red magma. They were above the crater of the volcano now, gazing down into its maw.

Heat built beneath Balur. Too much to just be the volcano's presence. And Balur realize that the dragon had finally landed upon a way to remove this thorn from its mouth. When the flame roared up, out of its throat, there would be nowhere for him to hide. He would be cooked, and finally ready to eat.

The throat below Balur opened, released his foot. Yellow light filled the dragon's maw, racing up. For a moment Balur teetered on the brink of the abyss, poised to tumble down into that liquid brightness.

He denied it. Instead, bunching muscles, screaming his hatred, his fear, his grief, he smashed the clock arm straight up. Hard iron met the soft fleshy palate of the dragon, tore through.

Blood fell like a waterfall upon Balur. It clogged the throat of the dragon. Below him the spark of fire, flickered, was drowned. Balur spat and thrashed, tried to breathe beneath the deluge. Blood made his hands slick and slippery. Yet still he maintained his grip upon his clock arm. Still he thrust up, higher, deeper, feeling bone. He planted his feet on the convulsing throat of the beast, pushed upward, roaring, extending to his full height in a single burst of energy.

The sword smashed through bone, tore into brain.

The dragon stopped moving. Went utterly still.

Balur ripped the blade left, tore it right.

Then gravity abandoned Balur. A sense of weightlessness embraced him. The sword, lodged in the dragon's brain, was his only anchor point. His feet drifted, clattered against the dragon's teeth, just as the slack jaw opened.

The dragon was falling, tumbling lifeless through the air.

He had killed it. He had killed it! *He had fucking killed it!* Euphoria clutched Balur. A weightlessness of spirit as well as body.

He watched the world whirl around them through the frame of the dragon's slack jaw. The black rock of the volcano reached up hungrily for them. From one maw, Balur stared into another. Like a strand of cotton threading a needle, the dragon smashed down through the volcano's crater, body somersaulting off the lip.

Gravity returned to Balur, smashing into him like a spurned lover, savaging every vital organ he had. The clock hand jerked free from the roof of the dragon's mouth. He was slammed one way, another. He crashed into its teeth, shattered them, was scoured by enamel shrapnel.

Then the dragon's body smashed cataclysmically into the magma. Molten spray rose in a vast corona, a celebration of his titanic death. Its head half-rebounded from the viscous muck. Inside, Balur was flung upward by the impact.

For a moment, he half-emerged from the dragon's slack lips. He saw gold everywhere. The walls of the entire crater were lined with vast ledges, and each ledge heaved with gold.

*This is being the Hallows,* he thought. *Lawl is rewarding me.* And then he was descending, slipping back down into the mouth, and he scrabbled desperately, trying to hold himself up in that glimmering, golden light. But even as he fought he could see the dragon's body rupturing, blood and guts spilling free. And fire. Fire leaking out of the dragon, running down its flanks, landing in the magma. And where it landed, the magma frothed and spat. And just before Balur slipped back fully into the dragon's roasting skull, he saw the whole dragon split open, a great gout of fire rushing up, up, up, up through its body.

The world flared red, then yellow, then white. And then the dragon's jaws fell shut, and Balur was caught in total darkness as all around him the world exploded.

# 90

# Witness

Quirk looked in amazement at Hallows' Mouth, once the Consortium's lair, now its final resting place.

She had stared as Balur had mounted the red dragon. She had stared as he had been borne aloft. She, along with the whole army, had gasped as he had been shaken loose, and swallowed whole.

It had been over in that moment. All the hopes. All the dreams. All the plans. It had all come to naught. The prophet, whoever he was today, was dead.

And then, as if reality had had second thoughts, as if maybe the gods did give a shit about Kondorra after all, the dragon had started to convulse in the sky, and then fallen down, straight into the volcano's mouth.

The whole army stared, unsure what to do. Was this victory? Had they won? Quirk had nothing to tell them. For all her learning, she was no wiser than they were.

Then the volcano erupted. A massive geologic orgasm, thrusting fire up into the night. The shock wave slammed into her, sent her sprawling back, falling into the tumbling mass of humanity.

Blackness shuddered at the corners of her vision. She fought her way back. Screaming and panic were rising all around her, buoying her on her journey back to consciousness.

Boulders and fire were arcing through the sky. They crashed down around her. Lives were swallowed by flame.

Quirk tried to scramble free, to get mobile, to get out of the way. Her ears were ringing. Her limbs felt distant and shaky. All around her, people wrestled and thrashed, an unstable bed of limbs that gave her no chance to gain purchase.

She could see a massive jagged shape—black against the dark blue of the night sky—plummeting toward her, implacable, unavoidable. A great black slab of death aimed from the heavens straight down to her.

*But I was the one who told them not to raid the hexed temples,* she thought desperately. It all seemed terribly unfair.

The object smashed to the ground twenty feet shy of her, skidded across the ground. She was showered with mud and gravel. A smell like bacon filled her nose.

Finally she wrestled herself free from the collapsed crowd, clambered to her feet. To her right another volcanic missile smashed to the earth. She skittered away, cowering. But the screams were short-lived.

The heavens were silent. Just the slow, steady rumble of molten rock spilling forth, ash rising into the sky. But for a moment the terror was suspended.

Quirk stared at the boulder that had almost ended her life. No…not a boulder. Not some chunk of cooling magma. And she should run. There could be another blast. This place was not safe. But she could not suppress the scientist inside. So she sniffed the air again…She could smell…meat? She moved closer, trying to make out details in the flickering light of the flaming battlefield.

And then she realized what she was looking at.

A dragon's massive, roasted head. It must have been blown clear off the dragon's neck, sent spinning up out of the mountain, cooked in an instant by the heat of the explosion.

Gods. A head. She had her own dragon's head. It was hers alone to explore. And cooked! She could taste it. Gods. Her belly was full of fluttering. She stepped out, hand outstretched.

The head convulsed. The jaw twitched.

Quirk reeled away. The horror of it all was suddenly apparent to her. The head was severed, but the brain had not finished firing. Somehow, impossibly, the dragon was still alive, trapped in the confines of its own roasted skull.

Gods. The agony must be almost overwhelming...

The head convulsed again. Quirk fought against the urge to vomit.

And then the jaws cracked open, tongue lolling wide. And stepping out, upon that tongue, as if it were a carpet rolled out for a conquering emperor, soaked in blood from head to foot, clutching a gore-slick clock hand in one fist, strode Balur.

Victorious.

# 91

# The Morning After the Night Before

The sun rose on a slaughterhouse scene. Broken bodies lay everywhere. The smell of charred meat filled the air. A volcano rumbled and boomed.

Balur flinched awake. He had been dreaming. A vision of gold. A mountain lined with gold and full of fire. Everything reaching up to encase him. Being swallowed by gold…

Blearily he scraped dried gore from his left eye. Staring down at himself he realized he was crusted in blood from head to foot. And from the noises slowly puncturing his consciousness it sounded like there was a party going on somewhere nearby.

Then it came back to him. The dragon. Clinging to its flank. Fighting to stay alive in its mouth. Stabbing its brains. Plunging into the volcano. A glimpse of impossible wealth. Then the explosion. Flying through the air, feeling the meat of the heat cooking around him. Smashing to the ground, cushioned by what was left of the thing's tongue. Forcing his way out of those locked jaws. The screaming, the cheering, the roars of joy. Raising his weapon high.

And then on the heels of those pieces of the night that he had managed to stitch together, meaning followed.

He had been killing a dragon. Him. *Alone.* They had taken to the skies. Tooth and claw. Two beasts desperately tearing the life from each other. Him, and the dragon. And who had emerged? Who had strode away?

He was vaguely aware that the gold was lost. That the volcano had erupted and turned a world's worth of wealth to nothing but slag, but it seemed an insignificant detail now. He was covered in the blood of his foe. He was coated in the proof of his victory.

They would sing songs of this. And they would be glorious.

He could see the head of his vanquished foe nearby. Black, crisp, and smelling faintly of pork. He would eat it later, feel the strength of his enemy enter him and be turned to nothing.

Beyond that, he could see the corpse of the yellow dragon, its throat torn out, lying in a lake of congealing blood. A black body lay nearby, guts splayed open, organs pulled free of the corpse. Its pale white ribs pointed to the heavens. And there were the green and brown bodies, sloping hills of death. There was someone still standing on the corpse of the green, still hacking away with some improvised club, working out the last of his rage on the slain beast.

They weren't the only corpses, of course. Thousands of human bodies lay scattered about the field. Some were barely recognizable. Some were just charred ash. Others were lying in pieces where talons had torn them apart. Some were in even smaller chunks, spilling out of the torn open stomachs of the dragons who had eaten them.

And there were two other corpses. Two dead bodies lying at the heart of the rough circle described by the battle.

Slowly the thought that he had killed a dragon soured in Balur's gut. Victory tasted like ashes in his mouth.

Then he spat. It turned out there actually were ashes in his mouth.

He tried to ground himself in the world. To get out of his own head. The noise that sounded like a celebration turned out to be exactly that. A hundred yards back from the scene of the fight, in every direction, were the survivors. There were more than he would have expected. Fifty thousand perhaps. At least forty-five. And truly, only ten or fifteen thousand dead was staggeringly good considering the beasts they had been up against. The sudden outburst of pent-up rage, it seemed, had all been too much for the dragons. They had been engines of destruction, no doubt, but they had not had the chance to warm up.

So he could understand the survivors' desire to celebrate. He could understand the ale being poured, the minstrels playing, the rowdy chanting of choruses, the cheering, the laughing, the sudden camaraderie between forces that had hours ago been ready to tear each other limb from limb. He could understand it all.

He just could not join it.

No one approached the dragons' bodies. Only that lone, raging figure hacking away. Everyone else stayed back, so he was alone as he approached the center of the field. The place where two wagons had burned. Where lead had—inexplicably—caused the Consortium army to switch sides.

He was alone as he approached the spot where Lette had died.

It was difficult to find the exact place, but he found a place churned up with mud and splattered with blood and gore. It was black with ash, and the lead lay nearby. *It would be doing for now,* he thought.

He stood, ignoring the celebrations, and for once in his life embraced silence and thought. Thoughts of Lette, of his tribe, of his being alone in the world.

"I was killing a dragon, Lette," he said to the ashes. "Just like I was saying I would. Dragonslayer. That was a job you were never suggesting for me."

He could almost hear what she would tell him. *Because I'm not a suicidal fuckwit, arsehole.* He smiled at the thought.

"They're talking about you, you know," said a slurred voice from behind him.

Balur wheeled round, instinctively grabbing for his hammer. But it was lost, lying at the bottom of a lake. And his clock hand was still buried in the brains of the red dragon.

But it was only Firkin. Thin, and dirty, and drunk.

"Flap, flap, flap go their little jawbones," he went on. "So much flapping you'd think they might fly away, you would." He cocked his head to one side. "Probably be calling that a miracle if it happened. Be saying you caused it. Miracle of the flap-flappy jaws."

He shook his head irritably. As if trying to dislodge a fly from his nose. Or, this being Firkin, possibly a whole colony of flies from the tangle of his beard.

"They would be saying it was me?" Balur half-repeated.

"Well," Firkin hawked and spat. "You're their prophet now, aren't you? Great big fucking thing. They like that. On and on about size, like it is of great import. Physical stature isn't everything, I tell them. Got to go around a few blocks, know what to do with it. But, oh no, eight feet tall has them all hot and sweaty and flapping away. Oh prophet this. Oh prophet that."

*The prophet. They are still thinking I'm the prophet.* Balur had to give it to the natives of Kondorra. They were stubborn when it came to hanging on to their delusions. You almost had to admire that sort of blind tenacity.

"Will was being the prophet," he said. "And Will is being dead."

Firkin looked at him oddly. "Will?"

Balur rolled his eyes. "Tall for one of you pink fleshy things. Blessed with an ability to be coming up with godawful plans. The one who was stealing my kill of Mattrax. The one who was going and prophesizing this whole mess."

"Mess?" Firkin's frown deepened.

"Yes," Balur growled. He was losing patience with being questioned. "Dead bodies. Dead friends. Blood being everywhere. That is being a classic definition, I am thinking."

"I know Will. I know messes," Firkin snapped with surprising anger. "I know fuck me, I'm a poor sad lizard stuck with a valley that worships me like a god. Oh boo-hoo all the way home." He hawked and spat. "I've been sad. I've lost whiskey bottles, you whipper of snappers. I know pain, like you cannot believe. But I still have my balls in my britches. Didn't know you gave yours to the lady friend. Did she lend them to Will so he could plow her?"

Balur was in what he might have described, if he had been inebriated enough, as a fragile mood. Firkin's shit was not something he had patience for at the best of times. And fragile moods were far from the best of times.

He crossed to Firkin in two paces, had him by the neck, then had him off the ground. "Be listening, you little turd," he hissed. "I have been losing my tribe today. And I am mourning my tribe. And I am not being above snapping your neck."

"Alone," cackled Firkin. "A lonely lonesome. I was alone once. Happened to me too. Few hundred years is what it feels like. My memory is a little hazy. I was drunk for most of it. Most of before it too, truth be told. It's brilliant being drunk, did I tell you that?" Feet dangling from the floor, Firkin seemed almost oblivious to Balur's hand at his throat.

"Don't think I was killing any dragons when I was drunk," he said. "Don't remember the adoration of thousands. Don't remember any worship at all. Might have paid for it once or twice. Hard to be sure. Might explain where all the money went. Might not. It's brilliant money. Little bits of copper and you give them to someone and he gives you booze. And you pour it into yourself and you just don't give so much of a shit anymore. Have you tried booze?"

"I have been trying booze," Balur growled at Firkin.

"Wasn't sure," Firkin said, attempting to nod, and doing a pretty poor job of it. "What with you being such a limp-dicked little crybaby and all."

Balur was actually shocked at that. He dropped Firkin and stared at him as if he was something rabid.

*Who said that? Who, with a hand around their neck?*

He reached for his hammer again, found it absent again, cursed again. Still, he could kill Firkin with his bare hands. It might even be more satisfying that way.

"Tribe!" Firkin yelled. "You are having no tribe?" He was scrambling back as Balur advanced. Even he could recognize this level of danger. "You are crying over losing a tribe of one? What did they do in the Analesian desert? Teach you to count up to the number of dicks you have?"

There was an audacity to that that even Balur could admire. He would maybe take some pride in tearing Firkin's spine from his body and flaying the man with it.

"You have a tribe of fifty thousand souls, you dolt!" Firkin screamed as Balur finally stood over the man. "You lost one and gained every other stupid fuck in this valley. You are number-one tribe man now, dumbarse! You say tribe, they say fuck yes, oh prophet of the tribe! You say go do tribe-y things, they find out what they are being, and then they do them. It's all tribe, all the time now, baby. Tribe of the prophet. You prophet. Prophet is dumbarse, but nobody is giving a shit because of all the prophety shit." Firkin appeared to notice that Balur was no longer attempting to kill him, dusted himself off a little bit, and said in a more reasonable tone, "And the dead dragons."

Balur was hesitating. He looked up at the inhabitants of the Kondorra valley. Drunk on victory and dragons' blood. Just like any good tribe should be.

"Why are they thinking that I am their prophet?" he asked.

Firkin had the audacity to look outraged.

"When five big, old, flappy fuckers land down from the sky and go about torching everything, and everybody stands around clutching at their drawers trying to keep the poop from sliding out, and then one giant bastard is letting out a roar like

he just got a hard-on he can use to beat a dragon to death—
people go and notice that sort of shit." He nodded sagely. "For I
am wise in the ways of the gods and I know such things."

Balur found his rage rekindling. "You are being about as
much a priest as I am being a prophet. If there ever was being a
prophet, he is being very burnt and toasty right now."

Despite being around three feet shorter than Balur, Firkin did
his best to look down his nose at him. "People," he said, "say
you are a prophet. You say you are not. You have one vote. They
have fifty thousand. You are a prophet. That's democracy."

Balur's patience was done. "That is being horseshit, and the last
shit of yours I shall be listening to, unless you are shitting yourself in terror as I am murdering you, or in an involuntary reflex
when you are dying. Because that is happening sometimes."

Balur sort of wished he didn't know that.

"Do you want a fucking tribe or not?" Firkin spat.

Which brought Balur up again.

Fifty thousand...Humans, yes. But fifty thousand. Perhaps
forty-five. But all his tribe. *His.* An Analesian could do a lot with
forty-five thousand soldiers. A lot of...

What? Good? Bad?

He wasn't sure, but he did have a sneaking suspicion it could
be fun.

But Lette...

Lette was dead. His tribe was dead. And an Analesian without his tribe was dead.

He had been without a tribe before, though. He had been
dying before in the desert. And he had found a new tribe then.

Firkin rolled his eyes. "Walk with me," he said in magnani-
mous tones. "Meet your people. Tribe. Whatever."

So Balur walked. Against his better judgment perhaps, but
what other choice did he truly have? To die? To mourn, and
weep, and drown his sorrows. Until...when? What then? A
time when nobody cared?

People cared now. They cheered as he approached. They roared. They hooted, and hollered, and screamed his name.

"Prophet! Prophet! Prophet!" The world shook with their cries. And then, as he drew closer still, they fell silent. They drew back. They bent their knees. They bowed their heads.

Balur came to a stop in the middle of the crowd. And as he looked out, all he could see were women, men, and children, down on one knee with their heads bent. Before him, Firkin was the only man standing. He spread his arms, spun around. A broad smile was smeared across his face. The message was clear.

*See what I give you.*

Balur looked back at the corpses of the dragons, and where Will and Lette lay dead, nothing more than piles of ash.

What would Lette have really wanted for him?

*A whore, an ale, and a good fight, you big dumb lizard,* he heard her voice inside his head.

*How about an army?* he asked that echo from the Hallows.

*Close enough.*


Quirk found him a few hours later. He was in Will's old tent, which a few enthusiastic worshippers had found and erected over him. They had made him a throne, and brought him a dragon's horn full of ale, and someone was working on the whore, and he was pretty confident it wouldn't be hard to find a fight.

She pushed her way through the tent flap flanked by the guards he had posted—large men previously of the Consortium army. They were armed with halberds, and he liked the way it looked when they dropped the weapons to form an X blocking people's path. Above the tent he had posted one of the remaining griffin riders, just because it looked awesome.

Still, mighty tribe leader that he might be, he found himself rising up and running forward to seize Quirk in a great hug that took her off her feet. He was surprised at how good it was to see her. But she was someone who had been there since the beginning, someone who had walked the same path as him.

"Quirk!" he boomed. Then to the startled-looking guards, "Ale! Much more ale!"

Still bundled in his arms, Quirk cleared her throat. Balur set her down with a twinge of embarrassment. "It is being good to see you," he said by way of explanation. Though he wasn't sure a prophet should have to explain himself. "I am being excited by my vision of this happening," he said to the guards, then realized he was explaining himself, which didn't seem prophetlike either. "Ale!" he shouted again for good measure.

Quirk was straightening her clothes as best she could. She was still dressed as a merchant, though now the clothes were ripped and stained.

"So," she said when she had finished. "You seem to have made yourself at home."

"These people are being my tribe," Balur said. "And I am being their prophet, it is turning out. I am being as surprised as anyone is being. But it is being quite convenient."

Quirk took that in without passing judgment. Balur liked that about her.

"Will?" she asked eventually. "Lette?"

Balur felt a cloud pass in front of the sun of his day. "They are not making it," he said quietly.

Quirk seemed genuinely shocked by that. "Oh," she said. "Oh, I didn't expect...It just seemed...He was so confident."

Balur nodded. "He was being a prophet after all. I was seeing it with my own eyes."

And so he explained it to her. How the wagons had been chased through the Consortium army by the dragons. How they had broken free. How the dragons had surrounded them, set them on fire. How the lead had come spilling out. And then how—

"Wait," Quirk interrupted him. "Lead?"

Balur shrugged. "It was making the Consortium army crazy. Mad. Just like he was saying. Like he was *prophesizing.*"

"Lead?" Quirk said again.

"Yes," Balur said, a little testily this time. "That is not seeming to me to be being the big point here. The army went crazy. He had prophesized—"

"Lead?" Quirk said again, her voice ratcheted up to an even higher notch of incredulity.

Balur threw up his hands.

Quirk shook her head. "I mean, I'm sorry, but that just doesn't make any sense. Gold doesn't turn to lead. Not alchemically. Not magically. It doesn't happen. It's impossible."

Balur narrowed his eyes. "Impossible? You are meaning it was a miracle?"

Quirk hesitated, then shook her head again, more definitively this time. "No," she said. "Not a miracle. It's just..." She paused again. "Impossible," she said.

"Well," said a voice over by the tent flap, "there may be a chance I could explain that."

Balur spun. And then stopped.

Then the whole world stopped.

Mostly it stopped making sense.

Grinning, Will stepped into the tent.

# 92

# Excuses and Explanations

Will's expression, Balur thought, could best be described as smug. Then after half a second he revised his opinion. It could best be described as the sort of smug that should be removed from someone's face by force. Balur stepped forward to do just that.

But then Lette slunk into the tent behind Will, gave him a half grin, and said, "Hey."

The next thing Balur knew, he had her in a bear hug and she was yelling that he was going to break her ribs.

"You are living!" he cried.

"Not for much fucking longer, you arse. Put me down."

She was turning a little blue, so he did as she asked. Still, it didn't feel to Balur as if quite sufficient a fuss had been made. He turned to Quirk. "She is being alive! They are both being alive!" he boomed. Try as he might, he couldn't get the volume of his voice to truly express the depth of the emotion welling in him. There had been a void and now it was full again. A piece of him he thought lost forever was returned to him. He thought his grin might split his face, and he didn't care.

"Yes," Quirk said carefully. She was studying both Will and Lette, as if searching for flaws. "The thing I'd like to know is, how?"

Will's smug expression was coming back, but Balur found he didn't mind it so much this time. He placed a vast hand on Lette's shoulder, left it there even when her knees buckled slightly.

"Okay," said Will, "about that."

"Yes," Quirk agreed, "about that." She sounded like a disapproving Analesian brood mother to Balur's ear. What she had to be so sour about, he had no idea.

"So," said Will, and Balur could tell he was bursting to tell them, but hesitant too. Most likely because he feared reprisal for jerking all their chains. Balur quietly reserved the right to beat Will's head down into his neck once all was explained to his satisfaction.

"Well," Will started again, "obviously the plan was a little more complex than the one I told you all about. But in my defense my feet were buried in the guts of a spy when I came up with it and I was feeling a little bit paranoid. If the Consortium knew of any part of it..."

He read their expressions and clearly saw that he wasn't winning anyone over. "Look, Lette already beat about five or six shades of shit out of me over the whole thing."

Lette nodded. Balur tousled her hair affectionately.

"Do that again," she told him, "and I'll take that hand and use it for a spittoon."

He smiled happily to himself.

"I really was worried about the spies," Will said. "I swear."

Balur was getting tired of this. "Be stopping making the excuses and be telling us how you are being alive before I am making you dead again."

"Well," Will said, "all of you know bits of it." He pointed to Balur. "You knew I'd come to you and said I'd changed my mind and that you should mobilize the whole army to attack. You must have suspected I'd gone to other people?"

"Why must I have been suspecting that?" That seemed like an unreasonable leap of logic to Balur.

Will gave him a pleading look, but before Balur could explain to Will that assumptions made asses out of you, and anyone else Balur chose to blame, Lette hit him with "I still don't see why a whole attack was necessary. And I still don't see why you didn't tell me."

"Because spies!" Will looked shocked that he needed to explain this again. "We're so large a group that people didn't know who the prophet was. How was I supposed to recognize a spy? The only reason we found that one was because he was terrible at his job. What if there had been a better one? And then when we were away from this camp, we were literally surrounded by enemies. It's the same reason I told Balur to launch the full attack. I figured if a Consortium spy had overheard about the feint then their army might not respond to the threat, which wouldn't let us steal the pay wagons. But the Consortium couldn't ignore the whole army coming forward."

"So why didn't you tell me when we were on the way from our camp to theirs?" Lette had that slightly murderous look in her eye that Balur always found so charming.

"Well..." Will shuffled his feet. "I didn't think you'd like the bit where I told Quirk to betray us."

"You did what?!" Lette momentarily looked as if her explosion would put anything Hallows' Mouth could muster to shame.

Balur stared from Will to Quirk. He wondered who he should kill first.

"It worked, didn't it?" Will said, managing to hang on to a scrap of his outrage. "We're all still here. The dragons are dead. Remember that before you judge me!"

Balur scratched at his head. "Be explaining to me why you were having Quirk betray you." He turned to Quirk. "And you be explaining to me why you did it."

Quirk met his gaze without flinching. "I did it because he told me to," she said.

"He was telling you to be going and being a merchant," Balur snapped back, "and you were having no problem to be telling him no. Then he is telling you to be pretending to be being a merchant and to be betraying him to the Consortium and suddenly you are having no problem?"

Quirk finally glanced down at her feet. She looked up, clearly resentful he had forced her to do that. "He said it would let me study them up close. He said it would help him save everybody."

"And it did!" Will put in.

She wheeled on him. "There are ten thousand dead out there!"

"And fifty thousand people still alive." Will showed as little chance of bending as Quirk herself. "I will take those numbers, and I will skip happily to my grave."

"I thought it was some sort of noble sacrifice, you arse," she said. "I thought you would give yourself up in exchange for all the other lives."

Will threw his hands up. "Have you not been paying attention at all? Do you think the Consortium would have let anyone from our army walk away? And even if they had we would just have been condemning this valley to endless years of oppression. They had to die. And they are dead. And at risk of sounding a bit braggy: because of my motherfucking plan! Which worked!"

This, Balur suspected, was not quite how Will had hoped his explanation would go.

He pointed at Will. "Okay," he said. "She, I am understanding. You, I am not."

"I needed," Will said, with an exaggerated slowness that Balur found, quite frankly, a little rude, "to piss them off, to tempt them out into the open. I needed them to be exposed. So I told Quirk she would likely be captured and dragged before them. And I asked her, when that happened, to tell them all the insulting things I had said. And then, when she heard sounds of fighting, to tell them I was stealing the gold."

Quirk nodded, a little of her fire dampened. "It did happen that way," she said.

Will nodded as if it were obvious. "And that was perfect because Lette and I had been telling everyone all day that the pay wagons were full of lead."

Balur held up a hand. He was still trying to sort everything out.

"You had the dragons attack you on the wagons on purpose?"

"Erm..." Will said, his defiance deflating a little

"This," said Lette, interrupting, "is where I kicked his arse. Because yes, he did. Without telling me, he had me jump into a wagon knowing full well that five dragons would attack me."

"Well," Will said, "that was the other bit of the plan I thought you might object to. But I thought you'd make for the safety of our army straightaway, not just run away."

Lette rolled her eyes. "Oh yes, because that's where every thief heads—toward the armed combat."

"Well, the dragons turned us around," Will said, "so it all worked out."

"Don't make me kick your arse again."

Balur was starting to get a headache. "Why were you wanting to head back toward us?"

Will shook his head as if he couldn't believe they didn't get it still. "So that everyone could see the dragons breathe fire on the wagons."

"You wanted everyone to see you die?"

"No." Will sighed. "I wanted everyone to see the dragons torch the pay wagons. That was the important part. Because of the lead."

Balur decided that he didn't care about the explanation that much and he would settle for just caving Will's head in. He curled his fists.

"Oh!" Will threw up his hands. "I forgot a bit. I'm sorry. Of course. I'm an idiot."

Balur looked over at Quirk to get a read from her. She was dancing a small flame along her knuckles. He didn't unclench his fists, but he didn't advance either.

"We'd told them that dragon's fire turned gold to lead," Will said.

"But it doesn't," Quirk said quickly.

Will nodded. "No. Of course not, but they didn't know that. They just knew everyone was saying that the dragons were out of gold and that one of the possible explanations flying about was that dragon's fire turned gold to lead. And then we took the pay wagons out so everyone could see the dragons breathe fire on the wagons. And then they all saw the lead. And suddenly the main reason the Consortium soldiers were all there was gone. They were being robbed basically, by these arsehole dragons. And they knew that the dragons could die, because of the skull you'd been dragging about all day. And they were all ready for a fight. So when they saw that, they lost their shit, and they attacked."

"But," Balur said, "you were driving wagons. So that the dragons would be destroying them. So that everyone would be seeing you die too."

"Which," Will said, "I thought was pretty clever, because if there's one way to stop people coming and looking for you, it's dying in front of them."

"But you would be being dead," Balur insisted.

"Yes," Will agreed.

"But you are not."

"No," Will agreed again.

"This," Quirk put in, "comes back to the 'how' part of the question that we started with."

"Oh," said Will. "Yes, of course. Well, I mean, if you get a horse panicked enough, if say you steer it into an angry army and have dragons chase it, then at some point you can be pretty sure it's just going to keep on going and you don't have to steer it much anymore. So you can jump free and let nature take its course."

"Which is why," Lette inserted with enough heat to sear a

steak medium-rare, "you should have let me know the fucking plan."

Using his keen powers of detection, Balur detected something unspoken. "If you were not knowing the plan," he said to Lette, "how were you knowing to jump?"

"Because," Lette said, wheeling on him, "this jackass," she thumbed at Will, "leapt from his wagon onto mine, then carried me off it, and used his body to cushion my fall. Which"—she allowed her expression to soften infinitesimally—"is about the only reason he's still alive."

"It worked," Will said, shrugging.

"Jackass," she said, but Balur could see she was smiling.

Quirk wasn't. "It worked?" she said, sounding peevish. "You mean you planned for Balur to crash a dragon into a volcano destroying all the gold you were so concerned about?"

Balur couldn't help but smile smugly at the memory. He checked Lette for her reaction. She rolled her eyes.

"Fine," she said in response to his outraged look. "I will admit that riding a dragon into a volcano and being the only one to walk away is passably impressive."

"I was escaping in its cooked head," Balur pointed out. "That is being what the bards are calling fucking epic shit."

Lette shrugged. "Fucking bards."

Balur's grin was threatening to do some serious damage to the integrity of his skull again.

"To be fair," Will said, "that was not exactly part of the plan."

"Not exactly?" Quirk arched an eyebrow so high it almost left her forehead.

"Not part of it in any way, shape, or form," Will conceded.

"You mean we were meant to be able to walk into the volcano and plunder every last penny, don't you?" said Lette, with a less than charitable look in Balur's direction this time.

Will nodded again.

And yet, Will was still grinning. And truly, Lette was not as upset as perhaps he would have expected her to be at this point.

Of course, there was the chance that Will had not noticed Lette sliding the knife into his back. That had happened to Balur once, though if memory served he had been drunker than a lord at the time.

But from the look in Lette's eyes, that was not what was going on. "What is it being?" he asked them.

"What?" said Lette.

*One day*, Balur thought, *she is going to have to be learning to do a better impression of being innocent.*

"The thing that you are not saying." Balur's impatience was returning.

"Rrright." Will dragged the word out. His smugness has resurfaced like a corpse that refused to stay tied to its anchor. "So the lead thing."

"Because," Quirk said, "dragon's fire doesn't turn gold to lead."

"No," Will agreed. "It doesn't. I thought we'd discussed that."

Balur cracked his knuckles. Loudly.

"Why don't you all step outside," Will said quickly, and pushed open the tent flap.

Balur looked questioningly at Lette. She nodded. "Don't worry," she said. "You'll like this bit."

So they pushed out into the camp. The sun was high and the wind had changed. The plume of smoke from Hallows' Mouth blew away from them now, stretching off toward the horizon, leaving clear skies above them. The sound of celebrations rose up all around.

And parked directly outside the tent were Quirk's two merchant wagons, with their colorful silk coverings. A man with a hard face whom Balur didn't recognize sat holding the reins of one wagon.

"Cattak?" Quirk said to the man. He tugged his forelock back at her.

"Yes," Will said. "You see, he and I got to talking after you introduced us. And I asked him if he could assemble a few tons of lead in a few days. And once he got past cursing me out for being a crazy man, he set down to work, and he did it."

He smiled at Cattak. Cattak tugged at his forelock again.

"So," Will said, "once that was done, Cattak and Quirk drove two wagons full of lead into the Consortium camp, disguised as merchants' wagons."

Balur stared at the wagons, did the mathematics. "There is being no way," he said, "that you could be moving several tons of lead from those wagons to the pay wagons before the dragons were attacking."

Will nodded again. "That is true." His grin was back. "But it was pretty easy to move the false silk covering off our wagons onto the dragons pay wagons."

Cattak clearly had his cue. He reached behind him, gripped the silk fabric, and tore. A great swath of it came free. Beneath was a solid wooden wall, painted black and banded with iron.

Balur felt his jaw go slack.

"You see," Will went on, "Cattak had been acting as a scout for a while, so he knew exactly what the Consortium pay wagons looked like. So he could create replicas easily enough. Then we just filled them with the lead he'd looted, disguised them with a silk covering, and drove them into the Consortium camp. Then when everyone was distracted by the fighting, he moved the coverings from our wagons to their pay wagons. Then Lette and I jumped on the fake pay wagons full of lead, and went off to have them be burned. We jumped off just in time, and went and hid. Meanwhile, Cattak took Quirk's merchants' wagons and went and hid as well. Then once everything had all died down, we all headed back here."

"So." Balur licked his lips. "Those wagons. They are being full of all the gold the Consortium was going to use to pay fifty thousand soldiers?"

Will's grin was particularly smug this time, but Balur didn't care one jot. "Yes," he said. "We did it. We ripped off the dragons. We stole so much of their gold we can write the words, 'Fuck off, dragons' in eighty-foot-tall letters right across this plain."

He beamed at them all.

"We're rich."

# 93

# One More Thing

There was whooping. There was hollering. There was cheering and dancing.

Quirk slipped away from it all. She was, she supposed, happy for them. And Will was right, she grudgingly admitted to herself. His plan had saved far more lives than probably any other could have done. But she had no real interest in joining in their celebrations. The corpses of the dragon were too close, their call too loud.

She approached, scattering crowds of gathering crows. Already the stench of rot was ripe in the air. She ran her hand over a rim of ragged meat, tracing the course of an exposed artery, already mentally cataloging it for later.

*So much dragon and so little time...*

She clambered into the splayed-open corpse of the dragon, feeling the meat slick beneath her feet. She followed the course of the vein, counting its branches, trying to discern the muscles it passed through. As she worked, and tried to control the quiver of excitement in her hands, she thought she could perhaps understand the celebrations of the others a little better.

After a few yards she found the vein's passage was blocked by a lump of hardened magma. The whole corpse was spattered with cooling chunks of black rock sprayed by the volcano that ranged in size from pinheads to apples. She plucked this one off the corpse, careful not to disturb the tissue beneath.

As she moved to toss it away, something caught her eye. A

sharp yellow glint she had only just exposed. She hesitated, examined the rock more closely, wiping and picking at it with her thumb.

Out of the rock emerged a small nugget of gold. It gleamed dully in her palm. Beauty incongruous in the battlefield.

Slowly Quirk took in the whole breath of the plain they all stood upon. Splatters of magma were everywhere. They spread out across the field of battle in a slowly dissipating arc to the west of Hallows' Mouth.

The gold had not disintegrated when the volcano blew. It had not been scooped up by the hand of some god and whisked away to the heavens. It had been melted. It had mixed with the rock. And it had been spread over this field.

Tons of it were being slowly churned into the mud by cavorting, drunken soldiers.

Standing in the corpse of a dead dragon, Quirk rolled the nugget of gold between her fingers.

She was not proud of much of what she had done in Kondorra. But looking back on everything that had brought her to this point, she could say she had gone out into the field, studied the beasts, and survived. She had seen them up close. She would have their corpses to study. She could take samples, and interview people here. She had more than enough information to write the definitive text on dragons. And when she returned to Tamathia, she would be the most famous thaumatobiologist alive. Her debt would be paid. The kindness of others would be rewarded.

There were happier endings, perhaps. But she was a realist. Perhaps this ending was happy enough.

She looked over to Lette, and Balur, and Will, They were dancing and drinking now. Just like everyone else. Would any more gold really improve things? From what she'd seen, too much wealth wasn't really good for people actually.

After a long moment, she pocketed the nugget, and silently went back to her work.

# 94

# Being Better People

Will's afternoon passed in a happy blur. A lot of it was spent lying out in the grass. Lette was resting her head on his chest for most of it, and he had a mug of ale in his hand more often than not.

"So," he said to Balur, as the sun started to dip behind the mountains on the distant horizon, *"you're* the prophet now?"

Balur shrugged. "You are being dead. Somebody was having to step up."

Will wasn't sure if the logic of that statement hung together perfectly. Still, it hung together well enough that he wasn't the prophet anymore, and he could definitely live with that.

"So," Lette said, "is that it then?"

"That what?" Balur took a long draft of his ale.

"Your better life," she said. "The one we came to Kondorra to find. This prophet thing, that's your answer?"

Balur considered this. "To be fair," he said, "the whole better life thing was being far more of your idea than mine. I was being completely happy with continuing to murder folk for coin."

Lette nodded. "That sounds like most religious leaders I've known."

Will decided he would sleep better at night if they changed the topic.

"What about you?" he said to Lette. "Who are you going to be, with all your newfound riches?"

Lette looked at Balur. Just for a moment. Then down at her ale.

"It is being all right," Balur said quietly. "I am understanding. In Analesia there is coming a time sometimes, when a tribe is getting so big that the desert can no longer support it. Then we are gathering together all the weak little pussies we are no longer wanting to be in our tribe, and we are shoving them off to find their own place to live. Or more often die."

Will had a strange sensation that that story was meant to be touching.

Lette nodded. "Our tribe of two has grown too big for these parts?"

"Well." Balur shrugged. "My tribe is having fifty thousand more people in it now. And I am not sure there is being enough room for deadweight like you anymore."

Lette weighed that, and smiled and put her arm around Will.

"Personally," she said, "I've always felt like two is the right size for a tribe."

If Will had died at that moment, he would not have considered his life poorly spent.

But he didn't die. Instead he saw Firkin walking toward them, and his moment of sunshine-bright happiness disappeared behind a cloud.

"Oh shit," he said. Because if there was one person who might not be thoroughly convinced that Will was dead...it was Firkin. Indeed, Firkin might well prefer Will to be his prophet— someone he could push around, someone who was not big enough to push back.

"Good morrow," the old man slurred as he approached, waving a wineskin at them. Then he looked at the wineskin. "Wait," he said. "This isn't morrow. It's wine." He put it to his lips, tilted his whole body back. He came back up smacking his lips. "Yes," he said. "Definitely wine."

He looked around their group, squinted, tilted his head on his side. "Morning, Will," he said, and sat down heavily.

"Evening, Firkin," Will said.

"Tiring shit, this being this mouth-of-the-prophet thing," Firkin said. "Lot of shouting." He rubbed his throat. "Parched half the time, I am." He took another hit of wine.

"Right." Will nodded. He felt curiously alone in this moment. None of the others seemed to want to save him. "And, erm..." He struggled for an angle of approach. "How is the prophet?" he said.

Firkin arched an eyebrow. "Why don't you ask him? Sitting right over there." He nodded at Balur.

Will felt relief so overwhelming it almost bowled him over and left him lying on the floor.

"Balur's the prophet?" he said, not quite trusting this was as good as it sounded.

Firkin shrugged. "Was telling me he was. Said the prophet wanted beers and whores in that order, and he was the prophet so I should listen to him, so to get them for him pronto. And I said 'beer and whores, thus spaketh the prophet' and suddenly they were everywhere." He blinked several times, and rubbed his bald head.

"But..." Will was terrified of pushing the subject but he had to know. "He told you back in Athril that I was the prophet."

Firkin nodded. "You said you weren't. He said you were. Now he goes and says he is." He shrugged. "I just say what the prophet says. I'm not going to argue with him. Look at the size of him."

Will looked at Balur.

Balur nodded. "I am being pretty magnificent in the size arena, it must be being said."

Will wasn't sure what to make of it. Because it seemed amazing, and he wasn't sure that amazing things happened to him.

Firkin grinned a gap-toothed grin at him and clapped him on the shoulder. "We did it, Will," he said. "Just like we used to talk about on those long, lazy days years ago. We took down all the dragons, we freed the people, and we got rich doing it." He suddenly and unexpectedly grabbed Will in a tight hug. "I'm really fucking proud of you," he said in a voice thick with emotion.

Will was struck dumb. He stared.

"All right," Firkin said, standing up. "Off to spread the good word and all that. Like butter on bread it is. Except using your mouth of course. Can't do that with butter. Well, maybe you could but the bread would be getting all wet." He shook himself. "Only stopped by to rest my legs."

And then he staggered away, sipping occasionally from his wineskin.

Will watched him go. The clouds seemed to be lifting inside his head.

"You realize," Lette said to Balur, "that you're stuck with him now. Oh prophet."

Balur shrugged. "I can be keeping him in line. Look at the size of me."

Lette snorted out a little laugh, turned, and looked at Will. "What about you, then?" She leaned forward, kissed him. For a minute the world was all about the softness of her lips, and the smell of her hair. She pulled away. "What are you going to be?"

Will kept staring after Firkin for a moment longer, then looked at her. At the world beyond. The celebrating crowds. The dead dragons. The blue sky and the white sun. And suddenly he knew exactly what he was going to be.

"Happy," he said. "I'm going to be happy."

# Acknowledgments

I have wanted to be an epic fantasy author since around the age of nine. Now, for better or worse, I am one. These are the people who helped me get here, and whom I can never thank enough. My parents, who indulged my geek side, and took me on my first trip to Middle Earth. Greg McClenaghan, who introduced me to D&D and lent me the Dragonlance Chronicles—I wouldn't be half the nerd I am today without him. Adam Brown, the self-proclaimed comedy genius and my first partner in literary crime. Paul Jessup, Natania Barron, Michelle Muenzler, Jacques Barcia, Jaym Gates, Harry Markov, Berit Ellingsen, and the rest of the Broken Circles writing group, who are a constant source of inspiration and amusement—everyone should be lucky enough to know people as good as them. Jeff and Ann Vandermeer, who introduced me to my agent. Howard Morhaim, the aforementioned agent, and quite possibly the only real wizard I have ever met. Will Hinton, my editor, who took a chance on me and this series, and whose advice and enthusiasm have been utterly invaluable. And finally, my wife, Tami, my muse, my first editor, my champion, and the princess in the tower who rescued me. Without her none of this would be possible.

# extras

orbit

# introducing

If you enjoyed
FOOL'S GOLD,
look out for the next Dragon Lords novel,

## FALSE IDOLS

*by Jon Hollins*

# 1

## Big Thaumatobiologist on Campus

Quirkelle Bal Tehrin dreamed of fire. It kindled in her sleep, licked at the feet of her desires and fears, then rose—wings spreading—to the sky, and tore through her subconscious. It was a roiling ocean of flame. It obliterated everything in its wake. She would come awake in the cot she kept in her garret above the Tamathian University, sheets soaked with sweat, and her palmprints scorched into the sheets.

She had yet to work out if the racing of her heart after these nightly visions was from terror or pleasure.

And yet, despite this, there were some things Quirk was certain of in life. That she knew more about dragons than anyone else alive. That such knowledge made her position at the Tamathian University more secure than a princess's chastity belt. And that the Tamarian Emperor's palace was not quite as impressive as he thought it was.

She sat now at his dinner table, two seats away from the man himself. She was flanked by his wife, the Empress, and by his daughter.

The Emperor himself was a small man, in his late fifties, balding, and with his remaining hair cropped to short gray stubble. He was wreathed entirely in gold. Great swirls of fabric encircled his arms, his torso. A great gold neckpiece—which probably weighed almost as much as his birdlike wife—sheathed his neck. His deeply lined face, emerging from its depths, appeared somewhat inadequate in comparison. Religious iconography dangled from him. A medallion inscribed with the scepter of Lawl, king of the gods, bobbled over the neckpiece. The open palm of Klink, god of commerce, was etched into his broad earrings. The wheat sheaves of Toil, god of fertility and the field, were upon his rings.

He had invited her here, as was now his weekly custom, to dine with his family, several highly esteemed courtiers, and a smattering of visiting dignitaries. At first she had served more as a conversation piece than as a source of conversation. Still, over time she had managed to change that.

At that precise moment, his eminence was attacking a small roast partridge and coming off the worse of the two combatants. Orange grease was smeared over his fingers, rings, face, and fabric. He kept spitting small bones in the direction of his plate and missing badly. More than once he had swallowed and then had to signal at a bodyguard to throw an elbow into his sternum so he could hawk up whatever had lodged in his throat.

On the plus side, he had not yet called for the beheading of the chef. He knew now that Quirk did not like that.

"So," the Emperor said around a mouthful of gristle, pointing a partridge thigh at her like a miniature rapier. "What is it that you make of this business with the Elven king?"

Quirk felt thirty pairs of eyeballs come to rest on her. Nobles, lords, ladies, the Emperor's cousin, two of his bastard children, three ambassadors, and a visiting dignitary from Verra. They all watched her and they waited.

The truth was, of course, that her knowledge of the world made her woefully inadequate to answer the question. She had for most of her life lived in seclusion, first as the personal weapon of a murderous demigod, and then as a hermitlike academic lost in the warren of tunnels of the Tamathian University. The one time she had ventured out into the world she had witnessed the death of seven dragons and just over ten thousand of the inhabitants of Kondorra. It was not a period in her life she would necessarily describe as successful.

And yet, they all waited. They all wanted to know what the world's leading thaumatobiologist and expert on dragons would say.

She wondered if any of them had actually read her papers. Had attended her lectures. She could not imagine the Chancellor of the Exchequer really coming to grips with the inner workings of *Varanus draconis*'s digestive tract. He was having enough trouble getting anything other than alcohol into his own.

*On such things,* she thought, *the fate of nations fall.*

The specific matter the king was referencing was the death of a white hart at the hands of several of his huntsmen. The hart had wandered from the forests of the Vale—which the Elven Court claimed as their own—and into the path of the several huntsmen looking for boar in the Emperor's abutting forest. Not being the sort of men to question providence when it stood in the way of a full purse, the huntsmen promptly shot the hart, skinned it, and sold the hide for a profit that would make even a city merchant blush. Which was all well and good until the Elven king delivered a message stating that the hart was his sovereign property, that the huntsmen were thieves, and that unless they were handed over to him for execution then the consequences would be dire.

Well... that was if she paraphrased the specifics of the Elven dialect. More directly the message had read: "So-called Emperor of all the round-eared fucks in the shit-stain empire of Tamar, give me the round-ear fucks who stole my fucking hart, or I shall come and fuck you. His highest eminence, master of the bowstring, slayer of the round-ear fucks, commander of the Vale forces, fine-aspected Todger IV."

"Well," Quirk said, as delicately as it was possible to do so, "given the tone, and content of the letter, I do not honestly believe that King"—she hesitated—"Todger"—she managed as gracefully as she could—"should be entertained in this manner. And furthermore, I do not believe that he can necessarily follow up on his threat to, erm..." She hesitated over this one. "...to violate you."

"So fuck him," said one of the nobles, and brayed with laughter. Several other followed suit. There was much stamping of feet, and pounding of golden goblets on the red velvet tablecloth.

Quirk winced, and not just because she was being reminded of the red velvet tablecloth. Sometime she really did need to speak to the Emperor about that particular detail. She raised a delicate finger to indicate that she was not quite done.

"However," she said, but no one was listening anymore.

The Emperor coughed loudly. All noise stopped. All attention returned to the richest, most powerful man in the room. He glared around at them, then looked back to Quirk. "You were saying?" he said.

Small he might be, but it was rumored that the Emperor had personally throttled two assassins to death after they had killed the rest of his personal guard.

"However," Quirk said again, "there doesn't seem to be much point in purposelessly angering"—again she hesitated over the name—"King Todger. While he cannot... violate anyone here, his forces can certainly make things difficult for border patrols, and nobody here wants to actually go to war with the elves."

"I wouldn't mind," said one lord, who then seemed to realize people could hear him.

"Truly, Lord El Sharred?" said the Emperor. He had a harsh, nasal voice. "You would like to take your cavalry into thick forest and have arrows rain down upon you while you chase men who disappear like ghosts among the branches?"

Lord El Sharred appear to vacillate momentarily between whether he should capitulate to his lord's greater wisdom or attempt to save face in front of his peers. He chose wrong.

"We should burn the place down around their ears," he said defiantly.

There was more pounding of goblets. The Emperor rolled his eyes. Quirk smiled at him. A question about fire she could answer.

"Have you ever tried to burn living wood, Lord El Sharred?" she asked. "To be honest, I doubt you've even tried to burn dry wood. You have people to do that for you after all, so why bother?" She smiled sweetly and watched as the insults passed over the man's head. "Living wood does not burn like the fire in your hearth at home. It is slow, and smoky, and reluctant.

If you were able to get one tree to burn before the elves turned you and your men into novelty pincushions, I would count you very good at your job."

Now, finally the Emperor laughed. And when he laughed, everyone laughed. Even Quirk laughed. Lord El Sharred turned very red, and nodded, and managed a quick, "I daresay I am," before retreating back to his goblet.

"As ever," said the Emperor, once the general mirth had died down, "you have proven yourself of greater wisdom and experience than many of the men who sit here, Professor Bal Tehrin. I ask again, and pray that you can answer without interruption, what would you advise?"

"Merely to send him ten of our own harts, slain, and ready for roasting so that he may feast at our expense. Lives will be spared, and honor will be satisfied."

The table held its collective breath as the Emperor considered this. Finally he clicked his fingers. Instantly a servant was at his side, eyes angled obsequiously low.

"Tell the huntsmen to kill ten harts and prepare them for delivery to King Todger along with a message expressing my deepest regrets at the unfortunate situation."

The servant nodded and backed away. The Emperor picked up the last of his partridges, looked at it distastefully, and cast it over his shoulder. "Let's just get to the fucking dessert, shall we?"

No one disagreed.

# introducing

**If you enjoyed
FOOL'S GOLD,
look out for**

## THE CITY STAINED RED

**Bring Down Heaven: Book 1**

*by Sam Sykes*

*STEP UP TO THE GATES*

*After years in the wilds, Lenk and his companions have come to
the city that serves as the world's beating heart.*

*The great charnel house where men die surer than any
wilderness.*

*They've come to claim payment for creatures slain, blood
spilled at the behest of a powerful holy man.*

*And Lenk has come to lay down his sword for good.*

*But this is no place to escape demons.*

# PROLOGUE

*Cier'Djaal*
*Some crappy little boat*
*First day of Yonder*

*You can't lie to a sword.*

*It's a trait you don't often think of between its more practical applications, but part of the appeal of a blade is that it keeps you honest. No matter how much of a hero you might think you are for picking it up, no matter how many evildoers you claim to have smitten with it, it's hard to pretend that steel you carry is good for much else besides killing.*

*Conversely, a sword can't lie to you.*

*If you can't use it, it'll tell you. If you don't want to use it, it'll decide whether you should. And if you look at it, earnestly, and ask if there's no other way besides killing, it'll look right back at you and say, earnestly, that it can't quite think of any.*

*Every day I wake up, I look in the corner of my squalid little cabin. I stare at my sword. My sword stares back at me. And I tell it the same thing I've told it every day for months.*

*"Soon, we reach Cier'Djaal. Soon, we reach a place where there are ways to make coin without killing. Soon, I'm getting off this ship and I'm leaving you far behind."*

*The sword just laughs.*

*Granted, this probably sounds a trifle insane, but I'm writing in ink so I can't go back and make it less crazy. But if you're reading this, you're probably anticipating the occasional lapse in sanity.*

*And if you aren't yet, I highly recommend you start. It'll help.*

*I've killed a lot of things.*

*I say "things," because "people" isn't a broad enough category and "stuff" would lead you to believe I don't spend a lot of time thinking about it.*

*The list thus far: men, women, demons, monsters, giant serpents, giant vermin, regular vermin, regular giants, cattle, lizards, fish, lizardmen, fishmen, frogmen, Cragsmen, and a goat.*

*Regular goat, mind; not a poisonous magic goat or anything. But he was kind of an asshole.*

*When I started killing, it seemed like I had good reasons. Survival, I guess. Money, too. But the more I did it, the better I got. And the better I got, the less reason I needed until killing was just something I did.*

*Easy as shaking a man's hand.*

*And when it's as easy as shaking a man's hand, you stop seeing open hands. All you see, then, is an empty spot where a sword should be. And will be, if you don't grab yours first.*

*I'm tired of it.*

*I don't live in lamentation of my past deeds. I did what I had to, even if I could have thought of something better. I don't hear voices and I don't have nightmares.*

*Not anymore, anyway.*

*I guess I'm just tired. Tired of seeing swords instead of hands, tired of looking for chairs against the wall whenever I go into a room, tired of knowing lists instead of people, tired of talking to my sword.*

*And I'm going to stop. And even if I can't, I have to try.*

*So I'm going to. Try, that is.*

*Just as soon as I get my money.*

*I suppose there's irony in trading blood for gold. Or hypocrisy.*

*I don't care and I sincerely doubt my employer does, either.*

Or maybe he does—holy men are odd that way—but he'll pay, anyway. Blood is gold and I've spilled a lot of the former for a considerable sum of the latter.

Ordinarily, you wouldn't think a priest of Talanas, the Healer, would appreciate that much blood. But Miron Evenhands, Lord Emissary and Member in Good Standing of the House of the Vanquishing Trinity, is no ordinary priest. As the former title implies, he's a man with access to a lot of wealth. And as the latter title is just cryptic enough to suggest, he's got a fair number of demons, cultists, and occult oddities to be eradicated.

And eradicate I have, with gusto.

And he has yet to pay. "Temporary barriers to the financial flow," he tells me. "Patience, adventurer, patience," he says. And patient I was. Patient enough to follow him across the sea for months until we came here.

Cier'Djaal, the City of Silk. This is the great charnel house where poor men eat dead rich men and become wealthy themselves. This is the city where fortunes are born, alive and screaming. This is the city that controls the silk, the city that controls the coin, the city that controls the world.

This is civilization.

This is what I want now.

My companions, too.

Or so I'd like to think.

It's not as though anyone chooses to be an adventurer, killing people for little coin and even less respect. We all took up the title, and each other's company, with the intent of leaving it behind someday. Cier'Djaal is as good as any a place to do so, I figure.

Though their opinions on our arrival have been...varied.

That Gariath should be against our entrance into any place where he might be required to wear a shirt, let alone a place crawling with humans, is no surprise.

Far more surprising are Denaos's objections—the man who breathes liquor and uses whores for pillows, I would have thought, would feel right at home among the thieves and scum of civilized society.

Asper and Dreadaeleon, happy to be anywhere that has a temple or a wizard tower, were generally in favor of it. Asper for the opportunity to be among civilized holy men, Dreadaeleon for the opportunity to be away from uncivilized laymen, both for the opportunity to be in a place with toilets.

When I told Kataria, she just sort of stared.

Like she always does.

Which made my decision as to what to do next fairly easy. This will be the last of our time spent together. Once I've got my money, once I can leave my sword behind, I intend to leave them with it.

Their opinions on this have been quiet.

Possibly because I haven't told them yet.

Probably because I won't until I'm far enough away that I can't hear my sword laughing at me anymore.

VISIT THE ORBIT BLOG AT

# www.orbitbooks.net

FEATURING

## BREAKING NEWS
## FORTHCOMING RELEASES
## LINKS TO AUTHOR SITES
## EXCLUSIVE INTERVIEWS
## EARLY EXTRACTS

AND COMMENTARY FROM OUR EDITORS

WITH REGULAR UPDATES FROM OUR TEAM,
ORBITBOOKS.NET IS YOUR SOURCE
FOR ALL THINGS ORBITAL.

WHILE YOU'RE THERE, JOIN OUR E-MAIL LIST
TO RECEIVE INFORMATION ON SPECIAL OFFERS,
GIVEAWAYS, AND MORE.

# imagine. explore. engage.